Indebted

"I never expected to find such delightful curves beneath your hideous gowns, my dear. But I fear the unmasking is not complete." He tugged off her spectacles and reached to set them on a nearby table. "You have lovely amber eyes. It's a shame to cover them needlessly."

Eva locked onto his gaze, some sanity returning. "It is a shame to torment me as you have, Your Grace."

A second chuckle filled the room. His green eyes dipped to examine her mouth.

Leaning forward, he whispered against her lips, "Tell me you want me, Miss Black."

In spite of his outrageous antics, the corners of her mouth twitched. "I am powerless to resist you, and you well know it," she murmured.

The School for Brides

CHERYL ANN SMITH

BERKLEY SENSATION, NEW YORK

THE BERKLEY PUBLISHING GROUP
Published by the Penguin Group
Penguin Group (USA) Inc.
375 Hudson Street, New York, New York 10014, USA
Penguin Group (Canada), 90 Eglinton Avenue East, Suite 700, Toronto, Ontario M4P 2Y3, Canada
(a division of Pearson Penguin Canada Inc.)
Penguin Books Ltd., 80 Strand, London WC2R 0RL, England
Penguin Group Ireland, 25 St. Stephen's Green, Dublin 2, Ireland (a division of Penguin Books Ltd.)
Penguin Group (Australia), 250 Camberwell Road, Camberwell, Victoria 3124, Australia
(a division of Pearson Australia Group Pty. Ltd.)
Penguin Books India Pvt. Ltd., 11 Community Centre, Panchsheel Park, New Delhi—110 017, India
Penguin Group (NZ), 67 Apollo Drive, Rosedale, North Shore 0632, New Zealand
(a division of Pearson New Zealand Ltd.)
Penguin Books (South Africa) (Pty.) Ltd., 24 Sturdee Avenue, Rosebank, Johannesburg 2196,
South Africa

Penguin Books Ltd., Registered Offices: 80 Strand, London WC2R 0RL, England

This is a work of fiction. Names, characters, places, and incidents either are the product of the author's imagination or are used fictitiously, and any resemblance to actual persons, living or dead, business establishments, events, or locales is entirely coincidental. The publisher does not have any control over and does not assume any responsibility for author or third-party websites or their content.

THE SCHOOL FOR BRIDES

A Berkley Sensation Book / published by arrangement with the author

PRINTING HISTORY
Berkley Sensation mass-market edition / April 2011

Copyright © 2011 by Cheryl Ann Smith.
Excerpt from *The Accidental Courtesan* by Cheryl Ann Smith copyright © by Cheryl Ann Smith.
Cover art by Jim Griffin.
Cover design by George Long.
Cover hand lettering by Ron Zinn.
Interior text design by Laura K. Corless.

ISBN: 978-0-425-24050-2

BERKLEY® SENSATION
Berkley Sensation Books are published by The Berkley Publishing Group,
a division of Penguin Group (USA) Inc.,
375 Hudson Street, New York, New York 10014.
BERKLEY® SENSATION and the "B" design are trademarks of Penguin Group (USA) Inc.

PRINTED IN THE UNITED STATES OF AMERICA

10 9 8 7 6 5 4 3 2 1

Acknowledgments

There are many people to acknowledge with a debut book. First I'd like to thank my wonderful agent, Kevan Lyon, who took a chance on an unfinished manuscript because she loved the story idea. For her encouragement and faith, I have to say . . . we did it!

Second, many thanks to my awesome editor, Wendy McCurdy, for buying a book about a courtesan rescuer from a new author and for helping to make my crazy dream come true. There is no way to properly express my gratitude.

For Duane, who has supported me while I worked tirelessly to become a published author, I could not have done this without you. And to Paige, Regan, and Ethan; you guys are the best.

To my sister, Michelle, you always knew I could do it, even after reading my very first manuscript. You are awesome. And thanks to Genny, for her support and for being the best unofficial promo person an author could ask for.

I also can't forget Patti, Starr, and Nicole for their insight and willingness to answer questions 24-7. Thanks guys!

But most of all, I need to thank my mom, Joyce, for all the years of proofreading my manuscripts until her eyes crossed, and for knowing that this would happen for me one day if I kept going. You never wavered from your encouragement and you pushed me when I needed motivation. As my biggest fan, this book is for you.

Chapter One

"From this moment forward, you will not wear any gown that shows even a trace of areola, a length of thigh, or any other part of your bodies normally covered by an undergarment."

Miss Eva Black paused impatiently while muslin, crinoline, and satin rustled as several pairs of hands reached to jerk up unacceptably low necklines. A shadowy hint of the curved crests of at least one pair of rosy peaks disappeared from view behind stiff lace.

"Proper clothing is the first outward sign of a lady and the first rule that cannot, and will not, be broken." She sighed, resisting the urge to tug at the high, scratchy neck of her gray wool gown. In the heat of the parlor, she felt trapped beneath the heavy layers of her spinster's garments.

It took determination not to shuck off the dress and kick it into the overstoked fire with her slippered foot. With the rain whipping against the window, throwing open a sash wasn't a viable option. She really had to give the

maid simpler instructions on whether a fire was appropriate when the morning was warm, lest fainting become the
order of the day.

The next several hours loomed ahead like a dismal and
itchy fog, yet Eva forged on. Her suffering was unimport-
ant. An example had to be set for her young courtesans at
all times as they looked to her for guidance and the chance
to free themselves from their desperate situations.

She continued, "With one's breasts exposed, one can
expect every reprobate for fifty miles around to come running for a peek. This is an unacceptable situation I intend
to change over the course of the next few weeks. You must
behave like ladies, if I am to have any chance of finding
each of you a husband."

More giggles and a flurry of whispers followed her
pronouncement. The young ladies took a moment to settle
before five pairs of curious eyes turned back to Eva. She
pulled her fingernails away from her neckline and settled
her hands in her lap. A lady did not fidget nor show discomfort in public. Eva was always the picture of ladylike
serenity, even if she was no Lady by birth or marriage.

Lady Watersham's book, *Rules for Young Women of
Quality*, spelled out every societal rule in precise detail,
and Eva had eagerly read and memorized every page. Now
she passed those teachings on to others desperately in need
of guidance and a chance at a life outside a courtesan's lot.

So she wouldn't fidget, even if pushed to the brink of
insanity by the confounding prickles.

Out of sorts today for some unknown reason, Eva felt
her mask of stiff propriety settle in the shape of an invisible
noose jerked tight around her neck. Just once she wanted to
giggle like a ninny with other girls, slouch against the back
of the settee with her bare feet outstretched, or scratch her
neck like a dog overrun with fleas.

Though only twenty-three, at times she felt eighty-
three. She'd skipped the frivolity of youth for the weight

of responsibility. At times it was almost too much for her narrow shoulders to carry.

"But how will a fellow know what he's buying if he can't see the merchandise?" Rose asked, pulling Eva from her thoughts of self-pity. The tiny redhead was a confection in pink satin and enough lace to cover several gowns from hem to neck.

"Merchandise?" Eva asked.

The perfect heart-shaped face turned sober as Rose seemed to reach for the correct way to express her ideas. She finally nodded her head. "Miss Eva, a fellow always wants a taste of what he's purchasing before he proposes a contract."

Rose's bright blue eyes were remarkably innocent for a girl who'd spent the last four years of her life servicing an elderly duke. A loose curl settled over her right eye, making her look much younger than twenty-one. However, it was her frankness when speaking of her sexual experiences that gave her a decidedly less-than-innocent air.

Pauline, a buxom twenty-six-year-old blonde in yellow, nodded, nibbling on a knuckle. "A man will pay a higher price if he likes what he sees beneath a corset and drawers. Plump breasts and a nicely rounded bottom are most favored among the gentry."

The comment was so matter-of-fact it took Eva a blink for her spine to catch up with her ears and draw her back from her moments of inattentiveness. She straightened one vertebra at a time, exasperated that a woman had to care what any man, or men, thought about her figure. If a lady wanted to eat so many pastries that her bottom grew as wide as the Thames, she should be able to do so without the judgment of the male species.

"Except for Lord Fitz," Rose interjected with a knowing glance at Pauline before Eva could respond. The two friends nodded their heads in unison, setting their curls to bobbing. Rose put an open hand to the side of her mouth and lowered her tone to a loud whisper. "I hear he likes his mistresses to look and dress like footmen—"

"Let's move along, ladies," Eva interjected sternly. From deep within, and past the beginning of a headache, she hung on to a tiny thread of patience. All she wanted to do was pull the nearest pillow over her head to shut out the light and the world.

Running this school, as she called it, was never easy. Nor was it simple to turn her courtesans into proper ladies and match them with husbands.

However, the importance of saving young women from lives of servitude on their backs, with pompous lords riding them like grunting, sweaty jockeys, was the foremost reason for her to get out of bed every day and make the journey across town to Cheapside.

Each well-made match produced a rush of relief that there would be one woman less to end up broken-spirited and left to live in poverty and quiet desperation, once the line of rich and lecherous patrons dried up.

Any bedding these five courtesans would indulge in from this moment forward would follow a wedding in front of a vicar and with papers signed to legalize the union. That she'd make sure of.

Though her temples pulsed, she would get through this introduction to the rules, send the women off to contemplate the lesson, then rush home to put a cool compress on her head and take a long nap between soft sheets.

"A man should choose you as his partner based on your intelligence, your disposition, and the joy you bring to his life. Not, Pauline, what you have beneath your corset. So, that said, you shall never again, for any reason, wear fabrics thin enough to see through outside your marital bed." Eva scanned the room and was satisfied all the women were now decently covered. "Advertising one's wares to the masses is no longer permitted if you intend to change your circumstances and find a respectable mate."

Audible groans and hushed whispers again sounded from around the modest yet tasteful blue room. Change did not come easily for her courtesans. However, Eva was confident that by the end of the month all her charges would step forward to meet the challenge she set forth: to make her, and themselves, proud.

"Trust me, ladies. You will have no difficulty finding a husband once I am finished with your instruction," Eva said. "And he will care more about the strength of your character than the circumference of your breasts."

Pauline knitted her hands in her lap and screwed up her face. Several emotions played across her delicate features.

Eva watched as a measure of understanding dawned in the young woman and the start of a new way of thinking passed through Pauline's pretty hazel eyes. Satisfaction filled Eva's heart; one enlightened courtesan and four to go.

The five women were of different ages, were from varied backgrounds, and had varied educations. They were all brightly wrapped from head to slippered toes in a selection of red, pink, blue, orange, and yellow feathers and bows, like exotic hens preening as they sought a cock with whom to mate.

Eva squelched a frown as she contemplated each in turn, perched together on the pair of rose-patterned settees. There was no dull mouse in the lot.

The women had been instructed to wear simple, unadorned clothing this morning. Perhaps next time she should be more specific about the cut and color of the gown. If this was the best each could come up with, a day of shopping was clearly in order.

Truthfully, catching the attention of a breathing, wealthy male had been their life's work up to this moment. And the second requirement was likely more important than the first.

"But His Grace says a woman is judged by her beauty and figure," Rose said innocently as she smoothed out her skirts. "And education is wasted on a woman. As long as she knows how to please a man and walk upright, she needs no further instruction."

Eva scowled. "His Grace needs to be horsewhipped. Walk upright and service men, indeed! Next time the old buzzard visits, Rose, jerk his cane away from him and beat him senseless with it."

Rose's eyes widened, then the corners of her mouth twitched in response to the peals of laughter of the other girls. A spark of mischief lit her face. Clearly this courtesan did not share the view of her ancient patron. "I think I shall do just that. It would do the wretch a wealth of good, and his wife and daughters would certainly be grateful."

While Eva sat shamefaced over her outburst about the arrogance of noblemen, the other women voiced various treacherous ways to make the old duke suffer for the crime of ignorance.

"Let us turn that stallion into a gelding," said Abigail softly as her cheeks pinkened beneath wisps of brown hair that framed her round face. She was twenty-four and had been a year into her career as a courtesan, since her father, a tenant farmer, died in a fight over ownership of a flock of sheep. Only her beauty and some education had kept her from selling her wares on the docks.

"Stallion?" Rose said with a laugh and pressed her fingertips to her mouth. Her eyes flashed. "A suckling colt has more vigor with a mare."

The jesting continued until all but the stern-faced Sophie were happily satisfied the duke had been verbally battered to a pulp. Though Eva suspected this particular gaggle of young women could try the patience of even the most stoic magistrate seated on a high court, she found she enjoyed their company. With all the darkness that marked her days, laughter and silliness were a welcome diversion. She even managed a smile at the image of the old duke slathered in pudding and covered with duck feathers.

Still, she had lessons to complete, and now was not the time to socialize if she were to keep on schedule. "As enjoyable as it would be to geld the duke, we are fresh out of rusty medical instruments to do the deed." She waited a moment until she had their full attention. "Now, let us continue. I have matched former courtesans with husbands for three years, and I understand how difficult it is to give up your seductive ways. Yet, none of you were chained up and dragged here to sit through my teachings, and each of you is permitted to leave any time you choose. Harold informed you before he brought you here that the school is entirely voluntary. As you saw when you entered through the front door of this town house, the solid oak panel does not have metal bars."

A secret network operated by word of mouth had brought each woman willingly to Eva's door. Since most of the courtesans had worked from the time they were young, this made her efforts challenging. They'd been taught early that earls, dukes, and barons cared less about what lay above the neckline than what treasures could be found below. It was her job to change their perception of life and themselves. They had value beyond their bodies, and by the end of the month all five would know just how high their worth was.

"Henceforth, the only time any of you will show any private parts to a man is on your wedding night and beyond. Your pasts are almost behind you now, and a new life dawns. If you follow a few simple rules, you'll be ready to wed before the month is out."

Unfortunately, the task was never quite so easy. Especially for those like Sophie, who'd worked as a courtesan for twelve years, since the tender age of seventeen, when her parents died and left her penniless.

Older women like Sophie and Yvette had played the coquette for so long they used seduction and their beauty to keep a roof over their heads and food in their bellies. It was difficult to break free of such a past and accept the idea that life held other possibilities. But Eva enjoyed a good challenge and her rate of successful matches was high.

"A gentleman does not need to see your parts exposed in order to make a proposal. A marriage proposal." She leveled a glare on each woman in turn and pursed her lips. "If any one of you does not see your future as a proper wife and mother, Harold will bring the coach around. I will not waste my time and your monies on a futile endeavor."

The courtesans peered at each other and then back to her. All shook their heads in unison. Two blondes, two brunettes, and Rose the redhead. All highly paid in their previous profession. Some wanted children, some wanted a home of their own, and some just wanted one man in her bed to love. Whatever their reasons, Eva would find them their perfect mate.

"Excellent. Let us get started." Eva walked over to the bookcase and pulled a thick volume off the shelf. The women watched, openly curious, as she returned and settled into a high-backed chair.

"From this moment onward, you will not use vulgar terms for genitalia, breasts, or sexual positions as topics of conversation in polite company. You will stick to topics such as the weather, or Parliament, or current fashion. I care not which, as long as it isn't immediately followed by a man shoving his hand down your corset."

Several snickers followed, then faded quickly when Eva failed to join in. "You will learn deportment and manners and clever ways to begin a conversation, and all of you will learn to carry yourselves with the grace of a duchess."

Eva turned the book to show its gilded black cover. The women stared as if the words were written in Latin. Though only shy Abigail couldn't read well, five puzzled faces gazed at the large gold-inlaid word at the top of the cover.

Husbands.

Eva's eyes softened and she nodded. "I promise a husband is now within reach for each of you."

"I do so want a husband," Abigail said, sighing.

Eva smiled at the beautiful girl. "Then a husband you shall have, Abigail."

If not for the limited number of positions for which women could seek employment in this society, and the beauty of her charges limiting the chances of finding work in any household where a husband resided, she wouldn't have needed to use her matchmaking talents to this end.

Eva herself had no interest in marriage and considered the institution dreadfully archaic. But her ladies really had no other choices. So marriage it was for her courtesans.

"Inside this book are information and sketches of men seeking wives; they have no compunction about your lack of virginity." Eva opened to a page and turned the book so the girls could see the first face. "I asked each man to answer some questions. I wrote down the questions, and their responses, here." She pointed to the page opposite the sketch. "I've verified the information myself, so each of you will know exactly what kind of man you are choosing and what he expects of his wife. When a man is matched, we remove him from the book so there will not be any confusion."

She flipped to a page where the sketched face was blacked out. She'd kept his page in the book for an example to show the sort of man she would not tolerate. "Men who abuse women are immediately refused, as are men with drinking or gambling problems. These are respectable men who want a respectable wife."

"But why would they want to wed one of us?" Yvette, a twenty-six-year-old brunette with tired brown eyes, crossed her arms over a sizable bosom and frowned. She'd had eight lovers during her six years as a courtesan, and her unhappiness with her lot showed in the hard lines on her face. She would be the most difficult to place without substantial effort on Eva's part. "What is wrong with them? Hideous scars? Rotten teeth? A missing limb?"

"Yes." Pauline nodded, and the yellow feather in her upswept hair fluttered along the side of her round face. "Men do not marry women like us unless there is something awful they are hiding. I want a husband, but could not abide a twisted troll with claw hands pawing at my soft parts."

Eva's shoulder blades tightened. Odd, women who willingly bedded the highest bidder had lofty standards when it came time to choose a mate.

She grimaced. The itchy gown was making her irritable. Of course she should have a pleasing mate.

"I assure you there isn't a single troll in this book, but neither are there dukes or earls or kings." Blunt honesty sometimes was exactly what these women required. If they expected to someday be addressed as "Lady" anything, they'd be sorely disappointed. "Men of stature require a virginal wife of impeccable birth to wed."

At least until they whelped an heir or two to continue their perfect bloodline into the next generation. After that, they set up young women like these in apartments or town houses, away from their wives, and played their lascivious games.

The concept of unfaithful marriages was one Eva found distasteful. Once a man and woman wed, they should forsake all others. Perhaps if the matches were born of love and not for financial gain, it might be the case.

It was rare when a couple found true love. Even then, it did not guarantee a happy ending. She knew the dark side of love well.

Shaking off the press of bleak thoughts, Eva added, "Every one of these men is apprised of the general circumstances of your lives, and they have chosen to be included in this book." She turned a few more pages and revealed several more faces. Some of the men were quite handsome, and none had claw hands. "They include barristers and shopkeepers and even a baron's younger son. I do not hide what I do from my clients, and select them carefully for stellar character and financial security."

"Yet they look for whores as wives," Abigail said quietly, and shared a sidelong glance with Yvette. She plucked at the sleeve of her blue gown and sighed. "Perhaps you should explain to us their reasoning."

Eva did not judge her charges for the lives they had led, for many had sad tales of desperate circumstances that led them to a courtesan's path. But neither could she understand how resistant they became once under her tutelage.

They came to her.

By the time a courtesan reached Sophie's age, she was well past the first blush of youth and no longer able to command a high price for her services. Suddenly, with age came the realization that her charm, sensuality, and pretty face were waning, and younger courtesans were ready to take her place. It was usually then that the woman became desperate.

If a courtesan had the sense to put aside coin for her future, she could close up shop and disappear into genteel retirement, or flee to the Continent for new adventures.

For others like these five, who had spent most of what they earned on fripperies and were without means enough to retire into obscurity, finding a decent husband was their chance for security.

Eva closed the book. "The reasons vary with the men." She leaned back into her chair, the book settled on her knees beneath her flat palms. "Some have businesses to build and do not have the time to find a potential wife and court her. Some travel extensively and seek a woman of adventurous spirit to follow him to exotic locations."

"Oh!" Rose bounced up and down on her seat and raised her hand. "I love adventure!"

Nodding, Eva smiled. The saucy little redhead would be a wonderful companion and wife for several of her clients. She still had the enthusiasm and blush of youth that men craved. "Excellent. I'll keep that in mind, Rose."

She turned her attention to each woman in turn. Their beauty should be only one part of what men saw when choosing them. Not the main or only reason.

"Truthfully, there are some men who seek to marry only women of rare beauty, far above the type of young lady they could normally attract. They want a peacock on their arm, not a sparrow. For that privilege, they will overlook a questionable past. Over the course of the month, you will be able to study the book and choose several men you feel will best match you. Then we will have a party where the introductions will be made."

The courtesans fell silent. Each knew the men paid generous fees for Eva's services, and the arrangements were business-based. Even so, several of them she had tutored and their suitors went on to make love matches. It was an end to which many aspired.

"What differs from your old life is that you all have choices here in this house. You pick the man, you decide what kind of life you want, and I put you and your suitors together. It is up to you how the relationship evolves. If you reject one match, we shall find you another until you, and he, are satisfied and we finalize the arrangement with marriage vows."

Soft sighs filled the room.

"It sounds wonderful," said Yvette wistfully. Apparently, even the most hardened of courtesans longed for love.

Eva ran her hand over the book and thought of how lucky these women were not to have fallen in love with their benefactors. It had happened with several previous clients and ended with broken hearts. She let out a pensive sigh of her own and blinked back the press of tears. If only Charlotte Rose had had a place like this to turn to before she fell into the love trap, her circumstances could have ended differently.

She mentally shook herself. It was not the time to drift into gloomy thoughts. Today was a day of new possibilities.

"Though your suitors have no qualms about your pasts, they do require the public air of respectability. That is where my lessons become invaluable." Eva peered over the top of her spectacles. "They have mothers, sisters, and families who might not be pleased with a former courtesan as the wife of their son or brother. From this moment on, you will forget everything you've done, every man who once warmed your beds, and live a modest life. And if you cannot do this, you are free to go. I do not force anyone to follow my directives. From now on, your future is your own responsibility."

A sniff drew her attention, then Rose burst into tears. Pauline slid across the settee and squeezed her hand. "What is wrong, dearest?" She pulled a handkerchief out of her bodice and handed it to the distraught girl.

Rose dabbed her eyes and hiccupped. "Ever since my mother tossed me out on my bum when I was seventeen and her second husband took an interest in me"—she blew her nose loudly into the handkerchief—"I have relied on men for everything." The last word had a high pitch to it. "I've done things I cannot even confess to my priest, for fear God will hear and strike me down." She let out a low wail. "I don't know if I can take care of myself." She fell into a round of soft sobs. Abigail moved over and took a position on her other side. She rested an arm around Rose's shoulder and clucked her tongue.

"Miss Eva will help us," Sophie said firmly from the other settee. "And you will no longer have to suffer His Grace's cold hands and limp—" She looked sheepishly at Eva and cleared her throat. "She'll find you a man of adventure who knows how to love you as you deserve to be loved."

Rose dabbed her tears and peered at Eva with measuring eyes, then slowly nodded her head. "Then I shall put my trust in her hands."

"We all will," said Abigail, and the others nodded.

Eva set the book aside and stood, hope for a successful outcome to this class springing once again into her breast. Sophie's unexpected show of tenderness to Rose clearly had an effect on all the women. They were no longer facing this as five separate women, but as a collective and supportive group.

With one show of tears, Rose had done what usually took days or weeks to achieve. Togetherness.

Eva walked to Rose and pulled her to her feet. She tipped up the girl's chin and looked into her shimmering eyes. "You need not worry, my dear Rose. By the time I've finished with you, you will be well able to care for yourself."

With a wavering smile, Rose nodded and pulled her into a tight hug. Eva flinched but allowed the embrace. The other women stood and circled around, their excited chatter infectious. Eva had opened her mouth to offer further reassurance when her butler, Harold, came through the open door with a troubled expression on his face. Eva gently extricated herself from Rose's embrace and stepped away from the group.

A sudden chill seeped into her bones, and she shivered. She looked to the windows, certain one had blown open to invite the cool morning into the stuffy room. But the panes were securely closed and locked and the heavy blue drapes showed not a flutter.

Strange. This was the second time in a week she'd felt that same dank chill slide through her body. If she wasn't a woman of solid mind and not one to dabble in fits of fancy, she would worry that this chill was a sign of impending doom.

Rubbish. She shook her head to clear it and faced Harold. She was a bit ruffled by his intrusion, as her orders were clear: He was not to interrupt the lessons unless it was an emergency. She stepped close, out of earshot of the women. "What is it, Harold? Has something happened to Mother?"

He shook his head firmly. "No, Miss."

Harold led her to the open doorway by her elbow. Her butler was tall, nearing thirty, and built like a pugilist; a perfect guard for the door of both this house and her home. He kept the girls safe and the riffraff off her front steps.

And Eva trusted him with her secrets. All her secrets.

He leaned toward her and whispered, "A man, a gentleman, is at the front door. He insists he has business with you that cannot wait." He glanced down the hallway and scowled. "When I informed him you were not taking callers today, he said to explain to you that if I send him away, he will return with a Bow Street Runner in tow and have you arrested."

Chapter Two

A wave of worry infused Eva. Strange men did not come here to see her without an invitation, either by accident or by design. Not even her male clients, who first had to submit to being blindfolded and then transported in a coach with blackened windows, under Harold's careful watch.

This nondescript town house was a safe haven for the women who chose to stay under this roof during their instruction, as some had fled abusive patrons. Their safety, as always, was first and foremost. When Harold was with Eva, a second butler, Primm, kept watch in the evenings. To have a caller at her door making threats was completely unacceptable and, well, shocking.

Eva smothered her anxiety and gathered her wits. "Did he present you his card or give you his name?" she murmured to Harold, thankful that his massive frame all but hid her from view.

"He did not," Harold murmured back, his jaw tight. "But he is no common man, Miss. His coat alone must have cost a year's pay."

A man who called without an appointment and wore expensive clothing? Her worry turned instantly to puzzlement.

Perhaps he was an escapee from Bedlam? Harold could well protect her were that the case.

But her girls and their privacy must be guarded at all costs from the prying eyes of the neighbors. Bringing a Bow Street Runner to her door would be a disaster.

"Then I must grant him an audience." She forced a smile and turned to her ladies. "I apologize for the interruption, but there is a small matter I must attend to that cannot wait. If you ladies would kindly head to the kitchen, Doris, my housekeeper, will give you your next lesson."

Eva watched as the brightly plumed birds paraded off. Once the door to the kitchen closed behind her courtesans, Eva proceeded down the hallway, her giant protector, the one person she trusted with her life and her charges, at her back.

One year ago, Harold had stumbled onto her doorstep, injured by a footpad in the mews near her home in Mayfair. He was dirty and rough, and clad in torn homespun clothing, his dark blond hair matted with drying blood. Without hesitation she'd settled him in the servants' quarters and cared for his wounds, grateful for something to occupy her mind and keep her sane when despair over her mother's worsening health threatened to overwhelm her.

A bond formed between them during the two weeks he struggled for survival. She never asked for his history, and he never explained either why he wandered the streets in the middle of the night or how he'd found his way to her door. Harold repaid her kindness with fierce loyalty and friendship, and that was good enough for her.

"Did he give you any indication of his business?" Eva paused, and Harold moved around her to place his hand on the door handle. She scanned his hard face and for the thousandth time gave thanks for his comforting presence.

He shook his head. "Only that he wouldn't leave until he spoke to you." Their eyes met, and Eva's stomach knotted at the concern in his expression. "I tried to run him off by informing him he had the wrong address. He was having none of it. The threats started when I tried to close the door in his face. I have a bad feeling about this, Miss Eva."

"This is indeed worrisome. I hope the man has not come to collect on Mother's old debts."

"Say the word, Miss Eva, and I will beat him senseless and drop him in a ditch somewhere."

In spite of the dire situation, her mouth twitched. "I think not. Something is amiss, and it will be best to find out the reason for his visit." She squeezed his thick arm. "Though I shall keep the offer in mind should his actions require a firm hand."

Harold nodded. Despite his protective nature, he always did as she asked. So she quickly collected herself and lifted her nose when he pulled open the door and scowled darkly at the interloper.

"Miss Black, sir." Harold stepped back one pace, still within arm's reach should the tall stranger decide to launch a surprise attack.

The visitor stepped from the darkness of the storm into the light spilling from the wall sconce in the hallway, then paused, his shadowed eyes fully on her. An intense stare from beneath a sodden, narrow-brimmed hat pierced through her. The man was clearly incensed over being left to cool his heels in the rain. He resembled a viper, coiled and ready to strike.

Eva's breath caught. Danger, and a mesmerizing sexual potency, emanated from this stranger's every pore. Like the slightly demonic and tragically handsome hero of a gothic novel, his cloak flapped in the wind and fury of the rising tempest behind him.

His brooding intensity left her uneasy. Yet, she'd not be cowed.

The stranger dragged a measuring stare down her body, then quickly reclaimed her gaze. It was impossible to read the thoughts behind his disarming eyes, but Eva suspected they weren't pleasant.

"State your business," Harold said over her shoulder. The stranger glared. He obviously had no patience with her servant. He'd been left to weather the storm on the door-step and was likely chilled to his bones. Not exactly proper protocol when one calls on a household. But Harold was no common servant, and not above taking a bit of revenge for the threats against Eva.

"I'll not do it out here."

The man put a boot on the top step and Eva startled backward into Harold's massive chest. The stranger brushed by her.

In the dim flicker of sconce light, the man gave her a more thorough perusal as he dripped a large puddle on the polished floor.

"You are Eva Black? Interesting." The timbre of his voice held no trace of warmth to take the edge off the ice in his green eyes. "You are not at all what I thought a thief would look like, though I suppose I am unused to thieves of the fairer sex. Truthfully, I am disappointed."

Thief? Her? She quickly pulled her mind from thoughts of gothic heroes upon storm-swept moors, and let her critical gaze drift down his body.

Though not as tall as Harold, the stranger was taller than most men. He was draped in wool, and rain had stained his finely cut garments. It was clear to Eva that this was no debt collector, nor a merchant come to call.

From his square jaw, to the aristocratic cut of his long-ish nose, to the tips of his expensive boots, this man was the epitome of arrogant nobility.

She drew up to full height. "I fear you have stumbled onto the wrong stoop and the wrong woman, sir. I have stolen nothing from you."

His expression turned icy. "Do you think that I would lower myself to come to your door in this godforsaken storm if there were any chance I might be mistaken?" He paused and turned his attention to Harold. "It took my investigator over three months to find you, and I will not leave until you've returned my property to me."

The situation became more puzzling by the moment. He spoke nonsense. But she was reluctant to draw the attention of neighbors by continuing this conversation in the open doorway.

"Very well." She squelched an impatient sigh. "We will speak in the library." Eva turned and led the stranger down the hall and up the stairs. She paused outside the door as he passed into the small room, and leaned close to Harold. "Make sure the ladies are otherwise occupied until I've concluded this matter."

Harold scowled and clenched both fists. One word and he'd be on her visitor like a rabid dog. Unfortunately, bloodshed would ruin the gleaming floors.

"I do not like leaving you alone with him," Harold grumbled.

She patted his thick forearm. "I will be fine. Just keep the women out of sight. And have the footmen stoke the fire when we have finished. It's cold enough in here to make ice."

Drawing in a breath, Eva turned to meet her adversary. He stood near the fireplace and watched her cross the room. She was careful to keep a respectable distance between them, well out of arm's reach. Without Harold, she felt vulnerable.

"Now that we are alone, why don't you tell me who you are and what it is you want from me," she said tightly. "You have me at a disadvantage."

The stranger drew off his wet cloak and draped it carelessly over a high-backed chair.

"I like to keep the advantage mine," he said briskly.

"I gather you do not intend to offer me tea and cakes, Miss Black?"

The sardonic words raised her hackles. "Had you been invited, sir, I would have planned ahead for an afternoon of buttered scones and witty banter."

He responded with a hard smile. "Your appearance gave me momentary pause that I might well have received misinformation and arrived at the wrong house. But now I have no doubt you are the woman I seek."

Without his cloak for added bulk, he was not as large as she expected. But he had broad shoulders that tapered downward to a narrow waist and hips, followed by defined and muscular thighs beneath well-cut buff breeches. He was a fine male specimen, though she assured herself that her observation was only clinical, like examining teeth before purchasing a carriage horse.

"Sir, though I have no qualms about standing around trading insults with you until the cock crows at dawn, I have other matters to attend to. I ask again, who are you, and what do you want from me?"

"I am Nicholas Drake, the Duke of Stanfield."

Instantly, she knew his name and title, though she knew not why. Perhaps from the society pages, perhaps from gossip in the market, but his introduction revealed he was no lesser baron or coachman, but a duke with all the blue blood behind the name.

He paused and looked around the room. In this simple setting, with its pale green papered walls, musty old books, and a worn yet serviceable Oriental rug beneath a matching set of chairs, he overwhelmed the space, and her, with his presence.

Once his perusal of the room was complete, he turned back to her and stared down his nose. "I have come for Arabella. If you would fetch her, we will be on our way."

Arabella? "So that is what this is about?"

The puzzle began to take shape. His name was familiar because he was Arabella's former lover. According to

the girl, he was possessive and ruthless, though generous
to a fault. Still, not once had he ever asked Arabella what
she wanted for herself, and the courtesan's life was not her
desire. She'd longed for love and children. She could get
neither with His Grace. She was neither a virgin nor did
she possess an impeccable bloodline to be his duchess.
Mistress, yes. Wife, no.

When Arabella had tried to end the relationship, he
brushed aside her wishes and bought her half a dozen new
gowns, expecting a new wardrobe to soothe her. But she
had simply waited for her opportunity and disappeared,
right out from under his arrogant nose.

The right decision, clearly. Everything Arabella said
about His Grace had come to pass. He *was* possessive and
ruthless enough to hunt her down. The girl was right to
flee.

"I am sorry, Your Grace. Arabella is not here."

"Then tell me where she is, Miss Black. I want to see
her. She belongs to me."

"Surely I am mistaken, Your Grace, but did you insinu-
ate that Arabella is your property?" She widened her eyes
innocently. "Is she what you claim I have stolen from you?"

"Arabella is mine and under my protection." His jaw
pulsed. "This matter is none of your business, Miss Black.
It is between Arabella and me."

"Of all the ridiculous notions, Your Grace!" Her body
tightened with anger. "Perhaps you should have fitted Arabella with a diamond-encrusted collar and kept her teth-
ered to your bed with a length of rope, after you trotted her
through the park for fresh air and exercise like a pampered
poodle!"

He stiffened, and she went on. "The girl is not an object
to be bought and sold like a mare or milk cow. She is a
person, a human being. She was free to choose another path
for herself. She has done so, and is no longer your concern."

Thunderclouds crossed his face. He covered the few

steps that separated them and loomed over her, anger etching lines on his face. "Arabella is mine."

Eva refused to be intimidated. "She is not yours, Your Grace. She was never yours."

A pair of large hands clenched and released at his sides, as if measuring her neck for size.

"That is her decision alone, Miss Black. Not yours. Tell me where she is. Now."

Eva froze. It would take only a moment for His Grace to snap her neck with his powerful hands before she could scream for help. "I cannot," she whispered. "She isn't here."

Undecided whether to call for Harold or bolt for the open door, in the end she did neither. He wouldn't cow her, no matter what he did to her. She'd show no fear.

His Grace expelled a breath through clenched teeth.

In that moment, she saw something deeper in his eyes than a man looking for his property. Before she could put a name to it, his face closed back up and he shoved one hand through his hair. Clearly, he wasn't about to risk years in Newgate for the chance to choke her dead.

She waited silently for him to settle himself and hopefully regain some sense. This was a smart man, a man of means if not scruples. Once he realized he had lost this game, he would trot off to his mansion, lick his wounds, and move on to his next conquest.

"If it is money you want, I have enough to purchase the chit back from you, Miss Black," he said low and tight. "Name your price."

Eva stared at him. She understood the notion of men of rank taking mistresses, though she despised the practice. It was a practice going back hundreds, if not thousands, of years. The institution wasn't about to change because of her opinion on the matter. But for this man to offer her money to buy back Arabella made her angry all over again.

"How dare you come into this home and make such a boorish offer, Your Grace? Arabella is gone, do you understand me? Gone from London and never coming back. So you can hie yourself off to Almack's or White's, or wherever dukes go to drink and gamble, and forget you ever knew her. She is no longer under your protection. The sooner you give up this futile chase, the sooner you can find a new courtesan to warm your bed."

Eva stood, chin upright; a tiny terrier facing down a tiger. No matter how he intimidated her, she would not be the first to look away. One sign of weakness, and he'd rip her to shreds.

Thank goodness he couldn't see the churning in her stomach or hear the rapid clip of her beating heart.

"I will find her, Miss Black," he said through gritted teeth. "When I do, she will happily return to my bed and forget the silly notions you put into her head."

It took strength of will to keep her fist from smashing him right in the nose. Never in her life had she met such a vexing and stubborn man!

"Silly notions, you say? What, for Arabella to aspire to greater things than to be a plaything, a warm body, for a duke?" Eva lifted her hands lest he step forward. "And what of her husband and the baby she carries? Will you murder the captain and take the baby to raise it as your own? Will she accept the death of the man she loves and eagerly spread her legs for you because you command it, Your Grace?"

His Grace stepped backward, almost faltered, if a man like him could falter. The arrogant beast looked as if she'd dumped ice water down his breeches.

"Arabella is married and with child?"

"I watched the vicar pronounce them man and wife, and a letter last week confirmed she is with child." This time, Eva *did* see emotion pass through His Grace's eyes before he turned his head away. Fondness? Regret? Though he considered Arabella his property, apparently the man had some affection for the girl. It explained his desperate search for her, and showed his heart wasn't entirely a black lump of coal after all.

Perhaps there was a human being beneath his cold, arrogant, pompous exterior? Arabella had touched him in some way. Maybe there was hope for him. Unfortunately, Eva had neither the time nor the desire to find a shovel and dig for humanity beneath layers of aristocratic upper crust.

A life in America for Arabella with her beloved ship captain husband was her future now. His Grace would have to move on with his life without her. Even he wouldn't dare interfere with a marriage made in the eyes of God.

"As you can see, Your Grace, you cannot have her back," Eva said. "I am positive, should you make your desire for a new mistress known about London, there will quickly be young women lined up outside your door."

If Eva expected resignation in his eyes when he lifted them back to her, she was startled by the intensity and black rage she found there.

"I will not forget what you've done, Miss Black."

In the dim room Eva watched, transfixed, while he retrieved his cloak and jerked it around his shoulders. He said not another word as he stalked past her, nor when he gained the hall and then the stairs, heavy footfalls marking his passage to the lower floor. She flinched when the oak panel door slammed closed behind him.

Harold found her rooted to the same spot moments later when he returned to her side and placed his comforting hand on her arm. His mouth screwed up with concern.

"Miss Eva," he said, and bent to peer into her face. "Are you ill? Did he hurt you?"

"Oh, Harold," she said softly when she finally found her tongue. She rubbed the chill flesh of her exposed upper arms and felt the same strange brush of cold air she'd felt earlier. "I think I have made a powerful enemy."

Chapter Three

Nicholas swore under his breath as he climbed into the coach and pulled the door closed with a bang. He reached to rap on the ceiling, and the driver urged the horses on.

Blind fury filled his mind. Arabella was lost to him forever. Sweet, beautiful Arabella. Two years of wooing and seducing her away from the Earl of Seabrook. Hardly a year spent in her bed. All wasted. It took years of searching for a perfect mistress, and she was yanked away by a pinched-faced spinster unable to mind her business and stay out of his.

"Miss Black will regret crossing me," he vowed.

Leaning back, he pictured Arabella and remembered the moment he'd first laid eyes on her beautiful face. She was in a private theater box, watching some forgettable play, shadowed by a pair of heavy drapes so as not to ruffle the sensibilities of the Ton by being seen publicly on the arm of her lover.

She'd laughed at some witty comment from Seabrook, her blue eyes dancing, when she turned her head slightly and caught his eye. The connection lasted only a moment before she turned back to her companion, pointedly dismissing him.

But the hook was set.

At first he'd limited his pursuit to casual public meetings and mild flirtation, out of respect for the earl. Eventually, he'd chased her with a single-minded purpose, uncaring of Seabrook's anger. When he finally made her his, she'd proved to be everything he'd dreamed. Lovely, loving, and eager to please; in bed and out.

They'd laughed and played, and for most of their time together she'd seemed content. He was sure of it. Only over the last few months had he sensed restlessness in her that she'd tried to mask with good humor and passion. She'd been distracted and rushed when he visited, and several times she'd been late to arrive when he'd called. When he'd queried her about it, she'd shrugged her perfect shoulders and pulled him down on the bed with a passionate kiss.

Then one morning he'd arrived on their one-year anniversary, with flowers and a ruby necklace in hand, and she was gone.

Vanished.

The servants were as puzzled as he. At first he worried she'd come to harm, and sent a footman for a Bow Street Runner. Then he'd found her note, penned in her delicate scroll on vellum. She thanked him politely for their time together and left his gifts piled up in the center of their bed.

All of his gifts down to the last ruby. She'd left with only the clothing on her back.

It had taken months to hunt her down to the last place she'd been seen. A shabby town house in Cheapside with a door guarded by a bear of a man and occupied by a woman of mystery who was as secretive as she was plain.

Eva Black. Medium height, hair an uninteresting brown, eyes the color of deep amber behind a pair of oversized spectacles. A mouse of a woman so much beneath his notice, and without Arabella's sparkle, she might well be a piece of dusty, faded furniture forgotten in an attic. Her dress was drab gray muslin and shapeless, hiding any hint of the body beneath.

Compared to Arabella, this woman was a dried-up crone, a spinster, and not worthy of his interest. Had she not stolen Arabella away from him, he'd be satisfied to go to his dotage without ever having crossed her path.

What infuriated him most was her outright defiance of his wishes and the look of satisfaction on her face, and in her eyes, when she'd dropped a figurative anvil on his head with the news Arabella was wed, bedded, and with child.

For a flash, he'd wondered if the infant could be his, then dismissed the notion. He was careful with all his lovers, and certainly with Arabella. The last thing he wanted was his perfect mistress burdened with his bastard.

It wasn't as if he did not want children someday to carry on his legacy. Just not with his beautiful courtesan. He wanted children with a carefully chosen wife of impeccable pedigree and high social standing.

Under his breath, he cursed the damned Black woman again and felt rage well in his stomach to sour the hopes he'd had to reclaim Arabella this afternoon. What good were money and a fine name when he couldn't keep a beggarly little nobody from sneaking into his life like a thief and stealing away someone he treasured most deeply?

Now Miss Black was staring down the barrel of his pistol, and he intended to pull the trigger. Not literally, of course, but she had to pay for her interference. He wouldn't be satisfied until she was destitute and begging on the streets for moldy bread crusts, and hiking up her skirts for any man with the jangle of coin in his pocket.

A slow grin passed over his face. Such an unseemly fate would certainly wipe the pinched line off her spinster's mouth and knock the haughty and disrespectful glint out of her eyes.

The coach slowed. "Collingwood House, Your Grace."

Pulling his mind from thoughts of revenge, he looked out the window at his home, a monolith of gray stone and red brick, a pair of columns bordering the entrance of the mansion. The home had been his family's residence for two hundred years, ever since his great-great-grandfather won it over a hand of cards.

Nicholas always wondered if the old man had cheated. It wasn't common knowledge among the Ton that his ancestor sometimes donned a highwayman's mask to recoup his gambling losses, but rather a carefully guarded family secret. Any whispers of such a scandal had been only that, whispers.

The Drake name was one of the oldest in England and highly revered. Any ancestor who might have veered slightly off the proper ducal path to engage in nefarious behavior did so under the cover of darkness so as not to soil the family title.

Yet, with the money and power Nicholas had at his disposal, and Collingwood House, he still couldn't keep one mistress content under his care.

Perhaps she would still be happy had she not crossed paths with Miss Black. The woman clearly put thoughts in her head that had no place being there. Arabella *had been* satisfied with their arrangement. He was as sure of it as he was of his own name. And he'd been content.

Sighing, Nicholas climbed out of the coach and walked up the stone steps, the slightest of nods his only acknowledgment to his butler, Alfred.

Alfred nodded. "Your Grace."

All sorts of wicked possibilities for extracting his pound of flesh from Miss Black tumbled in Nicolas's head, each worse than the previous one. Most ended with her chained hand and foot for a year or two in a dank dungeon.

However, he knew he'd do her no physical harm. He couldn't go that far. No, she had to suffer in other ways;

deep, dark, devious ways that showed no scars. His father had taught him the art of subtle torment, and for a second he recognized the old man in himself. He quickly brushed off the association. Miss Black was not his mother. The woman deserved her comeuppance.

But he needed help with his plans, for a man of privilege did not soil his hands doing nefarious deeds.

He paused outside the library and turned back to Alfred. "I need you to fetch Mister Crawford. Tell him I have another job that requires his special talents."

Alfred nodded his graying head. "Yes, Your Grace."

Nicholas slipped into the library and poured himself a brandy. The high-backed leather chair conformed to his body as he tugged his cravat loose and let the heat of the fire ease some of the chill in his bones. This space was his favorite when he had troublesome thoughts on his mind. The smell of dusty old books, a painting of his mother over the fireplace, boyhood memories of her laughter as she pulled some treasured book off the shelf always filled him with warmth and contentment.

Not today. Nothing could ease his sour stomach and take away his anger. With Arabella in place, he'd begun to seek a future bride from the pack of freshly minted debutantes tossed into the marriage mart this Season. Collingwood House needed a duchess and children. It was entirely too long since laughter had filled these cavernous halls and children's footsteps had clattered across these marble floors. Hell, he couldn't remember the last time anyone had laughed with unabashed joy in this house.

He'd chosen Lucy Banes-Dodd as the best of the batch of beauties and had begun making preliminary overtures to her father. Though she was a bit flighty for his taste, she was an attractive chit with an impeccable bloodline. With Arabella in place to warm his bed and Lucy to keep his home and bear his children, he could have found himself quite satisfied that all was as it should be, with his plans perfectly organized and executed the way he ran every aspect of his life. Neat and tidy.

It had all tumbled to ruins with Arabella's disappearance.

"Damn that meddling woman," he muttered under his breath.

The door to the library opened and Mister Crawford walked in unannounced. Tall and stout, the shabbily dressed investigator loped across the room, his ungainly gait the result of an old injury to his left leg.

Though not the sort of man one would invite for afternoon tea, Crawford was very good at his job. He traveled on the fringes of society, dabbled in some disreputable dealings, and was loyal as long as gold continued to flow into his pockets.

"You called for me, Your Grace?"

"You arrived faster than I expected." Nicholas indicated a chair opposite him. The man dropped into it and stretched out his damaged knee. "Were you seated on my stoop?"

Crawford grinned and waved a thin hand. "I was coming to see you, Your Grace. I crossed paths with your footman at the corner. I wanted to see if your confrontation with Miss Black was successful."

Nicholas frowned and lifted his glass. Crawford had found the missing Arabella for him, but that was where their connection with the matter ended. He'd not gossip about his relationship with her, nor relive today's disastrous meeting with Miss Black with the investigator. His private life was just that, private.

"Arabella is no longer my concern," he said dismissively. He leveled a frown on the other man to make his point clear. "Her name will not be mentioned again between us."

The man shrugged. "Aye, Your Grace."

Satisfied, Nicholas knitted his fingers and brought them to his lips. "I have another job for you. I need you to find out as much as you can about Miss Black. Where she goes when she leaves that dreadful town house, who she spends time with, if she has outstanding debts. I want to know every time she blinks or visits the privy. Everything."

"Do you mind me asking why, Your Grace?" Crawford leaned back in his chair. Leather creaked. "She isn't the sort of woman who would attract the likes of you, Your Grace."

"No, she isn't." His lips turned downward. Not in the least. If he and Miss Black were the last two people alive on this Earth, he'd take up celibacy, or leap from the Tower of London headfirst before giving her a second look. "My interest in her is not personal. She stole from me, and I intend to return the favor."

A slow grin crossed Crawford's lined face. "I see."

Somewhere near age forty, the investigator had lived long enough to know London inside and out, and where to dig to find all sorts of salacious information about anyone. He dressed as a man without means, invisible, as it were. If Miss Black had dead bodies hidden in her wardrobe, Crawford would flush them out.

"This might cost you plenty," Crawford said, tapping a finger on his temple. "Miss Black was nearly impossible to find in the first place. The woman holds her secrets close."

Nicholas waved a hand. When he was done with her, her life would be laid bare for all to see. "Cost is of no consequence. I want this done quickly and quietly."

"I will begin right away, Your Grace." Crawford stood, nodded, and hobbled to the door. "When I'm finished with Miss Black, you will know her better than her own mother does."

With a grin, he tottered out the door.

After a moment, Nicholas stretched out his legs and braced his elbow on the arm of the chair. The spinster had faced him down like a growling mutt, her amber eyes filled with scorn, as if he were something vile she'd scraped off the bottom of her shoe.

When he was finished with Miss Black, she'd be on her hands and knees, begging for some kindness and consideration of her plight.

He chuckled and poured another drink.

Eva climbed into the coach and removed her spectacles. She rubbed her eyes with her fingertips, then removed her bonnet and began the slow process of taking the multitude of pins from her hair. The routine of the simple task and the sway of the hack as it rolled through the streets eased some of the tension behind her eyes.

She'd be home soon, and safe.

The day had gone on slowly, long and troubling. After His Grace left, she'd tried to reclaim her schedule with the ladies, but found her mind occupied elsewhere. The enraged look in Nicholas Drake's ducal eyes left her fearful she'd fallen into a viper's pit and faced poisoned fangs. He was a powerful man with powerful friends. He could make her life a nightmare.

Still, to him Arabella was property. There were many young and beautiful women in London, eager for a man like him to keep them in luxury with coin and baubles in exchange for sexual favors. Surely one wayward mistress would not be missed very long, no matter how much he thought he cared for her. Men such as he ultimately cared for no one but themselves.

"And yet, he'd spent months searching for Arabella," she whispered. That worried Eva most of all. Obviously the girl had meant something to His Grace. But was it the fact she'd left him that had him so disturbed? Or did he actually care for, or perhaps love, Arabella?

Eva dropped the pins into her valise, then reached to remove the heavy wig. Released from bondage, a tangle of red-gold curls fell across her shoulders and tumbled down her back in a path of sunshine and fire.

As she began to braid the mass and the rented hack rumbled slowly toward Mayfair, she hoped His Grace would soon claim a new courtesan and forget her, and his former mistress. It irked her that he blamed her for Arabella's defection, as if she'd kidnapped the girl from under his long nose and dragged her screaming before a minister. Arabella had made her own decision to leave him. And had no regrets.

"If only His Grace had seen, or cared, how unhappy she was," Eva said softly, and tied a blue ribbon around the loose braid and replaced her bonnet. "Maybe the sting of her rejection would not be so great."

The moment the girl and Captain Greenhill had met, they'd both fallen deeply in love.

If His Grace knew his courtesan had taken up with a lowly American ship captain, well, Eva hated to think what his opinion of such a situation would be. The British nobles thought the sun rose and set on their command, and His Grace was no exception. How dare Arabella leave him? How dare Eva interfere?

She'd dared, and she would never regret Arabella's joy or that of her handsome husband. In many ways, Eva envied their love and happiness. She might not believe in love or marriage for herself, but she wasn't above enjoying the delight it brought others less jaded.

The town house was quiet when Eva arrived home a short time later, emotionally overwrought and exhausted from worrying about His Grace. After she hung her cloak on a peg and removed her prim gray bonnet, she took a moment to look around the simple but elegant green entryway and vowed that from this moment on, she would never give another thought to the duke. He could rage all he wanted and cut a swath of destruction across London, but he'd quickly learn that in spite of his power and wealth, he couldn't always have everything he wanted.

"There you are, Miss." Bessie walked out of the parlor.

The dour pinch of worry evaporated from her plump face and eased the lines around her eyes. "I was beginning to worry. You are not usually out so late."

"I was detained by a situation beyond my control, and it put me behind schedule." Eva blinked the duke's handsome visage out of her mind, and straightened. "How is Mother?"

"Miss Charlotte is resting in her room." Bessie Clark had lived with Eva and her mother since right before Eva was born. She knew everything about Charlotte's past and the circumstances of Eva's conception, yet she never judged. Like Harold, the housekeeper kept their secrets and watched over both women like a broody hen. "She was doing well this morning but took a turn after her luncheon. I believe she was thinking of your father again. She had that look in her eyes."

Eva nodded slowly. Whenever her mother thought of His Lordship, it was as if ten years hadn't passed since his death. She'd slip into a trancelike state, then fall into a deep melancholia once she realized he wasn't coming back to her. Ever.

"If you could ask Cook to make us a tray, I'll go to her." Eva headed for the stairs. As tired as she was, her mother always took comfort in her presence. If she was in a state, only Eva could ease her quiet suffering. "Oh, and perhaps you could include some of the lemon cakes. Mother does adore them."

"Yes, Miss."

Though it was still light outside, her mother's room was dark behind drawn drapes, and not even rose pink walls and a soft pink quilt could brighten the space. Propped against pillows, Charlotte Rose Winfield, once the most celebrated courtesan of her time, lay sleeping, with a cloud of gray-blonde curls spread out around her head and shoulders.

A floorboard creaked beneath Eva's foot, and her mother's blue eyes opened. A slow, sleepy smile crossed her face, in it a hint of the beauty she once had been, and still was.

"Evangeline. There is my angel. Come sit with me." Charlotte lifted her hand, and Eva moved to her side and took a place next to her on the bed. The soft odor of rosewater, her mother's signature scent, filled her senses. "You look tired, dearest. When I spoke to your father today, he agreed that you are working too hard. Though I know you like to help those poor destitute women, you must also watch out for your health."

The household, and her mother in particular, thought she assisted impoverished widows to find work. Only Bessie and Harold knew the truth. Society as a whole scorned courtesans and courtesans' bastard daughters, so she and her mother kept to themselves, hidden away from Charlotte's past.

Because of her mother's history and the circumstances of her own birth, Eva would already have more than one black mark against her in the eyes of society if the truth were known. To further lower herself by helping courtesans to a better life, though some might find it a noble calling, would horrify most people. Society would view her as lowering herself to speak to someone of such low rank.

The humor in this was that, unbeknownst to her acquaintances and lofty neighbors, she was a member of that same lower rank, a bastard offspring of a whore. A situation Eva found amusing in spite of the sadness that normally came of such a state of affairs.

Truthfully, she was content with her lot. She had her mother, a nice home on a pleasant street, and her work to keep her busy. What more could she desire?

"I will rest tonight, Mum, I promise." She looked down at the delicate hand in hers. Theirs was an odd pairing. Mother had become daughter, and daughter, mother. The roles had reversed that awful morning when Father's solicitor came to the door, hat in hand, with the worst news imaginable. Father had died in a horrible coach accident on an ice-slick road while on his way to visit them one snowy night.

The already fragile Charlotte had plunged into a gray place in her mind for close to a month. Only through Eva's forceful will had she taken any food. When Charlotte finally broke free of her deepest mourning, Eva had become her caretaker, Mother a near invalid. If not for her beloved child, Eva was certain her mother would have succumbed to her grief and followed her lover to his grave.

"God was smiling on me when he gave me you, sweet Evangeline." Mother squeezed her hand and smiled softly. "Did I ever tell you how happy your father was when I told him I was with child? He was happier than I've ever seen him. After ten years together, we finally had you."

"I know the story well, Mum." Unhappily wed to a shrewish woman of perfect breeding, Father chose Mother for love. A love he had no right to give when he had a wife and children at home. Still, Eva had loved him with childish innocence. His loss had shattered her heart, and she'd never quite managed to piece it back together. "Yours was history's grandest love affair," Eva teased. As grand as a love match could be when one of the two parties belonged to another.

Her mother smiled wistfully and closed her lids. "All women should be so lucky in love."

Lord Seymour and her mother cared not what society thought of their arrangement. They lived and loved with their hearts. However, in the end, Charlotte had ended up alone with a bastard child to raise and a small monthly stipend from his estate that her father had seen fit to put into place at Eva's birth. His wretched wife had tried, and failed, to discreetly cut off Charlotte and Eva from their inheritance.

Finally accepting defeat in the courts, and risking public shame by pursuing the matter further, Lady Seymour and

Eva's two spoiled half sisters faded off to Kent to enjoy the massive bulk of the family fortune, without giving another thought to Charlotte or Eva. And Eva was happy to be left in peace.

"He loved you dearly, you know, angel." Charlotte opened her eyes and deep sadness filled the blue depths. "You were his little love, his treasure."

"I know." Eva tucked the coverlet up to her mother's shoulders. "He was a wonderful father. I miss him every day."

Turning away, Charlotte tucked her arms to her chest and sadness filtered through her eyes. Once she began to fade away to her memories, there was no pulling her back into the present. "I will sleep now."

Eva sat in the chair for a while until her mother's breathing evened out and she slept. Half a lifetime of loving one man had come to this. Her mother suffered for love, a tragic figure alone in a bed, grieving still for her knight who had died alone on a dark road while traveling to spend two nights in her arms while his wife was off visiting family.

Love. A condition Eva chose never to experience if her mother's fate was to be her example. She'd long ago vowed never to love a man, any man, if this was the way such grand love played out. Love was not worth the price one paid when one life ended.

So she devoted herself to her mother, and her courtesans, for they had no qualms about love and marriage. And she was content. Never would a duke, or any man, come looking to the far reaches of the Earth for her, obsessed by what he'd lost, determined to drag her back into his life and bed.

To the world outside she was a poor young woman whose wealthy merchant father was lost at sea. She took care of her widowed mother, ill from a weak heart, or so the neighbors thought, and kept mostly to herself. Charlotte Rose, once a beautiful and celebrated courtesan, had vanished years ago, following her lover's death, into obscurity and speculation. No one would ever put Eva's mother and the courtesan together as one.

Out of the ashes of her father's death, thirteen-year-old Eva had grown up fast in the following ten years and made a new life for them, free of the shadows of her mother's former profession. And she'd do whatever it took to keep their secrets from destroying them both.

Chapter Four

"I do not understand this." Eva stared blankly at Mister Smith, her solicitor, as if he'd grown a giant wart in the center of his forehead. The man was pale beneath a mop of brown hair, his face screwed up with concern. "Mother's town house was a gift from a, ah, friend. The note should be paid in full."

Mister Smith picked through a stack of financial documents, then removed one from the bottom. He slid it across the desk, and she pulled it to her with her fingertips.

"This should explain everything, Miss Winfield," he said.

Eva went first to the heading and then to the signature to verify the document was an official bank document. She began to read the neatly penned text slowly, careful to make certain she understood it in its entirety. If she was facing ruin, she wanted to know exactly how she got there, and why.

Mister Smith was correct. With every word she read, the floor was crumbling beneath her feet and launching her and her mother into a dark abyss.

"Unfortunately, four years ago Mrs. Winfield used this town house as collateral for a loan of some size." Mister Smith laid another note near her hand. Eva examined it as if the paper was laced with poison before she picked it up. "I believe she wanted to purchase a necklace of sapphires and diamonds."

"A necklace?" What necklace? Eva pressed a hand to her temple. There had been several odd purchases during a two-year period when Mother was at her worst. She'd battled a number of serious health issues, and her mind seemed to take a turn downward with each.

"Nearly every week a new package was delivered to the door, only to be immediately returned to where it came from," she said. "Unusual things like ostrich feathers and men's shoes, and a very strange-looking dog with a large head. I thought I had returned them all."

He shook his head. "Apparently not everything, Miss. We still don't know about any recent debts. There is also a plot of land outside of York. I took the liberty of investigating its worth, and I fear your mother was taken in by the previous owner. It is worthless, too wet to plant a sustainable crop." Mister Smith hesitantly pushed another note to her. "Between these two and a few smaller notes, this town house is heavily in debt."

Eva wanted to rail against the heavens with an upraised fist, or rather, at her mother, one floor up. But Mother was incapable of understanding the consequences of her actions or how to resolve them. It was up to Eva to muddle through the mess and find a way to save their home.

"Mister Wellsley should have notified me of this situation immediately upon its discovery," Eva said. "I cannot believe he would have made her a loan when he was clear on her condition.

"I need to speak to Mister Wellsley immediately."

Two spots of red appeared on Mr. Smith's high, sharp cheekbones.

"Mister Wellsley retired a year ago to Scotland. His position was taken over by Mister Tew." Mister Smith shuffled papers and avoided her eyes. "Apparently the majority of your mother's older debts were purchased by an anonymous third party who has decided to call in the notes. The man is putting the bank on notice to pay up, and there is growing pressure to force Tew to sell this house to cover the notes."

Eva fought both panic and a pressing headache. She envisioned Mother and herself buried from their toes to their chins in receipts, with boxes of her mother's silly purchases scattered in the foyer for them to step around as they were escorted out the door and their home was closed and locked behind them.

"What can we do?" Her voice sounded high and frantic in her ears. "Perhaps I can speak to the man who bought the notes and work out some sort of monthly payment schedule?"

Mister Smith slowly shook his head, his eyes deeply troubled.

Frustration filled her like beach sand, heavy and wet.

She wanted to throw herself across the desk, wrap her hands around his skinny neck, and shake him until his teeth chattered. Sadly, he was only doing his job.

"I fear not, Miss Eva." He shuffled from one foot to the other, then, under her glare, took two steps backward. "He has asked to remain anonymous. He will contact you in his own time."

The desire to choke him faded. He was just the messenger, the puppet made of wood and stuffing. Someone else was manipulating the strings.

She dipped her head and circled her fingertips on her temples. "So I am to wait for him to decide what he intends to do with us? My mother is ill. Surely you can do something."

He twisted his hat in his hands.

"I will do what I can, Miss Winfield."

He put his crumpled hat on his head and left her in a flapping of coattails as he quickly fled the room.

Only then, when the house fell silent, did she give way to tears, sobbing softly.

How could this happen? She'd been so careful. Mother was watched closely when she was out, so as not to cause trouble for herself or others. Still, sometime, somewhere, she'd managed to sink them into a pit of debt.

Eva lifted her hands to her face and brushed aside the tears with her sleeves. There must be something she could do.

Surely the holder of the notes had some compassion in his heart. He could not be so cruel as to cast out two women alone and without a protector. Then again, that was how many courtesans turned to their profession.

It was the shame of allowing such a disaster to fall on her family that sickened Eva. She had done her best to hide her mother away and to protect her in her illness. She'd find a way to settle this to a satisfactory conclusion.

Knuckles sounded on the door. Harold opened the panel and stuck his head in. "Miss Eva, there is a messenger at the door with a note. He has been given instructions to speak only to you." He frowned. "Did Smith give you bad news?"

She shook her head firmly. "Mother has some very large debts, and the largest noteholder is pushing to get paid." She forced a stiff smile. "Please don't worry. It is nothing I cannot handle."

Eva scrubbed her cheeks one last time, sniffed, and took a few deep breaths. She pushed up from the desk and walked from the room. Standing at the front door was a man in livery she didn't recognize, holding a letter. Once she confirmed her identity, he handed over the note and walked away.

"Who is it from?"

Eva turned the note to stare at the unfamiliar seal. Harold moved close and peered over her shoulder. "I have no idea." She ripped open the envelope and unfolded the missive. The words were clipped and to the point. "It is from my creditor. He asks me to meet him alone at his town house in one hour, as we have many things to discuss. The address is here at the bottom."

A shiver passed through her. There wasn't a signature or any hint of her creditor's identity.

It was suspicious. If he was a man of sterling character, there would not be a need to hide his identity. Clearly, something was amiss, and she feared she was about to face the executioner's axe.

"You should not go alone." Harold crossed his arms, and muscles bulged beneath his coat. "It could be a trap."

"A trap? What could be worse than what I'm facing now? He holds my entire future in his hands." Her mother's future, too. "If he wants me to scrub his floors and darn his socks, it will be a little price to pay for keeping our home."

"Any decent man would not ask that of you." Harold took the note, read it, and handed it back. "We will go together."

"I must go alone," she said firmly. "I have to find out his reasons for this strange behavior, and I suspect he will not be pleased if I come with a guard." She folded the note and shoved it back into the envelope. "You will take me. Stay at the corner, and I will walk in alone. If I am not back in a fair bit of time, you have my permission to storm the battlements."

Though clearly displeased, Harold would do as she asked. He might not be a servant in the true sense of the word, but he was employed by her and did her bidding. "I will ready myself." She brushed her hand over her hair and went to the drawer holding her wig and spectacles. "Meet me outside with the carriage in half an hour."

* * *

The ride was not long, and Eva spent the time running every possible situation through her head. If this man was up to something untoward, Harold would be near. If his plan was to ruin her, she wanted to know why. As far as she could imagine, she had no real enemies, as her social circle was more of a tiny dot.

Well, there was one possible enemy. The duke had blustered about Arabella and made veiled threats.

It could not be him. Could it?

Surely His Grace had moved on with his life over the last two weeks. Men of his stature used and cast aside women as a matter of course. Arabella was sweet and beautiful, but one mistress could easily be replaced with another in a city the size of London. There were many young women eager to do anything for shelter and a way out of a hopeless existence.

Such a virile man as His Grace would want a woman in his bed posthaste. Still, her mind could not dismiss him as her tormentor. He'd stalked off enraged.

Harold stopped the carriage as she instructed, and a last brief argument ensued. Eva won, though the victory was hollow. She walked the remaining distance to the town house with his last warning to be careful echoing in her ears.

It was a three-story, simple structure built of sandstone without excessive adornment. The plants along the sidewalk were without spring color, and the door was simple oak without intricate carvings in the wood. It gave no hint of the owner's identity as Eva strode up the walk.

Compared to the finer homes on the block, there was nothing to make it stand out as belonging to a man of wealth.

Eva patted her wig to assure herself it was in place and adjusted her spectacles. Her black cape covered a severe brown dress with a neckline that came up under her chin.

She hoped to come across as formidable, lest he think she could be easily cowed, or had a mistaken belief she might be willing to trade her body to satisfy her debts.

With her stomach tightly knotted and her knees twitching, she reached for the knocker.

"I am Miss Black. I have an appointment with your employer," she said to the stern woman who answered the door. Deep grooves lined her forehead and ran between her eyes. Her mouth was pinched into a thin line. Her clothing indicated she was the housekeeper.

"Yes, come with me." Clearly the servant had little to smile about. Her employer must be a harsh taskmaster.

The ominous cloud darkened over Eva's head.

Eva followed the woman deep into the house and up the stairs, passing several rooms as they went. The floral decoration favored throughout appeared to have been chosen by a woman, perhaps the wife of the owner. The thought gave her some relief. If a wife was lurking nearby, the man would be less likely to misbehave.

"In here." The starchy housekeeper frowned, waited for her to pass into the small parlor, and quickly withdrew.

"Wait," Eva exclaimed, but it was too late. The doors were closed in her face with a loud click. She waited for a key being turned in the lock, rendering her a prisoner.

The only sound was the tap of footsteps of the retreating housekeeper.

Eva expelled a breath and examined her surroundings. Patterned in roses and vines, the tapestries, rugs, settees, and chairs were covered with fabric in an explosion of flowers in pinks and reds. The walls were papered with green and pink stripes, and several vases of pink and red roses, fading with age, covered every table surface.

The cloying scent of roses in the small space made breathing a chore. She felt as if a flower cart had overturned upon her as she walked down the sidewalk and buried her beneath a garden of blooms.

Clearly the mistress of the home had questionable taste, yet the wealth to buy out-of-season blooms. A few roses, yes, but this? How could one entertain friends in such an overwhelming room? One's mind could not focus on conversation when eyes were watering and sneezes were threatening.

So caught up was she in the contemplation of bad taste, Eva did not hear the door open behind her.

"Arabella chose the decor." The deep voice startled her, and she turned with a gasp. "It is a bit overwhelming. Fortunately, she had other talents."

"Your Grace." Her heart raced. Her worst fear had come to fruition. The man who held her notes, who all but owned her, was the same man who hated her. And in his rage, he'd managed to find the ideal way to exact his revenge. The one thing women feared most in this world of male dominance.

Poverty.

The duke stood in the open doorway in his shirtsleeves. His savage and handsome face was etched in a tight frown beneath the casual fall of dark waves across his forehead. Buff breeches encased muscled thighs to sinewy perfection, and just the hint of dark curls peeked out from beneath the open collar of his snowy shirt.

He was powerful and mesmerizing in his raw masculinity. It was all she could do to remember to breathe.

If not for the hatred for him that turned her stomach into a painful lump, she could easily be caught under his sensuous spell, as doubtless many women had been.

She wanted to run to the window, throw open the sash, and cry out for Harold to rescue her. But that would gain her little. She had to hear what he had to say and work out a plan to save Mother and herself. And if he decided to strangle her right here in this room of roses, Harold was too far away to stop him anyway.

Thankfully she'd chosen a gown with a high, stiff collar

to aid in strangulation prevention. Only a collar of thorns would make better armor.

"What do you want from me?" she asked, her voice thin. She watched his frown turn into a malevolent scowl. Fear sizzled down her spine. He was the devil himself.

"I want Arabella back."

Eva's shoulders slumped. She wanted to drop into the nearest chair but feared showing weakness. All she could do was puff up her feathers and make a show of confidence.

"I thought that matter was settled, Your Grace."

He stepped into the room and closed the door. "Oh, yes, it was. You are the reason she is not sharing my bed." He moved over to one narrow window and pushed it open enough to allow in a cool breeze to ruffle his shirt and hair, but not enough to allow her the space to launch an escape.

Unfortunately.

"Pity." She failed to sound sympathetic. "If you walk down Bond Street and crook your finger, Your Grace, I am certain you will have a full dozen eager would-be lovers to choose from." She made a face. "Your bed will not be empty for long."

His face went stony.

She had the grim feeling of being a mouse batted about by a playful cat before it finally decided to gobble down the helpless creature for its supper.

But if His Grace thought her helpless in his claws, he would be in for a surprise. She might be financially beholden to him, but she was no weak ninny. Hardships in her life had turned her spine to steel. It would take more than this setback to break her spirit.

So she walked to the nearest settee, where she settled herself, taking great care in spreading her cape and skirts around her as serenely as if she were invited for tea. When she finally lifted her eyes to his, she arched a brow and clasped her hands in her lap.

"I understand, Your Grace, that you have purchased my

notes." She hoped for some indication of his thoughts, but his face was impassive. "Perhaps you would like to tell me what kind of torment you plan for me in your desire for revenge. Cleaning your chamber pots? Throwing myself over rain puddles so you do not ruin your boots? Mucking out your stables?" She stared into his eyes. "Pray do not keep me in suspense a moment longer."

Nicholas watched the silly creature make a show of bravado, but she couldn't hide the tremor in her hands no matter how tightly she clasped them together. She was afraid of him, from her wide, worried eyes to the nervous leg twitch beneath her horrid brown gown.

Without her servant guard to stand over her like a wall between them, she was at his mercy, fully and completely.

And she knew it.

If only he had some shackles to rattle or a crop to tap against his boot. He bit back a grin.

He was enjoying this.

"I have learned many things about you over the last two weeks, Miss Black. Saving courtesans from ruin? What a foolish notion. Many chose their life as a way of saving themselves from backbreaking poverty. Would you rather see them starving and defiled in dark alleys for crusts of bread and a sip of ale?"

"Th-there are other options."

"As a seamstress or lady's companion or maid?" He snorted. "How many positions are available to the multitude of women who come to town seeking employment, Miss Black? A couple dozen? Less? And what of those women like Arabella, who draw the attention of men? Do you think a wife will accept her presence in a household with her husband?"

"I do not offer them employment," she said.

"No, you give them husbands."

"Mock me as you will, Your Grace, but I have had much success." She put her hand to her heart. "You are wealthy and a man. It is easy to dismiss my endeavors on behalf of these desperate women."

She had a point, though he'd not tell her so. He had always gotten everything he desired. It was difficult to imagine worrying over every scrap of food or finding shelter at night from the dangers of the city. Still, he hadn't the time or desire to quibble with her over the state of women when his mind was on revenge.

The spinster settled back on the settee, not as confident as before. She was tightly wound and appeared ready to dart for the open window if he moved too quickly. Since he had not yet sprung the trap, he slowly crossed his arms and leaned back on his heels.

"You are curious why I've asked you here and why I have purchased your debts. I suspect you believe I have nefarious plans for you, and you are correct. I did not take over your finances out of concern for your welfare." He paused, watching worry filter into her eyes. "As you know, I am without a mistress at present, thanks to you and your interference. I believe that makes you obligated to replace Arabella."

Her mouth gaped, and he continued before she could protest. "I understand you have several courtesans at your town house in Cheapside that will do nicely." She began to sputter as color infused her pale face. He bit back a grin. "I shall give you a list of the qualifications I desire in a lover. You shall choose one of the women for me and make the introduction."

"I will not." Outraged, she jumped to her feet. She had to look up to meet his eyes. "How dare you propose such a vile thing? Those women have had enough of being used and degraded for the baser needs of men. I will not hand one of them over to you on a leash, no matter what it costs me."

He lifted a brow. "Oh, I believe you will, Miss Black. I have you hanging from a cliff by your nails. You will do as I ask."

"Over my rotting corpse." She jutted out her chin. "I will not barter one of my courtesans to save myself."

Her stoicism surprised him. Most women would be in tears. But not this stiff spinster. She had nettle drawers and needles in her corset.

Evidently, he had to notch up the threats to get her to whimper. "What of your mother, Miss Black? What consequences should she pay for your refusal to cooperate?"

Her jaw tightened and her expression changed into that of a fierce tigress. "Leave my mother out of this, Your Grace."

Clearly, he had struck a nerve. She might not give a fig whether she ended up in poverty, but her mother was another matter. The cat had claws. He'd better not expose his back to her or he'd find his flesh shredded.

"My offer is simple, Miss Black. Find me a courtesan and I will turn over your notes; if she proves to be a satisfactory lover first, of course." He paused and watched her eyes darken and her face turn an odd shade of plum. "Then you can be assured your mother lives the rest of her days in the comfort she deserves."

"You are a despicable man." Her voice dropped and cracked as her thin shoulders slumped slightly forward. "My mother is ill. Surely you can find another way to torture me. I cannot give you one of my young women; they are not mine to give."

Nicholas watched defeat cross her face, and for the first time he noticed her delicate cheekbones and the long lashes framing her fierce amber eyes. It seemed an unusual moment to see there was actually a real woman beneath her colorless exterior, and not a wooden shop display.

If not for her drab clothing and dull brown hair, she might be considered mildly interesting to look at. Not enough to stir one to great passion, but not unpleasant to peer at over a table when breakfasting.

Suddenly he realized the perfect way to torment Miss Black and steal some of her starch. He'd known she would never accept his directive, and truthfully, he had no interest in any of her courtesans. He only wanted to see how far he could push her before she broke.

In her trim little frame she had more steely strength than he'd expected. Even without her giant bulldog of a servant to loom over her, she held fast to her convictions.

No, the stakes had to be raised.

And he knew how to push her over the edge. "Perhaps I can suggest another solution."

Chapter Five

Nicholas saw her stiffen and dig her nails into the arm of the settee. She was braced for his next assault on her morals and sensibilities. He wouldn't disappoint.

Though he had no plans to hurt her physically, tweaking her mind a bit had its rewards. Perhaps it would lessen some of her starch and dull her saber-sharp tongue.

Some of his anger had abated over the past few days, until his thoughts turned back to Arabella. Then he'd become angry all over again. He missed his courtesan's sweetness, her passion, and her laughter; all because of this prickly spinster and her outlandish desire to end the institution of mistresses and courtesans.

"Wh-what sort of solution?" she asked tentatively, obviously expecting the worst of him.

She had no idea.

"I propose a solution that will be satisfying to us both, Miss Black." He stressed "satisfying" and saw her stiffen. It was time for a full assault. He lowered his voice seductively and locked onto her gaze. "You are an intelligent woman. Undoubtedly, you have felt the connection between us."

She swallowed, her fingers plucking at the folds of her skirt. "I—I am sure I do not understand your meaning, Your Grace."

Slowly, he swept his gaze down her body. Though there wasn't much of interest to see in her person, he was positive he could find something attractive about her if he had a full day to pick her apart. He carefully examined every visible curve. Miss Black had a decent figure, if one had a taste for slender women.

He smiled. "I believe you do."

He walked around the back of the settee and placed his hands on the seat back on either side of her shoulders. Not touching, yet close enough to worry the tightly wound spinster.

Nicholas leaned low and caught the light scent of her lilac perfume drifting off a perfect, white, and well-hidden neck. It was positively delightful.

Beneath his breeches, he felt his cock stir for this bland spinster, and almost succumbed to a sudden urge to press his mouth against the narrow band of exposed skin beneath her dull brown hair. He had found something attractive about her. The surprise was his.

"Deny my words, but I know women." He dipped his face until his mouth was dangerously close to touching the spot right below her left ear. She shivered. "I intrigue you, Miss Black."

He grinned and exhaled warm breath onto her neck. She let out a small gasp and jumped to her feet. She pivoted and backed toward the door as he rounded the settee and stalked toward her.

"Just to make myself clear," she said, "there is nothing, nothing, about you that pleases or intrigues me. I would find a toothless rat catcher more appealing than you, Your Grace."

A chuckle escaped him. She was a fiery little wench.

"I am wounded, Miss Black," he said softly as he scanned the curves of her full, pink, and slightly parted mouth. "For I find you desperately appealing in your stiff and humorless way."

She gaped. It was impossible to tell if she suspected he was toying with her or was serious in his claims of attraction.

"I think it best if we forget this conversation in its entirety and keep our dealings to business. I would like to discuss a reasonable plan to repay my debts."

"I thought we settled this matter already, Miss Black," he said. "Your debts for a courtesan."

"I will not do that."

Blast! He would settle for one whimper, one lip quiver, and this would all be over and they would never need to cross paths again. She could send him a halfpence, a shilling a month to satisfy her debt and he'd be content. All he truly wanted was for her to suffer a small measure of the unhappiness he felt over losing Arabella. Yet, she clearly felt no remorse for his loss or any emotion for her financial ruination, as if her heart was stone.

"If you are unwilling to hand over a courtesan, I see no other option than for you to take Arabella's place." Her stubbornness reminded him of just how much he disdained everything about her, her delightful neck—hell, her mouth too—aside. He twisted his lips downward. "Though I fear you will be lacking in all areas of lovemaking, I will be happy to teach you how to please a man."

Her slap jerked his head sideways.

"You are a horrible and disgusting man," she ground out between gritted teeth. "I would rather lie down with swine."

He worked his jaw and shot out a hand to grab her arm as she stomped past him. Spinning her about, he pulled her against his chest and locked her into his embrace.

The softness of her lush body took him aback. She was

not as thin as he'd suspected. She possessed a few fine curves after all. However, it didn't matter. She was Miss Black all the same.

Eva struggled. Fire flicked through her eyes.

"You have a choice," he growled. "Accept my offer or hand over one of your courtesans. I'll have your answer at the end of the week, or I will have you turned out."

Eva pushed against him, and his hold on her waist slackened. She tried to step back, but he slid a hand behind her neck and pulled her face up to his. She looked terrified, yet was there was something, else? With each breath her modest breasts pressed against his chest and her heart beat erratically, hard enough that he could almost hear the beats. But it was her lips, pink and tipped up slightly at the corners and parted with her quivering breaths, that drew his full attention.

Without warning, he kissed her, hard.

Heat flashed down his body to ignite his erection. Her lips tasted of tea and mint and all things feminine. She let out a muted cry at the back of her throat and went limp. He probed her teeth in a silent call for entrance into her mouth, and for a moment he thought she would allow him to deepen the kiss.

He cupped her breast and teased the nipple.

She unclenched her jaw.

Then a set of teeth clamped down on his bottom lip. Nicholas grunted and released her. He pressed his fingertip to the throbbing injury. She turned, and fled the room in the rustle of heavy skirts.

A hard smile tugged at his mouth. He wanted to chase after her and paddle her bottom red. But it was an unexpected discovery that stayed his feet and set his mind reeling. In the moment she'd spun about and raced for the door, he'd noticed a lock of burnished gold and fire red tumble out from beneath her severe brown bun like the hues of breaking dawn.

There was much more to the dowdy spinster than he ever suspected. And he intended to discover all her secrets.

Eva raced down the sidewalk toward the waiting carriage. She pressed a gloved hand to her mouth and swiped the duke's taste from her lips.

Erasing him from her mind would be more difficult. In the instant between his kiss and her bite, her body had exploded in a riot of unexpected sensations. She'd felt flushed and confused as the most intimate part of her pulsed with what she could only think was a visceral reaction to the kiss.

Even now, as the cool wind blew around her, she felt both feverish and cold at the same time. The despicable duke had marked her with his kiss, stolen bits of her with his sensuous assault, and she feared she might never get those pieces back.

It took will to keep her feet moving forward when she wanted to slump to her knees in despair. The wretch had kissed her! No man had ever taken such liberties. Even now she felt one of his hands on the small of her back and the other hand, rough and male, encircling her neck as he bent his face to hers.

She steeled her emotions. "Please, Harold, take me home."

Harold helped her into the carriage, looking back at the town house with a vicious scowl.

Eva rushed to soothe his anger. "His Grace did not hurt me. Not physically." Then she looked away to hide the blush on her cheeks. Not by hand or weapon anyway.

Harold tensed. "So it was the duke."

She nodded. "Yes."

It wasn't until later, when she'd locked her bedroom door behind her, that she dissolved into a fit of weeping. Her

need to help courtesans make a better life for themselves
was turned around on her when he suggested she become
the very thing she reviled. A woman forced to bed a man
in order to survive.

Sweet Arabella saved, and her vile protector's desire for
revenge, and now Eva was on the cusp of losing everything.

But it was not the lost money she feared, nor homeless-
ness, if she had only herself to worry over. No, it was her
mother, her school, and her innocence that she grieved for.

The monthly stipend was enough to live off but not
to cover the piles of debts Mother had incurred. And she
would never turn over one of her ladies to the duke or allow
her mother to suffer the desperation of poverty, and he well
knew it.

If there was any other way to solve her situation, she'd
grasp it as a lifeline. There was nothing.

He would soon own her body, if not her soul.

There was no more perfect way to distract Eva from her
troubles than a visit to her courtesans and to plunge
into another lesson. When she returned to the town house
in Cheapside late the next day, the young ladies were in the
garden having tea. The sun had chosen to make an appearance after nearly a week of clouds and rain, and the five
women were having an animated conversation under the
shade of the huge oak tree.

"Miss Eva!" Rose exclaimed as Eva rounded the path
and came into view. In spite of their slightly inappropriate
low-cut gowns, not an areola was showing, and the bright
gowns, covered in feathers and bows, were a burst of color
lighting Eva's dim mood.

"Come and join us," Pauline said, reaching for the teapot.
"We have just finished learning to mend a hem. Abigail taught
us. She has perfect stitches."

Abigail smiled, her face pinkening. "I had to learn. Mother

could not be bothered, and would not spend the coin necessary to hire a seamstress to make needed repairs."

"My mother was too busy keeping that bastard husband of hers out of my bed to concern herself over domestic pursuits," Rose interjected. "The only time I used a needle was to stab him in the hand when he shoved it up my skirt." She sighed. "I was tossed out that very morning."

There were murmurs of sympathy all around.

"Well deserved, Rose," Yvette said, frowning. "You should have stabbed him in the heart."

Rose and Pauline giggled. "What about you, Sophie?" Rose asked. "Was your mum the domestic sort?"

"My mum was a courtesan," Sophie said, her voice emotionless. "She lived to pleasure her lovers. She left the sewing to the maids and my care to her sister. Auntie Jane's only concern was her next drink."

Smiles faded, and the women fell silent. They all had different, yet similar, tales of woe and managed to find laughter and hope anyway. Eva had once considered herself lucky to have had a father who looked after her. Now she was not so different from her courtesans.

In a few short days, Eva had gone from their protector and instructor to standing on the cusp of becoming one of them; a woman without options who gave her body to the highest bidder.

That they all had not become angry and bitter was miraculous. She hadn't yet been taken to bed by His Grace, and she was already feeling both emotions. A sense of despair had been with her since their encounter the previous day, along with waves of anger. And with his hated face ever looming in her mind, she thought the darkness of his presence would follow her always.

"I am pleased to find you all together." Eva changed the topic before it became too grim. She forced a smile and hoped the dark circles around her eyes weren't noticeable. Her meeting with the duke last evening had made sleep fitful. She'd woken up several times, her body drenched with sweat and her nipples pressed against her thin night-dress as if her body was readying itself for a lover.

Eva shifted uncomfortably on the chair. "I thought per-haps we could discuss what you learned yesterday from Cook. Perhaps Abigail would like to start."

They spent the next hour discussing everything one needed to know about supervising a kitchen and staff, and how to plan a menu when entertaining.

"Who knew there was so much to learn?" Abigail said softly. "The marquis has a staff in place. I need do nothing all day but await his visit."

"I thought your lover was a baron?" Yvette asked.

Abigail flushed from her roots to her neck. "Did I say baron? The baron was my first, ah, lover. The marquis is the current one."

Eva turned the topic back to their lessons. "Soon you will be in charge of all aspects of your homes while your husbands work," Eva said. "And if some of you are blessed with children, you'll have to hire a nanny and tutors, too. It is a lot of work, but running a household smoothly is very rewarding."

Pauline sat back in her chair, her eyes troubled. "I am not sure I can do this." She worried her bottom lip with her teeth. "I did not even choose my own gowns. His Lordship had them brought to me by the modiste."

Indeed. That explained the cut of Pauline's corsets and how her large bosom was hiked up so high it defied gravity.

Eva frowned. No matter what dismal fate His Grace planned for her, she vowed he would never rule her life as these women's had been ruled.

"I have planned shopping for us tomorrow afternoon, Pauline, and you will be able to purchase gowns of your choosing." Eva wondered if His Grace liked his lovers with their breasts aloft and their buttocks thinly veiled. She pushed the thought aside. "We will cut a swath across

London and learn everything there is to know about clothing, from the skin out."

"I do love to shop." Rose clapped her hands and wriggled in her chair. "The duke preferred me in pink." She indicated her gown and grimaced. "I think I shall choose everything blue."

Even Sophie managed a smile. "It will be nice to wear something new that isn't mended until the cloth can no longer hold a stitch. The earl pinched each farthing until it cried out for mercy."

It took Eva a moment to realize stern Sophie was making a jest, and she chuckled. The other women chuckled as well. Eva realized there was more to Sophie than just the hard edge she presented to the world. It might take longer to find her a husband than the others, but Eva would rise to the challenge.

"On that note, why don't we discuss how to budget the household allowance?" And Eva spent the next hour doing just that. The dull talk kept her mind off the duke.

The sun had barely begun to cast a few tentative threads of gold across Hyde Park when Eva broke the morning fog on the back of Muffin, the little mare her father had given her for her tenth birthday. Most would consider the dapple gray horse quite tame and certainly a dull ride, as the mare was nearing eighteen, but for Eva, Muffin represented a time when her father was still alive and Mother and she were truly happy.

For years of good memories and a sweet disposition, Muffin resided in a place of glory in the small stable behind their town house, along with their one carriage horse, Benny, and would remain there as long as she drew breath.

"The day will be a hot one, don't you think, darling?" Eva ran her gloved hand down the side of Muffin's neck as the cool morning began to warm nicely with the sun. "Perhaps you can roust yourself for a bit of a run today?"

Eva breathed in the cool, wet air and sighed with longing. Muffin had one speed: slow. Eva would need a different horse if she ever wanted the wind whipping through her hair as she raced along the park's winding paths.

Clad in a simple gray riding habit, she'd chosen to don her wig beneath her matching gray hat, and perched her spectacles on her nose, out of fear His Grace had spies lurking behind every potted plant and bush along the street outside her home.

As long as she held tightly to her disguise and repelled him with her plainness, she might be able to convince him to seek his vile pleasures elsewhere and leave her be.

It was a notion she very much worried was futile. The duke longed to make her pay, and what better way than to force her to suffer his lecherous attentions?

Eva urged Muffin on when she stopped to nip at a clump of grass. The mare snorted and clopped slowly down the lane with bits of grass hanging from the side of her mouth. Since the park was empty at the early hour, Eva had plenty of time to think without interruption about her most troubling topic: His Grace, and how to defy him.

Eva was so caught up in her worries that it took her a moment to realize Muffin was walking in an uneven gait. She drew the mare to a halt.

"What is this?" She dismounted and tipped back her hat. "Have you picked up a stone?" She led Muffin a few steps down the path to discover the injured foot, then lifted the mare's leg for an examination. Sure enough, a small pebble was wedged in her hoof, just sizable enough to cause discomfort. "Oh, dear. Let me see what I can do to get that out."

Eva pulled off one glove and dug at the area around the pebble with her nail. The pebble seemed quite determined to stay where it was. She released the hoof and looked around for something to pick it loose. At that moment, a squirrel darted across the road and Muffin shied into Eva. A hoof came down on her foot before she could jump out of the way.

Eva yelped as the full weight of the plump mare ground into her toes. Pain shot through her foot.

"Well done, Muffin," she said scornfully. "You put full effort into crushing my toes."

Unconcerned, the mare lowered her head to push a leaf around with her lip.

"I did not plan to consummate our arrangement in the park." A sardonic voice floated out of the misty fog. "But I suppose I can find a large bush behind which we can have some measure of privacy."

His Grace appeared out of the bleak backdrop atop a huge bay. Muffin swung around, her rotund belly heaving, her legs splayed for flight. Eva gripped the reins to keep Muffin in check.

His Grace was clad from hat-covered head to Hessian-covered feet in black, except for a white shirt with a high collar that brushed his cleanly shaven cheeks. He sat confidently atop the bay as if raised in a saddle, even as the beast pawed the ground and tossed his head in an effort to get closer to Muffin.

Were she not familiar with the duke and his hidden devil horns, she'd have admired the cut of his fine figure in spite of his arrogant smirk.

The man was so very handsome, from the strong cut of his jaw, to his green eyes, to the sculpted mouth that made her shiver with unwelcome attraction. She hoped he would never know how his punishing kiss had affected her.

The duke handled his restless horse with ease, his eyes never leaving her face. A hint of dark humor tugged his hard mouth as if he knew secrets about her he'd never share. Perhaps he was picturing the night he'd have her at his mercy.

Eva shuddered. Muffin lost her desire for flight after a few sniffs in the bay's direction, and the two horses eyed each other warily.

"As delightful as it would be to frolic in the wet grass with you, Your Grace, I regret I must decline." She fought a wince as she put weight on her injured foot, and stared with what she hoped was a good dose of disdain. "Unfortunately, I am on my way to rut with a drunken hackney driver, in the gutter, and I fear I am quite late." She ran a slow perusal down his body and back up. "Though, if you don't mind waiting, I can come back for you when I'm finished."

The smirk on his face turned into a malevolent grin.

"If you think you have the strength to accommodate two men, I can certainly wait . . ." He let his voice trail off.

The impossible man! What would it require to take him down a peg or two? Eva flushed. "I would rather bed an entire ship full of French sailors than spend one second behind a bush with you, Your Grace."

"And yet, you will grace my bed or hand over a courtesan," he said blandly and shifted in the saddle. "Or else you will lose that house of yours. The choice is yours. It makes no difference to me."

"Oh." She wanted to knock him from his horse and let Muffin trample all over him with her small, yet lethal, hooves. Never had she met anyone so infuriating. Clearly he took pleasure in the needless suffering of others. He probably spent his days kicking street urchins and stray dogs!

"As if I have a choice in the matter. You've pushed me into a corner and blocked my escape." She twisted the reins in her hands. "What can I do to convince you of the error of this revenge? Certainly you can see Arabella deserved more than she had with you. If you ever cared for her, you'd take some pleasure from her happiness."

He lifted a brow. "Oh, I am quite happy she has found

contentment in her situation. Believe it or not, I cared deeply for her and do wish her happiness."

"Then why must you press me into this bargain?" she said, her voice desperate. "Isn't it enough to know how dreadfully unhappy I've been since our association began?"

He seemed to ponder her plea, and she took some hope. Perhaps there was a ray of light in the blackness of his heart.

"Though your unhappiness pleases me greatly," he said finally, amused, "I find the thought of sharing my bed with you, Miss Black, gives me greater satisfaction than your concern over your financial difficulties."

She huffed. "You are despicable." Tears threatened. What started as a lovely ride had turned into a nightmare on two levels. The man was stubborn and unreasonable. A satisfactory revenge depended completely on her degradation and submission. He'd accept nothing less.

But she would not allow herself to cry in front of him. Her toes hurt, but no worse than her heart.

Dismissing him, she hobbled around the mare while searching frantically for a stick to dig out the pebble.

"What have you done to yourself?" he asked.

"It is nothing," she said.

His Grace nudged his horse close and swung down from the saddle. Eva tried to lead Muffin out of his path, but Muffin seemed smitten with the stallion and fought her efforts. The mare bobbed her head and nickered as their noses touched. Traitor.

"You've hurt yourself, Miss Black."

With a sigh, she nodded. "Muffin stepped on my toes."

He cast a quizzical glance at the mare. Eva explained, "It wasn't entirely her fault. She'd picked up a pebble." She pulled back the hem of her riding habit just enough to show her scuffed boot. "When I spend time with Muffin, I need to be watchful of where she puts her feet, lest my toes are trampled."

He looked at the crushed boot and nodded. "Then we shall care for the mare, after we discover what kind of damage she has done to your foot." With that, His Grace bent, took her high into his arms, and settled her against his chest.

"Your Grace!"

"Be still," he commanded. His strides were sure as he carried her to a patch of grass beneath a large oak tree. She had had little time to notice how powerful his shoulders were beneath her hands or how wonderful he smelled, when he slowly lowered her, rump first, to the ground.

Dazed by his strength, she was only partially aware Muffin and the bay had followed along behind them like a pair of well-trained poodles, their reins dragging. There was something fascinating about the ease with which her body responded to him. Even now, her body longed to be scooped back up in his powerful arms.

Unaware of her inward confusion, His Grace lowered to one knee at her feet and removed his gloves. He paused, peered into her eyes, then lifted the hem of her habit to fully expose her boot, without an invitation to do so.

"Your Grace, this is not proper. If you help me mount, I will be on my way."

He reached for her boot's laces and jerked loose the bow. "Not until I have a look. You might have broken your toes."

For once there was no hint of lecherous intentions as he eased the black leather boot off her foot with infinite care. In fact, she saw only concern on his face.

The image didn't fit with what she knew about the man and his heavy-handed ways. His touch was gentle as he set the boot aside and closed his fingers around her ankle. The duke settled her foot onto his thigh and softly caressed her toes with the lightest touch. She winced. He pulled his hand back. "I fear it may be worse than I originally suspected."

She nodded, noticing how thick and dark his lashes were

against his golden skin. With his lids lowered as he looked down at her foot, the fan of lashes hid his intense green eyes. She skimmed her gaze downward along his nose to his perfect mouth; the same mouth that had, for a brief moment, stunned her with his hard and probing kiss.

The kiss that haunted her nights.

"I must remove the stocking," he said.

From somewhere outside herself, she nodded absently as her attention turned downward when he eased her habit's hem up over her knee to expose her garter. She barely noticed the chill on her leg or understood the intimacy of the act. Her focus was on his large hands as they casually skimmed her thigh when he tugged at the garter. Her skin tingled, her lips parted, and her breath escaped little bits at a time.

His Grace untied the pink ribbons with skill and care. Eva kept her eyes from his, fearful he might see in them the shameful feelings he'd fanned to flame with his bold touch. The warmth of his bare fingers on her flesh caused her to tremble with an unwanted mix of sensations.

She heard his breath quicken and involuntarily darted a glance upward. For a few heartbeats they locked gazes. His hand tightened on her knee for a second, then he blinked. He quickly drew her stocking down her leg to expose her foot. His examination was brief.

"Hmm." Cupping her heel, he lifted her toes into view.

Eva wanted to whimper at the sight of four slightly purple toes. Only the smallest had been spared. "Are they broken?"

His Grace tenderly manipulated each one in turn. Eva clenched her teeth to keep silent. After a few minutes, he shook his head. "I see nothing to indicate a break."

"Thank goodness." Her shoulders slumped. She'd escaped a worse problem than a few bruises. It would be difficult to stay abed long enough to allow the bones to heal when she had courtesans to teach and a mother to care for.

The warmth of his hands seeped into her foot, and her toes felt less pained. She realized then how exposed she was with her foot on his lap, her stocking removed, and her skirt lifted to her knee.

She blushed. "Perhaps you should replace my stocking, Your Grace, before someone happens along to discover us. I would hate to ruin your impeccable reputation."

Her tart comment brought a grin. He retrieved the stocking and shook it out. He rolled it over her foot and began a slow procession up her leg. Eva struggled to ignore the shivers spreading out from his knuckles. He took his time replacing the garment, now that his concern for her foot had been assuaged. In fact, there was a hint of mischief on his face when he spoke. "If I'm to risk my reputation, Miss Black, I would prefer us both to be discovered wearing much less clothing."

The devil duke had returned.

"I will not be your whore," she said, and raised her nose a notch. She didn't care if his tone was teasing. He was the same man he was before his concern for her foot turned him toward an act of kindness. The gentleman in him had dissipated as quickly as smoke on the wind once he realized she was not seriously injured.

"Unless you agree to my other solution, Miss Black, you will." He worked the stocking into place and made a grand show of tying her garter.

"Then be about your seduction, Your Grace." She dropped her arms to her sides and expelled a heavy sigh. "I haven't the entire day to waste."

He chuckled. "You are a puzzle, Miss Black. One moment stiff as starch, the next, offering me favors in the park." He finished his task, lowered her skirt, and helped her to her feet. He moved around her, shaking out her skirts. "However, I do like my courtesans agreeable, and your offer is tempting," he said, and lowered his mouth to her ear. "Though I have a suspicion, Miss Black, you have never been agreeable."

With his mouth dangerously close to her lobe, Eva forced herself to concentrate on the antics of a pair of larks on a nearby bush.

"And you, Your Grace, are spoiled and childish. When you can't have your way, you throw a tantrum and make those around you suffer."

"That I do." He chuckled again. "You would not believe the happiness this moment brings me."

The tips of his fingers danced over her, removing debris as he went. She couldn't think beyond the light brushes of his hands. The duke was playing lady's maid, but there was nothing innocuous about his intentions. Beneath his touches was something deeper, seductive and dangerous.

After a time, his fingers found a few loosened strands of mousy-brown hair, freed from the wig, and she held her breath. If he sought to pull her hair from its tight knot, he'd discover her disguise. That would be a disaster.

Instead, he turned her to face him and released her hair. His eyes were dark and impenetrable pools of deep green. He followed the curve of her mouth with his eyes. "You are tense, Miss Black."

"You would be tense, too, if you were about to be violated in the dirt, Your Grace."

It was as if the world around them had faded to black. The only thing she could see, feel, was his fingertips dancing across the skin of her jaw, one finger tracing the curve of her lower lip. He was playing a seductive game, and she loathed her response.

Oh, she despised him. She hated his arrogance. She knew, without seeing his face, that there was smug satisfaction in his eyes. He'd elicited a sexual response in her, and he knew it. Her body was pliant in its betrayal.

The spicy scent of male mingled with horse and leather to add to his unwelcome appeal.

" 'Violate' is such a harsh term, Miss Black."

With his smug tone came some sanity. "What do you

really want from me, Your Grace?" she breathed, and closed her hand around his wrist to stop his exploration before she dragged him off into the bushes and begged him to ease her suffering.

"I only ask you to live up to your part of the bargain, Miss Black."

Chapter Six

B argain?" she said. "I have not agreed to a bargain."

   She attempted to step away, but her foot gave way beneath her, and she wobbled. His Grace caught her tightly against him.

"Easy. I have you."

She tipped her head back and peered up. The look in his eyes stunned her. Her disguise hadn't repelled him one lick. The desire in his eyes was acute.

She became aware of a hard ridge against her leg the moment he leaned to drag his mouth across her temple.

He was steely hard with desire. He wouldn't be satisfied until he had her.

Panic gripped her. He was a debaucher of women, willing or otherwise. She was certain of it. But her body ached for his touch with a shocking intensity she didn't understand.

Perhaps she was a whore after all.

Eva felt her eyes burn. Somehow she found the strength to whisper, "No, please. No."

His Grace stilled and lifted his head. Slowly he released his hold and his hands dropped away. He was quiet for a moment, then, "As you wish."

The duke turned abruptly and walked to Muffin. He lifted her hoof and dug out the stone. Eva wanted to call him to her and slip back into his arms. But the moment was lost. His face was set and his jaw tight as he returned and lifted her into his arms without ceremony.

The little mare barely acknowledged Eva as the duke settled her back in the saddle. For a moment, their gazes met.

Eva gathered the reins and gently kicked Muffin into a run.

Nicholas watched Eva nudge the mare into a jarring lope up the path, his gaze burning across Eva's back and down to her trim rump. The surprise of discovering a warm and responsive woman in Miss Black had unsettled him. There was an instant, when he held her, that she'd molded enticingly to his body, close enough for him to feel the delightful curve of her breasts; breasts that she kept well hidden.

She'd flattened the firm flesh somehow during her previous visit. He shook his head. Her surprises were endless.

Not once, when he'd stumbled upon her hobbling about in the mist with her fat gray pony, did he expect she would so easily accept his offer to help.

Instead, she'd sat stiff and quiet while he examined her toes, seeming to accept her fate. There was no weeping and wailing, no begging for mercy, no cutting barbs as he nuzzled her temple. He'd known the moment when she'd surrendered her body to him. And it wasn't just the same resignation he'd felt at first. He felt her stiff spine bend against his hand on her back and heard her breath catch, then grow uneven. It was desire in its purest form.

Her desire had taken him aback. The feel of her erect

nipples against his chest had certainly left any question of her hidden sensuality undisputed. There was a hunger in her that was deeply buried beneath her ridiculous costume.

He'd bedded women who feigned desire, and Eva wasn't one of them. Her response to him was instinctual and passionate.

When he proposed she become his courtesan, she'd responded, as expected, with a biting refusal. Never once did he believe she'd accept any part of his outlandish plot. He'd never forced himself on a woman and didn't plan to do so now. He expected that even if she did agree, by some queer twist of insanity, she'd come to his bed and lie stiff, cold, and prickly while he made quick work of getting to his release.

A very unsatisfying thought he couldn't stomach.

This encounter changed everything. Whereas he once looked toward taking revenge on her with trepidation, he now anticipated making her purr. Perhaps he shouldn't release his hold on her just yet, when there was much about her left to explore. Revenge had turned into a single-minded focus of seduction. He would peel the layers of her spinsterhood away and see all that was hidden beneath.

Eva stared down from the shadowy second-floor landing at the wolf pack of creditors standing in her entryway with stacks of bills clutched in their hands. There were rumbles of discontent and a few upraised voices as they insisted upon a meeting with her. Harold stood sentry over the lot lest they get unruly, and refused their request.

Every shop her mother had visited, every order she'd placed over the last several years, and obviously hidden, had come back to haunt her daughter. Eva counted a full dozen men and wondered how many more were outside awaiting their turn to confront her and demand money. Obviously, His Grace hadn't purchased all her debt. She could easily surmise the reason they had sought her out this day and who had sent them.

The devil was at work to torment her. He knew she was balancing on a razor's edge and needed a final push.

"His Grace said to ask for Miss Black." A portly man in a suit waved a fistful of notes in Harold's face and nodded to a tall, thin man beside him. "This bill has been past due for nigh six months. When can I expect to get paid?"

Eva blanched. She'd been so careful. Mother hadn't been allowed to venture out without an escort for several years. When had this debacle happened? She ran all the options through her head and came up with the only conclusion.

Mary. She was the one person who couldn't refuse her mother.

The girl was an efficient maid, but a ninny. If her mother wanted to circumvent her jailer, Mary would not be difficult to distract. Place a handsome footman in her view, or wave some trinket before her nose, and the girl would be trotting the Bond Street shops like a panting pup.

Mother was not always as fey as Eva feared. She still had enough sense to devise a plan to get what she wanted. If Eva lifted Mother's mattress, no telling what sorts of treasures would spill out.

She'd have to get Harold to check. Some of the hidden trinkets might be worth selling.

"I will no longer extend credit until these bills are caught up," one man protested as Harold began to slowly remove the men from the pack one at a time and ease them out the door.

Another shouted, "I am owed one hundred pounds!"

She wasn't sure what Harold said to the crush to finally get them all out, but when the oak panel door was closed and locked behind the last man, she felt deflated.

After her meeting with His Grace in the park this morning, she'd rushed home to hide in her room and pace. Her body aches and fevered flesh didn't subside with time or angry grumbling. Truthfully, the more she thought about the dark duke, the hotter she became, until she was certain she was coming down with some dreadful illness.

She felt trapped and ready to wring his manly neck. A few moments in his strapping arms and she was ready to throw aside all her principles to see what other kinds of sensuous games he could teach her.

Even now, distanced from the devil duke, she could think of nothing but the way he'd nuzzled her neck and how desperately flushed she'd become. She had turned into another person, not Miss Black with the dowdy gowns and bland wig, but Evangeline Winfield, daughter of a once celebrated and scandalous courtesan.

She couldn't understand what was happening to her. Perhaps if she'd had more dealings with men, her experiences would offer an explanation. She hated His Grace with all of her being—if he were crushed beneath a mail coach, she'd not shed a tear—so why did her body not recoil at his touch?

Worse yet, in the moments after she fled from him and plodded home on Muffin, she'd envied the year Arabella had spent in his bed.

Truly and fully envied Arabella!

Gads. She leaned her elbows on the rail and dropped her head into her hands. What was she to do? He had her trapped in a fox hole. His Grace was pacing above, waiting for her head to emerge so he could snatch her up with his large paw.

And devour her with his hot mouth.

She let out a low groan and dropped back against the wall. Below, Harold walked toward the kitchen, unaware she'd been spying. He was her protector, her only friend. And she'd never felt more isolated than she did in this moment.

Eva could not confide in him. Not this time. His Grace wouldn't be safe from her enraged servant if he knew what liberties His Grace had taken with her. And what she'd allowed!

Slowly, she limped down the hall to her room and closed the door to her sanctuary. But even in this place with the tiny blue flowers on its papered walls and coverlet in a matching hue, she could not close out His Grace, not completely. He was a specter ever floating over her, watching, waiting.

The mirror beckoned. Facing her reflection, she looked for marks on her skin, some evidence of His Grace: handprints, red splotches where his mouth had pressed against her skin. Nothing.

It was as if he'd never kissed her there, never caressed her face, never run his lips across her pliant flesh.

Frustrated, Eva looked down at her breasts. She never gave more than casual thought to the pair. They were just another part of her body and her femininity. But His Grace had touched one without invitation.

They were no longer hers alone.

If she went to his bed, would he play with them? She cupped the full flesh over her bodice as he had done. Would he kiss them, lick her nipples; suckle them until she cried out? Would he kiss her neck and touch her bottom and do all sorts of deviant things to her until she finally succumbed to pleasure?

Would she like these things? Would she encourage his exploration, invite his possession, or fight with every ounce of will she could muster?

Eva shook her head, dropped her hands, and backed away from the mirror. She no longer recognized the woman reflected there.

"I cannot become my mother," she whispered and sat on the bed. The grim hand of fate had intervened to connect her and the demonic duke. He would never set her free until he tired of her. Eva flopped back on the coverlet and stared blindly at the ceiling. Would he be satisfied with one night?

Deep inside her she knew the pull of His Grace was too powerful to fight. He owned her; he'd sent the creditors to her today to prove his power and force her hand. He'd woven himself into her life and left her open and vulnerable.

"I cannot let him touch me again," she whispered, disheartened. "I will not be his whore." And yet, she knew she would be. He'd weakened her with her desire until all she could think about was how desperately she wanted him. How the taste of his mouth had left her wanting to explore further the silent promises his body had offered and her body ached for.

When he came for her, she wouldn't refuse him.

Downtrodden and defeated, she pushed from the bed and called for a bath.

A coach has arrived for you, Miss Evangeline." Mary walked into Eva's room as she was giving her appearance a last glance in the mirror. The girl's voice held a touch of awe as she clasped her hands to her thin chest. "'Tis from a duke."

Eva kept her face calm and inspected her clothing. Everything in her costume was in place. Evangeline was deeply buried beneath Miss Black. She hoped it would be enough.

Mary examined her gown and grimaced. "I can fetch the blue gown if you like, Miss Eva," she offered timidly. "'Tis a lovely shade and fitting for an outing."

The blue would be a fine choice if the duke were a suitor. Since he wasn't courting her, and debauching her was his plan, he'd have to make do with the brown. His happiness was the least of her worries. "Thank you, no, Mary. This is perfect."

"Yes, Miss." Mary shot her a puzzled frown and withdrew.

When she'd requested the bath, Eva knew he'd send for her, sensed it to her toes. Her benefactor was not a patient man, and he was on a hunt for a bedmate. She'd felt the press of his desire against her thigh this morning. She knew time had ticked away, and the hour to accept or refuse his request had gone.

Arabella had left him months ago. Unless he visited prostitutes, he'd lived without a mistress for a long time.

Smoothing her skirts, she smiled tightly. The brown gown was little better than the one Mary was wearing and without ribbons and bows. It had a severe collar so high and tight, her neck rivaled that of an ostrich. She wore her wig under her oldest bonnet, and her spectacles were in her valise.

She was dressed for war. If His Grace thought she would climb into his bed warm and willing, he was sorely mistaken. He would have to fight for her with all the seductive talents he possessed. She would be no man's easy whore.

With a last sigh, she left the room.

His Grace's rose-decorated town house was dimly lit when she arrived an hour later. The footman led her into a large dining room.

The stuffy space was lit with a row of burning candles along the center of a long table, and two huge vases of flowers of every color were placed as centerpieces on the wood surface, with not a single rose mingled among the blooms.

His Grace sat at the far end of the table. He was casually attired in his shirtsleeves with his shirt partially unbuttoned at the neck. A glass of some sort of spirit was in his hand. The candlelight flickered over his features, framing him in gold against the backdrop of shadowed walls.

He brought to mind a handsome gothic romantic hero

of legend, tucked away in a castle waiting for an innocent virgin to come along to chain to his bed for his pleasure.

Chained for pleasure? Eva tried not to imagine herself reaching out her chained hands to caress his broad chest, but the image came unbidden. If she was his captive, how far would she go to gain her release? Would she kiss him? Would she let him remove her clothes and touch her breasts? Between her legs?

It was a shocking image—but even more shocking was her aroused reaction to it.

He sipped his drink, staring at her over the rim of the glass.

"Miss Black."

"Your Grace."

She stood in the doorway after the butler withdrew, trying to hide her apprehension. She marveled at the darkness in this handsome man who would force her into this bargain without a care for her feelings. But of course, men of his stature felt entitled to take what they wanted. And for some unexplainable reason, he wanted her.

Eva breathed in. Her tightly boned corset left her little room for more than a shallow breath. She tugged at her neckline. "That dress is hideous, Miss Black," he said bluntly.

"I'm sorry it does not please you," she responded stiffly. Beneath her clothing, her body burned in the stuffy room. Perhaps so many protective layers hadn't been a good idea. She swayed slightly.

He continued to regard her with a scowl.

"Strip," he said sharply.

She blinked. "What?"

"I said, 'strip.'" He drank the spirit and poured another glass. "The night is warm, and you seem to be in some distress. Perchance wool wasn't the best choice of garment?"

The shock of his command froze her limbs and she couldn't move. "I c-cannot," she whispered.

* * *

Nicholas watched the color drain from her cheeks. The woman seemed to have gained a stone since their last meeting. He suspected that beneath her dreadful gown, she had on enough petticoats and chemises for three women. It certainly would make breathing difficult and lead to light-headedness. There was only one way to ease her suffering. Less clothing.

"I do apologize, My Lady. It seems I have offended you." He leaned forward with his elbows on the table. "I thought to offer wine and poetry befitting your beauty but suspected you'd prefer a direct approach. Was I wrong?"

Fire returned to her eyes, and he hid his satisfaction when she crossed her arms over her flattened breasts. Her annoyance would keep her upright.

"Your seductive skills are certainly lacking, Your Grace," she scolded. "I confess I cannot fathom how you ever manage to entice women into your bed."

His chuckle lifted her chin. "You do amuse, Miss Black." He watched her watch him. Her eyes caressed his face and moved down to his open collar. While her mind balked, her body was his. All he had to do now was convince her to put aside their differences and enjoy the pleasures two people could share. "I will show you my talents once you have taken off some of those layers of clothing, lest you faint dead away."

If there was ever a moment tonight where he felt her balk or panic, he'd stop immediately. When she came to his bed, he wanted her willing and as eager for him as he was for her. His intention was to bring her to heel and teach her a lesson about what her interference had cost him in losing his dearest Arabella. Not to leave her battered and abused.

Oddly, the anger he'd felt over losing Arabella had vanished the moment this spinster bit his lip. Eva Black had a fire in her that Arabella lacked, and she intrigued him with her starch and fight. Before this night was over, he intended to make her burn.

"If you cannot undress, Miss Black, I shall be forced to strip you myself." Nicholas set his glass down, stood, and walked over to her. She flinched but remained where she was, as if her feet were nailed to the floor.

The scent of lilacs drifted around her. She lowered her lids, and soft brown lashes fanned out over her lovely eyes. Those eyes were the windows to her every emotion.

Nicholas lifted his fingers to the strings of her bonnet and paused with gray satin tangled in his fingers. "May I?"

Without meeting his eyes, she nodded weakly. Her skin had a moist sheen. With two tugs, the bonnet was in his hand. He fanned her with it. She was heated, but not with desire. This wasn't the seduction he'd imagined.

The gloves quickly followed and were cast aside. He wanted to free her hair but decided to leave it to last. Miss Black could keep her mask of spinsterhood. For now.

Nicholas came to a halt behind her and slid a knuckle down the row of buttons that ran from the base of her skull to the curve of her lower back.

"An unfortunate choice of gowns you made this evening, Miss Black." He leaned to her ear and breathed into the soft shell. The scent of her skin stirred him to the beginnings of an erection. "I am an expert with buttons."

He thought he caught the slightest hint of a whimper as he began a downward procession through the tiny buttons. When he reached midback, he eased the drab gown down until her pale shoulders and creamy white neck were exposed to his inspection.

From his advantage above her, he let his gaze caress the delicate curve of her neck. His spinster was a delightful mix of softness and strength.

He pressed his lips to where her neck joined her shoulders, and a few short, stray crimson-gold hairs peeked out from beneath the hideous brown wig. They were a siren's call he couldn't resist.

His senses flooded with the scent of lilacs and sunshine as he nuzzled his face to the spot.

The taste of her soft skin was nearly his undoing.

Eva closed her eyes tightly as His Grace pressed his lips against her neck. His breath and a light dusting of beard shadow tickled her skin. The whirling room began to slow as the heat eased slightly, now that she was free of the itchy collar of the gown. If her arms weren't weighted beneath her clothes, she'd pull the remaining layers off herself.

For a second time in two days, he was caring for her, though tonight it was as much for his own benefit as it was for hers. Still, he could use her weakness to his advantage but did not do so. Yes, he was undressing her, but her fear was lessening. Once he had her unclothed and cooled, the game would change.

The gown fell away. "Better?" he asked and came around her.

Eva tried to breathe deeply, and failed. "I'm still having difficulty." She tugged at her corset. He brushed her hands away and worked the lacings.

"You have certainly sacrificed your comfort to arm yourself against my invasion." He tugged firmly at the corset. "We will remedy that shortly."

Eva expected the creamy swell of her breasts to escape when released from the boned structure. However, the layers of lacy chemises held fast and saved her modesty. There were many levels of undergarments to shuck off before she could be free.

"I considered stitching a gown of thorns," she retorted breathlessly. "Then I decided your determination to bed me wouldn't be put off by anything less than yards of broken glass and steel spikes. And I was completely out of those."

Good humor returned to his eyes. He dipped his fingers beneath two chemises and held her gaze. Then, with a jerk, he rent the delicate cloth open to her waist. She gasped.

"Two removed, and"—he tipped his head to look down into her partially exposed cleavage—"four chemises to go."

Eva was certain her breasts swelled with anticipation of what he might do to them once they were freed. She was both alarmed and confused. Part of her wanted this seduction to end. At the same time, she wanted him to take away the restrictions of her spinsterhood and allow her to experience, just once, how it felt to be desired and loved by a man.

His Grace was without a doubt the finest figure of man she'd ever seen, and he knew how to use his seductive talents to invoke her response. In spite of her distaste for the man, she was finding it difficult to stay detached with the scent of soap and brandy swirling around her, and the warmth of his hands at the ribbon on the outer chemise.

"I think you are not as repulsed as you'd like me to believe," he said softly, and ran a fingertip along the skin above the lace trim. Her heart tumbled erratically and her eyes drooped closed. A sigh escaped her lips.

"There is an attraction between us, Miss Black. You feel it, too."

Eva opened her eyes with a scowl. He circled her and slid the chemise off her shoulders, to her waist, and then to her hips. Breathing was much easier now, and his hands bolder, splaying across her buttocks as he eased the chemise ever downward.

"You delude yourself, Your Grace, if you think I am not suffering. You cannot know how deep my hatred is." She could not make the words sound convincing, even to herself. It was impossible to think when the duke was caressing her rump.

He chuckled. The chemise dropped into the pile of discarded clothing at her feet. He bent forward to press his cheek against hers and gathered her into his arms. She nearly melted in his embrace. "Perhaps we should wait until you have spent the night in my bed to decide if you hate me still."

Such arrogance! "Make no mistake, Your Grace." As he caressed her ribs, then slid his hands up to pause just below her breasts, a low moan escaped her and she arched back against his chest. The duke needed no further invitation. His hands splayed open to cup the full flesh. Gently, he teased her nipples through the thick layers of cloth, and they hardened beneath his play. She gasped. "I will loathe you to my dying breath."

Her body ached deliciously in places it should not. He released her and continued with chemise removal. He nibbled the exposed skin of her shoulders as he peeled off her clothing, one item at a time. She couldn't focus on anything besides his hands and mouth, and the deep, powerful need inside her.

It was the coolness of the room that alerted her to her near nakedness when her drawers slid down her bare legs. With a last burst of virginal modesty, she tried to cross her arms over herself to keep the last thin chemise. But he loosened the laces and the thin cloth gaped. Her hands kept her breast from exposure. Cotton and wool were piled up to her knees already, but she couldn't give up this one final barrier.

He bent and swept her into his arms, kicking aside the garments. Then he lowered her back to her feet, placing himself behind her. She was so intensely aware of him that he didn't need to touch her so that she could feel him infuse her with his presence.

"Please," Eva begged as his hands cupped her hips and moved lower to caress her thighs. His chest pressed intimately against her back, and she felt a hard ridge at the cleft between her buttocks. She was weak and hot, unable to put into words what she wanted. There was no previous experience to guide her.

A chuckle broke his silence. He walked around her, always touching, and ran a fingertip down the curve of her jaw. She could no longer use her clothing as an excuse for her intense and wavering emotions. She wanted him. Desperately.

"I never expected to find such delightful curves beneath your hideous gowns, my dear. But I fear the unmasking is not complete." He tugged off her spectacles and reached to set them on a nearby table. "You have lovely amber eyes. It's a shame to cover them needlessly."

Eva locked onto his gaze, some sanity returning. "It is a shame to torment me as you have, Your Grace."

A second chuckle filled the room. His green eyes dipped to examine her mouth.

Leaning forward, he whispered against her lips, "Tell me you want me, Miss Black."

In spite of his outrageous antics, the corners of her mouth twitched. "I am powerless to resist you, and you well know it," she murmured. Her hands skimmed up his stomach and twisted into his shirt.

A slow and wicked grin crossed his lips. "I was forced to give up Arabella because of your interference." He teased the corner of her mouth with his thumb. "I think it only fair you give me something in return."

The advance continued until he touched her wig. She stilled. It was the last of her costume to hide behind. Once it was gone, she would be completely exposed to him as Evangeline. Miss Black would be lost in his eyes forever.

"It is not a fair trade, and you well know it. She never truly belonged to you." The man was as stubborn in his convictions as he was spoiled and arrogant.

"Then we are of different opinions, Miss Black," he said simply. "For I think the trade very fair."

"And how often should I expect to be called to your bed before my debt is paid, Your Grace?" Eva tipped her head up and arched a brow. She felt his rapid heartbeat beneath her hands and lifted her eyes. A slight shift, and her thigh pressed intimately against his. "Once? Twice? Thrice?"

His eyes darkened, and he caught her around the waist. His large hands kneaded her flesh. "Are you so certain you will be satisfied once the bargain is met, Miss Black?" he said, holding her gaze. "You may discover spending time in my bed not as abhorrent as you believe."

Eva sighed and leaned into him. With nothing but a chemise and his clothing between them, she felt the entire length of his muscled body from her breasts to her knees.

She could no longer pretend that she did not want him.

She lifted onto her toes and pressed her breasts hard against his chest. "Kiss me, Your Grace."

Chapter Seven

Nicholas stilled. Along with desire, there was a touch of fear in her beautiful amber eyes that took him aback. In spite of her unexpected request, he sensed her hesitation and felt tremors ripple through her body.

The last remains of her spinster disguise. If Crawford hadn't discovered that she was a courtesan's daughter, Nicholas would suspect she really was an innocent.

Impossible. Not once, when he pressed her to replace Arabella in his bed, had she claimed virginity in an effort to keep him at bay.

Impatience welled. Tonight he would show this spinster that he wasn't a brute, once and for all.

First he would finish her unveiling.

He reached out and pulled the wig free. Hairpins tinkled across the floor as a mass of red-gold hair tumbled across her shoulders and down her back.

He went hard. Lud, she was beautiful!

Eva grabbed for the wig, but it was too late. Before she could react, he cupped her head and pulled her mouth to his. Full and sweet, her lips, her kiss set off a firestorm down his body. Eva clutched at his shoulders, trying to push him back, but she was pinned against him. She let out little sounds of protest as he explored the seam of her mouth with his tongue.

Never had a woman so ensnared his mind, his body. He had no fear of another bite as he nibbled her lips. He'd take the punishment if it meant the nip would end with her consent to allow him to plunder her sensuous mouth.

Eva tasted brandy and felt his erection press against her belly as she tipped her head to accept his tongue. He paused momentarily, arms slack, then clasped her to him and thrust deep. A centuries-old mating dance began.

How she wanted this! Her body hadn't been her own since his first touch, and she couldn't take the confounded aching anymore. There had to be a way to ease her suffering, and she knew this dreadfully handsome duke was the key. It was he who had started the firestorm in her; it would be he who would put it out.

She lifted to her toes to mold her body closer to his. The duke's hand slid down to cup her buttock and ground her body against his erection. The intimacy shocked her. Still, she could not find the strength for any more regrets.

The junction between her legs throbbed as she snaked her arms around his neck and kissed him with everything she had. Tongues tangled, Eva became a wild thing, shoving her hand in his hair as he tangled her locks in his. She wanted to feel his bare chest beneath her hands, to run her fingers through the dusting of hair there.

No more games. What Eva now wanted was for him to show her all the delights a man of experience could teach a woman.

It was he who pulled back and stared, stunned, into her eyes. Her mind found its way through the fog. "I despise you, Your Grace," she managed to say before she drew his head down for another searing kiss.

Nicholas Drake, her enemy, scooped her up into his arms and carried her from the dining room, heedless of any servants. She broke the kiss and nuzzled his neck, raining a trail of kisses up to and along his hard jaw. She inhaled his scent while he carried her up two flights of stairs to a large chamber at the end of a long, darkened hallway.

He pushed open the door, then kicked it closed behind him. A small picture frame wobbled and crashed to the floor. He dropped her to her feet and bent to kiss her while tearing at her thin chemise. Eva eagerly released her claim on the cloth. She clawed at his shirt, pulling it up and over his head as her chemise slid to the floor. She followed her instincts, knew what she wanted, and by the look in his eyes it was enough. She felt positively wanton and wicked.

Naked, she felt no shyness. The raging desire in his face made her powerful, and she reached to run her hands over the wide expanse and planes of his broad, muscled chest. The warm skin beckoned, and she paused to trail her fingertips over his nipples.

He groaned and pulled at his breeches, popping the buttons open. Eva stared when he shoved the cloth down over his narrow hips and his erection sprang free. She clasped her hand around him, fascinated by her first look at a naked man.

And he was magnificent. But her exploration was cut short when he clasped her to him, reclaimed her mouth, and pushed her backward, his hands everywhere from her hair to her thighs and back, touching her in her most intimate places.

The duke edged her toward the bed, holding her in the circle of his arms lest she trip and fall.

When the backs of her knees hit the mattress, she fell backward with a small laugh, and scrambled on hands and knees to the center of the bed. He followed her, flattening her beneath his outstretched body, and kissed her deeply. The duke braced himself over her, easing open her thighs, the tip of his erection poised and waiting at the entrance of her body.

"So beautiful," he breathed, and lowered his head to suck a nipple into his warm mouth. "Delightful."

She let out a small cry and arched her back. He suckled for a moment, then turned his attention to the other breast, nipping gently at the peak. She played with his soft hair as the magnificent beast teased her with his expert mouth, eliciting sounds of delight before reclaiming her lips.

Eva ran her hands over him eagerly, breathlessly, impatiently. She pushed aside regrets and hatred, and instead reveled in the feel of his hard frame, both soft and warm, muscled and lean.

When he lifted his head to peer into her eyes, his hair fell in disarray around his handsome face.

He grinned wickedly. "Do you want me to stop?"

"No," she moaned. He then turned his attention to her nipples again, and rained kisses across her stomach and up her neck until she could no longer tolerate the raw, aching throb between her legs. Instinctively, she knew she would not be satisfied until the coupling was complete.

Desperate, she lifted her hips to press his cock against her throbbing core. "Please, Your Grace." And he was quick to oblige her. With one swift movement, he sheathed himself inside her. She whimpered in pain when he breached the barrier of her innocence with a deep, penetrating thrust.

His Grace paused. "You are a virgin?"

She nodded. "No longer."

And in that moment their frantic coupling changed. His face softened and his touch gentled. He leaned to kiss her lids and the prickle of virgin tears at the corners of her eyes.

Eva looked up at him shyly, and the tenderness she saw in this duke as he peered softly down at her shook her deeply. With gentle care, he began slow, measured thrusts into her, allowing her to adjust to his body and to ease through the dull pain of her lost innocence.

He kissed her mouth, her chin, her neck, nibbling and teasing as she became accustomed to his body and pleasure built inside her. Little gasps and whimpers escaped. He drove into her gently and thoroughly, driving her to the brink of insanity with his magnificent body. Eva cupped his buttocks and kneaded the firm flesh. When she felt she could take no more, and she called for mercy, he deepened his thrusts and drove her over the edge to a stunning release.

She cried out and tumbled back on the bed. The duke groaned and buried himself to the hilt as he found his own satisfaction.

Spent, Eva sighed and ran her fingertips over his back and across his buttocks when he lowered himself on his elbows over her and kissed her. She wasn't at all sure how she had gotten to this place and into this bed; the details where hazy. She only knew she'd been thoroughly made love to by her despised duke, and she couldn't work up a single regret.

His Grace moved off her after a moment and stretched out at her side, his head resting on his open palm. Their legs tangled together. His normally tight face was relaxed, giving the dark devil duke an almost boyish cast.

"You may not believe this, but taking you into my bed this evening was not my intention." He brushed a stray hair out of her eyes. "I thought you would club me with a candlestick and run away."

Eva narrowed her lids. "So I am to blame for this?" she said tartly. "You could have voiced your honorable intentions while I still had the chance to flee with my innocence intact."

His mouth twitched. "In all fairness, I didn't know you were a virgin. You seemed so intent on seducing me, I found I could not resist, or risk disappointing you."

She gasped, and slapped his hand away from her breast. "I seduced you?"

"That is the way I remember it, Miss Black."

Of all the notions! Eva sputtered and placed her hand on his chest when he dipped his head to kiss her. "You are such an insufferable man. I was innocent, and you, a man clearly of great experience. You took advantage of me in a time of weakness. In fact, you own me. I was forced to comply."

The smile left his face. "It was never my intention to force you into my bed." He slid up and leaned against the headboard. "I was angry. I'm still angry. You had no business interfering in my life. And in spite of what you believe, I cared for Arabella. We were ideally matched." He ran a hand over his head and scratched the back of his skull. "She wasn't always unhappy with our arrangement, Miss Black."

If he'd seduced Arabella as he'd seduced her, she could believe her friend had found some satisfaction in their physical arrangement.

But Arabella was happy now with a new life, a husband, and soon a new baby—none of which she would ever have had if she'd remained the duke's plaything.

And Eva had taken her place. "The past is just that, the past, Your Grace. The sooner you move beyond your disappointment, the sooner you will be able to find peace."

It took a moment and a pointed stare before he spoke. He trailed a fingertip between her breasts. Humor returned to his eyes. "What we shared here has gone far to mend my anger, Miss Black."

Heat crept up her neck. "You may call me Eva, or Evangeline, if you prefer, Your Grace." She looked down at her swollen nipples and crossed her arms over them. Her eyes drifted down his naked body to his softened cock. "I think Miss Black is a bit formal after what transpired here."

* * *

It felt odd to think of her as anything but Miss Black. "You did have a choice, Eva. A single no, and I would have released you. Yet, you kissed me and undressed me as eagerly as I did you. You cannot say I forced you."

After a pause, she slowly shook her head. "You did not force me. I came to your bed willingly."

Thank God. He rose to his knees and knelt in front of her. He drew her up off her rump until they were face to face. "If you ever come to my bed again, it will be because you want me, not for any other reason. I will not use your debt to manipulate you again. You and your mother will always have a home."

Not touching, they looked into each other's eyes. He watched a procession of raw emotions flicker through her. He wanted to take her into his arms and make love to her again and again, until she had no more regrets. He wanted to make love to her until he no longer saw Miss Black, the spinster who upended his life, in her, but the elusive Miss Winfield—Eva—who hid from the world. He wanted to know every inch of the woman behind the spectacles and wig.

He wanted her, the beautiful courtesan's daughter.

"I think I shall call you Nicholas, Your Grace," she whispered finally as she spanned a hand in the center of his chest. "Your Grace seems too formal for this situation."

Nicholas grinned as she wrapped her arm around his neck and drew him down to the bed.

Nicholas tucked a hand behind his head and the other around Eva. Her explosive passion had both shocked and delighted him. Even now, as he listened to her breathe, her soft hair tangled beneath his shoulder, it was impossible to believe Eva Black and Evangeline Winfield were one and the same.

How easily he'd been tricked. He'd been so angry with her since their first meeting; he'd refused to see beyond her costume. He wanted so much to punish her, to bring her to heel, to make her beg for mercy.

But it had been she who had knocked him senseless.

A virgin? A courtesan's daughter had been an innocent. Had he known from the first, would it have made a difference? Perhaps. But they were beyond regrets. She'd been thoroughly made love to. There was no taking these moments back, nor did he desire to. He wanted her just as she was now, soft and pliable beside him in her sleep.

The question now became what he was to do with her. Certainly, taking her innocence had satisfied his desire for revenge. He'd ruined her more effectively than purchasing her debts ever could. He should free her. Yet, somehow he knew it would not be that simple. She'd crawled under his skin with her beautiful amber eyes and surprisingly passionate nature.

If she agreed to continue their arrangement and become his courtesan in truth, would she be satisfied to remain in the background when he married?

She helped courtesans escape their protectors. It was impossible to imagine she would be satisfied to live her days as one of them, lounging about in a scandalous gown on a settee, awaiting his pleasure while reading some inane poetry book.

The idea broke a smile across his face. He imagined her outrage and the scathing words she'd use when expressing her refusal. Though he'd spent only a handful of hours in her presence, he knew enough to know she wouldn't be pleased with the offer to become a kept lover.

In the darkness he studied the soft angles of her lovely cheekbones and slightly pointed chin, but came up with no solution. Perhaps he should think on it in the morning, when her thigh was not draped over his and a breast was not pressed against his ribs. How had he ever found her plain and uninteresting?

It was nearly impossible not to plot to keep her as his mistress when she was so near.

Eva shifted in her sleep and let out a small sigh. Nicholas tucked the quilt over her breasts, less for worry she'd catch a chill than for his own desire for rest. The generous globes were all too tempting. And he was spent.

It was early the next morning when Nicholas's carriage took her home. It was just before dawn, and the black sky was fading to gray as Eva leaned back on the seat, worry furrowing her brow.

She had been made love to three times during the night and was immensely satisfied by the encounters. For those stolen moments, she would never feel regret for her loss of innocence. As for the duke, the repercussions of her actions in his arms weren't so clear. He'd opened up emotions and sexual desires she'd always intended to keep buried until her death.

Outwardly, though she looked the same, inside she'd changed. She was no longer innocent. She'd lost her virginity to a man who was everything she hated: arrogant, vengeful, and a duke. His wealth and power were enough to send her diving under the nearest bed and away from gossips. And her willingness to allow him to love her, time and time again, troubled her greatly.

The future she'd plotted for herself did not involve marriage, so there was no risk of a husband discovering her lost innocence. And since she had no intention of ever returning to the duke, unless he'd gotten her with child, their interactions were concluded.

To continue to see him was to risk not only a baby, but her heart, if she was foolish enough to fall in love with this man who would never love her.

She'd seen what her mother had given up to love her father; hidden away from the world, never able to claim him fully as hers. Though Father did love her mother deeply, there were rules they both had to follow.

Eva knew Nicholas could never wed her, and she would not be satisfied to live in the shadows of his wife and children.

Thus, she would continue her life as it was, and put Nicholas behind her. And now and then she'd think back to her night with the dark duke, and be warm with the memories.

After instructing the coachman to let her off behind the town house, she walked through the garden, enjoying the last few moments of solitude to collect herself. When Harold opened the kitchen door, a scowl on his face, she walked past him without a word, to find refuge in her room.

Eventually, she would face his scorn, but for now, she needed to sleep.

"The color is delightful on you, Sophie. You look lovely," Rose said, laughing as Pauline spun Sophie around for inspection. The day dress was green with a respectable lacy neckline and a froth of lace circling the short, puffed sleeves.

"You are the lovely one, Rose," Sophie said, staring at Rose in the mirror. The change in Sophie after a few short days had been unexpected. She had lost some of the hard lines on her face, and smiled more often.

Rose's enthusiasm for life had proved infectious, and not even the hardened Sophie and Yvette were immune. Yvette occasionally entertained them with a racy story and became somewhat of an older sister to Rose, Pauline, and Abigail when they needed advice.

Eva handed a cream-colored dress to Yvette and listened to Rose and Pauline chatter about patterns and fabric with Abigail, who was stripped to her chemise. Rose was clad in pale blue, and the two women were indeed stunning in their new frocks.

Madame Fornier and her assistants scurried about, eager to show the latest fashions as they envisioned a large sale. Eva had planned to take her ladies shopping the day before, but drenching rain kept them inside. So they'd spent the previous afternoon going over topics one discussed over tea and at parties, and of course, current events.

Eva wanted her ladies ready for any social situation.

Her wandering mind, and unsettled nights, kept her from fully focusing on anything but the most mundane tasks. In spite of her best efforts, she could not get His Grace out of her thoughts. She'd tossed on her bed last night, feverish and aching for his body. She could not walk down the street without hoping for a glimpse of his handsome face.

"What do you think of this one, Miss Eva?" Abigail asked. Eva snapped back to attention. The dress was pale yellow with tiny matching flowers at the neckline. "The dress is pretty, but the color makes your skin sallow." Eva moved over to a table and picked up a bolt of deep burgundy fabric. "If Madame can make the same dress in this color, it will be perfect."

Abigail smiled. "Miss Eva is right. I will take this in the other color."

Eva smiled back at the girl. Even Abigail had begun to blossom from her deep shyness and reserve to show a quick wit. She'd quickly become a favorite. Eva hoped to make her a match with one of three men she'd selected of similar temperament. Abigail would make any of them a fine wife.

All the women had something to offer a suitor. Eva already had several men in mind to introduce to Rose and Yvette. Once she had a firm grasp of her courtesans' personalities, it was just a matter of making introductions to the suitors, then letting attraction take over.

While the women stripped for the next selection of gowns in the private fitting room, Eva wandered the shop, fingering fabrics and trimmings. After the women had discovered the joy of garments made of fabric one couldn't see through, giving up their courtesans' gowns had not been difficult.

A flash of black caught the corner of Eva's eye. She turned to see a tall, caped figure slip into a room at the back of the shop. She looked around for Madame Fornier, but the dressmaker seemed to have vanished.

Curious, Eva walked to where the man had disappeared, and gingerly peered around the open doorway. A gloved hand shot out and grasped her by the wrist. Before she could cry out, she was jerked inside the storage room, and the door was closed behind her.

"Let me loose," she whimpered the instant she recognized the spicy scent of her captor. "Your Grace?"

In the dim light seeping under the door, Eva molded to his body as he swept his hat off his head with one hand and circled her waist with the other. "Were you expecting someone else?"

He turned to press her back to the wall and bent to hungrily claim her mouth. Heat rocked Eva as she wrapped her arms around his neck and tipped her head to a better fit. She let out a low moan of sheer happiness as Nicholas kissed her breathless.

When he finally lifted his head, her heart threatened to leap from her chest. She knew she should push him away, yet she hadn't the will to do so. He was warm and hard, and she longed to feel him naked above her, plunging into her body. If not for the inappropriate setting, she'd have tossed up her skirts and let him have his way with her.

"Why are you here?" she whispered, clutching his coat. "Someone might have seen you. Do you plan to ruin me?"

"That was my intention," he teased. "I knew your curiosity would bring you to me." He tipped his head and nipped her ear. "I saw your carriage and planned only to walk past. My solicitor is two doors down. When I saw you through the window, I was drawn inside." He lowered his hand to caress her rump. "I could not resist a bit of fondling."

Oddly, she found his admission pleasing. She arched a brow. "You must be familiar with the shop, Your Grace, to find this room. It is somewhat hidden behind the shelves."

"I have been here once or twice." Doubtless, with previous lovers. He sucked her earlobe.

Eva giggled quietly and leaned her head back to allow him access to her neck. Her wig slipped and blocked his advance. He groaned and lifted his head. "I hate how you hide your hair, Eva. Why do you feel the need to do so?"

Eva released him and settled back against the wall. "You would not understand, Your Grace. Your life has been open to the world since your birth. I am not so lucky. I need to keep my two worlds separate. Miss Black belongs to the courtesans and Miss Winfield belongs to me."

"Interesting. You hide only from your courtesans?" He lifted her face with his fingertips and peered into her eyes. "I know about your mother's history. Is that the real reason why you hide behind Miss Black?"

Eva lifted her head. "You know?" She bent and slipped out from under his arm. She faced him, frowning. "How could you know?"

She felt sick. All the years of hiding the truth, and the duke had discovered her deepest secret in a few days. She crossed her arms protectively. "Oh, yes. You made it your mission to discover all about me so you could drag me though the gutters and ruin my life."

"Eva"—his voice turned stony—"I would never expose your secret, despite my vengeful plotting. I ended the investigation as soon as I recognized Charlotte's name."

Her stomach twisted at the familiar way he said "Charlotte," and she whispered, "You know my mother?" She pressed her hands over her mouth.

The duke nodded. "She was a casual acquaintance of my father. I met her once in Hyde Park when I was a child. She was stunning and also kind. She allowed me to ride atop her coach with the coachman as she took a turn around the park. It was something my father would not allow." He stepped close. "My investigator knows nothing of her identity. I made certain of it. Charlotte is safe."

Tears welled in her eyes. She'd never known anyone who'd been acquainted with her mother when she had been young and vivacious. Eva had needed to cut all ties to her mother's courtesan life to protect her and her fragile mind.

"She is ill, Your Grace," she said weakly. "If anyone finds out the truth of her past, I don't think she could bear the scrutiny."

Nicholas clasped her arms and made her face him. There was no sign of thoughts of revenge or anger in his shadowed face; only compassion, and a touch of sympathy, as he bent until they were almost nose to nose. "You have my word, Eva. I will take her secret to my grave."

Chapter Eight

How could she trust this man? He'd set out to destroy her in spite of his current words to the contrary. The change in him since their night together was undoubtedly but a temporary diversion. Fevered couplings would not change the fact that the duke was ruthless and selfish and arrogant.

"No matter what transpires between us, Eva, I will not betray Charlotte," he said tightly, as if reading her suspicious thoughts. "To do so would be cruel."

Eva nodded. "Thank you, Your Grace."

Troubled, she backed out of reach.

"I should get back before the ladies grow concerned," she said, looking away. She could not bear to see that vengeful devil duke in the face of the man who'd loved her so passionately for one magical night, and had held her tenderly while she slept.

She felt him watch her for a moment, and she reluctantly looked up to see his hooded expression. His posture was stiff and his jaw tight. A chasm had developed between them with his admission of knowing her mother, and Eva knew he felt it, too.

Nicholas nodded sharply and replaced his hat low on his head. "Good day, Miss Black."

"Good day, Your Grace."

Without another glance, he left her alone in the dark.

.

Eva returned home a few hours later, exhausted. She'd left the women at the school, buried in boxes of gowns and hats and gloves, and had taken the opportunity to slip away. They were happy to spend their meager funds on gowns, and Eva made sure each purchase was reasonable.

Her feet throbbed from endless hours standing, and she felt the strain of the day press against the backs of her eyes. Harold had said nothing to her all day, but a permanent scowl was present on his face as he drove them from shop to shop and helped them with their packages.

She wondered if he'd seen the duke enter the shop and suspected an assignation. Even if the meeting had led to a brief romp on the storage room floor, she owed him no explanation. As a grown woman, her decisions were her own. If she deemed it necessary to take a new lover each day for a week, it was her decision. She'd never asked about his romances, and he should not concern himself with hers.

"Do you plan to talk to me, Harold, or am I to live the rest of my days suffering under your brooding silence?" She stopped just inside the foyer and tipped her head up. His fair brows were nearly knitted together above his nose. "You might as well say your piece and be done with it. I cannot stand the infernal silence."

"You are making a mistake," he grumbled, and pulled his hat off. He crushed the narrow brim in one hand. "His Grace will destroy you, Eva. He will take and take until you have nothing left to give, then leave you as your father left your mother. What will you do then?"

"My father died," she snapped. "It is not the same."

"Is it not?" He took her elbow and steered her into the parlor. Once the door was closed, he turned to her. "He is using you for his own ends. Make no mistake about that, Eva. And once he has your heart ensnared, he'll vanish without cause or explanation."

"Mother and Father were in love, and he died. He died!" Ire rose in her breast. "I am not in love with His Grace." It was the truth. She would be a fool to fall in love with a man like him. He was above her in wealth and situation. He would pluck a beauty from his own class and wed her. Eva was but a temporary diversion, and she had no grander hopes. "Nor will I ever be."

"You deny it now, but what about next week, next month?" Harold scrubbed a hand along his jaw. It was several days since he had shaved, and the bristles were becoming pronounced. "Even were he to fall in love with you, he could not wed you. You know that." He paced, and did not allow her to comment. "Would you be satisfied to accept the arrangement your parents had?" He shook his head and scowled. "I know you, Eva. Knowing you were whoring for him while his duchess waited at home would kill you inside."

"How dare you say such an insolent thing to me?" she cried. "You have no right."

"Someone has to," he countered, and stalked about the room, his body tense. "You are under his spell and cannot see daylight."

The frank words chilled her, and she crossed her arms around her waist and walked to the window. Clouds gathered in the sky and a light mist began to fall. The grayness of the day matched her brooding mood as she stared across the rain-spoiled yard to the street beyond.

She knew Harold was right, and in the moment, she hated him for knowing her so well. She also hated that he was her only real friend and that protecting her mother had left her so isolated from the closeness women shared.

How could a man understand a woman's heart fully? How could she explain how those stolen moments with His Grace had made her feel alive for the first time in her life? She had shared passion with the duke without thinking about her mother or her courtesans or how she had to hide from her worries and fears every day. She'd been naked, both physically and emotionally, and strangely, she'd trusted His Grace that night with both her body and her heart.

"I will speak of it no more." She felt sickened. Harold had turned her into a whore through ignorance and accusation. Though no money had passed between her and the duke, and there was no arrangement in place, she had bedded the man without a word of affection or the promise of a future between them.

Harold saw her as she refused to see herself. Was she a whore because she'd given in to temptation with His Grace?

In that moment, she began to understand her courtesans as she never had before.

She'd helped them, she'd taught them, she'd found them husbands, but as a virgin spinster, she'd never really known what drew so many women to choose, and stay in, that life.

The night with His Grace had taught her how powerful desire could be. And she'd wanted him so desperately with her body, if not her mind and heart. Even now, she longed to welcome him into her bed, to feel his hands playing with her, driving her to madness. She wanted to taste his skin, to feel him thrust into her with long, deep strokes. She wanted to listen to his heart beat beneath her ear as he slept beside her, her head on his chest, his arm tucked around her.

She wanted to take back the day he showed up on her stoop and erase him from her mind. She wanted not to see the disappointment in Harold's eyes because she'd given her innocence to their enemy.

"You may not want to speak of His Grace, but I can see in your face that he has his hooks in you." Eva looked over her shoulder as Harold grasped the door handle and turned to her. "Be careful, Eva."

Don't forget Lady Pennington's ball is Friday, and the Banes-Dodds will be in attendance." Nicholas's mother, Catherine, shuffled through a stack of invitations beside her breakfast plate. She divided them into piles based on priority, as she did every morning over strawberry pastries and overcooked eggs. "I'm sure Lucy is eager to see you again, dearest son. Several weeks have passed since you made an appearance at any function."

Nicholas lifted his head from the newspaper and frowned. Since the day he'd lost Arabella, his pursuit of Lucy Banes-Dodd had been lackluster. Hell, since the day he met Eva, she'd become his entire focus, raised to an obscene level after he'd taken her to bed. In fact, he could hardly recall the face of the pretty Lucy.

He'd been so intent on first punishing, then seducing, Eva that he'd allowed everything else in his life to fall by the wayside.

"Weeks?" He racked his brain for the last party he'd attended. It was the Wilksbury masque nearly a month ago. He'd gone masked and danced several times with Lucy, who was dressed as a shepherdess, and with several other potential duchesses. The evening had gone along pleasantly enough, but his mind wasn't fully engaged in flirtation. He'd been in the midst of searching for Arabella. The evening had been distinctly forgettable.

He was often restless of late. The excitement of youthful entertainments had waned with his advancing age, and he no longer pursued the enticements of gambling and emotionless couplings with lovers whose faces he couldn't recall the next day. Though he'd worked very hard to become the man his father wanted him to be, he knew there were certain things he would want to do differently.

"You're distracted of late, love." His mother's curious green eyes explored his face. She dropped an invitation on the correct stack and leaned forward to better examine him. "Rumor has it you misplaced your mistress."

Nicholas grimaced. He was the subject of gossip, again. It was a place he hated to be. But it was the curse of his class to twitter about things they knew nothing about. Scandal after scandal entertained society, and if none was forthcoming, stories were invented.

To have his proper mother mention his mistress at breakfast made him cock his brow. "I did not lose her, Mother. We have parted company. Amicably."

Another face had replaced both Lucy and Arabella in his mind. A face he'd be well off to forget.

His mother didn't need to be privy to such information.

Deep inside, he understood the feisty Miss Winfield was trouble, a thorn in his well-run life. If he wanted to regain some sanity, he needed to find another interest. Quickly.

"Then you have no plans to throw yourself from a bridge and end your grief." His mother's lips quirked.

He leveled a glare at her still beautiful face. Her dark hair had begun to gray, but her face was as lovely as ever. Men fell over themselves to speak to the wealthy and charming widow. It was her unhappy past that kept her from marrying again, and a steel spine that had kept her chin high when her marriage had crumbled. She was completely satisfied with her social functions and charities and raising her son.

It was his bachelorhood she fretted over.

"You can assure the gossips I have no plans to leap to my death from any high surface." He'd never care so much for a woman that he would consider death preferable to losing her. He lifted the newspaper and scanned the page. "In fact, I will attend the ball, Mother. It is high time I return to society."

A young lady is at the door wishing to speak to you, Miss Eva." Mother's elderly butler, Edwin, cast a quick glance at the dough between her hands and up her arms. Eva took to cooking whenever she was troubled about something. It calmed her and allowed her to think through her problems. Today the loaves of bread would be plentiful.

He continued, "She claims she is some sort of relation, though she is tight-lipped about the details."

A relation? Aside from her mother and some half sisters she'd never met, there was no one she could claim as kin. Mother's family was dead, and Father's was out of reach.

Curiosity kept her from sending the visitor away. "Settle her in the parlor. I will wash my hands and be right up." Eva dropped the dough and cleaned her hands, her mind whirling. It was her month for strange visits. First His Grace, and now some woman claiming to be a long-lost relative.

Eva was relieved her mother was upstairs sleeping. If the visitor was truly family, Eva would discover the motives for her unexpected arrival and handle the situation from there.

Brushing the flour off her dress, she smoothed it as best she could. It was one of her oldest, and slightly frayed at the cuffs, but she had no time to change. She patted her hair, tucked a stray lock behind her ear, and left the kitchen with trepidation. She looked around for Harold as she walked to the parlor. He was absent. She suspected he'd gone off to Cheapside to check on the courtesans.

She paused outside the open parlor door and took a few deep breaths for calm.

When she stepped into the parlor, the stranger was staring at the painting of her father over the mantel. Handsome and stately, he had the hint of humor in his amber eyes. She'd loved that look as a girl, as if he knew deep and shocking secrets he chose not to share.

Her heart tightened. She missed him so. However, it was the petite figure in dove gray who now held her attention. The dress was expensive despite its simple cut, and her matching bonnet did not fully cover her pale hair. From the back it was difficult to guess her age, but Eva suspected she was young.

Eva took a step into the room, but a soft voice from beneath the bonnet drew her to a stop. "He was so handsome, was he not? I hear you have his eyes, Evangeline."

Slowly the woman turned around, her heart-shaped face shadowed by her bonnet, but there was no mistaking the eyes that stared at her from under the brim. The eyes Eva, Father, and this girl all shared. An unusual shade of deep amber with the hint of gold around the pupils if one looked closely enough.

The room tilted. Eva stumbled over to a chair and sat. Her throat closed and her hands trembled. She did not need to see a certificate of birth to know her sister. Though their hair colors were different shades entirely, this girl would be easily picked out of a crowd as Eva's kin.

The question was, which sister was she, and why was she here, now of all times?

"I fear I have shocked you, Evangeline." The young woman slid the bonnet off her head and walked to Eva. She was taller than Eva by an inch or two. Her pert nose had a few freckles and her mouth was gently curved. She was lovely. "It was not my intention. I worried you would not see me and thought it best not to announce my name."

She clasped her gloved hands together. Perhaps she was shaking, too. "I am Noelle. I was born two years before you. Our sister, Margaret, is between us. She is the serious sister."

Noelle's eyes danced. She certainly had their father's mischievous nature. "Perhaps you need a moment to gather your wits. Shall I call for tea?"

"No." Eva pulled in a deep breath and shook her head to clear her unease. She had always known about Noelle, but to have her now sitting in her parlor had shaken her. "I fear I'm confused. I was led to believe you knew nothing about me; or rather, you did not want to know me. I am not the kind of woman a lady of title would claim as kin."

A blonde brow went up and Noelle appeared puzzled. "Why ever not? We share a father. We are not at fault for the choices he made." She smiled brightly. "I've known about you for years, from overhearing conversations between my mother and Aunt Beatrice." She glanced at the portrait. "Mother would not let me see you while I was growing up. I am now old enough to make my own decisions. I just had to come see you."

Eva felt as if her world was crumbling. First His Grace, now another person had come from the shadows to threaten everything. She was paddling against a high tide and was about to be dragged out to sea.

"I think it best if you leave and never come back," Eva said softly. "There is nothing for you here."

Hurt flashed on Noelle's face. She watched Eva for a long moment, then placed her hands on her hips. A spark of defiance replaced the hurt. "I came here without my mother's knowledge or permission, and against Margaret's advice. I risked everything to meet you, my sister. Now you want to toss me out when we have just met?" She tapped a toe. "You may have me removed by force, but I am not ready to take my leave just yet."

The girl was stubborn, a characteristic they shared. She was also charming and defiant, traits Eva normally found enviable. Her own rebellious streak had been replaced with responsibility.

Eva felt some of her ire fade. It would not hurt to discover if there was a darker reason for the visit. It helps to know one's enemies when mounting a defense.

"You are Lady Noelle Seymour. Why would you want

to know a courtesan's daughter?" Eva clasped her hands. "My bloodline does not change the circumstances of my birth. Our father betrayed your mother. I cannot see why you do not despise me."

Noelle dropped into a chair and sighed. Clearly, she had no intention of leaving without having her say. It would take the missing Harold to remove her from the building.

"If you knew my mother, you would understand why he sought a warm bed elsewhere," Noelle said. "Mother is cold and cares for no one but herself. My sister and I were largely an inconvenience, part of her duty to continue the family line. She deeply regretted not having a son."

"How horrible," Eva responded, sympathetic in spite of herself. Her mother had certainly not been perfect, but Eva had always known that she was loved. Never once in her life had her mother ever expressed regret over her birth. "Still, if you are discovered here, you will be ruined. The scandal would rock polite society."

Eva cared naught for the snobbish Ton but knew that if Noelle was to make a suitable match someday, she had to keep their connection secret and her reputation pristine.

"Pish-posh." Noelle waved her gloved hand. "No one need know we are sisters. We will claim we are reunited distant cousins. You can hail from some obscure corner of Northumberland and have come to visit me. No one in society need know any different."

Her words bounced around in Eva's head.

"You can't be suggesting that we be seen in public together. You must be mad."

Truthfully, Eva wasn't sure she wanted to know Noelle at all, publicly or otherwise. She sensed that the whirlwind who was her sister could cause her loads of trouble. There was much to be said for being an only child.

Noelle shook her head and sighed. "I do believe my sister is afraid of a little adventure. I must say I am quite aggrieved." She looked around the room and rested her attention on a small elephant figurine. "Did you know our father spent time in India and America? He traveled many places and saw many things. He was an adventurer in his youth." Noelle's face turned grim. "What would he think of his daughter if he knew she was fearful of her very own shadow?"

One vertebra at a time, Eva straightened. "Since you know nothing about me, you cannot make such a judgment. I've had plenty of adventures." She could not tell Noelle about the courtesan school or her relationship with His Grace. They were her secrets. She shot Noelle a look with narrowed eyes. "I suspect, sister, you are throwing down a challenge you believe I will not be able to resist."

The young woman was a stranger in all regards, yet there was something about her that intrigued Eva. She had a streak of wild in her. Eva suspected her mother, Lady Seymour, had tried and failed to curb the streak. After all, she'd come from Kent to meet her bastard sister at great risk to herself and her family.

Then the thought of pricking the woman who'd almost stolen her father's stipend from them lifted her spirits. Lady Seymour would suffer an attack of apoplexy should she discover the whereabouts of her elder daughter.

Still, getting acquainted with Noelle privately was one thing. As for public outings, she would never agree to that foolish notion.

She smiled at her odd sister. "Would you like some tea, Noelle? I think it is time we became acquainted."

For nearly two hours they chatted about everything from the mundane details of their lives to stories of their father. Eva's reserve toward Noelle faded bit by bit when she failed to find any dark motive for her arrival. Noelle appeared genuine and open.

They laughed a little, cried a little more, and discovered a genuine fondness for one another. Eva learned a bit about Margaret and understood the two sisters did not share the same view of their half sister. Apparently Eva would never meet Margaret. It was more than enough to know Noelle and spend a few hours with her.

Later, when Eva sought out her bed and the house grew quiet, she was happy and content. All her worries were put to rest. She felt certain Noelle would be satisfied with the meeting and return to Kent and her life there.

With no harm done.

Chapter Nine

Pens scratched on parchment as the former courtesans added numbers and tallied columns. Eva walked between them, a starchy schoolmarm in gray. Teaching women to keep books was an unusual undertaking. However, it was a valuable tool for them. One never knew when proficiency with sums might be useful.

"I can't do this," Rose whined, dropping her pen in the ink pot. She stared at her open palms and the ink stains on several of her fingertips. "I am terrible with sums."

"Let me see what you've done, Rose." Eva leaned over her shoulder and began to add the numbers in her head. Halfway down the column she found the mistake. "Here is where you went off. You put a six in this spot instead of an eight."

Rose leaned over and inspected the parchment. "Hmm." She retrieved the pen and made the change. After another minute she returned the pen to the ink pot a second time and gleefully rubbed her palms together. "I did it!"

Eva smiled. "Yes, you did. And since you've completed

this most satisfactorily, I have a surprise for you." She paused until all eyes were on her. "A look through the Husbands book."

Rose let out a squeal. "I do so want to look." She jumped to her feet and clapped her hands. "I get to be first."

Several envious stares followed her across the room. Eva walked to the bookshelf and pulled out the heavy volume. They were almost at the end of their instruction and nearly ready to be matched with a mate. Choosing potential suitors was exciting for the women, and for Eva, too.

She caressed the cover of the book. "Settle yourself on the settee, Rose." Rose dropped into the indicated space and held out her hands. Eva's mouth twitched. Rose wasn't timid. It was part of her charm. The girl was more akin to a wiggly puppy in her enthusiasm for life's adventures. "This is the culmination of your learning."

"Why did you to start this school, Miss Eva?" Abigail asked. She dipped her pen in the ink pot.

"Well, it was quite simple, really," Eva said. "What started out as a simple conversation about unrequited love with the shy young artist who painted my mother's portrait blossomed into a way to help courtesans. It took several years and countless hours of work, but I am satisfied with the result."

The story was true. She left out the part about her mother's history and how it had gotten her to this place. The two stories cobbled together had convinced her to help courtesans find love and escape.

"Tell us more about the artist," Pauline urged.

Eva smiled as she continued. "As it happened, Mister Bennett was looking for a wife and was deeply infatuated with Miss Hale, the mistress of a count. I intervened and discovered a surprising knack for matchmaking. Soon they were very much in love. The pair was so pleased with my efforts, they asked for help with matching Mister Bennett's brother. Through word of mouth, and a string of unhappily unattached friends of Mister Bennett's, my school was born. Now Mister Bennett recommends and sketches the suitors while Mrs. Bennett tends their growing brood of five children. Of course I make the final selections of who is included in the book."

It was an exceedingly successful arrangement. In three years of matchmaking, she'd not heard a single complaint from any of the husbands or wives.

"Once the rest of you have finished your sums," Eva said, opening the cover to the first face, "you may also have a peek."

The sound of pens furiously scratching on parchment followed the pronouncement as Eva handed the book to Rose. With everyone occupied, Eva looked from woman to woman, painfully noting the absence of Yvette. No one had seen her since yesterday, when she went out on some secret errand and had not yet returned.

Eva knew Yvette was finding the transition from courtesan to wife most difficult. The struggle had left her withdrawn over the last two days. She'd sold her body for so long, she wasn't sure if she would be satisfied with a simple life.

In spite of this, Eva had been positive Yvette was still willing to turn her life around.

Now she wasn't so sure.

Had Yvette gone back to her abusive lover without telling anyone? From what Eva now understood, when he lost a purse gambling, he'd slap Yvette. When a business venture downturned, he'd give her a black eye or a bruised lip. He took any reason to vent his frustrations on her. Yvette had suffered greatly, making it impossible for Eva to understand how she could consider returning to the man.

Unfortunately, he was a mystery. Yvette had refused to name him when asked. Without the information, it was impossible to discover if Yvette had renewed their relationship.

According to Sophie, a woman of a certain age with her livelihood slowly coming to an end, Yvette had taken the abuse with stoic acceptance until she'd found her way to Eva's door.

"I'm next!" Pauline pushed aside the pen and parchment and hurried to take a choice seat next to Rose. Soon the two women were chattering happily and perusing sketches.

Eva went to the window and looked up and down the empty street. As the young women giggled behind her, she felt darkness grow in the pit of her stomach. There was something not right about Yvette's absence. She sensed it, felt it, and was certain that wherever Yvette was, she was in serious trouble.

In a city as large as London, where did one begin looking for a missing courtesan? If she did begin a search, would Yvette want to be found?

Eva knew she could do nothing at the moment and needed to keep her attention on the remaining courtesans. They weren't worried yet about Yvette, and Eva knew they'd follow her example. If she exhibited calm and confidence that Yvette would return, so would they.

"This one is very handsome," Abigail said, and Eva turned back, discovering a trio of heads bent low over the book. Parchment crinkled as they turned the pages. Sophie quickly finished her sums and joined them, leaning over the back of the settee.

"This one has an overbite but he has very kind eyes," Rose said. "I do adore a man with kind eyes."

"Look at that one." Sophie pointed to a face. She squinted to read his information. "It says he's a solicitor." Her face brightened. "A solicitor? He must have a lovely house."

Sophie lifted her eyes to Eva, who had joined her behind the settee. Eva peered at the book over her spectacles. They were clear glass and of no use.

"A solicitor he is," Eva agreed. This was one of the men

she had selected for Sophie. "He is looking for a woman of some maturity and without children, to run his household and travel with him when he visits clients. He is quite wealthy."

"He would be perfect for you, Sophie," Pauline interjected eagerly. "I'll bet he cuts a fine figure in court."

Sophie tried to hide her interest, but her eyes shone. Eva would send his invitation immediately.

"Why don't all of you make a list of potential suitors and give it to me?" Eva walked to the desk. "I will send invitations next week." She smiled at the women. "You have proven to be fine students. We should complete our lessons in the next few days."

To look at the women now, one would find it difficult to recognize a former courtesan in the group. They were respectably dressed and free of face paint and gaudy adornments. Each had a lovely spirit that made her delightful to spend time with.

Eva suspected her male clients would be pleased to take any one of them as his wife.

H arold took Eva home a few hours later, giving one-word answers and avoiding her questions about where he had been. He was still put out with her, and she with him, but at the moment she had more pressing worries than her disgruntled servant and friend.

Yvette's absence nagged at her. Not once, since that day when they had gathered for their first meeting, had Eva believed Yvette regretted her choice to give up the courtesan's life. Though she had not taken easily to instruction, she had settled in and satisfactorily completed her lessons.

And in the last few days, Eva had seen Yvette smile more easily and appear less resentful of her circumstance. Though Sophie assured her Yvette was just adjusting to the restrictions of her new situation, and would return to Cheapside very soon, Eva wasn't so certain.

"Where is my mother?" Eva asked a passing maid, and was directed to the garden. She found Mother resting beneath a tree with her nurse hovering nearby. At Eva's arrival, Mrs. Brown nodded and wandered back to the house.

"Good afternoon, my darling." Charlotte smiled and took Eva's hand as she settled into a chair beside her. Her hands were cool. Eva tucked her quilt higher around her lest she take ill. Charlotte buried her fingers in the folds. "I could not stand another minute in my room. I just had to get some air and watch the birds play."

"Today is a perfect day to do so." Eva agreed. Her mother was too pale. Months had passed since last Mother had allowed Eva to take her on an outing. She preferred to remain shut in her room with her memories. "The sun is hiding, but it is neither too hot nor too cold. I think summer will soon be upon us."

Charlotte nodded. "It is almost time for the Season to start full swing. I used to love to attend the parties." She let out a small sigh, and her eyes took on a dreamy cast. "There were so many beautiful gowns and such handsome men to dance with every night. It was glorious."

The parties her mother was invited to were outside of polite society. Still, she had traveled on the fringe of the Ton. Those parties and balls could be just as fine, if not more extravagant, than those given by a duchess or a wealthy countess. Eva could imagine the crush of men who'd fought to dance with the beautiful Charlotte Rose.

It was during her first courtesan ball that Mother had fallen in love. One look at the dashing Lord Seymour, Eva's father, and Mother had never again danced with another man.

"I do remember how you loved parties, Mother," Eva said. "Father took you out many times, and you looked so beautiful . . ."

"You remember?"

"I do." Eva squeezed her hand. Her parents had been a magnificent couple. "You had a blue gown with a sheer overlay sprinkled with tiny glass beads. It was the color of a summer sky. When you walked, it shimmered like stars."

Charlotte nodded. "I still have that gown." Mother looked into her eyes. "I saved it for you."

Eva startled. The gown had to be very out of fashion. It was surprising that her mother had kept it. Perhaps it was the memories she savored when looking at the gown. It was what she wore to one of the last functions her parents attended before her father's death.

"I would love to have it, Mother." Eva blinked back tears, remembering their happiness. She'd envied their love at the time. Her mother's suffering after his death had cast a pall over those memories. "Unfortunately, I have nowhere to wear such a treasure."

"Oh, but you will, darling." Charlotte smiled wistfully. "I believe one day a man will carry you off to his castle. Then you will wear my dress and remember how happy your father and I were, a long time ago."

Eva sensed Mother slipping away, so she rushed to keep her in the present. "I met someone who claims to have known you before I was born. His Grace, the Duke of Stanfield."

The name chased the shadows from her mother's eyes. "Nicholas?" Charlotte's mouth twitched, and she placed a hand to her cheek. "He was such a dear boy, so charming but a bit wild." She peered at Eva, and light danced in her gaze. "He must be a devastatingly handsome rake now."

It seemed to Eva that her entire body flushed. "He is handsome," she admitted. Her mother did not need a description of the sculpted muscles beneath his clothing or how he used his body so expertly in the art of love play. It was a secret she'd keep to herself.

She resisted the urge to tug at her high collar and tried to forget His Grace's magnificent mouth. When had the day gotten so hot?

A funny look crossed Mother's face. A sly stare followed. "His Grace owns a house that is nearly a castle, Collingwood House, here in London. Perhaps you will soon have occasion to wear my gown after all."

Eva struggled to retain serenity on her features. The mere thought of His Grace was enough to send delicious tremors across her skin. If her mother sensed the tiniest bit of interest in him, she'd never let it rest.

"Don't be absurd, Mother, it isn't a castle." It was nearly as large, though, and a fit setting for a duke. "We do not travel in the same circles." Eva traveled in no circles at all. "We have met twice quite casually. I would not sit by the door awaiting an invitation to join His Grace and the dowager duchess for tea and cakes."

She hated to lie about their connection, but the hours she'd spent writhing with the naked duke in his bed was something she could not discuss with anyone. It was difficult enough to suffer Harold and his grim scowls. If her mother knew she'd briefly become the duke's lover, Charlotte would have impossible visions of a summer wedding settling in her head.

"Well, I would not be so quick to dismiss him as a suitor." Mother yawned behind her hand. "My daughter would make a fine duchess."

Sighing, Eva held her tongue as Mrs. Brown came to retrieve her patient. The nurse helped Mother to her feet. "It is time for your nap, Mrs. Winfield."

Smiling sadly, Eva gave Mother a kiss on the cheek and watched her make her way gingerly up the path. Eva could never be a duchess. The ridiculous notion was the product of her mother's confused mind. A courtesan's daughter could never become a duchess.

However, another idea came to the fore. If anyone could help her find Yvette, it was His Grace. His investigator had uncovered her secrets with very little difficulty. Perhaps Nicholas could be persuaded to allow the man's talents to aid her in this matter. Yvette needed to be found, and quickly.

Suddenly feeling lighter, Eva hurried into the house to change into something suitable for a meeting with His Grace.

Since Harold was missing and Eva did not want him to know her destination, lest they have another argument, she chose to hire a hack to take her to His Grace's town house. She hoped he had not yet returned to Collingwood House. She could not visit him where the dowager duchess resided.

He'd mentioned once, during a quiet moment, that he'd taken up temporary residence in the empty town house to get away from his mother's fussing. She wanted him to marry and produce grandchildren for her to dote on. The duchess encouraged his pursuit of the young misses.

Eva had listened, silent, as the conversation left her oddly saddened that she would never experience the wonder of motherhood. Not once before that moment had she considered becoming a mother. Afterward, it was often on her mind.

The hackney coach slowed. Dusk had fallen by the time she'd set out to visit the duke, and she felt darkness lessened her chances of discovery. She was an unmarried woman visiting an unmarried man without a chaperone. Not that she had a reputation to ruin.

It was only after she knocked on the town house door that she realized he could be entertaining a woman, or women, if that was his predilection. He'd kept Arabella here, and probably a whole line of mistresses before her. And likely after her, too.

After their last encounter, he'd clearly been unhappy with her. It wouldn't be beyond reason that he'd found a woman with a more agreeable temperament. A man such as His Grace certainly wouldn't go long without female companionship.

The thought stopped Eva's hand on the knocker before she could drop it again. She tried to untangle the sudden feelings of resentment she felt at the idea of His Grace replacing her so quickly. It irritated her that she cared, and that at this moment he could be nibbling the breasts of another woman.

An urge to flee had spun her around when the door was jerked open, and the duke himself glared at her, surprised.

"Eva?" There wasn't a smile of welcome, nor a hint anywhere in his cold expression that he was even slightly pleased to see her. His dark hair was ruffled and his shirt untucked from his breeches. He looked like he had right before he'd shucked off his clothing and pushed her down on the bed. It was very possible a naked woman awaited his return.

Pained, Eva swallowed past hurt. "This was a mistake. I should leave." She stepped back. His arm reached out to catch her wrist. He pulled her over the threshold and into the dim entryway. His housekeeper walked into the hallway. His Grace waved her away.

"You have already intruded on my evening," he said tightly as he pulled Eva along behind him. "You might as well state your business."

Annoyance welled. Three days ago he'd made passionate love to her. Now he acted as though she'd arrived at his door covered with oozing sores. She wanted to give him a set-down, but worry for Yvette stilled her tongue as she stumbled along beside him.

Once they reached the library, Eva twisted out of his grip and took a few calming breaths. She looked around the space and felt a touch of envy over his floor-to-ceiling bookshelves. Though she had had little time to read of late, she enjoyed burying herself in worlds outside her own. If she had a library such as this, she might never venture outside its comforts.

"Intruding was not my intention, Your Grace."

Without comment, he walked to a sideboard to pour a drink, then settled into a chair. He did not offer her tea or a seat. Clearly he was still angry with her.

It was the silence of the house she felt most deeply. Unless he had hidden a woman somewhere on an upper floor, he was alone. This pleased her immensely.

But his affairs, or lack of them, was not her pressing concern. She had not returned to share his bed, so she ignored his glare and straightened her shoulders.

"I have come to ask a favor of you. It is a situation of grave importance." She pulled in a deep breath to steady her rapid heart. "One of my courtesans is missing. I would like to hire your investigator to find her."

Chapter Ten

The woman did have a steel spine. He'd give her credit for not cowering under his glare. Even after his assurances he'd not expose Charlotte's secrets, and though she had allowed him untold liberties with her body, he was certain she still distrusted, and possibly still despised, him with everything inside her.

Yet, his spinster-courtesan had come to ask him for help in spite of those feelings. She was a puzzle.

Truthfully, Eva had every reason to feel nothing but contempt for him, and knowing she would not fall in love with him was a relief. He desired her, and nothing else. If only he could convince her to continue a physical relationship without strings, it would be mutually satisfying.

Love had no part in such agreements.

He swirled the brandy in his glass. "Why would I agree to such an ill-advised endeavor?" he said, keeping his voice bland. He'd hoped that after she'd become his lover, his stubborn busybody would give up her efforts to change courtesans into wives. Obviously, he'd been mistaken. It was another reason to limit his interactions with Eva to those of the carnal kind. She was entirely too rigid in her beliefs. "If a courtesan chooses to stay with her protector, it is not your place to interfere."

The argument was old between them and should've already been put to rest. But Eva could not see that her actions would not alter the tradition of wealthy men taking lovers outside marriage. Men always had their mistresses. One woman would not change history or the future.

"I understand your disdain, Your Grace, though I do find your thoughts a mite confused. The courtesans come to me. I do not seek them out."

She visibly struggled to control her anger.

"But I do not believe Yvette is with her lover, Your Grace." She pressed a palm to her head. "He abused her."

He clicked his tongue. "You have proof of this?"

She shook her head. Her delightful mouth thinned. He remembered how it felt when she kissed him and nibbled his jaw, then moved down to press kisses on his chest. He hardened despite her serious tone, and he shifted to hide the bulge in his breeches. She was driving him mad!

"It is more of a feeling." She turned her palms up, pleading. He struggled to concentrate on her words when what he really wanted to do was rip off her clothes and take her, up against a bookcase. "It cannot hurt to prove me wrong."

A feeling? That was her proof?

Feelings muddled up every interaction one had with women. It started at birth and grew until there was no reasoning with them most of the time. She was distressed over this . . . feeling?

"The woman has likely found herself another lover and is happily settled into a cottage or town house, counting her good fortune," Nicholas said and waved a hand dismissively. He had more important matters to discuss. Like how to relieve the strain in his breeches.

Eva stiffened. "I do not think so, Your Grace."

Nicholas expelled a harsh breath. Eva was a bottomless well of arguments. She could argue with a man until he was ready to hang himself with his cravat.

Evidently, her mouth needed something else to keep it occupied. Once he settled the case of the missing courtesan, he had a few ideas in that regard.

"If this Yvette has gone off and gotten herself into a fix, it is not my worry, or yours," he said. "She'll eventually turn up from her adventure, perhaps a bit the worse for it, and ready to resume her studies."

Studies? He bit back a snort at his choice of words. As if it was possible to change the essence of a woman, a courtesan, and make her a proper wife. A foolish notion it was. That was why most men didn't make their mistresses their wives. Their nature lacked the moral discipline to keep faithful to one man. A man should know with absolute certainty that he was the father of his own children.

"Do you lack even a single drop of compassion in that noble body of yours, Your Grace?" Eva said, her voice rising. "You may see women as less than your equal, but Yvette is a good person and she has people who care about her and her safety. I am not asking you to spend your gold to pay for this, as you call it, ill-advised endeavor. I only ask you make the introduction."

It wasn't her snide words that captured his attention. It was the way a few silky strands of her hair had escaped her bonnet and curled delightfully down and around her neck. They trailed across the creamy skin above the square neckline of her simple gown. There was something about her flame-licked hair that took his breath away. It was such an unusual shade.

His arousal pressed against his breeches to a seam-splitting degree. He vividly recalled the lilac scent of her skin and their eager couplings, as if they had just come from frolicking in his bed. She came across prim and pinched like a schoolmarm, but once she was extricated from her clothes, she was a wild entity.

Slowly he walked around her, dipping his head now and again to inhale the sweet scent of her, not touching, keeping a modicum of distance between them. He saw her go rigid, yet he sensed she was not entirely immune to him, anger aside.

"I believe I might be more inclined to help if you had on a few less clothes." He suppressed a smile when her spine stiffened beneath a row of tiny buttons. The curve of it was expertly made for marking a trail for kisses. "I am finding it impossible to concentrate on your plight when my cock is occupied with other thoughts."

She let out a low sound that was somewhere between exasperation and rage. He watched her hands curl into fists.

"You are the most maddening man." She turned around to face him fully. Her face was pink and her neck mottled. "Irksome, vexing, and vile. A woman's life may be in danger, and all you can think about is your baser needs."

He reached to trace a finger across her stomach. "My baser needs?" He cocked a brow and cupped her hips. She tried to step back, but he held tight and bent to press his mouth against her shoulder. "You cannot tell me your courtesan was your only reason for darkening my door this night. You are as eager to return to my bed as I am eager to have you in it."

This wasn't entirely true. His desire for her was tenfold hers at the moment. If he did not get her to bed quickly, and her legs draped around his hips, he was in dire danger of spilling his seed in his breeches.

But Eva had other ideas. She twisted awkwardly and sidestepped, leaving his arms empty. He drew up and watched as she walked a few paces away, her hips swaying enticingly.

"I think, Your Grace, you have long become accustomed to having everything your way." She shot him a perilous glance over her shoulder, promising him ill will. And yet, there was mischief tugging at her mouth. "But I, too, have difficulty taking orders from others."

He crossed his arms. "I hadn't noticed."

A single lamp marked her passage as Eva crossed to the back of the room and leaned against his desk. "I think, though taking to your bed is clearly pleasurable to a certain degree, that I gain nothing by giving in to your demands." She reached up to push a cap sleeve off her shoulder, exposing creamy skin.

Nicholas squelched a groan. She saw his game and was playing with him. The question was simply how far she would go to get what she wanted.

"Nothing?" He dipped his head and ran a sidelong gaze down her body. Unlike her previous visit, she'd left off all but a minimum of layers beneath her gown. The cream-colored material flowed down her body to accentuate each curve. He itched to shove his hands up her skirt and explore the silky patch of curls between her legs. "I think your moans and cries indicate otherwise."

In the candlelight, the color of her cheeks deepened to rosy red. It was the only indication that she remembered their night together as vividly as he. Still, she didn't waver.

"Have you always been so confident of your skills as a lover, Your Grace?" She shrugged, and the other sleeve dropped off a perfect white shoulder. "Perhaps I was only falsely playing to your immense ego to keep you from taking away my home. Perhaps the pleasure was yours alone."

The chit did have a pair of steel stones beneath her drawers. She was not the least intimidated by his ducal rank. Her stubbornness and aggravating need to thwart him at every turn now became a challenge. He'd discovered that she made love just as passionately as she fought for her courtesans, for her mother, and for herself. She was unlike any other woman he'd ever known. Everything about her was a whirl of color and a mass of everything contrary.

Each time he thought her captured and bent to his will, she'd slip from his fingertips and thwart him. Not this time.

"There was nothing false about the way your body responded under my tutelage. I know as well as you that you want me." He grinned wickedly. "I have a few more tricks to teach you, Eva. You must give me a chance to prove your words as lies."

Eva frowned. There was no denying the attraction between them. Even now her body called to him to take her with passionate fervor. However, she was not about to put off her reason for her visit while he made her lose focus on Yvette's plight.

"If you truly want to give me what I desire, then you will agree to introduce me to your investigator." She leaned forward under the pretense of smoothing her skirt and watched him through a fringe of hair. His attention dropped to her neckline, where her breasts threatened to spill over frothy lace.

Never had she lowered herself to use her body, her charms to get her way, but her relationship with His Grace was no normal situation. If she had to play off his desire for her to get to the investigator, then so be it. The time to cling to her morals, and her virginity, had passed. He wanted her, and to have her he needed to give her something in return.

She could suffer regrets for her fall from grace once Yvette was safe.

He stared at her for a long moment, his hooded eyes telling her nothing of his thoughts. His linen shirt was open at the neck, and the sleeves were rolled to the elbows to show a fine mist of dark hair on his forearms. His black breeches were sculpted to his thighs and molded to the hard ridge of his erection.

The sight made her mouth go dry, and her body flushed with heat. He was a fine specimen of a man, dark and dangerous. If she were to crawl into the murky water between fighting for her soul and becoming his courtesan in truth, or to turn around and walk away from him forever, she wasn't sure which she would choose.

"I will make the introduction tomorrow," he said finally, through harsh breath and gritted teeth.

"Thank you, Your Grace." Eva nodded. She locked into his eyes and walked slowly toward him. His intensity drew her in as she slid into his arms and cupped the side of his face. She touched her tongue to her bottom lip. "Now you must show me those tricks you promised."

She lifted to her toes, pressed her mouth to his, and tasted brandy on his lips. In an instant, his arms closed around her, cupping her buttocks and crushing her against his erection. Her last bit of reserve—pride, as it were—fled with the brush of her breasts across his chest as he shifted to pull her closer to his hardness.

Eva hated the ease with which she'd become his lover, his courtesan. She hated how much she desired him, too. And as she tangled her tongue with his, she knew she would always feel vulnerable to his seduction.

Though she wanted to believe she'd gone to his bed under force and fear of her future, there wasn't a requirement in the arrangement that she'd actually find pleasure in his arms.

Her pleasure was his gift to her.

Nicholas reached to free her hair from the chignon and it tumbled sensuously down her back. She knew some of her features were quite ordinary, but with a mass of extraordinary hair infused with flame, she'd enticed a duke to take her to his bed.

"I will not become your courtesan," she said softly as he waged a sensual war on the curved shell of her ear. He nibbled around the edge, then buried his face in her hair. He inhaled deeply. A soft sigh escaped her.

" 'Tis a bit late for that, love." He trailed kisses down her neck and nibbled her collarbone. "If you prefer another term, I'll not quibble."

Eva felt cool air on her legs and realized her slippers were gone and her skirts were sliding up her legs, twisted in his long, lean fingers, and she was arched back over the desk. He quickly loosened her bodice, and the plump flesh pressed up to a precarious level.

The man had skills aplenty. While his mouth was occupied with hers, he'd managed to get her halfway undressed without her knowledge. She'd spoken often to her young women about the need to keep certain parts covered at all times. And now her own nipples were peeking out from behind the creamy lace of her bodice, and she was extremely pleased.

Regrets raced through her. She taught her courtesans all about propriety, and this was entirely improper. However, the duke was not about to allow her a moment to rethink this agreement. He dropped to one knee before her and shoved her skirts up to her waist.

Shockingly exposed in the candlelight, she had only a moment to feel herself being eased up onto her back on the desk before his hot breath touched her clitoris.

"Your Grace, please, you cannot." She tried to close her legs, but his head and shoulders prevented such an action. She was trapped. She felt him part the curls with his fingers, and she whimpered a protest. He brushed her nub with his thumb, and she gasped at the flash of pleasure.

"I can, and I will." She lifted onto her elbows and watched in surprise as he dipped his head and replaced his thumb with his tongue. She let out a cry as he took the nub in his mouth and suckled gently. The shocking intimacy of the act dropped her back on the desk's surface and she began little whimper-moans as her body responded to his egregious behavior.

As if she could take any more, he slipped one finger

inside her wet sheath, then another. She bucked, her heels pressing against the desk as he licked and suckled and drove her to the brink of insanity. When she finally tumbled headlong into her release, she screamed his name and fell back, her body replete.

His Grace gave her no time to recover. He rose to position himself between her legs and tore open the buttons on his breeches. She pulled him to her as he entered her in one slick movement and buried himself to the hilt.

Eva met him thrust for thrust. She felt as if her body had taken flight, and could not feel the earth beneath her. He kissed her; he suckled her nipples, and pulsed inside her until she lost all sense of time or place. And when he cried out hoarsely and spilled his seed inside her, they fell together, collapsing on the hard surface of the desk, breathless and boneless.

"I will not be your courtesan," she said sleepily as his erection slowly softened and slid out of her body.

"You *are* my courtesan," he replied. He lifted her off the desk and carried her to the Oriental rug by the fireplace, gently settling her on the soft surface. There was the real fear of discovery by a footman or maid, but Eva could not lift a finger to cover herself. She smiled lightly, imagining the mortified face of a servant were he or she to come through the door and find Eva splayed out, her skirts bunched to her waist and parts only a husband should see exposed for anyone to take a peek.

Nicholas tugged her skirts into place.

"Thank you, Your Grace." She touched his hip with one hand, the only part of her able to move. A hazy, damp sheen covered her skin, cooled by the chill of the room.

"You're welcome, Miss Winfield," he said, matching her formality.

Eva realized it was the first time he called her anything but Eva or Miss Black. She supposed their intimacy was as confusing to him as it was to her. Though he was a man with certain needs, she sensed he did not usually commit such, ah, intimate acts on his desk.

Nicholas rolled onto his side and lifted a damp lock to his nose. "I never seduced Arabella in this room, Eva, if that is what is screwing up your face." He grinned. "In fact, I have decided to sell this town house. A new mistress needs a new house of her own."

She wrinkled her nose. His uncanny ability to read her thoughts was disturbing. If he ever lost his title and fortune, he could find work with a troupe of gypsies telling fortunes. "Then I hope she will be very happy there, Your Grace."

His bark of laughter filled the tall room. "Stubborn witch!" He leaned to kiss her.

"Arrogant beast," she replied, grinning, and they shared a slow and intimate kiss. It was so seldom that Eva heard him laugh, and she committed the sound to memory. There would be years ahead without him, so she also memorized his scent, the feel of the rough patches on his palms when he caressed her, the taste of his mouth. Even the way he scowled and his brows came together with a deep groove between them. She did not want to forget anything about her first and only lover.

Eva broke the kiss. "Tell me about your home," she asked, and leaned back on the rug. "A man of your position must find this town house restricting."

He positioned his head on his open palm. "Collingwood House? My mother and I live there when she is in town, though she prefers to stay in the country. When the Season is fully upon us, she rushes to London and casts about at various functions for my perfect future wife."

Wife. The word soured her stomach. Of course, he would have a wife someday, and they'd discussed the matter before. Nicholas was almost past the age when most men wanted to produce a passel of heirs. And the idea of Nicholas sharing such recent scandalous intimacies with another woman was profoundly difficult for her to imagine. Still, he'd had sex with women before her and would continue his amorous liaisons after she'd faded back into obscurity.

She forced a light tone. "And has she whittled down a list of young beauties?"

His brows went up. She hoped she hadn't sounded overly interested in his private matters. It was easier to keep their interactions purely of a physical nature. It was the dreaded curse curiosity making her ask. It wasn't as if she'd didn't have other topics to chose from.

"She has. I agree with her choice." He rubbed his chin. If he found the conversation odd, it didn't show. It was possible he'd spoken of the same topic with Arabella. A mistress knew her place. Speaking of a wife would not be unusual, though likely not common. The two lives should and would be kept separate.

Strangely, she felt a sudden rush of resentment over Arabella and her time with His Grace. She knew it was absurd to feel it, but she couldn't stop herself.

"Before Arabella left, I had made overtures to Lucy Banes-Dodd. Her father was encouraging the match." He twisted the lock of her hair. "I've been distracted of late. I promised Mother I would renew the courtship soon."

Eva hated herself for the bleak turn of her mood. She should change the topic to the weather. Instead she pressed, "And what of Arabella? Would you have continued your relationship with her after you married?"

"I expected to do so."

The confidence in his words irked her, as if Miss Banes-Dodd wouldn't be put out to share his bed with another woman. Eva knew it was an arrangement common to men of wealth, and their wives pretended not to know where their husbands spent their time and money. She supposed when one married for wealth and position, and not for love, the wives likely were relieved when their husbands slaked their needs elsewhere.

Her father had found love with her mother.

"I could not agree to such an archaic practice nor accept my husband finding comfort in another's arms," she said. "If I were to marry, it would be for love. I'd expect total faithfulness and devotion."

Wide shoulders shrugged. "A noble idea, but impractical." He reached to place a hand over her heart. "Love is for ballads and plays. Most women are more realistic. They know a good marriage can be the difference between comfort and protection, and poverty. You have a monthly stipend. If not for that, what would you do?"

What would she do? She couldn't help her courtesans, nor could she afford to stay in her home. Truthfully, she could end up entering into a contract with some man like His Grace.

"Women are slaves to the whims of men." Her voice was so low she wasn't sure he'd heard her until he nodded.

"I can give you riches beyond your imagination, Eva."

She nodded. "For the price of my soul, Your Grace."

The softness in his face fled and his jaw pulsed. "You enjoy the pleasures of my bed, Eva. We share a passion most people will never experience. You should give me leave to spoil you as I wish, as my courtesan."

She looked into his eyes, disbelieving he'd all but likened her to a possession. She rolled onto her knees. She'd almost forgotten that beneath the handsome face, and his clothes askew from their frolicking, was still the man who all but called Arabella his property. He saw her the same way.

A fleeting sadness tangled with her anger. "You do not, nor will you ever, own me. Take your money and your baubles and fill the pockets of your precious Lucy. All I ask for is a chance to repay my debts fairly without bullying from you." She jerked her bodice in place and leveled a pointed glare on him. "I think I have earned that right."

Eva stomped over to the desk and retrieved her slippers. She bent to pull them on, then straightened and walked to the door. Never had she been so incensed with anyone. He had a way of jabbing at her until he drove her mad with his opinions.

"I hope you have much happiness with your Lucy, and I wish her the best of luck." She opened the door and stepped out. "She'll need it."

Chapter Eleven

"Have you gone batty?" Eva stared at her sister and shook her head. It was difficult enough to comprehend that she had a sister who wanted to know her. She'd not be dragged off to parties she had no possible reason for attending. If anyone discovered her identity, the scandal would be far-reaching and life-ruining.

And after her confrontation with Nicholas last evening, she wasn't in the best of moods. She wanted to be left alone. Noelle was having none of that.

"Members of the Ton may hide their true natures behind closed doors, but publicly they hold to their rules like talismans of honor," Eva said sharply. "I will not attend Lady Pennington's ball with you."

Noelle leaned back on the settee and stretched both arms across the back. Her expensive green day dress took up the better part of the patterned surface. In the light from the window, she sparkled like an emerald. "Why ever not?"

Eva stared, exasperated. Noelle must have difficulty

hearing. It seemed to come and go, based on the topic and whether she was in agreement on the issue or not.

Noelle was impossible. She was bossy and pushy, and oftentimes reminded her of the duke. Neither understood how hard she'd worked to protect her mother and herself from prying eyes, and how lonely she'd become because of her sacrifices. But it was her life, and she wasn't about to risk everything on the whims of a sister she'd known for a few days.

"My mother was a courtesan, remember?" Eva reached for her tea and sipped it. "Though her time as a courtesan was brief and her lovers limited to Father, Mother was one of those rare beauties people remember years after they fade into obscurity. Lady Pennington will not be pleased if I show up at her ball and flaunt myself about."

Amber eyes flashed. "Who's to know you are Charlotte's daughter? You are my long-lost cousin from Northumberland. Remember? We have recently made contact through letters and have become fast friends. Lady Pennington will not deny me a second invitation."

"You cannot be so confident." There! The argument was over. Lady Pennington had a well-planned guest list. She was very particular about whom she invited and posted footmen at the door to keep out riffraff. The only way to gain entrance to the ball uninvited was to climb through a window. And she would not do that for anyone. "I understand guest lists are often filled weeks in advance."

Noelle smirked. Eva very much hated it when she smirked. "Aunt Penn is my godmother. She will not say no to me."

Eva's eyes widened. "Lady Pennington is your godmother?" she said dumbly. This association with her sister was getting worse. Eva hadn't known how well connected her father had been. Mother rarely talked about that aspect of his life. She liked to speak only of the times when he was with them.

At Noelle's nod, she leaned back and sighed. "You think she will not question the arrival of this relative she has never met? I hear she is a dragon with the ability to expel smoke out of her nose." The situation had the makings of a disaster. "What of your mother? She will take one look into my eyes, Father's eyes, and realize the deception."

"Oh, Aunt Penn isn't as fire-breathing as is rumored. She can be a dear." Crinoline rustled as Noelle stood. She put her palms together and tapped her fingers. "Mother will be in Bath. She's felt poorly of late, suffering with headaches, and is in seclusion. Aunt Penn may consider herself an expert on families of the Ton, but she doesn't know everyone. Father has cousins scattered all the way into Scotland."

Though she knew Noelle's idea was absurd, the thought of attending a ball caused a stir of intrigue inside Eva. She'd never attended a party, much less a ball the magnitude of the Pennington ball. Most of the newspapers called the yearly event the official start of the Season. Everyone who mattered would be there, polished to shine.

It was a world closed off to Eva and her ilk. If the Ton knew her history, they'd have her drawn and quartered.

She lifted her nose and frowned at Noelle. "No one will believe such an outlandish story. No, I will not attend, no matter how deeply you scowl. If there is even a small chance of discovery, well, I cannot risk it."

Slippered footfalls moved back and forth as Noelle began to pace. Eva's stomach tightened. She understood enough now about her sister to know that Noelle didn't like to be told no. She had a determined look in her eyes that worried Eva. She braced herself for a fight.

"Who besides the housekeeper and Harold know about your mother's history?" Noelle asked.

"No one."

More pacing. Her hands became very animated when she was plotting something. Eva wondered if anyone had ever told her no and lived to tell.

Noelle stopped and spun to face Eva. "Then how could anyone find out? Your mother has virtually vanished from this earth, and it's been more than ten years since she was seen publicly on Father's arm." Noelle stopped, and her eyes brightened. "You will spend the weekend with me at the town house so your position as my visiting cousin will be established and accepted. Then you will disappear back into the northern wilds as quickly as you appeared, with none the wiser." She danced about as if she had just invented a cure for the plague. "It is brilliant."

Eva knew her chances of escaping the plot were thin. And spending time in her father's London home would be glorious. She'd always hidden herself, tucked away; lingering outside the bright light of society and his legitimate family. To spend time surrounded by his things would make her feel close to him again.

"What of the current earl?"

Noelle smiled. "Uncle Arthur is in India studying plants and birds. If he had his druthers, he'd never return to England. His man of affairs pays the bills, and Mother oversees everything else. The staff aside, we will have the house to ourselves."

Though everything inside her knew she was standing in front of a speeding coach, Eva could no longer summon the will to throw her body from the path and save herself. Her long-squelched sense of adventure wouldn't allow it. She'd just have to pray for good luck.

"There will be hundreds of guests," Eva managed weakly, her will crumbling. "Perhaps I'd be lost in the crush and spend the evening unnoticed if I wear something plain . . ." She let her voice trail off as Noelle's shriek damaged her hearing. For a Lady, her sister didn't always act as a proper blue blood should. Eva ought to give her a copy of Lady Watersham's book to read when she wasn't plotting mischief.

"I have just the gown for you, Eva. I bought it yesterday."

Eva glowered. "You were awfully certain I would agree to this madness, sister." She took one look in Noelle's bright eyes, and her stomach dropped to her toes.

After Noelle took off for home to see to the gown, Eva carefully portioned out part of Father's monthly stipend to Cook for supplies and to pay the small staff. She set aside a handful of shillings and a few other coins from her school earnings, what she could afford, to make a modest payment to His Grace. It would take years to settle the debts, but she couldn't face the prospect of owing him forever. The weight of the financial burden was bearable if she reminded herself that one day, she'd be free of him.

She'd met with the investigator, Mister Crawford, and made a visit to Cheapside. The women were now as worried about Yvette as she was, and Eva assured them she had hired someone to look for the missing woman.

Pauline had wrung her hands. "I think she's in danger, Miss Eva." She refused to meet Eva's eyes and examined the tips of her slippers. Her voice dropped to a whisper. "I know she's in danger."

Eva was startled, and the women all stared at the buxom blonde. Her bottom lip quivered. Pauline seemed on the brink of an emotional breakdown. "Have you a reason to believe so, Pauline?"

The courtesan nodded slowly, and tears welled in her eyes. "The night she left, when everyone else was asleep, I stumbled into her in the hallway upstairs. She was wearing her cloak and carrying a small satchel." Pauline sniffed and dabbed an eye with her knuckle. "It was after midnight."

Eva handed her a handkerchief. "Where was she going?"

Pauline blew her nose. "She swore me not to tell. But under the circumstances, I must." She sucked in a ragged breath. "She wanted some things from her town house. Her lover was very generous after the beatings. Every time he hurt her, he'd buy her a trinket to assuage his guilt. She'd somehow heard he was at his country home for the rest of the month. She believed it would be safe to return if she slipped in and out unnoticed."

"Oh, Pauline," Eva said. Her heart twisted, and she put a hand over it. "You should have told me right away."

The girl sobbed quietly into her hands. Rose circled an arm around her shoulder and looked hopelessly at Eva.

Eva lifted her eyes to Harold, who stood in the doorway, his face grim. She took no comfort in his expression. He was as concerned as they all were. She wanted to send him off to pummel the mysterious lover, but had no clues to who he was or where to find him.

She suspected the situation was dire. If Yvette had been misinformed and her protector discovered her sneaking around the town house, there was no telling what he might do to his runaway courtesan.

"I never noticed any bruises," Abigail said softly and turned her gaze on Harold. There were gray smudges under her eyes as she seemed to silently beg him for help. Worry over Yvette had taken a toll on her, on all the women.

Sophie nodded. "I once had a lover who was rough. I never saw any signs of it on Yvette. If not for our shared confidences, I'd never have known."

"None of us suspected," Eva said. She turned back to Harold. If only he had been notified of Yvette's dangerous plan immediately, he could have stopped her. "Harold, is it truly possible this lover has kidnapped her?"

He crossed his arms and shrugged. "I haven't heard anything. If she's being held somewhere in London, gossip will find its way to me."

In all the time she'd known Harold, Eva had never once questioned his loyalty or asked him for information about his past. Now, as she looked into his hard expression, she wondered if she should have used more vigilance when she accepted this man so willingly into her life. It was easy to forget that some men had darkness in their souls that could be deadly when they were crossed; a darkness that was hidden until it was too late.

Still, even now, when she saw cold anger etched into his features, she knew he'd never hurt her and her courtesans. The man who'd kidnapped and possibly killed Yvette was the one in danger. Harold took his position as their protector seriously. If anyone dared hurt one of his flock, he'd see them punished.

That was what worried Eva.

"I'm afraid when we do find her, there will be little we can do against the culprit," Abigail said simply. She turned away from Harold. "There are different rules for those with a title and those without. Even if he murdered her, if her lover is high-ranking, he will not be punished. His friends will do what they can to cover up the crime. No one will care about a dead courtesan."

The bitterness in Abigail's voice shocked Eva. She wondered about the young woman's history. Truthfully, Eva knew nothing about her, about any of the women, really. Just a few tidbits of shared information casually dropped into conversation. Eva rarely became close to any of her charges. Once they left her care, they began new lives and put their pasts behind them. And Eva was part of those pasts.

Abigail had kept to herself and followed her instructions without complaint. Eva often wondered how the quiet beauty had become a courtesan and if her anger at noblemen came from experience. Whenever one of the other women had pressed for details of her life, she'd quietly changed the topic.

"It's true, Miss Eva," Sophie said. "I once knew a girl who was the lover of Lord Applegate. She vanished without word to anyone. There were rumors he'd killed her in a jealous fit after he caught her speaking with another man. There was a brief investigation, then the matter was dropped. To this day, she is still missing."

Eva wanted to dispute the outlandish charges. However, there was truth in it all. Men like His Grace had to be caught strangling someone in the center of Grosvenor Square, in front of a hundred witnesses, before any justice would be meted out.

A grim prospect indeed.

Eva looked at her charges, and there was deep worry on all faces. Though the five courtesans were not all friends, they'd developed a bond over the last several weeks while working toward a common goal. Now, one was missing and they wanted to know the truth.

"We must all hope for Yvette's safety," Eva said. She had to distract them. "My, ah, friend assures me the investigator is excellent in his profession. He will find her." Eva knew just how competent Mister Crawford was. He'd flushed out most of her secrets. When he was finished, Mister Crawford would know what kind of jam Yvette ate on her toast and what her favorite perfume was. If she had come to harm, they would know soon. "Why don't we go out into the garden, ladies, and have tea? It is a lovely day."

D o you really think Yvette is alive?" Harold asked hours later when they arrived home. He took Eva's cloak and hung it on a peg by the door. Sounds filtered from the kitchen, where the evening meal was being cooked, and the scent of cinnamon drifted through the household. Eva took no comfort from the familiar sounds and smells. The day had been exceedingly trying.

The speculation about Yvette's fate had not been squelched by her attempts to get the women focused on other topics. There was a constant undercurrent of apprehension lingering in all of them. Until Yvette's fate was established, there would be no peace for anyone.

Eva lifted her face to his. A common concern over the missing courtesan had given them a brief and tenuous truce today. Still, she knew Harold hadn't gotten over his displeasure with her. His frustration still simmered beneath his stoic surface.

"I don't know." She turned and led him to the parlor. "My greatest hope is to find her well. However, I am worried. If her protector is a violent man, he may have punished her for trying to leave him. I fear the depths of his anger."

Pulling off her bonnet and the pins from of her hair, she removed the wig and spectacles and set both on a low table. Harold crouched and banked the fire. The glow of the flames took away some of her chill as she moved to the settee and settled on its overstuffed cushions. In her home, she normally felt safe from the ills of the city outside its walls.

If not for her father's generosity, she could well have ended up like Yvette, like any of her courtesans. But the press of disaster always lingered now, with His Grace holding her debts over her head. These walls had been breached time and again, and she could not build them high enough to keep His Grace out of her life.

"I am to blame for this," Harold said, and stood. "Had I been vigilant, she would not have gone off alone."

"How were you to know of her plans?" Eva protested. "You cannot be with our courtesans constantly. They must make their own decisions. Even had you suspected anything, she would have found a way to sneak off. You couldn't chain her to her bed."

"If I wasn't occupied with other matters," he said simply, "I would have spent more time with the women and sensed something untoward."

He didn't accuse her directly, but the implication weighed on her shoulders. In his opinion, if not for her relationship with His Grace, Harold might have thwarted Yvette's escape.

Tiny hairs prickled the back of her neck. "You will not

blame me for what has happened." She couldn't believe Harold could be so cruel. Hurt filled her. This could not be just about whom she bedded. There was a deeper reason for his cutting anger. Something she could not see. "Yvette is responsible for sneaking out in the middle of the night."

"She became involved with a man she mistakenly hoped would protect and care for her as she aged," Harold countered sharply. "She saw his wealth and his title, and her defenses disappeared. She didn't see his cruelty until it was too late. Now she might be dead."

"Our situations are not the same," Eva cried. "She was forced into her life by circumstances she could not overcome. His Grace is not a cruel man, and he does not own me."

"What of His Grace?" Harold asked sharply. He leaned against the mantel and glowered. "What will he do once he tires of you, Eva? Will he throw you out of this house? If he calls in the notes, and you cannot pay, will debtors' prison be your next address?"

"His Grace has promised Mother will always have a home here," she snapped. Frustration sent burning bile up the back of her throat. "He will not break his word."

"You know him so well?" he sneered.

Truthfully, she knew almost nothing about the duke. The doubts Harold had raised were similar to the doubts keeping her awake most nights. Her future had become tenuous, confused. Though she believed Nicholas would treat her mother well, his plans for her were less clear. What kind of man was he really? How well did she know him outside of his bed?

When she took a moment to look at those around her— Harold, Noelle, His Grace, the courtesans—she was surrounded by strangers. What did she know about any of them?

She jutted out her chin and refused to succumb to tears. Never had she felt so adrift, without arms to pull her back into the boat. If only she'd allowed herself to get close to others as she grew up. Then she wouldn't feel so alone now.

"It is not your concern, Harold."

"Not my concern?" He shook his head slowly as anger flushed his face. "It worries me every day that you and your mother could be left destitute on the whims of that man you bed. Has he made you any promises? Will he wed you?" At her silence, he threw up his hands. "I have sacrificed to watch over you, Eva, and you say it is not my concern?"

Sacrificed? Eva felt her resolve slip. She had never thought he might have a family, a profession he'd given up to stay with her and be her companion. Still, she had never asked him to sacrifice for her. Whatever he'd given up was of his free will.

Harold *was* her friend, as much as he could be, but he was still her employee. Now she wasn't so sure which Harold she wished him to be. As a friend, he felt free to express his opinions. As an employee, he'd crossed into dangerous territory where His Grace was concerned.

She'd chosen to become the duke's lover. Though she'd broken their tie, His Grace still had the power to force her back to his bed, though he had not yet done so. Was he plotting another seductive attack on her eager body? Could she ever be sure of his intentions?

If Harold did anything to jeopardize the tenuous relationship between her and the duke, he could cause them all irreparable harm.

She would send Harold on his way before she would risk her mother's health and situation. "I don't expect you to understand my reasons, Harold. They are my own." She stood and faced him. "However, you need to remember this. You talk of sacrifices. I, too, have sacrificed. I have my work and I have my mother and I have you. I do not go to parties, I do not socialize. I have never had, nor will I ever have, a suitor who brings me flowers and asks me to take drives in the park. So if I allow myself a few stolen moments of pleasure in the arms of a man, you of all people should understand."

Eva did not wait for his comment. She squared her shoulders and walked stiffly away.

Harold watched her disappear and felt her hurt. Guilt kept him from following her. From the day he'd come to London and begun watching over Eva, he had left everything in his life behind. Oddly, the trio of footpads who had beaten him and stolen his purse had done him a service.

He'd had to find a way into her household without rousing suspicion, and his injuries had done that. And she'd never questioned him about his previous life. She'd simply cared for him until he was fit and then offered him a position in her household.

What had begun as a simple business agreement had grown into something deeper. He'd truly come to care for Eva and Charlotte. They were the family he'd lost. And he hated to see her lose any chance of happiness by giving herself to the duke, a man who would use and discard her. Yet, he knew how painfully lonely she was. If only she'd chosen a man who would love and care for her forever. Then he'd not begrudge her even one moment of happiness.

Harold knew he should sound a warning, but worried about the consequences of confiding all of Eva's secrets. He'd already betrayed her, though she didn't suspect it. Once he made his report, his part in this deceit would be finished and he'd be free to return home. It was the tangled threads of betrayal, and saying good-bye, that would be more difficult to settle in his already beleaguered conscience.

When the investigation of Miss Winfield had been proposed, he'd tried to refuse. But he was living in desperate straits with his coffers empty. An offer was made for a chance to live comfortably, in exchange for a few months' work. Before he realized what was happening, he was dressed as a footman and in a coach on his way to London.

No. He would keep this to himself, for now. Eva was in no real danger, and a broken heart was survivable. Not that his employer cared what happened to Eva or her mother.

Harold winced. He cared.

Knowing Eva as he did, her heart was already engaged. She had given the man her innocence. She couldn't separate her mind and body, though she might convince herself she could. One day soon, when the duke turned her out, she would crumble.

And it would take all the strength inside him not to go to Collingwood House and beat the bloody duke senseless.

Chapter Twelve

The silver ball gown was so lovely, like a shimmer of heavenly light, that Eva frowned at her reflection. The clinging fabric molded to her upper body as if she'd spent hours in fittings, and fell in delicate yards of silk and lace, shot through with lighter silver threads, from the bodice to the floor.

The color set off the hints of gold and copper in Eva's upswept hair as she scowled. No fairy godmother with magic powers could have turned her so perfectly into a princess. She sparkled.

Eva met her sister's eyes in the mirror. Noelle was immensely satisfied with herself. She hadn't stopped humming since she'd arrived with the gown draped over her arm.

"This is your idea of plain?"

Noelle, resplendent in rose satin, smiled. Her fair hair was twisted at the back of her head in an elaborate creation that must have taken her maid half the afternoon to produce. Ruby earbobs dangled from her lobes and crystal-encrusted pins sparkled in her hair.

"I had the modiste take off the ribbons and bows to make the gown simpler," Noelle offered with a shrug. She moved behind Eva and leaned over her shoulder. The light scent of roses drifted around her. "You look lovely. I could not have made a better choice myself."

Eva narrowed her eyes. "You did choose it."

Noelle giggled and reached for a jar of powder. "I did, didn't I? I must have excellent taste."

"And you are modest, too, sister." The term "sister" no longer felt odd on her tongue. Only the two of them, and Harold, knew of their connection. Noelle had been passed off as a new friend, and the servants and her mother accepted it as fact.

Eva knew she should run to the wardrobe and pull out one of her drab spinster costumes, but could not bring herself to do so. She'd never had the occasion to wear such an exquisite creation, and vanity overcame any desire to take it off.

"With my beautiful sister at my side, it will be impossible to hide in the crowd," Eva said. "The den of lions will be licking their chops with anticipation."

The only thing Eva could do was pray she would not trip over the duke. He was the most ferocious beast of all.

"Nonsense." Noelle put the jar down. "The only slavering happening this evening will come from the eager young bucks begging for an introduction to you."

Eva worried her bottom lip. The dratted whisper of reason reared up, and she faltered in her resolve to enjoy the ball. Young bucks? Was she up to the task of flirting and dancing? Would she shame herself and her sister with her inexperienced bumbling? She had no formidable chaperone to hide behind if she desired a moment to collect herself, or to save her from an overzealous suitor.

Harold had promised to linger outside with the coach, on the chance she might need to make a speedy exit. Inside the manor, she was on her own with only Noelle for protection. The idea did not soothe her in the least.

What if His Grace attended the ball? It was not beyond comprehension that he would be there. He was trolling for a bride, and there would be many young women to choose from; a veritable flock of well-bred pigeons cooing for his attention. If Miss Banes-Dodd refused him, he'd have to do nothing more than stretch out an arm and collect a dozen young marriage-minded misses tottering along at his coattails.

Her frown deepened. He would laugh and dance and pick out a wife without giving a moment of thought to her. She, Eva, was utterly inconsequential to his future; a mistress easily replaced with another when he became bored.

The frown deepened to a scowl.

Suddenly, there was nothing more she wanted to do at this moment than to rush off to the ball and flirt with every man between eighteen and eighty who crossed her path.

The duke be damned.

Eva touched the tiny diamond earbobs she'd borrowed from her mother. Mother had been wearing them the night she met Eva's father. Charlotte always considered them lucky.

If anyone needed luck tonight, it was Eva.

She hooked her arm through Noelle's. "Shall we go?"

Candles flickered from every window on the two lower floors of Pennington Manor as Noelle's coach stopped in a line of other coaches. Eva peered out the window at the four-story brick monolith that overshadowed the smaller houses on either side of it in fashionable Grosvenor Square.

Eva's initial rush of excitement was tempered slightly as Noelle pointed out each home they passed, with a brief description of the families within, including Collingwood House, which was two streets over. She had no business being in this world, and she knew it. Seeing Nicholas's huge home confirmed again she'd never have a place at his side.

Women of questionable birth dared not dream such dreams.

She'd kept her face bland when Noelle spoke of the handsome, unattached duke, but her heart fluttered dangerously in her breast while unease settled in her bones. Noelle was a picture of serenity, but Eva was a jumble of nerves. Everyone who mattered in society's inner circle would be attending this ball. He would be there, she had no doubt.

There was more than a chance this house of cards would tumble down and Noelle would be left picking through the devastation. If His Grace chose to unmask her as his mistress, nothing would save either sister.

"I think we should end this madness before it's too late." Eva touched her clasped hands to her mouth. "We can return home and eat fig cakes until our seams pop."

Noelle brushed a piece of lint off her cloak. "Nonsense. I have the chance to show off my lovely sister, and I intend to do so proudly. Of course, we will introduce you as my cousin, but nonetheless I plan to laugh gaily and dance until my feet hurt. Then we shall dine on fattened pheasant and gritty oysters until we must let our corsets out. And if a handsome young man kisses my hand, I shall giggle like a silly goose and bat my lashes until he is desperately smitten."

Eva giggled. Noelle was like an untamed wind blowing through the eaves. It was impossible not to get caught up in the vortex.

The coach inched forward. Noelle leaned out the window. "It takes longer to get to the front of the line than the ball is long. Cannot the guests disembark at a less leisurely pace?"

"Patience, Noelle. We are nearly there."

Eva examined Noelle's serene face. Was it possible Noelle hoped that she would be exposed and ruined? It was a strange thought, but it would certainly explain her sudden arrival on Eva's doorstep and her insistence that Eva accompany her this evening. Or maybe she hoped to somehow scandalize her uncaring mother. What better way to accomplish that than to flaunt a bastard sister around London?

She leveled a pointed stare on Noelle. "Why are you really doing this, Noelle? I am nothing but a shameful secret, a product of our father's indiscretion. Yet, you are risking everything to treat me like a princess tonight. Why?"

Noelle looked at her with surprise. It took a moment before she smiled softly in the dim light. "You are my sister. Regardless of your birth, you are my family."

"There must be more," Eva interjected. She wouldn't get out of this coach until she had answers. "Tell me the real reason for this game."

With a sigh, Noelle leaned forward and reached for Eva's hand. "Father and Mother hated each other, and seldom spoke unless it was to ask to pass something at mealtime. I often wonder if Meg and I are not the offspring of the gardener." She bit her bottom lip to stop it from trembling. "Your mother and we girls were his happiness. I cannot begrudge Charlotte's giving him moments of joy. So yes, I risk much to claim you as kin. I will have it no other way."

Thankfully the shadows hid the shimmer of tears in Eva's eyes as she smiled and shook her head slowly. "You are an odd and wonderful young woman, Noelle."

Noelle grinned. "You would not change a thing about me."

Eva drew in and released a big sigh. She squeezed her sister's hand. "No, indeed, I would not."

The overwhelming scent of perfume and thousands of blooms, in overflowing vases, caused Eva to falter slightly as Noelle led her, arm in arm, toward the ballroom. The hall was packed with people, men in their finery and women in vivid gowns, as if each was fighting to outdo the others in color and design.

Eva struggled not to gawk like a ninny at the high ceiling in the foyer, painted a pale blue with a smattering of fluffy white clouds scattered across the surface. Whoever the artist was, he was very talented. It was almost as if Pennington Manor had no roof and she was staring at a bright summer sky.

"This house is a palace." She leaned close to Noelle's ear in order to be heard over the sound of dozens of voices.

"It is grand." Noelle gripped her tightly as a man in a peacock blue coat brushed past. "Aunt Penn does have a desire for the dramatic. Last year she insisted all her women guests dress in red and the men in black. It was stunning."

"I can imagine." Eva cast one last glance at the ceiling before they left the hall. She could spend hours lying on her back on the marble floor, just staring at the clouds and daydreaming.

"See that man over there talking to the woman with the green feathers in her hair?" Noelle pointed discreetly behind her fan, and Eva looked where indicated. The man was tall and thin with a decidedly boyish face. "Last year Mother pushed me to accept his suit, until he was caught by Margaret in a compromising situation with one of our footmen. They were both dismissed quite handily. Now Mother has given up trying to match me. She believes her only chance for grandchildren rests with our sister."

It was impossible to picture Noelle heavily laden with child. Noelle often deemed herself unfit for marriage, and was quite content to allow the rest of society to repopulate.

Eva took a turn to tease. "I would not disavow men completely, sister. You might find one tonight who sweeps you off to his castle. Then you will spend the rest of your days happily filling out a branch of his family tree."

Noelle grimaced and cast a quick glance around the hallway outside the ballroom. "I would have a better chance of getting hit by a falling star than that. Men prefer women who cling to their every word, not question everything they say." She winked. "My mother calls me impossible."

The two sisters giggled, and Eva teased, "On that, your mother and I agree."

They waited until a large family moved to the front of the line and then slipped unannounced into the ballroom behind them. Eva thought it better that way. Though she was dressed like a sparkling silver Christmas star, the less attention she drew to herself, the better their chances to survive the evening unscathed.

This was to be her first and last society ball, and she planned to enjoy it to the fullest. Unfortunately, they had taken only a few steps inside the massive ballroom when a voice broke through the crush and stopped Noelle. She tensed.

"There you are, dearest." A woman of middle years, in a frothy concoction of deep green topped with an overlay of delicate gold lace, crossed between clusters of guests to come to a halt before Noelle. She took Noelle's hands and said crossly, "I worried you'd taken ill, Noelle. I thought you'd come early and help me welcome my guests."

Noelle accepted a tight-lipped kiss on both cheeks. "I apologize, Aunt." She stepped back to indicate Eva. "My cousin, Evangeline, has just arrived from the country. We were rushed to find her something suitable to wear."

A pair of hawk eyes snapped to Eva's face, and in them was a full measure of suspicion. She now understood why Lady Pennington was called a dragon. She was a formidable force. Eva braced herself and struggled to keep her composure beneath the painfully sharp glare.

"Evangeline? You have no cousin named Evangeline."

"That is what makes this so delightful, Aunt." Noelle slipped an arm protectively through Eva's. They leaned lightly on each other. "I just discovered Uncle Edward entered into a secret marriage after Auntie Bess, just before he died. A cousin, Roderick, was born of that union.

Cousin Roderick married Miss Eloise Solomon, and Evangeline is their only child. Sadly, Eva's parents died some months ago when their boat capsized in a swell. It was only then, through a delayed letter, that I happily discovered I had another cousin."

Eva managed to bite the inside of her cheek and look grim. She wanted to laugh at the sober way Noelle presented the outlandish lie.

"Lady Pennington, may I introduce Evangeline Harrington."

Lady Pennington's gaze bore into Eva as if digging deep for some hint of deception. Eva knew that the instant she had an available moment, the lady would dash off a note to Noelle's mother for confirmation. But it was too late to do so this evening, so for now, Eva was safe.

And as the lie was difficult to disprove, Lady Pennington could do but one thing as a hostess faced with a new and highly connected relation to Noelle. "Welcome to my home, Miss Harrington," she said with a tight smile. "I hope we will have time later in the evening to get to know one another."

"I would like that," Eva said. As much as she would like to rip off her clothes and dance naked through London. She made a note to be everywhere Lady Pennington wasn't.

Lady Pennington shot Noelle a dark, suspicious frown and walked off to greet arriving guests.

The air seemed to lighten, and it was easier to breathe without the dragon present.

"Do you think she believed us?" Eva asked, shooting her sister a sidelong and skeptical glance.

Noelle pursed her lips. "Not for a moment."

Their blended laughter turned several heads.

Eva spent much of the next hour being shuttled through introductions to Noelle's acquaintances. Since she lived most of her time in Kent, her close friends were at the ball. Eva carried herself with what she hoped was dignity and grace, thankful for her mother's girlhood teachings.

Charlotte hadn't known what kind of life her daughter would grow up to lead, but she wanted Eva to be able to fit into even the grandest situation. So it was easy to play the part of a country cousin, a lady of impeccable birth.

When a young man, reasonably handsome in spite of two crooked front teeth, swept Noelle away for a dance, Eva felt slightly out of sorts. Several pairs of male eyes turned in her direction, but she was still a curious novelty and they were unsure how to approach her.

So she accepted a glass of punch from a passing servant and let her attention drift over the crowd.

The sounds of laughter and the music, the sight of beautiful gowns and men in their evening attire, and the scent of candles and flowers infused Eva's senses. She tapped her toe beneath the hem of her gown and waited with impatience for one of the young men to summon the courage to ask her to dance.

She very much wanted to dance.

Casually, as she looked over the rim of her glass for an eye to catch, the crush parted for an instant, and an imposing figure came into view. Her heart stopped.

A tall man in black, his back to her, was in conversation with a petite brunette in a pale pink gown. The girl was smiling sweetly at him, as if every word spilling from his mouth was the most fascinating thing she'd ever heard in her young life.

Eva quickly dismissed her, for it was the dark hair and broad shoulders of the girl's companion that took her breath away. She'd spent time enough in his company, in clothing and out of it, to know him intimately from every angle, every carved and sculpted and muscled plane.

His Grace.

Like a rabbit confronted by a passing hound, she wasn't sure if she should flee or stay still, hoping she could remain unnoticed in the horde. Luck was not with her, in spite of her mother's earbobs. He turned, smiling, and froze.

From across the room, he stared at her, and all the laughter in the green depths of his eyes died. She felt ill and flushed and guilty. She had crossed an invisible line between their worlds, and by the dangerous downturn of his mouth, she knew he was furious.

All sense of time and place faded as she quickly turned and headed for a set of open doors to the terrace. She shoved her glass into a maid's hand without pausing in her flight. Eva had gotten halfway around a potted tree, a few steps from freedom, when a hand clamped around her arm. She turned to face Nicholas.

"What are you doing here, Eva?" he hissed, using his body to block the curious glances of guests lingering nearby. Holding on to her arm, he pulled her with him through the doorway. Casually nodding to a couple leaning on the rail, he propelled her along the terrace and into a shadowy corner. "Are you mad?"

She *was* mad. She was in a dark corner of the terrace, at a ball she had no business attending, with a man who knew her body almost as intimately as she did. Just days earlier he'd buried his face between her legs and given her a mind-numbing orgasm.

Slowly, she nodded, her face heating. "Clearly."

Nicholas expelled a harsh breath, then pointed a finger in the direction of the ballroom. "Do you realize just inside those doors are my future wife, my mother, nearly everyone of my acquaintance?"

So, the brunette *was* the perfect and soon-to-be duchess, Lucy Banes-Dodd. The woman who would someday soon share his bed, host his parties, and present His Grace with a passel of well-bred and exceedingly beautiful children. She would be all the things Eva could never be to him: an openly cherished wife and lover.

A press of the demon jealousy welled. He had his every desire, and she had nothing. She had lived most of her life behind the doors of her home, unable to enjoy the frivolous fun most young ladies of her age thrived upon. She had never truly resented her choices, until now. He'd not take this night from her.

"I have every right to be here," she whispered and tried to back away. A vine-covered trellis blocked her escape. "I was invited."

"Invited? Don't be absurd." He gripped her arms and leaned down. His warm breath brushed her nose. "Lady Pennington does not invite courtesans to her balls."

Anger flashed, and with it, hurt. Of course, to him, she was nothing but a whore, unfit to mingle with his grand friends and family. She was worthy only of his bed, and nothing more. And it would always be that way.

She bit her bottom lip to keep it from trembling. Pride lifted her chin. "I am not your courtesan."

The deep hurt in her eyes took him aback. He hadn't meant to be so cutting and cruel, but discovering her in the ballroom, on the night he planned to ask for Lucy's hand, had come as quite a shock. And her delicate beauty, framed in reflections of silver light off the threads in her gown, had stunned him and nearly taken him to his knees.

She was breathtaking. The moment he saw her, Lucy became one with the tapestries. All he could think about was dragging Eva off to some private place and peeling her out of her gown.

"Eva, I . . ." Words failed. He'd just all but called her a whore. How could he explain to her that she'd become more than a courtesan to him? That she'd stolen his nights and filled his days with unwelcome thoughts of her, and every day that passed without seeing her face had become torture?

Eva trembled, and her lips parted. He let out a low growl. Before his mind could overtake his body with a measure of sense, he pulled her against him and crushed his mouth over hers.

She let out a low whimper and went slack against him, opening her mouth to meet his thrust. He plundered her mouth and tasted the sweet infusion of punch.

Lud, he couldn't think about the danger of trysting with her in the dark, steps away from the open doors, when her perfect body was molded to his. He'd left his future betrothed to drag Eva out of the ballroom, not caring who watched. She'd been a sickness he couldn't control from their first brief and painful kiss.

Not even marriage to Lucy would cure his addiction.

Eva's hand snaked behind his head, and she tangled her fingers in his hair. She was perfection and madness, and her touch was enough to burn him with its fire. He pressed his erection against her belly, aching to release his cock into her slick heat.

He tore his mouth free and pressed his face against her hair. His breath was raw and ragged. "I cannot think of anyone else when you are near, sweet. You must leave now, before anyone else sees you and asks questions."

She met his eyes and lifted to her toes. A wicked smile tugged at her mouth as she pressed her breasts against his chest. "Kiss me again, Nicholas."

The only thing he could do was oblige. He kissed her hard, mating their tongues until she let out small sounds of delight. As his mind raced over all the places a couple could hide in the darkened garden to find stolen moments alone, the crinkle of crinoline jerked his head up. A trim blonde in a rose gown stood a few feet away, arms crossed.

"Unhand my sister at once, Your Grace."

His arms dropped away and he stepped back. "Your sister?" Crawford had never mentioned a sister in his report.

He looked from Eva to the woman and back. Yes, perhaps the eyes were the same.

"Noelle, I can explain." Eva smoothed her bodice with shaky hands in a futile attempt to right her mussed appearance. "Your Grace, this is my sister Noelle, Lady Seymour."

He stared at the blonde. Lady Seymour? Though they'd never met, he thought she was some sort of relation of Lady Pennington, a goddaughter perhaps? He'd known Eva was the by-blow of a lord, but Crawford had been unable to discover the connection before Nicholas had abruptly ended the investigation.

Now he knew her father was the late Lord Seymour, an earl of high standing and a peer. He had bedded Eva knowing her mother had been a courtesan. To know half of her bloodline was as old as his own settled a stone in his stomach.

Lady Seymour glared at him and walked over to take Eva by the hand like she was a naughty child. "Lord Barden seeks to dance with Eva. We cannot keep him waiting."

With that, his reluctant courtesan left him lurking alone in the darkness while she tapped along on the heels of her ruffled sister. Eva sent one last helpless glance over her shoulder as they vanished around the corner.

Nicholas scrubbed both hands through his hair. Lord Seymour's daughter? What a bewildering tangle he'd been dropped into. He tried to remember the old friend of his father, but the earl was nothing but a blur. The man had died some time ago. Who knew he'd fathered an illegitimate daughter in addition to his own brood?

He dropped back against the trellis and peered up at the starry sky. Clearly there would be no proposal tonight. It would be difficult enough to spend the next several hours pretending he and Eva were strangers. Adding his hawk-eyed mother into the mix, tension began to thump behind his eyes. If only he could convince Eva to vanish quietly.

Perhaps he could have maneuvered Eva in some way, but he suspected Lady Noelle wouldn't be so easy to sway. The minx. She'd brought her bastard sister to the biggest society function of the year, clearly without qualm or reservation. If the old gossips got wind of their connection, and his connection to Eva, the ensuing scandal would rock polite society to its foundation.

There was only one solution: to act as if nothing was amiss; keep Eva, Lucy, and his mother apart; and hope the growing pain in his head did not cause his brain to explode inside his skull.

Would you like to explain how I leave you alone for a few minutes, then find you kissing His Grace in the dark?" Noelle had closed the door to a small sitting room and faced Eva, her voice low and accusing. "Luckily, I saw him drag you outside, or you might well have been compromised."

Compromised by His Grace? If Noelle wasn't so angry, she might have laughed. He'd more than compromised her many, many times. Kissing him was mild in comparison to the delicious and scandalous moments she's spent on his desk, in his bed, on his floor.

"It isn't what you think." How could she explain their relationship? She couldn't blurt out, "I have allowed His Grace to happily violate me while I cried out his name with unabashed pleasure." Somehow she understood that Noelle would not find such a confession amusing. Her sister was no ordinary woman, but deep down, she'd had societal rules battered into her brain since birth. One day soon, Eva fully expected her to realize that befriending her bastard sister was a mistake, and that would be the end of their sisterhood.

Eva lowered herself into a high-backed chair. "I met His Grace several weeks ago. I won't bore you with the entire story, let us just say we have an arrangement, he and I."

Noelle dropped into the chair across from her, her eyes wide. "You're his mistress, aren't you?" She rubbed a hand over her forehead, and Eva nodded. "Certainly this was not your idea?"

At Eva's hesitation, Noelle had her answer. Her eyes narrowed. "I thought not. The bastard! Did he force you?"

Quickly, Eva shook her head. If Noelle suspected a hint

of coercion, she'd have His Grace gelded and dumped into the Thames, with Harold at her side wielding the knife.

"Certainly not. It is a complicated situation." She rose and went to the window. Several shadowed couples strolled along the garden path below. "I hated him at first. Then everything changed." She turned to face her sister. "There is something between us I cannot name. An attraction I try to fight with everything in me. But the moment he touches me, I am lost."

"Do you love him? Has he offered for your hand?"

If Noelle had asked her for her feelings a week ago, her answer would be clearer. Now she wasn't as certain what she thought of His Grace. All she did know was she must not fall in love with the unattainable duke. "No. I cannot love him. I am his lover. It can be no more than that."

Noelle glowered. "So he gets what he wants without consequences? I cannot believe this arrangement is satisfactory to you."

Her discourse unsettled Eva. It pained her deeply to see the disappointment in Noelle's eyes. She closed off her emotions to protect herself from another verbal battering. Harold's behavior had left her frayed. She couldn't take her sister's scorn, too. Not here, not now.

Perhaps now, Noelle would realize this tenuous connection between them would only cause her grief in the end. "I am a courtesan's daughter. I can aspire to no greater heights."

Angered, Noelle jumped to her feet. She went to Eva and clasped her shoulders.

"I will not have you say such things. You are my sister. It matters not what happened between our father and your mother, or what she was in her previous life. I will not allow a duke to take advantage of you without repercussions. I vow I will find a way to make him wed you."

Chapter Thirteen

Eva found flirting uncomfortable, in spite of her vast store of knowledge on how to engage in lighthearted banter. She had virtually no experience with men. Though she learned much about polite society from Lady Watersham's book, *Rules for Young Women of Quality*, and had watched the maids flirt with the footmen, complete with hair twisting and lash batting, putting the information to practical use at a ball of this size was overwhelming.

She had not been born to this life.

His Grace glowering at her from across the room made it worse, though she succeeded quite well at keeping her eyes from his. His displeasure was a colossal weight to carry.

Still, she would not allow him to chase her off. Noelle was determined to see them wed, and flung every eligible man who was able to stand upright into her path, as a way of forcing the duke take notice of her desirability to other men.

Though Eva had no aspirations of becoming a duchess, and tried to talk sense into her sister, she did find the idea of secretly tormenting Nicholas somewhat delightful.

He had ruled her life for weeks and bullied her for much longer. He'd called her a whore. Well, almost. The implication was there. It was time to turn things about and exact some bits of revenge on the lordly duke.

If nothing else, and in spite of his scowls, she knew he desired her enough to leave his future fiancée and drag her from the ballroom for a heated kiss. If he was so devoted to his Miss Banes-Dodd, he wouldn't care what Eva did tonight or with whom she did it. From his menacing carriage, she knew His Grace was ready to murder—all because of the line of beaux vying for her attention.

Eva bit back a smile. Let him suffer.

Her skin tingled with awareness of him as she danced with one man after another, barely having time to catch her breath in between. She laughed with carefree abandon while earls and barons and dukes tried their very best to learn her secrets. She carefully evaded any pointed questions about her birthplace or her connection to Noelle.

"You dance beautifully, Miss Harrington," Baron Tillbury's youngest son, Farrell, said and gave her a slight bow before leading her from the dance floor. He was very young, just eighteen, and had all the sharp angles of a boy on the cusp of manhood. Yet, he knew how to charm. And he was pleasing enough of face beneath a mop of fair hair to be a favorite of the young women. "Perhaps you might like some punch?"

Eva nodded. "I would love some punch."

He vanished quickly on his errand. Eva fanned herself, pleased to have a moment alone and a chance to breathe. The packed room was warm, and dozens of candles added to the heat of all the bodies. She looked about for Noelle and eventually caught a glimpse of her across the room, just inside the terrace doors, speaking animatedly with Harold, his face tight and hers sober. Whatever they were discussing was serious.

When the discussion was at an end, Harold walked out the doors and vanished into the night.

She frowned as Noelle met her eyes. Noelle waved her hand, indicating all was well, as a young gentleman in a green coat bowed, took Noelle's arm, and led her into a line of dancers.

If there was something amiss, Harold would come to her. He was likely snooping, making sure Eva was not getting into mischief. Perhaps Noelle had told tales of her discovery on the terrace and had included him in her plot to snag the duke. If that was their intention, they would be sorely disappointed.

His Grace was not the sort of man to be forced into an unwanted arrangement.

Casually, she lifted her eyes to where she'd last seen His Grace. He was speaking to an attractive woman in red, but his eyes were on Eva. Mingled with his unhappiness was an intensity she had seen only when he was ripping at her clothing, desperate to see her naked.

Beneath her corset, Eva's stomach flipped. The dark desire in his face stopped her breathing. Clearly, he had no plans to tend to his business and leave her to hers. He was stalking her from a distance, lying in wait to separate her from the herd before he pounced.

Eva was certain that if they were alone, he'd turn her over his knee and paddle her rump rosy red. Then rip off her gown and love her violently and passionately.

The idea brought a smile. Her open amusement deepened his frown until his brows were nearly one. A giggle bubbled and her stomach settled. There was safety in the crowd. As long as she did not venture outside, her rump and the rest of her body were safe.

Nicholas watched young Farrell return to Eva, two glasses in hand, and all he wanted to do was rearrange the young upstart's long, thin nose to a less agreeable angle.

If he allowed himself to pummel all the men who had held Eva in their arms this evening, there would be bloody noses scattered the entire length of the room and beyond. Each time one of the dandies whispered intimately in her ear or spun her about the floor, a red film settled in his eyes.

Eva belonged to him. Hell, he'd taken her virginity. He'd left his imprint on her, and no other man had the right to breach his claim. Yet, he could not go to her, claim her as his in front of such esteemed company.

This left him in a state of blinding frustration.

"You seem taken with Miss Harrington, my son." Mother tapped his arm with her fan. They both watched Eva laugh at some witticism from Farrell as he strolled with her about the crowded room. "You must be careful, or Lucy will take offense."

Nicholas forced his attention downward to his mother. She'd seen something in him when he watched Eva. Undoubtedly, deep groin-twisting lust. He had to squelch it before she was inviting Eva over for tea and pressing her for her history.

"About whom are you speaking, Mother?"

Her green eyes flashed. "The young lady in silver you haven't taken your eyes off all evening." She narrowed her eyes and peered at Eva. "I understand she's Lady Seymour's cousin from somewhere near the Scottish border. Though there is some speculation the tale may be tall."

"She is lovely," Nicholas conceded as casually as he could manage through gritted teeth. Farrell had been run off by a man of higher standing, the charming and handsome Earl of Wayborn. He bent to speak to Eva, and she smiled. The man held out his arm and she took it, tucking her hand under his elbow.

The blasted Wayborn led her across the ballroom and into the dining hall, where tables laden with food awaited the guests. The tinkle of her laughter drifted back to him even after she was no longer visible.

Perhaps there would be bloodshed this evening after all.

He forced himself to remain calm. "There are many lovely women in attendance this evening, Mother. Including Lucy. I have not devoted more than a glance to any one in particular."

"Indeed? Not more than a glance? Hmm," Catherine said. "Then why have you not danced with Lucy all evening? You seem content to glare at the mysterious cousin. Would you to like to tell me why? What is she to you?"

Nicholas wanted to deny it all, to keep his mother from discovering Eva's identity. But the duchess wouldn't be put off with half-truths. Since his birth, she'd known every lie he'd ever told, and punished him for each one. If he was to work his way back to sanity, his mother was the one to help.

"She is my mistress," he said bluntly. He paused, waiting for some expression of outrage, some gasp of surprise. Instead, she was oddly silent for a very long moment before she nodded.

"I see."

Those two words worried him. His mother was never one to hold back either her praise or her scorn. She spoke her mind freely, and more often than not, her intuition proved deadly accurate. If only she'd been as careful when choosing his father, she wouldn't have suffered so many years of unhappiness.

"That is all you have to say, Mother?"

Catherine held his stare. "What should I say, Nicholas? Why is she here? Who is she really? How does she know Lady Seymour? What about Lucy? What do you intend to do about this?"

Nicholas let out a sigh, squelching a smile. His mother had weathered bigger storms, including his dead father's propensity to openly flaunt his indiscretions all about London. To discover her son's mistress at the same ball as her friends and acquaintances must be low on her level of shocking.

"She is Evangeline Winfield. She is Lady Seymour's half sister. Lord Seymour fathered her out of wedlock with his cherished courtesan."

This time her eyes widened. Clearly his mother wasn't entirely unflappable. "You took an earl's by-blow, sister to Lady Seymour, to bed? Nicholas, what were you thinking?"

"In all fairness, Mother, I was just made aware of their connection this evening when I discovered her here, of all places. Imagine my surprise when our kiss on the terrace was interrupted by the furious Lady Noelle. Between the two women, I am lucky I still have my head."

Catherine gaped, then her mouth slowly melted into a smile. "You were taken to task by a courtesan's daughter and her Lady sister? If only I had been there to witness the confrontation! I would have found it far more entertaining than this evening has proved to be thus far." She paused. "In fact, the night is looking brighter."

Nicholas's mouth thinned at the raw good humor on her pretty features. There had been years during his childhood when she never smiled at all. His father's death had brought back her laughter.

"I am pleased you find the situation so entertaining, Mother. Now the question begs, how can I solve this situation?"

"What are your choices? Cast her to the gossips and ruin Lady Seymour; then shame Lucy and her family and ours?" Catherine nodded to passing guests and lifted her fan. "You should ask yourself what your feelings for Miss Winfield are and what *you* intend to do about her."

"What can I do?" He felt deflated. Lady Seymour had taken Eva out of the shadows and introduced her to society. Even if he could convince Eva that spending time in society could be harmful to her and her mother, Lady Seymour was a complication. The woman wouldn't accept a continued arrangement between himself and Eva. "By morning, she will be the most sought-after young woman of the Season."

Mother laughed lightly. "I have never seen you so out of sorts with any woman, Nicholas. This woman has wriggled her way into your head. And perhaps your heart."

His head snapped around. "I do not love her." The protest was too quick, and did nothing to remove her knowing stare. "I have seen what love can do. You loved Father, and yet he mistreated you dreadfully."

Finally, she sobered. "Oh, Nicholas." She placed a hand on his arm. "Do not allow your parents' mistakes to keep you from love. I was young and smitten by a handsome face. I didn't look inside to see the darkness in Charles." She shook her head sadly. "You are not your father."

"Miss Winfield would argue that point." He'd lived his life climbing out from under his father's shadow, only to treat Eva in as beastly a fashion as his father had treated his mother. He'd allowed his father's example to blind him to Arabella's unhappiness, too. He felt a flush of guilt. "There are many reasons for Miss Winfield to despise me."

The duchess turned toward the dining hall. "I think you are mistaken, Nicholas. Miss Winfield cares for you more than she knows."

She waved to an acquaintance, then faced him. "She watches you as you watch her. I think you should put off your engagement until you have settled matters with Miss Winfield."

Nicholas nodded, then noticed his mother go still.

"Dear Lord! Is she the child of Charlotte Rose?" At his nod, all the color fled her face. "Oh, Nicholas, you have stepped into a pit of mire." She took his arm and led him to a small padded bench in a private corner, then dragged him down beside her. "Charlotte Rose was the impoverished daughter of the Count and Countess Moreau of France. She was sixteen when her parents were killed, and she became the ward of her elderly English aunt, Lady

Cordelia Winfield Suttleby. I don't know all the details, but three years later, after Lady Suttleby died, her small fortune went to her one remaining male relative."

Catherine sighed, her eyes troubled. "The girl vanished."

Nicholas felt every word slam into his head. Eva was French nobility? He *had* stumbled into mire, up to his neck. He wasn't sure if he wanted to hear the rest of the tale. However, to know what he was dealing with, he needed all the details. "Continue."

"London was abuzz when she resurfaced several months later and caused quite a scandal in the Ton. There were so many rumors about her and where she'd been. All we knew for certain was that she was looking for a protector, and all the men desired to take their place in her bed. I knew this sorrowful tale because your father made sure I understood he planned to be the victor."

He knew Father was a bastard, but this went too far.

The duchess tapped her fan on her knee. "In spite of his best attempts, your father had to concede when she chose Lord Seymour. Then one day she vanished, this time for good. Eventually the whispers and speculation settled, and that was that. I guess we now know the final chapter of the story."

"Eva." His brain pulsed inside his skull. Eva was no longer just a spinster and a courtesan's daughter. She was a count's granddaughter, a lady's sister, his courtesan. He should run from her, marry Lucy, and retire to obscurity deep in the country. That would be best for everyone.

When had his orderly world become so upended? He scowled. Oh, yes, the moment he'd found out she'd stolen Arabella and had vowed revenge.

"Do you care for the girl, Nicholas?"

"Of course I care for her, Mother," he snapped. "We have shared intimacies. But do not look for more. I will not wed her, if that is what is spinning around in your head."

He scanned the room. Lucy was chattering with the dashing Mister Albright. No amount of will could summon up even a trace of jealousy. Even if she dropped to her back on the marble floor and invited him to take her innocence in front of this company, Nicholas wouldn't care. His every thought and desire had focused on Eva from the moment he discovered a few stray red-blonde hairs peeking out from beneath that damnable wig.

Deep within him, he suspected it would always be so.

"Perhaps you *should* marry the girl," Mother said softly. "Clearly, you are taken with each other."

It was Nicholas who was surprised. His mother suggested marriage to someone with Eva's background? It was outlandish to consider it. "Imagine the scandal, Mother. No matter the blue blood in her veins, her mother was a courtesan, and that cannot be ignored. I must choose a woman with an impeccable reputation."

"So you say." Mother shrugged. "Our family has weathered worse scandals. Your great-great-grandfather was a highwayman, though never caught, and your great-grandmother was a sixteen-year-old milkmaid. I think your great-grandfather discovered her walking along the road, became smitten, and ran off to Gretna Green with her that very day." She smiled. "Theirs was a long and loving union."

Eva walked back into the ballroom on the earl's arm, as comfortable with him as if they were old friends. Her beauty complemented the impeccably dressed man at her side. They were a handsome pair.

Frustration welled within Nicholas. Again. He had to put an immediate stop to the earl's pursuit, or Eva would be engaged to the rake and lost to him forever.

Her face drew him like a siren song. He gave his mother a quick nod, excused himself, and crossed the room.

"I would love to call on you tomorrow afternoon, My Lady," the earl was saying as Nicholas drew near. "Certainly, your entire day is not completely filled."

Eva had just opened her mouth when Nicholas appeared before her and took her hand. "I fear Miss Winfield will not be taking callers. She has promised me a picnic." He drew her away from her smitten suitor and onto the dance floor. The first strains of a waltz rose. He pulled her closer than was entirely proper.

"How dare you?" Eva managed to force a smile for the curious onlookers. "Who I spend time with is none of your affair, Your Grace."

He cocked a brow. "Is it not?" He spun her slowly around the floor. Her beauty challenged his ability to breathe. And for the second time this night, he found delight in having her in his arms. "Bedding you made it my business."

"Oh"—Eva turned pink—"you are insufferable."

"Indeed?" He grinned. "Most women find me charming."

Eva wanted to kick him in the shin, hard. Unfortunately, this was not the place to do it without setting the gossips buzzing. There was already too much speculation about her. She'd caused a stir among the men in the company. The young women, and their mamas, were not happy with her presence at the ball. She'd had to fend off several proposals, proper and otherwise, and ignore biting speculation about her true identity. If she gave in to the impulse to kick the duke, it would not help her cause.

"Charming?" She laughed scornfully to hide her hurt. "You called me a whore."

His face tightened. "A moment I gravely regret, Eva. I was shocked to find you here and I said something I didn't mean." He eased back enough for her to see his face. "I do not think of you that way."

The apology was heartfelt. Some of her hurt faded. "Apology accepted. I still do not find you charming. Not in the least."

A slow grin lifted his mouth. "Indeed? It is one of the things women love most about me, besides my handsome face and superior form, of course."

She choked on a laugh. He was simply arrogant to the bone.

And yet, in his arms she felt as if she were dancing on clouds. He was so male, so powerful, so handsome. Every part of her was aware of his presence, and a familiar ache grew within her. She wished they were alone.

"I suppose when one is hoping to marry a duke with an immense fortune," she said, "it would be to any woman's advantage not to mention your less than, um, attractive faults."

"Faults? Interesting." He turned his face into grim mask that didn't remove the mischief in his eyes. "Now that you have pointed out that I have some faults, I think you should make me a list so I can work on changing them all."

Eva struggled not to smile. After spending the evening glowering, his sudden change of mood was unexpected, and welcome. With one of his hands holding hers and the other circling her waist, she felt as if he was making a public claim to her. Of course it was just a dance, but for a moment, she felt as if they belonged together.

"Oh, dear. I do apologize, Your Grace. I fear the list would be far too long to write and would cramp my hand." She flexed her fingers on his shoulder to make her point. "I think the first ten should suffice."

"Hmm." He drew them to a halt when the music faded, but kept hold of her until the music swelled again. Several men lurking nearby frowned, then turned away. Nicholas seemed not to notice. "Perhaps I should help. Let's see. You have called me arrogant. I will give you that. One."

Eva bit her lip to hide a smile. He smelled of spirits and exotic spice. His high stock framed his manly jaw, and the cut of his black coat accentuated his broad shoulders to sinewy perfection. She suspected every unattached woman at the ball, and some married ones, too, envied her at this moment.

Remembering how it felt to be sensuously assaulted on his desk, her body tingled. If he asked her to run from the room and follow him to his town house, she would not refuse.

"Two. I agree I am spoiled and used to having my every wish fulfilled. You must blame my mother for that. As her only child, she refused me very little. Yet, there is much I still desire."

Somehow, under the weight of his perusal, she suspected he wasn't talking about horses and estates, but remembering their amorous encounters. If they were alone, he would make very good use of Lady Pennington's immense dining table to debauch her in the most delicious ways.

Her nipples budded beneath her gown. She very much needed to find something less arousing than His Grace and his vigorous lovemaking to occupy her mind and time.

"Insufferable, outrageous, domineering. Three, four, and five." He grinned, and she shook her head. He tightened his hand on her waist. It was proving difficult to hear him over the rapid beat of her heart. His warmth seeped through her, and she felt and saw nothing outside the circle of his arms. "Impossible, intolerable, infuriating, disrespectful. Six, seven, eight, nine." He seemed to ponder the last, which made her giggle in spite of herself. He *was* impossibly charming when he wanted to be. "I hope you do not consider my lovemaking skills as a fault, love," he said finally. "I do not think I could bear it."

"Your Grace," she scolded. A quick look about confirmed no one was near enough to hear, and she breathed again.

"I remember I kissed your neck and nuzzled your ears with gentle vigor," he continued casually, as if he'd not heard her protest. "I suckled your breasts sufficiently. Your moans bespoke your pleasure."

Heat sizzled through her body. A scandalized laugh caught in her throat and she choked out, "Please stop, Your Grace. Someone will hear."

"My thrusts were deep and enthusiastic. I plundered you fully until you reached cry-inducing orgasms." He locked onto her eyes and his gaze was all innocence. "You called out my name. More than once, as I recall."

Now she laughed outright. She caressed his shoulder and no longer cared who noticed. She was thoroughly enjoying herself with this man, her lover, at her first and only ball.

"You are such an exasperating man."

"Ten. Exasperating. Your list is complete." He whirled her around as their laughter mingled and drew dozens of eyes.

It was two women, standing shoulder to shoulder, to whom the dancing pair were of the most interest. Lady Noelle Seymour and Her Grace, the Dowager Duchess of Stanfield, whispered quietly, a matching set of frowns marking their faces.

"Miss Winfield is a woman of quality and good character?" the duchess asked, her keen eyes sharp.

Noelle nodded. When the duchess had approached her, she had worried that she had discovered the ruse and planned to have the two sisters ejected from the ball. To her delight, Her Grace had learned the truth about Eva's liaison with her son but was not outraged. In fact, she wasn't displeased with her son's clear preference for Eva over the other lovelies.

"She is. She was an innocent when your son seduced her." Noelle wanted to make certain Eva was rightfully portrayed as the victim, and her innocence in the seduction fully established in the duchess's mind. "I do not know the particulars, but it was not her intention to go to his bed."

The duchess nodded. "Nicholas has a certain charm with women."

They watched for a moment as son and sister lowered their heads to speak intimately as the music died. All eyes were on them. "They do make a magnificent couple," Noelle said, sighing.

"They do," Her Grace agreed, "delightful."

Noelle was only just learning about her sister, but knew she'd suffered for the sins of her parents. To see her with His Grace, laughing and happy, brought her joy.

Eva complemented his dark looks with her fire. Though she denied her feelings for him, Noelle saw the way Eva looked at the insufferable duke. She was ensnared by him. It would not be long before she was headlong in love, if she wasn't already.

"Will he wed her?" Noelle asked.

The duchess narrowed her eyes. "He will if I have a say in it. My son deserves to be happy. If Miss Winfield can bring him that, I will welcome her gladly into my family."

Noelle turned her head. The duchess seemed sincere. But there were secrets left to test Her Grace's goodwill. "There are things about Eva you do not know, Your Grace."

Green eyes met hers. "I know more than you suspect, Lady Seymour. Her mother's past is of no consequence."

This was a surprise to Noelle. She knew Her Grace had lived with humiliating scandal. Her husband had lived the life of a whoremonger, a man who carelessly drifted from affair to affair, with no concern for the feelings of his wife. When he died, all of London had let out a collective sigh of relief.

The duchess was immensely popular among society. Though they'd gossiped about her shame, they also sympathized with her plight. Now she was free, and there wasn't anyone who didn't think the heart seizure that took the duke had not been deserved.

Noelle mentally crossed herself for thinking such a horrible thought. This was a night of surprises, starting with finding Eva in an embrace with the duke. She would not tarnish her joy over her sister's happiness with grim and unhappy thoughts.

It must be all the duchess had lived through that left her sympathetic to Eva's situation. Whatever her reasons for accepting her sister, Noelle would not question them. As long as the duchess was on her side, Eva and His Grace stood no chance of escape.

"Then we have work to do, Your Grace."

Chapter Fourteen

Eva left Noelle in the hallway and walked to her room. It was a strange feeling to be wandering the same hallways, eating at the same table, enjoying the same comforts her father had enjoyed under this roof. These halls echoed with his laughter, his anger, his touch.

Here, he'd lived one life with his wife and children. With her mother and her, he'd enjoyed another life. They were two parallel worlds, carefully kept apart. As Noelle and Margaret were growing up here and at his home in Kent, Eva grew up in a town house in Mayfair, some miles away.

It took the curiosity of her sister for the two lives to collide. She no longer doubted Noelle's reasons for seeking her out. Noelle cared for her, as she cared for Noelle. It was a strange circumstance, yet not so, when one considered the source. Noelle liked to press against the boundaries of societal rules, and Eva was a part of that. Their becoming friends was a wonderful twist to this adventure.

Eva wondered what her father would think of two of his beloved daughters finding each other.

She suspected he'd be pleased.

It was impossible not to expect that at any moment he would appear in an open doorway and pull her into his arms for one of his hugs that smelled faintly of pipe tobacco.

"I miss you, Father," Eva whispered, and took a few deep breaths. She rubbed her arms and stopped outside her room.

In the last few weeks, she'd gone from an innocent to a mistress, then from being an only child to having a sister. Two, if she counted Margaret, even though she clearly wanted no part of Noelle's plans to meet Eva. No matter. She was quite satisfied with the sister she had.

Swept from the darkness of a sheltered existence into the light of the Ton, Eva was not at all sure how it would work out.

Truthfully, she was fearful that she was on a runaway horse racing toward the edge of a cliff, and no amount of sawing on the reins would stop the frantic beast.

Tomorrow, she'd pack her bag and return home to her orderly life, leaving Noelle to offer an explanation for her disappearance.

It was her sister's idea to drag her to the ball, and it was Noelle who'd have to make appropriate excuses when suitors called. Her sister would undoubtedly come up with a plausible explanation. Noelle loved a good tale.

Eva smoothed her hands over the gown and smiled. Once the clock had struck two and they'd left the ball, she'd turned back into a scullery maid. A well-dressed scullery maid. She wouldn't feel a bit guilty leaving Noelle to mop up the mess she'd created.

The house was quiet when she entered her room and lighted a wall sconce. The frothy pink bedroom was not her taste. Apparently, Margaret had chosen the colors as a child, and it hadn't been changed a whit since then. Eva imagined Margaret's pinch-faced displeasure if she knew the daughter of her father's mistress was spending the evening in her bed.

The idea brought another smile as she reached for the buttons on her gown. Undoing them proved difficult as she twisted to reach behind her. Perhaps she shouldn't have been so quick to dismiss the maid. Unfortunately, the girl liked to chatter, and Eva was not in the mood to listen to her endless selection of topics. She was pleasantly exhausted and wanted to be alone.

"Need some help?"

Eva yelped and spun around. On the far side of the bed and in shadow, His Grace sat on a spindly chair, his booted feet up and crossed on the deep pink coverlet, without a care for the fabric.

"What are you doing here?" she hissed, listening for hurried footsteps in the hallway. When no alarm sounded in response to her cry, she planted her hands on her hips and tapped her toe. "How did you find me? How did you get in?"

Thankfully, the room was near the end of the hall and the closest room to it was empty. If Noelle had discovered him lurking in her room, she'd have had him dragged out and horsewhipped under the light of the moon.

His teeth flashed in the dim light. "I deduced you might stay here as part of the ruse. I instructed my footman to find out which room was yours. The oak outside your window was an effective ladder. It was only a small jump to the sill and a fistful of ivy, and then I was in."

"You climbed the tree?" That was difficult to believe. From what she could see, he hadn't a scuff or a stain anywhere on his clothes. "You don't seem like the tree-climbing type."

"You would be surprised what mischief I can get into when I'm motivated." His gaze caressed her body and his eyes darkened. Her peaks hardened beneath her gown. "Tonight I could not resist the temptation drifting from your window. I had to climb up and help you undress."

"I see." She removed her earbobs and returned them to the case. Her body was filled with nervous tingles. He must have left the ball before she and Noelle had, from the arms of his almost-fiancée, to come to her. It made her ridiculously happy to know that he would rather be with her than the lovely Lucy. Again. "Noelle will have to instruct the groundskeepers to cut down the tree tomorrow." She returned his enticing gaze. "I wouldn't wish to be the cause of your death if you fall."

"I couldn't fall." Mischief spilled from him. "We have plans for this evening that I'd hate to miss, should I crack my head open in a tumble from the tree."

She arched a brow. "Funny. I do not remember making plans with you."

"Oh, make no mistake, love," he said confidently. "Every time you gazed into my eyes tonight, there was a clear invitation to have my way with you."

Eva flushed to the roots of her hair. He was correct. She *had* teased and flirted with him outrageously. Even when he was conversing with someone else, she'd managed to catch his eye, and her smiles had been meant as a call for him to return to her. She'd openly invited her lover to seek her out, and seek her out he had.

Nicholas had shucked off his coat and loosened his cravat. The latter hung in twists down both sides of his open shirtfront. His hair was mussed from his climbing the tree and a second-floor catlike leap to her window.

He looked devilishly handsome and quite at home.

Feeling mischievous, she sauntered over to where he sat and turned her back to him. She straddled his legs and sat on his lap. Almost instantly, she felt his erection against her.

She lifted her hair out of the way and waited. "I understand you are an expert with buttons."

Nicholas lowered his feet to the floor and leaned to inhale her scent as he brushed his nose against her neck. Warm breath caressed her skin as he plucked the buttons open, one at a time. The intimacy of the moment made Eva feel decidedly like a wife.

"Did I mention how lovely you were this evening, mistress?" He paused and pressed a kiss in the opening as her gown began to fall away.

She closed her eyes and sighed. He was perfection in the sensuous aspects of lovemaking. The duke knew just how to pleasure a woman, and she thoroughly enjoyed his efforts. "I don't recall. Perhaps you should remind me."

He eased the gown down her arms and leaned in to place a soft kiss on one shoulder. "Every other woman paled in comparison, sweet."

Another burst of happiness lifted her heart.

"But what of Lucy?" she asked casually, tamping down the unwelcome image of Nicholas sneaking into the girl's room with debauchery on his mind. The virginal chit would likely expire from fright. "I saw her. She's very pretty."

Nicholas quietly opened a few more buttons before answering. "I was to offer for her hand this evening," he said softly, and lowered the gown a bit more. The silver fabric fell away in the front to expose a full swell of cleavage. Only her nipples remained hidden beneath her chemise. "Your arrival changed everything."

"Oh?" A silly grin crossed her face. She was thankful her back was turned. Her presence at the ball had been perfectly timed, and she couldn't hide her satisfaction. His Grace was still unattached because she'd allowed her sister to bully her into attending. She silently thanked Noelle.

Poor wealthy and perfectly unengaged Lucy had gone home to a lonely bed while the duke climbed through her window, like a sneak thief in the night. For her.

Eva wanted to laugh for sheer joy. Instead, she wriggled her bottom and heard his breath deepen. In a matter of seconds, she was free of the gown and his hands were slid-ing around her waist as if seeking her breasts. Bracing her hands on his thighs, she stood and stepped away.

"Stay," she commanded over her shoulder when he moved to rise. She exaggerated the sway of her hips as she walked several steps and turned. His hint of a smile led her as she slowly wriggled out of the gown and placed it across the foot of the bed. She had his full attention.

Eyes wide, she asked, "Do you like it when I strip for you, Your Grace?"

At his nod, she loosened her corset, then paused. "And this?" He nodded again, as she pulled the laces open and slid it down her hips. She kicked it away. Instead of remov-ing the rest of her garments, she tugged the ribbon holding the neckline of her chemise closed. Her full breasts pressed the limits of the thin cloth and threatened to spill over.

He groaned. "You are a tease, Evangeline Winfield."

His words came breathlessly. She smiled and locked onto his stare. Slowly, hips swaying, she walked back to him and dropped to her knees. His position made freeing him from his breeches somewhat difficult, but after a few false starts, she finally managed to part the cloth and free his erection.

A deeper groan rumbled from his throat as she gathered the length in her hand and caressed the soft tip. How per-fectly his body was made to pleasure them both.

"You push me to distraction, mistress."

Eva smiled and pressed a kiss on the tip. "Indeed? I thought we were enemies." She released him, then stood and straddled his knees. He watched intently as she bunched her chemise and petticoat in her hands, drawing them up over her hips until only her drawers, garters, and stockings remained to cover the patch of curls from his eyes.

With care, Eva spread the opening of the drawers. With his help, she positioned herself over his erection and slowly impaled herself on his hard cock. Nicholas buried his face between her breasts and let out a harsh sound.

She slid up and down once, then lifted her attention to his face. His hunger was complete and blinding to see. Their previous encounters had not cooled his ardor. He wanted her as much, or more, now than he had the first time he took her to bed.

"You like this, Nicholas?"

"I do." He grinned as she leaned to capture his mouth for a brief, deep kiss. He swirled his tongue with hers, then broke free. He looked deep into her eyes. "I like it very much."

Eva ran her hands down the sides of his face and cupped his jaw. The smoldering desire in his intense eyes left her trembling and confused by the fluttering in her heart. In that moment, she realized all her fears had come to fruition. She'd fallen deeply and completely in love with her dark duke.

"I am a well-trained courtesan," she said lightly, struggling to keep the tiny cracks opening up in her heart from becoming deep fissures. There was no place for love here. It was all about passion and pleasure, and the mating of two bodies. So she closed off her heart and pulled his shirt free of his breeches. She drew it over his head and tossed it toward the bed. "I am here to please."

Splaying her hands across his chest, she teased his nipples and bent to inhale the warm scent of his skin as she pressed a kiss at the base of his throat. He tasted slightly of salt, and his body radiated heat. Nicholas plucked the pins from her hair, and the mass tumbled down her back. He cupped her hips and lifted and lowered her, burying his erection deeply inside her, again and again.

She rocked with his movements in a primal dance and found a position where she could brush delightfully against him for maximum pleasure. He sucked her nipples through her chemise, wetting the fabric and drawing small cries of delight from her. The spindly chair creaked in protest as their combined weight pushed it to the limits of remaining upright.

He plundered her flesh, two bodies moving in perfect synchronization until Eva felt the world around her explode in sparks of bright light. She threw her head back and cried out his name. Nicholas pumped into her deeply as he found his own release with a ragged groan.

Eva slumped on his chest, replete. Nicholas pressed his mouth into her hair and caressed her back in slow lover's strokes. She listened to his rapid heartbeat, wishing they could stay this way forever.

"You do please me, love," he said softly. "Very much."

With her face hidden, Eva sighed sadly as she took as much comfort from him as she could. Their time was limited. She needed to make as many memories as possible of his scent, his face, his touch. One day soon he'd officially offer for Lucy, and Eva would never see him again.

Blinking back tears, she forced a smile. "You please me, too, very much, Your Grace."

Later, Nicholas stared at the ceiling, where the glow of the fire flickered across plaster, and relished the warm feel of Eva as she slept beside him. Her soft breathing tickled his skin where she rested her face on his chest. The hint of flowers infused her hair, tangled around his shoulder and scattered in silken strands across his chest.

She was everything he desired in a mistress, yet all he feared, too. He was losing control when she was near. The ball was a perfect example. It wouldn't surprise him in the least if society was abuzz tomorrow with speculation about his infatuation with the beautiful stranger.

The chance to wed Lucy was all but destroyed. There was little chance his attraction to the mysterious Miss Harrington wouldn't get back to her and her parents. Only his wealth and position might keep her from refusing him.

Still, was Lucy his desire? Had she ever been?

Eva haunted his days and nights. Every thought, every dream was filled with her. She'd become his obsession.

At this moment, he should be engaged and ready to embark on a new chapter of his life. Lucy should be happily dreaming of a wedding. Instead, he'd broken into Lady Seymour's home and seduced her sister right beneath her nose.

Well, Eva had seduced him; completely and passionately and without a moment of hesitation or regret. She'd turned his desire for revenge into a desire for her, one he couldn't shake. When he looked into her eyes, he was lost.

He realized that the idea of spending the rest of his days and nights with the sweet but uninteresting Lucy Banes-Dodd had lost most of its luster. Hell, all of its luster. He wanted passion and fire, not milk and dry biscuits. Yet, Lucy would make an ideal wife. Why, then, was that no longer enough?

Eva murmured in her sleep and slid her arm around his waist. The flames in the fireplace had died to a smattering of embers, and her small hand was cool in the chill room. Her lips upturned at the corners. He wondered what sort of dreams she dreamt and if they were about him. With Eva, it was impossible to say.

His spinster-courtesan was a puzzle. Why she drove him insane was even more puzzling. They had nothing in common. He lived his life by stiff rules, by a code of conduct set forth as appropriate for his position in society. She mocked him and tormented him for everything he was and believed, yet the moment he'd seen her across the ballroom, he'd forgotten everything and everyone else. The spinster had engaged not only his body but his mind as well. He'd begun to see his world through her eyes, and had found many aspects of it lacking.

The slight smile on her face grew. Eyes still closed, she eased her hand down his chest, under the sheet, and over his cock. He twitched and began to harden.

"I was having the most delightful dream, Your Grace,"

she whispered as her eyes opened. "You were cast as the hero, and all the things you were doing to me were positively wicked."

Nicholas chuckled and pushed her back on the bed. Now he knew her dreams were filled with him, too. The thought gave him immense satisfaction. "Then you must tell me all about it, Eva love."

The last shadows lingered just before dawn when Nicholas draped one leg over the sill and paused to rake his gaze down her thinly clad body. Her dusky nipples were visible beneath the thin nightdress, and if he looked closely, he thought he caught a hint of the curls at the junction of her thighs. Whether it was truth or his heated imagination, it didn't matter. He knew every inch of her body intimately and could summon her curves in his mind whenever and wherever he chose.

"You can sneak down the back servants' stairs, Nicholas," Eva whispered, her voice worried. She had her hands curled into his coat. "This window seems very high up."

He drew her close, a hand around her back and the other in her hair near her ear. "I think the danger of leaping into a tree is far more enticing for a damsel such as my lovely Eva than my sneaking down and out a servants' entrance like a cowardly dandy."

Eva leaned out the window and looked down. "If you fall and break a bone, your screams will awaken the household, and the whole city will quickly know where you spent the evening, Sir Knight."

The concern on her face touched him. She no longer hoped for his violent, painful death. The idea pleased him. He pulled her tight and kissed her hard.

"Then I shall just have to be careful." He released her reluctantly and climbed onto the sill. She slowly untangled her hands from his coat. "Say a prayer, Milady."

Eva gasped as he leapt to the tree. He bobbled slightly but grasped the branch above his head. In an instant, he found his footing, thankful he wouldn't have to bear the shame of falling in an untidy heap while Eva watched. She let out a relieved laugh. "Well done, sir."

He flashed a grin. "I'm off to pillage and plunder, Milady." He bowed, wobbled, and righted himself. "Until later."

Without further fanfare, he climbed down the tree. After a last look up at her, framed in moonlight in the window, he made his way silently across the lawn and out the gate to the street.

Eva heard branches rustle, then the sound of Nicholas dropping to the ground with a thump. She couldn't see him, yet felt his eyes on her, and she lifted a hand. When the gate from the garden squeaked open and closed, she turned back into the darkened room and sat on the bed, her eyes and heart troubled.

What to do?

Love. Often spoken of and sung about, it was the most complicated of emotions and seldom a part of relationships. When one did find love, it was rarely part of marriage, or between a man and his mistress. It was easier to hate His Grace than to fall head over heels for him.

He was a drug so heady she craved him the way some craved the demon drug, opium. He'd promised her nothing but pleasure, and he'd fulfilled that promise. Not once in their most private moments had he given her any reason to expect anything more than stolen bits of time.

Though he called her "love," it was nothing more than an endearment in the moment of passion; a term of affection he used in the unguarded occasions when they were alone. Nicholas would never love her. He might feel affection, perhaps, but not love. It was not in him. He was practical. She was the slave to emotion.

Eva placed her hands over her face. He had cared for Arabella and he cared for her. She sensed it in the way he held her. But he came with limits. As long as she stayed within her boundaries, all was well. For the moment, he'd forgiven her for attending the ball. Once his mind cleared, he would be angry for her impertinence. He'd likely irreparably damaged his arrangement with Lucy. He'd not forgive her for that, as he had not forgiven her for losing Arabella.

She was the cause of both losses.

There was only one thing she could do.

Chapter Fifteen

"No news of Yvette, Miss Eva?" Abigail said as they settled down for tea. The four young women were very worried. Days had passed since their friend disappeared, and they all felt her absence. With the passage of time it became difficult to finish their lessons and to keep focused on the last details of their instruction. They were ready to be matched. Eva was pleased with how hard each of them had worked and the changes in all of them.

Even the book met with little enthusiasm when Eva suggested one last look in case there was anyone they might have missed. The party was a week away, and though they'd each chosen two men to invite, and Eva included several choices of her own, their concern for Yvette overshadowed the party.

Eva had hoped to withhold the information she'd received from Mister Crawford this morning until she had news. However, the fearful faces left her no choice but to tell them about the report. The women deserved the truth.

"The investigator has discovered the identity of Yvette's lover and has gone to his country home to have a look around. He has given me the man's name, and I have hope we will soon learn if Yvette has been seen there." Eva did her best to hide her worry. It was her greatest wish to find Yvette alive. "There was no sign of her at his town house."

"If the investigator finds her, what then?" Sophie plucked at the lace edging of her pink gown until the piece frayed. She smoothed it down and clasped her hands. "What if her lover has locked her in a tower and plans to starve her? What if she is chained in a cellar with rats?"

"Oh, dear." Rose's lips trembled, and she pressed a knuckle to her mouth. "What if he has sold her to slavers? She might end up in some far-off place and never be seen again."

Eva lifted her hands. She had to restore order before they worked themselves into a frenzy. "Ladies, please. We must not overwork our imaginations." Their minds had clearly sent their speculation in all sorts of dark directions. "To be of any use to Yvette, we must think positive thoughts."

"Miss Eva is right," Abigail offered. "We must allow the investigator to discover some clues. It is quite possible she has not been kidnapped at all. Perhaps she has found a new protector and is happy."

"We all hope for her happiness, Abigail." As Eva sipped her tea, a possible answer to the dilemma formed.

For the past two days, she had been avoiding the duke. He'd sent around a note, but she had refused to accept it. The only way to forget him was avoidance. Once he realized she was no longer available to him, he'd propose to his Lucy and get about the business of marriage.

But now, if Yvette was held being captive, Eva might have to visit His Grace one last time for help. He would know someone who could rescue her. Maybe enlist the Bow Street Runners.

Her heart ached for Nicholas, and she did her best to ignore the pain. It would be a constant presence once the final break was made and her heart was left in bits. She might as well get used to it now. They had no future.

Rose nodded. "I think we should choose two suitors for her. There was one man, a merchant, she seemed drawn to. Perhaps we can find another." She retrieved the book. The other women gathered around her as she turned the pages. "See, this one. He is a mature man of forty. He owns a tea shop and travels frequently to France to visit his brother. Yvette's mother was French."

"He is a fine choice," Pauline agreed as she turned the page. "And this one. He, too, is in his forties, widowed, with grown children. He seeks a companion to help fill his days." She smiled. "He might be perfect for Yvette."

"He very well might," Sophie agreed.

"Turn the page. I think I know of another," Abigail said. Excitement grew. "I believe there was a shopkeeper near the back. He was widowed and his children are also grown."

The women chattered happily as they examined all the men as possible husbands for Yvette. Eva was relieved that they had found something to focus on besides dark speculation about Yvette's fate.

"Turn to the last page," Eva said. "Just yesterday I added an American shipbuilder. He was recommended to me by Mister Jones." Pages ruffled, and several sighs followed. "The American plans to move his company to London and he is quite prosperous. I think we should consider sending him an invitation."

"He is handsome," said Pauline.

"Very much so," added Rose.

"He has an impeccable reputation. I have been assured of that."

"Then he must be included," Sophie said firmly. "We shall have to make a list and whittle it down to the best two"—she looked at Eva—"or three."

Eva smiled. Her courtesans had turned from objects of pleasure to young women of superior manners and quality. The men on her invitation list would be pleased with such a fine group, from the stunning Rose to the subtle beauty of Abigail. She could only pray for Yvette's rescue and successful matches for all five women.

"We must quickly finalize Yvette's list." Eva poured more tea. "I will send out the invitations tomorrow."

The next day, with the invitations sent, Eva went over the party menu with Cook. Since the gathering would be small, and in mid afternoon, there was no need to offer an elaborate meal. Tea, cakes, punch, and sandwiches would feed the guests nicely. And of course food was always a possible topic of conversation when one had to fill long stretches of silence.

Eva knew from previous experience that there would be very little eating. Though there wasn't pressure to choose a mate at the party, there was always anxiety the first time her former courtesans put their lessons to use.

How could there not be? This was the culmination of all their hard work. The women had been beautiful and charming from the first; Eva had just given them tools to pave a path to marriage. They would be tested, if only in their own minds, and each felt the strain.

Harold had taken the women to their final fittings for the dresses they would wear to the party. The excitement of the impending event was dampened slightly by Yvette's absence, yet there was lingering hope she would be found and returned to them in time. The women clung to that hope and forced themselves to continue as planned.

Eva wasn't sure of anything outside her own situation. She, too, forced herself to press through her days in a fog. She was unsettled and grim, as if a black cloud was following her and she could not outrun it.

She deeply missed His Grace. More than she had ever expected she would. She'd never been in love before. She struggled daily with the complications of that unwelcome emotion.

Prayers for Mister Crawford's swift return went unanswered. The wait was grueling. If all went well, the investigator would find and rescue Yvette, and Eva wouldn't have to face Nicholas again. Each time she saw his handsome face, it was a blow to her heart.

It was three days into her self-imposed removal from Nicholas's life, and she was short-tempered and grumpy. She was constantly biting her tongue so as not to snap at everyone, including her mother, over every little inconvenience.

What she desired most was to take to her bed for a fortnight, and weep and wail until Nicholas was washed away by her tears. He was likely engaged by now and looking forward to his wedding night. She could not see him allowing weeds to grow beneath his feet while his reluctant courtesan hid from him. He'd want to get Lucy quickly settled as his intended bride before another man had the chance to woo her away; then begin a search for a new lover. Men of his ilk never settled for the love of a wife. He'd seek a courtesan to warm his bed.

The kitchen suddenly felt very hot, and her head swam. She dropped the menu and whispered, "Excuse me."

To Cook's surprise, Eva rushed out the back door into the garden. Fearing she was about to be ill, she sucked in deep, damp breaths until her stomach settled.

It was cool and cloudy; not the sort of day to stroll through the garden. She felt an invisible sheen of moisture settle on her bare arms and face. The first spring flowers were in full bloom against the bleak backdrop, but she did not give them more than a dismissive glance. She hurried to the nearest stone bench and dropped onto its damp surface.

Tears threatened. Unhappiness settled inside her. The idea of Nicholas married was more than she could accept under the weight of frayed emotions. The only bed he should be sharing was hers! His children should be hers!

"Eva?"

Startled, she jerked her head up. Through the tears welling

in her eyes, she saw Nicholas coming up the path with the brisk strides of a confident nobleman. He wore a hat and cloak to fend off the threatening rain. She feasted on the sight of him as he drew close.

Quickly, she brushed her hand over her cheeks and stood. He must not see her pain.

"Your Grace." Her heart leapt as she peered into his face. She wanted to run into his arms, kiss him, and touch him all over to assure herself he was not imagined. But she kept her feet planted where they were. "This is the second time you have come here uninvited, Your Grace. I will not have it."

His jaw tightened at her curt words. "I was concerned when you didn't reply to my message. I feared you had fallen ill." He examined her briefly. His lips thinned. "I see you are in good health."

She braced herself for what needed to be done. "I think it best for all if we end our association, Your Grace. My sister is unhappy, I am unhappy, and soon you will be wed. Your Lucy will certainly be unhappy if you continue to bed me."

"Lucy has no bearing on the relationship between you and me, Eva," he said tightly. "I have not asked for her hand."

"But you will." Eva sighed. Why couldn't he leave her alone? Couldn't he see how difficult this was for her? "Either her or another blue blood like her. You have a family branch to fill out, and your mother will not be satisfied until she has a full dozen grandchildren to spoil."

"You do not know my mother's wishes." He tapped his riding crop on his boot and tipped his face toward the leaden clouds. "She has not once mentioned Lucy since the ball. In fact, she has not mentioned marriage at all."

Eva let out a harsh breath. She desperately hoped she had no part in his mother's attitude change. She didn't want to add the duchess to the list of people hurt by her actions.

"It doesn't matter which woman you choose; the end will inevitably be the same. Your marriage. Since I have come into your life, I have stolen your courtesan, I have invaded your world, and quite possibly have prevented your engagement. I think it best if you return to Collingwood House and forget you ever knew me." She locked and unlocked her hands together. "I will pay you monthly until my debt is cleared, even if it takes a hundred years."

"You think I care about the damned debt?" His voice boomed over her. She jumped. He scowled. "The town house has been gifted to you in your name, so your mother cannot borrow against it again. The rest of the debts will be paid once I have an accounting of them in entirety." He reached down to take her hand and drew her to her feet. "I made a mistake when I forced you to become my mistress through threats of debtors' prison."

How astonishing! She was free! She should be dancing for joy. But not even this could lift her spirits. "I thank you for your consideration, Your Grace. My mother and I are grateful."

"Damn it, Eva." He took her roughly by the arms and shook her lightly. He bent to look into her eyes. "I do not want your gratitude. I don't want you to feel you should come to my bed out of some sense of obligation. I want you to continue our association because you desire me as I desire you."

He dipped his head and brushed his warm lips over hers. Eva placed a hand on his chest and felt his rapid heartbeat. Just as quickly, he released her, and she wobbled. "I will not come to you again. You know where to find me. The decision is yours."

Wide-eyed and breathless, Eva watched him stalk down the path toward the back wall. The slam of the metal gate echoed in her ears long after she heard a coach pull away.

She slumped onto the bench and covered her face. Nicholas had removed her chains and gifted her with the return of her life. She no longer had to worry about her future or his powerful presence tugging at her purse strings. Mother was safe and Eva never had to see him again, unless she chose to do so.

"Oh, dear." She placed her open hands over her mouth and stared absently at a patch of blue hyacinths. His Grace had come as close to words of affection as she could ever expect from him. He'd freed her, yet he wanted her to stay.

There was no need to read poetry or to linger over words of love. He hungered for her, he cared for her. She'd seen it play out in his eyes and felt it in his kiss.

"I see His Grace has returned." Harold rounded a narrow hedge and came to a stop before her. He stared toward the back of the garden, his face a closed mask. "He is smitten with you, Eva."

"He cares for me," Eva agreed. No man would give such a grand gift unless he cared for her welfare. "He has forgiven my debts and signed over Mother's house to me." Her voice caught in her throat, and she stared up at Harold through stinging eyes. A deep swallow cleared her voice. "And he has left our future together up to me."

Harold worked his jaw for a long moment. It was clear he didn't want to give credit to His Grace for his selfless act. The two men were fighting for the right to protect Eva and her mother. Thankfully, there had not been bloodshed.

"I may have misjudged the man," he said finally.

Eva's eyes widened. It had taken much out of Harold to admit his mistake.

"We both misjudged him," she said.

After a nod, Harold scratched the side of his head. "Has he asked for your hand?"

"He has not." She lifted her chin. She was too overwrought to argue today. "I do not expect such an offer. I'm a courtesan's daughter." A few raindrops started to fall. She held back tears and stood. "Oh, Harold, I do care for him. I know not what to do. I'm no longer satisfied with the life I have. I want so much more. I want a family of my own."

Harold shrugged. "I cannot offer advice when it comes to

His Grace or your future. You must do what is in your heart. If he cannot give you what you desire, you must let him go."

Eva looped her hand under his elbow and rested her head on his shoulder. The damp wool of his coat was oddly comforting. She had missed their closeness over the last few weeks, and was relieved to have it back. "You are such a good friend."

He patted her hand and mumbled, "If you only knew."

Nicholas listened intently to Crawford until he finished his report. The investigator took a deep breath and added, "I'm certain the woman is being held somewhere in Highland Abbey. The earl's servants are whispering about a woman locked in a room on the second floor. I believe she is the missing, perhaps kidnapped, Yvette."

Kidnapped? Eva was correct to be worried. Her courtesan had not gone missing by choice but by force. Lord Maddington had had her kidnapped. The bastard!

"You told this to Miss Black?" It felt strange to call her by her spinster name, but it was better to keep Crawford thinking of her that way. Miss Black belonged to her courtesans. Evangeline Winfield belonged solely to Nicholas, and he easily kept the two separate in his mind.

"I left her and came here straightaway, Your Grace." The investigator stood by the fire, warming from his journey across town in the rain. His bones crackled as he flexed and released his hands toward the flames. "The lady was very worried, and also very generous."

Nicholas frowned. "You were not to take money from her."

"I tried to refuse it." Crawford grinned. "When I explained you would make the payment, her big servant forced a purse into my hand." Crawford chuckled. "I feared what he might do if I refused. I slipped it onto a table on the way out."

Grinning, Nicholas nodded. Eva wouldn't be pleased.

Harold was as persuasive as he was large. Nicholas imagined Eva, the servant at her back, refusing to allow Nicholas to pay any further debts on her behalf. Even without Harold, he suspected Crawford had been outmanned. She was a force of her own, and would be angry when she discovered the purse left behind.

Lud, he missed her!

Stretching out his legs to ease the tightening in his crotch, Nicholas leaned an elbow on the armrest and tucked his jaw into his hand. "Thank you for your efforts, Crawford. You have done an excellent job. I have instructed my butler to double your fee. You can see him on the way out."

Crawford tucked his hat onto his head and bowed. "If you ever need me again, just send a note, Your Grace." He walked out the open door and down the hall.

Muted voices drifted back, then the front door closed behind the investigator. A few minutes later a knock echoed through the house. Nicholas heard a female voice, and then the butler escorted Eva into the room.

"Miss Winfield, Your Grace."

Relieved to see her, Nicholas stood. "Eva." She was a vision of ethereal beauty beneath the hood of her sodden cloak. Water dripped onto the polished floor as she pushed the hood back and her hair fell about her in a tangled mass of damp curls. She'd left off the wig. He cleared his throat to recover from his surprise and tamp down a sudden flush of desire.

He casually reached for his glass and tossed back the last swallow of brandy in an effort to calm his body. An insurmountable task when she was near. "I didn't expect you, or I would have had tea prepared."

She stepped farther into the room, and the firelight flickered across her pale face. "I did not come here for tea, Your Grace. This isn't a social call."

The news of the discovery of Yvette's whereabouts was the likely reason for her visit. She was attached to her fallen birds, and with one chick missing, Eva had become obsessed with finding her and returning her to the nest.

"I saw Mister Crawford leave as I was arriving. So you know about Yvette." She extended her hands, beseeching. "I am desperately worried about her, Your Grace. We need your help."

Returning the glass to the table, he walked to her. With Crawford's information, he knew what Yvette faced, and could not allow Eva to put herself in danger. She had to be convinced to let professionals handle the situation.

"There is little I can do, sweet, but summon the Bow Street Runners and let them do their own investigation." He brushed a curl behind her ear. "Her lover is a peer. We must tread carefully."

"You think they'd care about one missing courtesan, against the murders and thievery that happen here in London every day?" she cried, curling her hands into fists. "If they investigate this at all, it could take weeks, months even, to find enough evidence to rescue her. By then, Yvette could be dead or sold into slavery."

The fear in her face twisted his gut. She had no idea of the size of Yvette's problem. The woman was in grave trouble, and he couldn't allow Eva to face the same by confronting Maddington. If any harm befell Eva, there would be hell to pay. "I have connections. I can hurry things along."

Eva pressed a gloved fist to her mouth. "We cannot wait. She's in immediate danger." She paced, trailing droplets of water in her wake. "We must come up with another solution. We know where she's held. Perhaps we can confront the staff and demand they release her."

"Eva . . ." He reached for her arm to stop the pacing. He touched the side of her face. The soft skin was clammy under his warm palm. "Sweet, I know Lord Maddington. They do not call him the Mad Lord for naught. He is a violent man. He almost killed a footman for dropping a vase.

If your Yvette is indeed at Highland Abbey, she is well guarded. None of his servants will dare betray him. They fear him too much."

Beneath his hands she shook. "Please help her, Nicholas." Her bottom lip trembled and tears filled the corners of her eyes. "We cannot allow her to be murdered!"

A sob broke from her. He eased her into his arms. Her shaking turned into quiet weeping as rain and tears soaked through his shirt. She felt small and vulnerable, tucked against his chest. Protective feelings welled inside him, and he murmured soothing sounds until she quieted.

Spent, she lifted her head and sniffled. "I apologize for bringing this to you, Your Grace. Yvette is not your concern." She stepped back and released her grip on his shirt. He cupped her face with both hands. He hated to see her so dejected.

"I promise I will do what I can for your friend." He leaned to press his lips to her forehead. "Allow me a day or two to see what I can discover. Promise?"

Slowly, Eva nodded. But the dark spark he saw in her eyes, just before she turned and walked to the door, narrowed his eyes and roused suspicion.

"Eva." Her hand rested on the door handle and she looked over her shoulder. The dull pain in her eyes had faded. She looked as if she was about to do something reckless.

Short of tying her to his bed, he had to remain confident that Harold would keep a watch over her while the Runners looked into the kidnapping. "Do not do anything foolish."

"I will not." She nodded stiffly. "Good day, Your Grace."

For the remainder of the afternoon, a sickening dread settled deep in his gut.

Chapter Sixteen

I cannot sit here in my room and do nothing," Eva said. She leaned back against the pillows on her bed, then leaned forward, turned, and punched the closest pillow into a downy pulp before slumping back against it. She felt so overwhelmingly helpless and frustrated. "Yvette is in danger."

Noelle reclined on an elbow at the foot of the bed and traced a finger around the floral pattern on the coverlet. Summoned by Eva, Noelle had rushed to the Mayfair house. Though Noelle didn't know Yvette, Eva was sure she sympathized with her plight. What woman would not? To be kidnapped and likely abused by a man with a history of violence was a terrifying nightmare all women could understand.

"Did His Grace not say he would help?" Noelle had faith in the powers of a duke on a mission. It was a faith Eva didn't share. No one man was all-powerful and able to work miracles. Not even the dark duke. "I think it best if you allow him a few days to see what he can do. A man of his stature can engage the Runners to action in ways we cannot."

The unshakable belief in His Grace rankled. It wasn't as if Eva didn't believe Nicholas could do what he said. It was the waiting she took issue with. Never patient to begin with, she felt each tick of the clock batter through her mind with piercing accuracy. Time was wasting, and she couldn't bear it!

"A few days? We might as well serve up Yvette to the earl on a platter with an apple in her mouth," Eva snapped. She crossed her arms and blew hair out of her eyes. "Lord Maddington nearly killed a man. Does that not warrant immediate action?"

"And what, exactly, does this immediate action entail?" Noelle said. She pushed up on the bed. "Do you ride up to his door on Muffin, dressed in medieval armor, and demand her release? Or roust the villagers, arm them with pitchforks and flaming torches, and launch an attack on the abbey?"

"I don't appreciate you mocking me, sister," Eva scolded.

Noelle leaned on one palm. She reached out to place her other hand on Eva's outstretched ankle. "I do understand your worry, and I apologize. However, if this man is as dangerous as His Grace believes, you must not cross him. His Grace will help. I know he will. He will do anything for you."

Perhaps not anything. He would not give her his name, a home, and children. But she had more urgent concerns right now. She would think about what to do about His Grace later, once Yvette was safe.

"I will allow him no more than two days," Eva said firmly. Two days loomed, seemingly without end. "No more. If Yvette is not rescued by then, I shall roust the villagers."

Eva shoved her black mourning gown into her satchel. The heavy wool garment was too small; it hadn't been worn for almost four years, since the death of her elderly nurse. Still, it was the only black gown she owned and would have to do as a disguise. She could live with flattened breasts and shallow breathing as long as she was invisible in the darkness.

She'd eaten her supper, read to her mother, and waited until everyone in the household went to bed. Then she wrote a note and packed two days of necessities after donning her spinster wig and spectacles.

It was just before dawn when she slipped from the house and hurried across the damp grass of the garden, running out to the mews. Boothe, the groom, was snoring loudly as Eva stealthily slipped into the small stable.

She'd seen Boothe saddle Muffin hundreds of times, and felt fairly confident she could manage without help. She pushed a note onto a nail by Muffin's stall to assure Boothe the mare hadn't been stolen, and set to work.

The plump pony yawned and chewed slowly on bits of hay while Eva worked with efficiency, though it took several tries to get the saddle positioned correctly. Soon the task was complete. She tied the satchel behind the saddle and patted the horse gently on the rump.

"Ready, love?" She led Muffin outside to a mounting block and slipped into the saddle. With the splash of orange and gold from the sun yet to make a full appearance, Eva pointed Muffin north, and prayed the mare could make the trip without expiring along the way from exhaustion.

The road was pitted and muddy but clear, except for an occasional coach or farmer's cart, as Eva and Muffin made the trip to the small village outside Highland Abbey. It had taken twice the hour or two most travelers needed to cover the distance. With many stops for Muffin to rest, it was early afternoon before she stabled the mare, took a room at the inn, and asked for food to be sent up.

Famished, Eva ate a hearty stew in her room and then settled down for a nap. Muffin had one speed, slow, and one gait, jarring. Eva's body ached in places she didn't know one could ache. Still, they had made the trip in its entirety without the rotund little mare dropping onto her back, dead, her hooves in the air.

A success indeed.

Once refreshed, she pulled her wig and spectacles back on and left the inn. She wandered about the tiny village. A few businesses dotted the one road passing through it, and a smattering of houses made up the rest of the ramshackle occupied dwellings. One could nearly toss a stone from one end to the other. Clearly, the inn was the only reason anyone had for stopping on the way to somewhere else, and prosperity was only a dream to its residents.

As casually as she could, Eva asked several villagers about Lord Maddington, in an effort to gain information about the man. She was met with glares and stony silence. The villagers were either fiercely loyal to the earl, who owned most of the property in the area, or too terrified to cross him and risk his wrath. She returned to the inn without any information to help her understand her adversary.

Knowing Yvette was less than a mile up the road, and she could do nothing for her right then, left Eva on the verge of tears.

She nibbled on some freshly baked bread and more stew, but the food sat like a lump in her belly. She finally pushed the bowl away and settled on the bed. It would be after midnight before she felt it would be safe to walk to the abbey and take a look around. She flopped back on the patched quilt and began a fitful evening of counting cracks in the plaster ceiling.

Several hours later, just as her lids were beginning to droop with the pull of sleep, a sharp rap on the door brought her upright on the bed with a start.

Eva tiptoed to the door and pressed her ear to the rough plank. She heard nothing. Placing a hand over her heart for calm, she lowered her voice to a rough tenor and barked out, "Who's there?"

"It's me, Rose."

Eva yanked the door open, mouth agape, to find several pairs of eyes staring back at her from the ill-lit hallway. Standing in a cluster and dressed like stable boys in homespun shirts, trousers, and caps were Rose, Sophie, Abigail, and Pauline. They smiled sheepishly, as if they'd been caught with their hands in someone else's jewelry box.

"Let us in. Quickly!" Rose whispered.

Eva stepped back as they stumbled into the room, rushing to get out of sight.

"What are you doing here?" Eva scowled as they pulled off their caps.

"We came to help you rescue Yvette, of course," said Pauline, looking around the simple room. She sat in the chamber's only chair, then stretched out her legs in a most unladylike fashion. "We would have gotten here sooner, but had to wait for a coach heading in this direction."

Eva frowned. "But how did you know where I was?"

"Harold came looking for you," Abigail said, brushing dust off her shirt. "He was terribly concerned when he discovered you'd run off. We all were."

"Rose overheard you speaking with the investigator about Lord Maddington and the abbey and suspected you were planning to rescue Yvette," said Sophie. "We knew you shouldn't face such a task alone. So while Rose distracted the grooms, Abigail and I borrowed some clothing from the stable behind that huge town house at the end of the street."

"You stole clothing?" Eva asked, aghast.

"We left a note. Unsigned of course," Abigail broke in. "We will return the clothes when we return to London." She worried a thumbnail between her teeth. "I'm certain no one saw us."

Eva's worry increased tenfold. Knowing they cared enough to risk prison for her and Yvette lifted her spirits, in spite of their risky behavior. They were the closest to true women friends she had ever had. However, their presence had muddled up her plans.

Though the company was welcome, she'd hoped to find a way to get to Yvette without drawing undue attention to herself or arousing the earl's suspicions. The arrival of the four young "men" would surely cause a stir in this small village.

"Were you seen sneaking into the inn?" Eva pressed.

"We took the back stairs so no one would notice us. The innkeeper thinks we are bedding down in the stable," Sophie offered. "One drunken sot out back was snoring and muttering in his sleep, but we came across no one else."

Thank goodness. "You should take the first coach back to London in the morning," Eva said, working her bottom lip with her teeth. "You risk yourselves needlessly; I can handle this matter alone."

"Indeed?" Sophie dropped on the bed, leaned forward, and rested her elbows on her knees. The other three settled on either side of her. "If His Lordship catches you snooping around his property, he'll have you shot. With five of us, we can create enough of a commotion to allow one of us to slip in and rescue Yvette."

A rap on the door stopped any further argument. Eva jumped and pressed a finger to her mouth to keep silent. Drat. The innkeeper must have heard something and become suspicious. If he tossed them out, there would be nowhere else to go at this hour.

It wasn't the innkeeper standing in the hallway when Eva opened the door with an apology on her lips.

Noelle stood outside the door, dressed in widow's black, with a lacy black veil covering her face and hair. It took Eva a second to recover from the shock, and then she closed a hand around her sister's narrow wrist and yanked her inside.

Locking the door tightly behind her, Eva slammed her

hands on her hips and swept an exasperated look around the room. So much for her plot to take a stealthy look around Highland Abbey. Stealth didn't include a sister and a gaggle of courtesans trotting at her heels.

"Have we forgotten anyone? Or should I go downstairs and ask the innkeeper for another room with a row of beds?" Eva sighed. "Would you care to explain why you're here, Noelle?"

Her sister swept off her hat and tossed it on the bed. She pulled Eva into a rib-cracking hug and kissed her on the cheek. "I was worried you'd come to harm, so I came to rescue you from your good intentions." She pulled back and stared at the other women, her brows up. "I see I wasn't the only one with that notion. The battalion has arrived in full force."

Eva scowled. Who knew she was so incompetent and helpless? "Clearly I am much in need of assistance."

She introduced everyone, leaving out her sisterly connection to Noelle and her sister's title. Proper decorum kept the former courtesans from questioning Noelle's unexpected arrival.

"We are Miss Eva's students," Rose broke in. She smiled prettily. "She is turning us from mistresses into wives."

Eva winced, wishing Rose had kept the information about the school to herself. Noelle knew too much about her already.

"None of us want to be courtesans anymore," Abigail chimed in, looking at Noelle, then down at her booted feet. "We cannot wait until the party next week, when we can find husbands!"

"I see," Noelle responded, with an ironic look at Eva. "An interesting profession you have, my dear."

All eyes on her, Eva shifted from foot to foot. She hadn't expected her sister and courtesans ever to meet. This had the makings of a disaster.

It was Noelle who came to her rescue with a quick change

of topic. "Now that we have gathered the army together," she said, "we must plot our troop movements. The enemy will be more numerous and better armed. We must use cunning and wits if this battle is to be successful and the prize captured."

At the upward cock of Eva's brow, Noelle grinned and shrugged. "I was once courted by a major."

Eva realized right then that she couldn't have chosen anyone better to plunge into this madcap and possibly fatal adventure with her than Noelle with her steel will and fearlessness.

She reached out and took Noelle's hand. They locked eyes, and no further words needed to be said. They would watch over each other, two sisters against a common enemy.

Drawing in a deep breath, Eva reached her other hand toward Sophie, and soon they all stood hand in hand in a crude circle. They drew on each other for strength.

"I know we believe Yvette is alive and we will be able to save her, but we must be prepared for the possibility that she may have perished." Eva hated to say such a dismal thing aloud, but as the leader of this ragtag band, she had to be truthful and courageous.

"We cannot storm the abbey and go right up to the door," she continued. "The earl is an evil man. We must get in and out of the abbey with stealth, without raising an alarm."

"Imagine his face when he discovers Yvette gone," Rose said with a giggle. Her blue eyes danced. "'Tis unfortunate we cannot geld him before we leave."

"No gelding," Eva said. She needed to speak with Rose about her often expressed desire to geld men. It would certainly not endear her to her husband. "He has a house full of servants, and we'll be outnumbered. He must not know he's been robbed until he discovers the treasure gone in the morning. By then, we'll be well away from here."

"And he will be free to torment another woman without suffering a single negative consequence for his behavior,"

Abigail said, her voice strained. "It is a grave injustice when a man like that can do as he wishes and not suffer for it."

"It *is* an injustice, Abigail," Noelle said. "That is why Eva helps her courtesans leave unhappy situations and why we will help Yvette. Clearly the earl is obsessed with your friend. That has kept her alive. It will be a small, if not appropriate, punishment once she's been taken from him forever."

Eva took a moment to ponder the comment. She hadn't looked at it that way. "Noelle is correct. Though the mad lord will likely never face true justice, he'll lose Yvette. I vow to take some satisfaction in that knowledge."

"I shall also," Abigail said. "Reluctantly."

"I still think we should have brought Harold," Rose interjected with an evil grin. "He could have gelded him easy."

Pauline snickered and swung out a foot to gently nudge Rose in the leg. Rose kicked back at her. Pauline narrowed her lids and frowned fiendishly. "For such an innocent face, you, dear Rose, have a very wicked mind."

Rose shrugged and released Eva's and Pauline's hands to tuck a loose bit of bright red hair under her cap. "My mum and her lecherous husband taught me not to trust anyone and to do what was needed to survive. If that includes having a bit of sport at the expense of men and their family baubles, well, I will not apologize."

Eva grinned at the image. Perhaps letting Rose geld the mad lord wasn't such an unwelcome idea. He deserved harsh punishment, and gelding would leave him unable to abuse women sexually in the future.

"If the need should arise tonight and the earl needs punishing, I promise it will be you, Rose, wielding the knife." Eva waited until the uneasy giggles passed. "Now let us get to business. We have a battle to plan."

Chapter Seventeen

Sophie and Rose managed to find breeches, shirts, and boots for Noelle and Eva. Eva didn't ask them for details as she pulled on the too-large boots and laced them tight. Their crimes were piling up, and by the end of the evening, there'd be more. Tomorrow, she'd make sure all the borrowed garments were returned.

Eva left the spectacles behind but kept her wig in place. The courtesans didn't know her any other way, and her bright hair could draw unwelcome interest.

"We will look for a way to sneak into the abbey and up the stairs," Eva said. "Mister Crawford learned the woman, whom we assume is Yvette, is hidden somewhere on the second floor. We must pray the earl is a deep sleeper."

"Caution is the only way to keep from getting caught." Noelle stood. With her hair secured in a tight knot, she could almost be taken for a young man at a distance and in poor light. Truthfully, none of them could bear close scrutiny. There were too many curves to be masked effectively with their simple disguises.

Eva shivered. She wanted to gather up her sister and courtesans and take the morning coach out of the village. They were all in danger because of her, and she was sick with fear. If any one of them was hurt, she'd never forgive herself. But the choice was theirs, and she could not squelch their desire to help Yvette.

She walked to door. "Ready?"

The abbey wasn't far, but in the dark, and with dread growing with each step, the walk seemed to stretch for an eternity. Each rustle of damp, musty leaves or the call of some night creature had Abigail's and Rose's knees knocking with fright. Even Eva, who normally wasn't fearful after nightfall, startled a few times when a rustle came close.

The tension built to a level where they were all seeing shadowy figures behind every tree or bush. When the spire of the abbey finally came into view under a thin slip of the moon, Eva's body went limp with relief.

"Do you think he has dogs?" Sophie whispered.

"Let us hope not," Noelle replied.

They fell silent, listening for hounds. When no baying was heard, Eva led them cautiously up the drive. Once they passed the last stand of trees, the abbey came into full view.

"It is beautiful," Pauline said, and crossed herself.

The place was a monolith of stone and stood three stories tall; three very tall stories, with several wings added sometime after the original structure had been completed. It had housed a rectory and convent when it was built late in the fifteenth century. Some two hundred years ago it had been converted into a private residence.

"Goodness," Rose gasped, "we'll never find Yvette in there."

"Have faith, ladies," Eva whispered. It was just after midnight, and the household was asleep. Not a single candle glowed in a window. She took it as a sign of good fortune. "Since we are six, we'll break into pairs, and each couple will search a section of the abbey. I'll take Abigail,

Noelle with Rose, and Sophie with Pauline. If there is any sign whatsoever of danger, you must leave the abbey at once and return to the inn."

Five heads nodded. Eva took a moment to summon up a few threads of courage. Looking at her band of miscreants, she felt a rush of affection. She wanted to hug each one tightly until their ribs bowed. Instead, she said a silent prayer for their safety.

Rose and Abigail were the most skittish of the six, and Eva knew she and Noelle would have a calming influence over the two women. "At a time such as this, there is no place for panic," she said firmly. "If anyone wishes to wait here, please say so now. Once we're inside the abbey, it will be too dangerous to flee in hysterics."

Even in the dim light, Eva saw shadows of hesitation on the faces of Abigail, Pauline, and Rose. But they nodded anyway. They had come together, and they would conquer together. And the mad earl be damned.

"Stay close." Eva led them silently to the back of the abbey, keeping near to the walls and their shadows. Eva and Noelle searched for, and eventually found, a small unlocked door where one of the wings was cobbled together with the original structure.

Where the door led to was a question. Built in a time of unrest, many old buildings had secret doors and passageways in which to flee marauders. Eva eased open the door and slipped cautiously inside; the room was clearly the kitchen. After taking a moment to listen for anyone moving in the dark, she waved for the women to join her.

The courtesans huddled together for comfort. Eva peered from face to face. She knew one squeak of a door or creak of a floorboard, and at least half of her army would flee as if their borrowed clothes were afire.

Eva drew Noelle aside. "I'm beginning to have reservations, sister. I think we might want to leave Rose and Abigail outside. They are jittery and on the verge of going to pieces. Any screams will wake the household and we'll be caught."

Noelle looked over Eva's shoulder and screwed up her face. "I believe you have a point. Perhaps we should leave them to keep watch outside. They can shout if they see anything untoward."

They returned to the women. The suggestion had barely left Eva's mouth when Abigail and Rose fled through the open door.

Down to four rescuers, Eva paired herself with Sophie and Pauline with Noelle. The four women joined hands, said a brief whispered prayer, and separated. Noelle and Pauline took the servants' stairs in the kitchen, and Eva and Sophie walked quietly into the hallway as the moon moved from behind the clouds and cast light through stained glass windows.

Their gasps were muffled behind gloved hands. It truly was an abbey. The high, rounded ceiling ran the length of the massive hall that had what Eva guessed was a floor formed of bits of colored glass patterned in a mosaic. Columns lined the open room that once had likely held rows of pews and an altar at the far end.

Highland Abbey was a treasure. Eva leaned to whisper to Sophie, "It is impossible to believe such a vile man owns such a sacred and beautiful home. The angels must be weeping from the sheer injustice of it all."

The hall was eerily quiet and nearly as black as pitch when the moon returned to its hiding place. Eva was certain that were they to listen closely, the whispers of spirits of long-dead occupants could be heard behind the columns and in the shadows.

She shook her head to clear it. "We must go quickly," she said softly.

It took several false starts to find a staircase. They stopped on the second-floor landing to get their bearings. On the left side were doors, and on the right side several narrow balconies overlooked the open hall. She and Sophie went to the balcony rail and took a brief peek at the expansive hall below.

"I think the kitchen stairs lead to the south side of the abbey, so we shall start here." Eva looked down the hall and counted doors. There looked to be a full dozen. "It's impossible to know which one is His Lordship's room."

"Look for a glow under the door," Sophie said softly. "On this chill night he will have a fire."

Eva expelled a quick breath. "Excellent."

Sophie's face broke into a grin. "I am quite used to sneaking about in the dark. My first lover installed me as a maid in his manor. He found it exciting to romp with me in his library, knowing his wife was one floor above."

Shaking her head disdainfully, Eva tried to imagine herself dusting the mantel during the day at Collingwood House and frolicking with His Grace in the pantry at night while Lucy slept innocently in their marital bed.

She would never allow it. She could never share Nicholas. If he had a duchess, she vowed, he wouldn't have her.

"We will have to check them all." Eva and Sophie began the task of opening the door of each room in turn. Every rusty hinge and creaking floorboard caused heart stoppage. Yet no alarm sounded in the darkness.

Most of the rooms were dark except for moonlight coming through the narrow windows. One had a glow under the door, but when they cracked open the panel for a peek, they found a middle-aged man and woman sleeping in the bed, emitting a pair of muffled snores.

By the time they reached the end of the hallway, Eva's muscles ached from the strain of tiptoeing about. Ice ran through her veins, and her hands and toes were stiff. She closed the last door and turned to Sophie. "Yvette can be anywhere or nowhere at all. There is certainly a cellar, and many outbuildings, too. We could search all night and still not discover every secret nook and hidden room."

Sophie matched her low tone. "Perhaps Noelle and Pauline have had better luck."

The two women followed the railing around to the south wing and listened for signs of the other women. There wasn't a single glow under any door, and Eva wondered if the earl was away. "It is possible he's spirited Yvette off, if he has held her at all," she said tightly. "The woman rumored to be hidden here could've been someone else."

"Wait, I hear something." Sophie pointed down the hallway. Hushed voices drifted around them. They clasped hands and carefully took a few steps. The fevered whispers grew louder. It took a moment for Eva to recognize Noelle's voice coming from behind a closed door.

"Noelle?" The two voices went silent. Then the door was eased open and Noelle's pale face peered out.

"Eva, thank goodness. We think we found her." She pulled Eva and Sophie inside the room and closed and locked the door. Noelle hurried toward the fireplace, and the others followed. She pointed to a panel on the left side of the stone hearth that was almost unnoticeably different textured wood than the other panels. "We heard a noise coming from here and a shuffle of what we think were feet. We think this is a hidden door."

"Could it be rats?" Eva asked as she tapped the panel. A small squeak sounded, like no rat she'd ever heard. She pressed her ear against the wood. "Yvette?"

A whimper followed. "Yvette!" Eva whispered sharply. "Tap twice if you are well."

Two taps. Sophie and Pauline fell into each other's arms and rocked happily back and forth. Eva felt around for a lock. But when she did find an indentation in the door and a lock, her joy was tempered. No amount of manipulating her fingertips around the metal loosened its locking mechanism.

"Ladies, we need to find a key."

Four pairs of hands began a frantic search of the room.

Pauline almost upended a vase, catching it just before it could hit the floor. She smiled sheepishly.

Eva pressed her ear to the door. She thought she heard muffled weeping. "Stay calm, Yvette, we'll get you out."

"There is nothing," Noelle whispered.

"There has to be a key," Eva hissed. She checked the mantel and the hearth. Nothing. "We cannot break the door down."

"Wait, I might be able to help." Sophie pulled off her cap and removed several pins from her hair. "My father was a thief. He taught me how to open locks when I was a child. I haven't had to use the skill for many years."

Eva, Noelle, and Pauline stared. Sophie smiled wryly and shrugged. "If you don't match me with a husband, I can always turn to thievery."

Pauline bit back a snort as Sophie turned to the panel and dropped to her knees. Eva watched intently. Her courtesans were full of surprises.

"Have you ever opened a lock in the dark?" Eva asked.

"I used to be able to open them blindfolded. But it's been almost twenty years since he died." Sophie examined the lock for a moment with her fingertips, then went to work. "I hope I can remember his teaching."

"Do your best," Noelle urged.

Pauline and Noelle clasped hands as the muted sounds of the hairpins against metal filled the silence. Eva knew it would be a miracle if this worked, but she had faith that someone was watching over them.

It took several unsuccessful attempts before a click finally resonated in the small room and Sophie jumped to her feet. "I did it," she said softly, and looked skyward. "Thank you, Papa."

With Eva's help, they swung the door wide.

Tied to a chair against a wall and wearing only a thin chemise and a pair of stockings, Yvette cried silent tears.

Her mouth was wrapped with cloth, and she struggled against her bonds.

Eva rushed to her and knelt at her feet. "Quiet, now. We will get you free." She started to free one of Yvette's feet while Noelle and Sophie worked on her hands. Pauline hugged Yvette's neck gently for a second, then unwrapped the cloth around her mouth. In minutes she was free. She wobbled as Eva, Pauline, and Sophie eased her to her feet. They held her in a tight embrace while Noelle watched the happy reunion.

"We're so happy to see you," Eva whispered as tears ran down her face. She held Yvette by the arms when she swayed, and peered into her red eyes. "We were so worried."

Sophie and Pauline pulled back to allow Yvette to breathe and give Eva a brief chance to check her over. There were no outward signs of injury, but some scars were impossible to see. There was no telling the level of mistreatment she'd been subjected to.

Traumatized, Yvette sobbed. "Thank you for coming for me, Miss Eva. All of you."

Of all of Eva's students, Yvette had been the most difficult to warm to. But over their weeks together, the hardened courtesan had broken down some of her protective walls and allowed Eva to see a hint of vulnerability. Just before her kidnapping she and Eva had built a tenuous companionship. She hoped it would continue.

Eva touched her face. "We had to come," she said, then hugged Yvette again. They held each other tight.

Finally Noelle touched Eva on the shoulder. "We must leave this reunion for later. It's best if we get out of the abbey quickly, before we are discovered."

With Eva on her left and Sophie on her right, Yvette was helped out of the room and into the hallway.

"The tight bindings caused my feet to numb," Yvette murmured. "I feel tingles now. Give me a moment and I should be able to stand unaided."

Helped along, Yvette gradually stood more firmly on her

feet. They had nearly reached the end of the hall when the light of a candle pierced the darkness behind them. The five women came to an abrupt stop and spun around as a man came around the corner.

The stranger holding the candle froze. "What is this?" His angry face glowed demonically in the flickering light. He seemed as outraged to see them huddled in the hallway as they were shocked to see him wearing nothing but a pair of breeches and boots below a stark white belly.

Yvette moaned. "'Tis His Lordship."

Eva was the first to recover. "Run!" She and Sophie turned Yvette, and they hobble-carried her toward the staircase.

"Stop," the earl roared. Booted footsteps pounded behind them at a full run. They heard a clatter and then his candle went out. Harsh swearing followed. Without a candle, he was momentarily blinded by the darkness.

Yvette hung heavy between them, but Eva barely felt her weight. Abject terror gripped her, and she could focus on nothing but the sound of His Lordship in pursuit and their group reaching freedom.

"Faster," Eva cried, and Sophie grabbed for the rail as they tripped down the first few steps. Pauline tangled her fingers in the back of Eva's shirt as Noelle grabbed Sophie's waistband to keep them from falling. "Almost there!"

Pauline cried out as they took the bottom step and stumbled from the staircase into the great hall. The earl was steps behind, and closing in.

Eva spun to get her bearings, and gasped when she ran into something large.

Nicholas's hard eyes stared down at her.

"Nicholas!"

No time for questions. He reached for Sophie, and pushed her and Yvette in the direction of the kitchen. Noelle and Pauline ran after them. He grabbed Eva by the hand and pulled her after the women as the earl took the last stair and stumbled to a halt.

The earl shouted a name, and a voice answered from somewhere within the immense hall. Eva sped beside His Grace. She caught sight of the women running through the open kitchen door and outside. Nicholas slowed as they rushed onto the lawn. They paused to look for the rest of the women, which gave the earl just enough time to catch them. Nicholas spun around to face their adversary, abruptly releasing Eva.

The earl squinted at Nicholas, his breath harsh and his rage clear. "I know you." He took a step closer. "Stanfield?"

"Maddington."

Though Nicholas was taller by a hand, the earl outweighed him by a good two stone, most of it around his midsection. The mad lord stood to his full height, closed his fists, and demanded, "Give me back Yvette, and we will forget you broke into my home."

"She is now under my protection." Nicholas reached out to block Eva when she jumped forward, sputtering in outrage. "And there she will stay."

Eva went weak with relief. She wasn't sure how Nicholas had come to be there or what his intentions toward her were, but clearly he had come for her and to save Yvette.

Thankfully, the earl had no power to take Yvette back. Lord Maddington was a mouse in comparison to the strength and power of her duke. Love welled in her heart for her gallant knight.

"You intend to pull rank, Your Grace?" the earl sneered. "I am well within my rights to have you shot. How was I to know the thief was a peer?" Maddington glanced at Eva. His tongue touched his bottom lip. "It will be my pleasure to teach the wench not to cross me."

A low growl rumbled from inside Nicholas, and he launched himself at the earl. A *woof* was expelled from the earl's lungs as His Grace caught him in his flabby stomach with his shoulder, and the two men fell to the ground.

Nicholas gained his feet first and punched Maddington

in the chin as he rose. Maddington stumbled back, shook his head, and charged.

The fight was violent and brutal. Fists connected with alarming accuracy and speed. Eva was only partially aware of Noelle's hand on her arm as she and Sophie ran out of the darkness to watch the fray. Nicholas took a blow to the face and returned a punch of his own to the earl's stomach. The man doubled over, and staggered back.

Nicholas grabbed him by the arm and raised his fist. A shot rang out, and Nicholas lurched backward. He just managed to keep his footing, and jerked the earl upright as a second shot pierced the night. The earl gasped and went limp. Nicholas released him, and Maddington crumpled to the ground.

Eva looked toward movement beneath a tree and saw a footman staring wide-eyed at the bloodshed and the earl lying lifeless at Nicholas's feet. He let out a low moan, dropped a pair of pistols, and ran.

"Nicholas!" Eva ran to him in time to keep him from falling. A dark stain spread beneath his coat. "Oh, Nicholas!"

Someone came running toward them.

"Get to the coach," Harold commanded, and Noelle and Sophie rushed away. He went to Eva and gently pulled her aside as Nicolas's eyes began to roll back. Grabbing Nicholas about the knees, he hoisted him up and settled him over his wide shoulder. He didn't waver under Nicholas's lifeless weight.

Eva ran her hand over her lover's dark head, tears scorching her cheeks. She loved him, and now she might lose him.

"Please don't let him die, Harold," she begged.

Chapter Eighteen

Harold carried His Grace to the waiting carriage. Eva and Noelle helped him get the injured duke inside, where the other women huddled together in the cramped quarters. All eyes were wide with fear over the terrifying way the rescue had ended. Yvette wept quietly in Sophie's arms.

The mad earl was dead. He'd been killed, accidentally, by one of his own footmen who was attempting to murder Nicholas. Knowing Lord Maddington wasn't alive to take revenge offered little comfort to Eva at the moment. She lifted Nicholas's feet to put them on the seat, and felt his dead weight. His shallow breathing kept her from full despair. He was alive, but for how long?

She stifled tears. His face was so pale. If he died, it would be her fault. If only he'd stayed in London and left her to save Yvette alone.

When Nicholas was settled on the seat, Eva dropped to her knees and opened his coat for a better look at the wound. The moonlight clearly revealed that he was losing a great deal of blood.

"Oh, dear." Abigail fanned her cheeks with her hands.

"If you faint, Abigail, I'll shove you out of the carriage," Noelle snapped. Abigail shot her a dark glare. "Eva and her duke need us to be strong."

"Duke?" Abigail's voice was a tight squeak. "We were rescued by a duke?" Muffled whispers followed. Eva paid them no heed. She'd pressed her hand over the wound, and blood was seeping through her fingers. Harold ripped open Nicholas's shirt in order to examine the bullet hole more closely. The ragged edges of the wound brought gasps.

"He is bleeding to death," Eva cried as Harold knelt beside her. "He needs a doctor."

"Steady, Eva. Hysterics will not help your man." Harold gently probed the area. "Take off his cravat," he said as he pressed his hand to the wound. "We need to stop the blood loss. We'll worry about the bullet later."

Eva quickly removed the cravat and handed it to Harold. He folded the cloth tightly and pressed it against the wound. "Reach behind him and see if the bullet went through." She slipped her hand under his body and felt around with her fingertips. There was no blood.

"I feel nothing." Her voice caught. Nicholas was so strong and invincible. It terrified her to think she might lose him. "The bullet must still be inside."

Harold silently packed the wound, tearing off parts of Nicholas's shirt as he did so. The bandaging was crude but serviceable. They couldn't go back inside the abbey for help. Not with the earl lying dead on the lawn.

A hand reached out to touch her head. It took Eva a moment to realize the hand belonged to His Grace. She lifted her eyes and scanned his face in the moonlight. Her heart leapt. His eyes were closed, but the corners of his mouth twitched. "I despise that wig."

Eva laugh-cried and pulled it from her head. Her hair tumbled about her shoulders and over his hand in a tangled mass. Whispers rose again. The courtesans had never seen her without her disguise. "I will burn it tomorrow, I swear it."

A sob broke from her throat as he wove his fingers through her hair and coughed. She cupped his free hand to her face and kissed his palm, wetting it with her tears.

"No time to crumble, love. I need my feisty spinster now." Nicholas opened his lids slightly, and her chest tightened. The light in his intense eyes had dimmed. It was a very bad sign. "Where is Maddington?"

"Dead," Harold said. A dog bayed in the distance, and Harold's movements quickened. The entire household must have been roused by the shots. Confusion would give them a few precious minutes to make certain Nicholas was out of immediate danger.

Nicholas nodded. His hand slid from her hair. "If I survive this, I'll thank the footman."

Eva cupped his face. His skin felt cool to the touch. "You will survive. I'll not have it otherwise." She leaned forward and placed a soft kiss on his slightly parted lips. "My revenge for your insufferable behavior is not yet complete. I still have a list of tortures to heap upon your arrogant head."

A slow smile crinkled the corners of his eyes. "Then I shall look forward to many years of suffering ahead, madam."

He slumped back on the squabs and his eyes closed. Eva whimpered and reached to press her fingertips to his neck. Her body felt drained of blood until her fingers found his pulse.

"Keep the cravat tightly pressed to the wound," Harold said, and stepped quickly out the door of the coach. "I need to get us safely away."

A shout came from somewhere in the darkness. Searchers must be scrambling to look for the earl's killer. The household would be in a panic. The coach rocked as Harold climbed into the driver's seat and called to the horses. The coach jerked, sending Eva onto her rump as the women huddled tightly together on one seat. She quickly returned to her knees and positioned herself to put pressure on Nicholas's wound.

"He is a strong man, Eva," Noelle said, and reached out to put a comforting hand on her arm. "He will fight for himself and for you."

Tears began anew. Eva felt warm rivulets trickle down her cheeks. "I cannot live without him, Noelle. I love him."

Noelle climbed down beside her and placed an arm around her shoulders. "I know you do, dearest." She placed a hand over Eva's, and the two of them held the bandages tight. "We will fight for him together, sister."

A sharp intake of breath came from behind them, followed by speculative murmurs. Discovering their Miss Black was not only in disguise but also kin to Noelle came as a shock to the courtesans. Another of Eva's secrets was exposed.

At the moment she didn't care. Once Nicholas was under a doctor's care, she could sort all this out.

They passed through the trees and onto the road. Moonlight flooded the coach. Seconds later Sophie gasped. "I know him. He is His Grace, the Duke of Stanfield. I have seen him riding in the park."

Eva knew she could not take her secrets back. Her courtesans were too bright to accept weak lies. Before she could untwist the muddle in her mind and find a reasonable explanation, Noelle turned her head.

"Miss Eva is my sister," Noelle snapped. "I'm Lady Noelle Seymour. We have just recently become acquainted. His Grace and my sister are, uh, friends. So I ask that you kindly stop your infernal speculation until he is safe and cared for."

The coach fell silent except for the squeaks and groans

of its wild flight and Harold's calls to the horses. It seemed like hours before they finally came to a stop. Eva's legs were numb from crouching, and her hands tingled where they pressed against the wound. Harold clambered down and jerked open the door. For a moment she saw the light of a single lamp outside a large house before Harold climbed into the carriage.

"Where are we?" Eva asked.

"We'll have time later for explanations." Harold bent and lifted Nicholas off the seat. It took Eva, Noelle, and Harold some awkward maneuvering to get the duke out of the coach and over Harold's shoulder. An old man in a nightshirt, cap, and thick spectacles squinted in the lamplight as everyone tumbled out of the coach.

"My Lord?"

Harold brushed past him. "Send for a doctor." The women rushed to keep up as Harold headed for a wide staircase. Eva couldn't register anything more than that the house seemed somewhat worn as she kept in step behind her servant. All she could hope was that the owners of the manor house would not refuse to help the nine strangers who had arrived on their doorstep.

Harold paused briefly at the top of the stairs, then turned right and headed for a room at the end of the hallway. He kicked the door open, carried Nicholas to the bed, and eased him onto the blue coverlet. The old servant appeared in the doorway and impatiently brushed past the clutch of women.

"I sent for the doctor, and rooms have been opened for your guests, My Lord." He peered over his shoulder at the young women dressed as men, and blinked. "Shall I escort the, um, ladies to their rooms?"

"Thank you, Edgar, and see that they are fed." Harold turned back to Nicholas and began to remove his shirt. "Bring me water and something for bandages."

"Yes, My Lord."

"My Lord?" Eva stared at Harold. It was the third time he had been addressed that way. He carefully avoided her eyes as he ripped away the bandages to expose the wound. She joined Harold on the bed.

"The man is clearly feeble of mind," he said tightly.

Eva had no time to press. Caring for Nicholas had become her focus. She and Harold cleaned away the blood. The bleeding had slowed to a trickle as it dried around the wound. Somewhere in her exhausted mind she registered the sound of a boy's voice advising Harold that the doctor was attending a difficult birth and would be delayed indefinitely.

Harold nodded grimly and dismissed the lad. He returned to the bed, his face tight. "We will have to remove the bullet ourselves."

Eva shook her head. "I'll not have His Grace die during a botched surgery I helped perform. There has to be another doctor." She probed the wound and felt the bullet below the skin. Thank God it hadn't gone deeper.

Harold stared into her face. "There is no one." He dipped the bloody cloth into the basin. "Do you trust me, Eva?" She paused for only a blink, then nodded slowly. He was one of the two people she trusted completely. "Then let us get this bullet out."

Working with quiet efficiency, Harold dug the bullet from the flesh just below Nicholas's rib cage. The duke thrashed on the bed in his delirium but did not regain consciousness. Harold then stepped back while Eva closed the wound with tiny stitches. When the duke was finally bandaged and settled beneath the coverlet, she slumped in the chair, her face in her hands.

Harold slipped quietly from the room.

Nearly two hours later, Nicholas stirred. Eva rose from the chair to place her hand on his head. So far fever had remained at bay. Infection was always a worry despite Harold's skilled bullet removal. She sat beside Nicholas and took his hand. His eyes flickered open.

"Your Grace?" she brushed his hair back from his eyes and scanned his beloved face. He was pale, yet some color was returning to his cheeks. His lower lip was slightly swollen, and several black-and-blue smudges resembling the shape of knuckles rimmed his right eye. "Can you hear me?"

"I feel like I've been kicked by a mule," he rasped, brushing his hand over his ribs. He grimaced. "Did you allow a butcher to tend me?"

Eva smiled. "It was Harold. He took the bullet out."

He snorted, "Doubtless, with a dull, rusty blade." Nicholas shifted weakly and straightened his legs. Eva helped him into a more comfortable position, then tucked another blanket around him. "I should thank him for not burying the blade in my belly."

"You should." She brushed hair out of his eyes. "He did a fine job. I think he has warmed to you."

One eyelid dropped closed as he peered sidelong at her. "Warmed may be overstating his feelings. I would settle for no longer wanting to snap my neck."

With a shrug, Eva rubbed gooseflesh on her arms. She tried to ignore the rush of affection in her heart and to remain stoic. Now that he was safe, she pulled back, intending to shield herself from further hurt. Nothing had truly changed between them. Love couldn't close the chasm separating them.

"He is very protective, and you were a beast. Forcing me into your bed! Did you expect him to invite you to billiards and conversation like you were old friends?"

"Touché, love." His hand snaked out and closed over her thigh. A shiver thrilled up her leg. The warmth in his eyes set her heart beating erratically. Clearly the bullet wound hadn't dampened his ardor. "I was not at my best."

She kept her eyes carefully averted from his lower extremities, thankful the coverlet hid his nakedness. She wasn't certain if she could withstand the sight of him without his clothes. It had been days since he'd touched her, and she ached to be in his arms.

"If you don't mind riding atop, you are welcome to join me in love play, sweet." Eva startled, and realized he must have seen the raw hunger in her eyes. Warmth crept across her face. "I'd not push you away."

It took all her strength not to do as he asked. Every emotion, every part of her wanted to throw aside caution and give herself fully—mind, body, and soul—to him. But there was still the matter of her future.

He'd become her joy, and she struggled under its weight. There were limits to what part she could play in his life, and she wasn't happy with the restrictions. So she ignored the comment and changed the topic.

"You are a hero, Your Grace." She stood and returned to the chair. She locked her hands together to stop their trembling. "If not for your timely intervention, the earl would have captured or killed us all."

"It was you I was worried about. When your man Harold came looking for you, I knew immediately that you'd ignored my wishes and gone to mount a rescue. Stubborn chit!" He scowled. "We came straightaway. I left Harold to guard the coach. I've been inside the abbey several times for house parties and knew I could find my way in the darkness. He would have slowed my progress."

"Harold must have balked at your orders."

Nicholas grinned and yawned. "The wishes of a duke trump those of a servant."

Eva sighed. "I am positive you played the card well." She could imagine the two men chest to chest, huffing and braying for the highest rung on the ladder. But there was nothing Harold could do against the duke. He would've been very angry to be left behind.

"I am very happy I did." Nicholas plucked at the bandage. "He saved my life. If anyone deserves our thanks, it is Harold."

For saving Nicholas, Eva would be forever grateful to Harold. He had proven his loyalty and friendship when she needed him most.

"Well, I'm happy you'll survive to return to London, marry Lucy, and have a dozen children. And I will match my courtesans and become a very stiff and dour old spinster as I ease into my dotage." Not even the lightness in her tone could ease the depths of her sadness. She wanted to curl up in a corner and cry. "Complete with a horrid wig and spectacles."

"I fear your plans will not come to fruition, love," Nicholas said. "I see no lonely spinsterhood in your future. Nor do I intend to wed Lucy. Not now, not ever."

Eva stared.

"I've decided my future lies with a certain fiery courtesan with beautiful amber eyes and hair that drives me mad with desire," he continued unabated. "She is the only woman who will be sharing my bed from this day forward."

His words made no sense. "Clearly you are suffering the ill effects of your injury. You are required, not by law, certainly, but by an ancient code, to wed a woman of impeccable breeding and to father children of pure bloodlines. I am not that woman." She drew back and set her chin at a stubborn angle. "There are too many bastards in this world already. As one myself, I will not bring forth any others."

Nicholas snorted. "Have I asked you to bear my bastards, my dearest Evangeline?"

"You have vowed we will continue to share a bed." She crossed her arms tightly over her chest. "Unless I prove to be barren, the chances are very high you will eventually plant a fertile seed inside me." Her cheeks warmed. "I will not have my child live the fatherless life I've lived."

"I may have already done the deed." He dipped his gaze to her stomach. "I did not take my normal precautions."

She shook her head firmly. "I do not carry your child."

Settling his green eyes on her, he scratched around the bandage with a finger. He grimaced from the movement.

"You are entirely too stubborn for your own good. I cannot believe that after growing up with my father and watching my mother suffer for her love, I have allowed you to capture my heart." He smiled softly. "I want you to be my wife, Eva."

Had the chair not been beneath her rump, she would have fallen into a heap on the floor. "Your wife?" she squeaked. "You are clearly delirious from blood loss. I cannot wed you. I'm the bastard daughter of a courtesan. I have lived my life hiding that fact and saving courtesans from my mother's fate. I cannot be a duchess. It would be scandalous."

Annoyance tightened his mouth. "I care not where you came from or who your parents were."

Eva jumped to her feet with a cry. "I care. Society cares. Once the gossips learn who my mother is, they will rip us both apart and push Mother into a darkness she can never escape." She backed away and pressed her clasped hands to her mouth. "We will not mention this again, Your Grace. Ever."

With that, she raced from the room.

Nicholas listened to Eva's retreating steps through the open door, his ire rising with each footfall. He'd finally come to the conclusion that he loved her and wanted to wed her, and she'd rejected him most soundly.

The woman was indeed stubborn down to her perfect toes. Shaking her until her teeth rattled wasn't an option in his weakened condition. Neither was dragging her off to Gretna Green and forcing a marriage. Knowing Eva as he did, forcing her to do anything usually didn't end well. She was entirely too independent. And he loved her for that, and all the other aspects of her character he'd once found trying.

"Your Grace?"

He looked up and saw Eva's sister standing hesitantly in the doorway. She was lovely in yellow, though the dress had seen better times. If he had a lick of sense, he'd offer for her instead. Lady Seymour had grown up in privilege and wouldn't balk at becoming a duchess. She could keep his home and entertain guests and bear him loads of children.

Unfortunately, she wasn't Eva. There was only one Eva.

"Enter," he grumbled. She walked across the room and took the recently vacated chair, perching uncomfortably on the edge.

"How are you feeling, Your Grace?"

"As well as can be expected after being shot by a footman, then carved up by a butcher," he grumbled. His mood was darkening by the minute. "I am lucky to be breathing."

Lady Seymour bit her twitching lips, clearly to smother a smug smile. "Harold did a fine job of patching you up, Your Grace. You should be grateful."

At the moment he felt anything but grateful. Surly, yes. Aggrieved, certainly. In pain, most definitely. The last thing he wanted was to launch into a string of idle chatter with this near stranger, not when stewing over Eva was the one thing he wanted to do most, alone. "What is it you want, Lady Seymour?"

Amusement finally flickered across her face. "I want you to marry my sister."

He stilled. This was an interesting turn. The woman was a curiosity. If he wed Eva, it would be difficult to keep the true nature of the sisters' relationship secret. Gossip had flared over Eva's appearance at the ball and hadn't waned with her just as sudden disappearance. If she became his duchess, the scrutiny would be intense.

For the first time he could see Eva's concerns through his own eyes. It was no wonder she balked at his proposal.

"Why should I marry your sister?"

"Because you love her."

The statement nearly took him off the bed. He raked his gaze over her face. Had his feelings been so clear to everyone but himself?

She continued, "And because you took her innocence, and she might well be carrying your child. Because in spite of your father's reputation, you are a man of character, though you tarnished it when you seduced Eva. Because she is warm and loving and wonderful, and you could do no better than to make her your duchess."

He cocked a brow and hid his amusement. "Are you always so forthright, Lady Seymour?"

She smiled. "It is my most endearing trait."

Nicholas chuckled. "I agree with the part about Eva making a fine duchess, and I do love her. And just to be clear, I asked for her hand and she refused me. She is fiercely protective of her mother. She believes our marriage would harm Charlotte."

Lady Seymour slumped back in the chair. "That is certainly a concern. Gossips do like to dig up dark family secrets and bandy them about. Charlotte is in no condition to have her past exposed. Eva is right to be worried."

They sat silent for a moment. "There has to be a way to solve this issue," Lady Seymour said. "I know you and Eva are meant to be together. It will shatter her heart to lose you."

"It will do me no better." Was it possible Noelle was right, and Eva did love him? She'd given him no sign she felt anything more than desire. If she loved him, it would certainly change everything. "I will find a way to assuage her fears."

A satisfied smile lit her face. "I have faith, Your Grace." She winked, then left him to ponder the situation.

With Charlotte at risk, he needed to protect her and still wed Eva. The years ahead of him would be empty and dark without her. He loved his courtesan-spinster.

He'd do anything to have her. Anything.

Chapter Nineteen

Eva brushed aside her tears and splashed tepid water on her face. All her life she'd known she'd never marry or be a mother. It was impossible when she had so many secrets to keep. Now the man she loved wanted to give her a family of her own, and she'd had to refuse him, though he knew everything about her. And didn't care.

Had he been born to a bookkeeper or a farmer and lived a quiet life, she'd have eagerly accepted his proposal. But a duke? Not only was Nicholas a duke, but a member of a powerful family and subjected to constant scrutiny from society.

Not even his scandalous father could keep the Ton from embracing his son and widow to their ample bosom as if they were royalty. But a courtesan's daughter was another scandal entirely. There were some lines one didn't step over, and this was one of them. Her mother was considered a whore, though she'd had but one lover. Her daughter could not become a duchess.

She'd be shunned, her mother would be exposed, and

Noelle and the phantom Margaret would be ostracized. A bastard sister was not unexpected, the way noblemen planted their seed far and wide. However, one didn't drag her from the shadows and parade her at a society ball.

Eva released a shaky sigh and left her room. Nicholas needed several days to recover, and though she wanted desperately to return to London and her mother, she couldn't abandon him. He'd saved them. She owed him the loyalty of caring for him until he was well enough to travel. Then she would leave him at Collingwood House and wish him well.

The women, except Noelle and Yvette, who were resting upstairs, were gathered in a small, simple drawing room. The excited chatter silenced when Eva arrived.

They were curious, and she couldn't blame them. The previous night had been one of revelations. She would offer her explanations later. Right now, she was too weary to deal with questions.

The furnishings were limited to a settee, a table, and three chairs, and the settee and the chairs were fully occupied. The fabric of the furniture and the drapes was faded and frayed, and the papered walls had crackled with age. Overall, the house had an air of neglect, and its mustiness was that of a house long closed up.

The owner of the house remained a mystery. If a family resided here, she'd seen no sign of them. Only a few elderly servants and several spiders appeared to call this place home.

"How is the patient?" Abigail asked, worried. She wore a faded pink dress that looked as if it had been donated by a housekeeper or maid. In fact, all the women were clad in frocks of cotton or wool in faded colors and sized to fit bodies of slightly larger girth and height. The women looked as if they had found a trunk of old clothes and were playing dress up.

"He's resting," Eva said. She looked down at her borrowed trousers and shirt, stained with blood and dirt. She hadn't given her appearance a moment's thought since Nicholas was shot.

"The housekeeper, Mrs. Moore, gave us these dresses." Rose grimaced when she leaned forward and her bodice gaped to show a yellowing chemise. "She found them in the attic. There was a trunk of finer gowns, but moths had rendered them unwearable."

"The baron and his wife had a daughter who died of a fever when she was sixteen," Abigail said softly. "Mrs. Moore said the things were hers. The family was impoverished for many years due to bad investments by the baron."

"There is a dress for you in Lady Noelle's room," Sophie said. "We didn't want to disturb you with His Grace."

"I shall have to thank the baroness for her kindness. Has anyone seen her?"

"There is neither baroness nor baron." Harold strode into the room, his face a stony mask. He carried a bottle and glass in his hands, and he'd changed into breeches and a coat of blue wool that fit his pugilist's body as if they'd been custom-made. The housekeeper must have spent some time rooting through trunks to find those garments. "The baroness drowned in the lake shortly after Louise died, and the baron passed away last year in his sleep. Mrs. Moore is responsible for the clothing."

Eva watched as Harold poured a draught of what she thought was whiskey and downed it in one deep swallow. Her brows shot up. She'd never seen him imbibe spirits. The night, and the shooting, must have troubled him more than she'd imagined.

"How do you know so much about the family, Harold?" she asked. Her suspicion grew. His clothing looked new, and he'd made himself at home as if he'd been here before. A quick glance out the window at the overgrown lawn and the house's distance from the road made her realize he hadn't stumbled on the place by accident. So she implored him, "No more secrets. Please."

Their eyes met, and he was the first to look away. He poured another drink and tossed it back. "The house is mine."

Abigail let out a gasp and went pale. With a whimper, she rose to her feet and raced from the room. Harold grimaced and tensed.

"It was my family who died here." He set down the glass and went to the window. "After my sister and mother died, I became estranged from my father for several years. It was only after his death that I returned, finding the house in ruins."

The courtesans had become silent as stones. This wasn't a conversation to be had with an audience. Eva motioned them to leave, and they did so reluctantly. She was left alone with her secretive friend.

Her stomach soured. She sensed the rest of his story would end badly. For her. He was a baron who had been masquerading as a servant. She guessed his arrival on her doorstep hadn't been accidental. She had to pray he was not an escaped murderer or wanted highwayman.

"Please continue." She braced herself and focused on breathing slowly and calmly. She owed him much, and he had the right to her full attention.

He drew his hands over his head to cup the back of his neck before he finally turned to face her. His stoic mask had changed to an expression of deep regret. "After Father died, I discovered he'd left me with nothing but this property and mounting bills. After I left here, I served several years in the army, working under a physician. Mostly I drifted around, working jobs to keep myself fed. I ended up in Kent, at Bridgeton Manor, as a groom."

Eva swayed. Puzzle pieces started to snap together. Harold rushed to her side, but she shook him off. She stumbled to a chair and slumped into it. "Noelle."

"No," Harold barked sharply. "Noelle's mother."

Eva clasped her hands and put them to her mouth. Hurt filled her. "That horrid witch! I thought the Dowager had accepted what she couldn't change and had moved forward." Eva lifted her eyes and let Harold see the depth of her hurt. "You betrayed me from the beginning." Her lower lip quivered. "The one person besides my mother I trusted, and it was all a terrible ruse put together by the one person in this world who wants to see us destroyed."

"Eva"—Harold dropped to one knee before her, pain etching lines into his face—"she offered me a way to live comfortably and to return this house to a usable property. She wanted to know everything about you and Charlotte, to see if I could find a weakness she could use against you."

It felt as if the air had fled the room. Her head began to spin. "You must have had much to report." Her mouth was dry, and it was difficult to speak. "Am I to expect guards from Bedlam, Harold, to drag my mother from my home in the dead of night?"

"No. Eva, please listen." He splayed his hands. "She knows nothing. You saved me when the footpads left me for dead. I knew then that I couldn't honor my contract with Lady Seymour. You and Charlotte became my family."

Closing her eyes against tears, Eva shook her head. He had been a spy for the enemy. He could be lying still. "You could have warned me of her intentions so I could protect us. How do I know anything you say is truth?"

Harold reached to place a hand over hers. "I fed her some false information and thought it best if I stayed and watched over you and Charlotte, lest she send someone else. Lady Seymour is driven by an insane desire to punish you for being born. There was no telling the depths she'd go to in her plotting. I couldn't worry you needlessly. I thought it best to keep silent."

"And Noelle?" Eva wasn't ready to forgive him. She understood his manly desire to protect her. It was the curse of all members of his sex. "She must have known something."

"She knew nothing about her mother's betrayal." Harold looked down. "Before I left for London, she asked me for a favor: to discover your address so that she could visit you in the future. She has always been curious about you."

Noelle had told her as much.

"I was surprised when she showed up at our door," Harold said. "It took much convincing for her to accept that I was there for a good reason. Once she discovered her mother's involvement, she quickly agreed to keep mum and allow me to continue as your protector. We both feared you would release me from your employment if you discovered the truth. Then you'd be left unprotected."

Eva pulled her hand free and stood. Harold rose to his feet. Forgiveness wouldn't be easy, even if his intentions were honorable. She needed to seek out Noelle. Her sister had her own explaining to do.

Until the last secret was revealed, she wouldn't rest. "I have much to think about. Somehow I feel this macabre play isn't over. There are always many twists before the end. You must give me time to think this through, My Lord—?"

"Lerwick." Harold said with the hint of a grin. "The Right Honorable Lord Lerwick, at your service. But I insist you call me Harold, My Lady."

Her mouth twitched. She took a step closer to forgiveness. She could not give up their friendship over what had been his desperation to save his home. Their paths weren't so dissimilar. She'd taken the duke to bed to save her home and her mother. "If you will excuse me, Your Lordship, I have a sister to confront."

It took Eva some time to discover Noelle in an animated conversation with Abigail near a small lake at the back of the property. The two women were clearly arguing. Raised voices carried across the meadow; though Eva couldn't understand the words. As she neared, Noelle turned her head, saw her arrive, and flushed guiltily. Abigail turned, and put her hand to her mouth.

"Eva," Noelle said sharply, "I—we—" She snapped her mouth shut. Both women's faces turned pink, a matching set of flushes high on their cheekbones. Abigail appeared skittish, ready to flee, and Noelle put a protective arm across her body.

Eva walked around a tree stump and stepped close. She sensed that the conversation she'd interrupted involved her. Her life appeared to be the topic of interest to everyone close to her, the subject of endless speculation. It rankled to be the subject of gossip. Her business was not anyone else's concern.

"Is something amiss, ladies? Noelle? Abigail?"

Abigail became fascinated with her hands. Noelle seemed suddenly stricken mute, an unusual condition for her. "If you do not tell me this instant why you're hiding in this weed patch discussing me"—Eva paused and put her hands on her hips—"I will drag both of you down to the lake and push you in."

Noelle darted a glance at Abigail, who refused to look up but visibly quaked under the scrutiny.

"Coward," Noelle said, and Abigail pulled her lower lip between her teeth and worried it for a moment.

"You tell her," Abigail finally said. Her voice dropped to a breathless whisper. "I cannot."

Noelle let out a sharp sigh, drawing the attention back to her. Eva focused on her face. Like Harold, her sister was clearly troubled. Several heartbeats passed before Noelle finally opened her mouth and her shoulders drooped. "Abigail is our sister."

"What?" Eva gasped. She'd expected hurdles while unraveling the tapestry of this confusing story, but not this. Her shock couldn't be greater. "We have a courtesan sister?"

Her mind fractured into bits. She couldn't pull together a single clear thought. After Harold's confession, she'd thought the worst of the secrets were behind her. No revelation made by her servant and friend compared to this one. She was in shock.

Noelle shook her head. "Abigail is Margaret."

Eva's expression of shock widened as she glanced from one face to the other. Why had she never noticed the similarities in the two sisters; the cut of their jaws, the likeness of their noses? She supposed it wasn't clear without the two standing side by side. Clearly Margaret favored the coloring of their mother, though she did have a hint of amber in her eyes.

The shyest of her courtesans was her sister. Eva slumped against the stump. Darkness called to her mind, and she blinked to keep from dropping to her knees.

Abigail rushed to her side and fanned her with a hand. "I think you should explain quickly, Noelle, before she faints."

Their eldest sister joined them, hesitant, as if she expected Eva to regain her strength and claw her eyes out. At the moment, Eva could do nothing but hold herself up. Two shocks in one morning had undone her. Had the sky chosen to fall at that moment, she wouldn't be able to lift her hands to cover her head.

"Actually, I forced Margaret to pose as a courtesan and made up a story for her," Noelle rushed to explain. "She was adamantly against it. She wanted no part of the deception."

"I wanted no part of you. You were a shameful secret better kept hidden, and I hated you," Abigail-Margaret admitted. She reached to take Eva's limp hand. "Mother cursed you and your mother every day of our lives. I thought you were a twisted troll and your mother was a deceitful sorceress who stole Father from her and was responsible for his death."

Eva flinched. Father was traveling to see them when his coach slid off an icy road and tumbled down a ravine. It was easy to see why the sisters would blame Mother and her for the tragic accident.

Margaret added, "As you have learned, it is impossible to refuse Noelle when she has her mind set. I finally agreed." She squeezed Eva's hand. "When I saw how you helped and cared for the courtesans, I realized I'd been so very wrong about you. Father's death was an unfortunate accident. And when you risked your life for Yvette, I knew that I would be happy to call you my sister."

Eva trembled, then burst into tears. "You two are the strangest pair," she sobbed as Margaret slid an arm around her shoulders and hugged her close. "You should run from me. I am the product of Father's betrayal of your mother."

Margaret smiled. "Mother spent her life making Father miserable. Charlotte gave him happiness. I know that now. We cannot change the actions of our parents, and if you can forgive us for our deceit, we can be sisters. Now and always."

Tears flowed freely as the three women held each other. Eva knew she should be angry, yet she couldn't fault them for wanting to know her, deception aside. She'd known about her sisters since she was a child and had grown up thinking they were spoiled wretches. To discover they were not was a delight.

Eva pulled back and looked into the pair of damp faces. "Please do not tell me there are other offspring from Father scattered about. I don't think I can take any more surprises."

Noelle shook her head and grinned. "I think we are the total of his children. Unless he had youthful indiscretions that bore fruit, he was completely devoted to your mother and to us girls. We were enough to keep him busy."

Margaret sniffed and rubbed her face on her sleeve. "I think we are about to add to our family," she said slyly. "A duke, if I am not mistaken."

It took a blink to discover Abigail-Margaret was speaking of her duke. "I cannot wed him."

Her sisters looked at each other. Noelle said, "Eva refused him. We shall see if he has the stamina to bring her to heel.

I suspect His Grace is not easily cowed, if last evening is an indication. He will find a way to protect Charlotte and to have his duchess. Wait and see."

"If only we all were so lucky in love," Margaret said with a sigh as they soothed Eva's concerns.

Later, Eva changed out of the soiled stable boy's clothing and into a patched green dress that showed a hint of ankle. The borrowed too-large boots appeared with each step from beneath the high hem. The only slippers Mrs. Moore could produce were several sizes too small, so Eva clunked around the empty rooms, out of sorts and with much on her mind. She was without a mission or family to turn to, and far from home.

She missed her mother.

Caged in what was a once fine if modest home, she felt like an invisible observer of her own life; as if the twenty-three years of her existence were a dream. Everything she thought she knew about herself was now taken from her, and the narrow gray view in which she saw her life had widened into bright color and light, all because of a vengeful duke and a pair of curious sisters.

She wanted to go to Nicholas and throw herself on his chest. Unfortunately, it was not a good idea to spend much time in his presence. Harold saw to his care, and she'd check on him when he was sleeping. She worried that she'd take one look deep into his eyes and beg him to wed her. Or bed her.

Either was unacceptable.

It was Mother's image that kept her feet from walking along the hallway to his door. Charlotte was, as always, her priority.

"Eva?" Noelle appeared at the top of the stairs. She was breathless. "Come quickly, His Grace has taken a turn."

Eva gathered her skirts and raced up the stairs, tripping

in her haste. She ran past Noelle, then shoved through the open door. Her heart pounding, she hurried to the bed, expecting to find him near death. Instead, he was sleeping peacefully, a slight flush on his face. She bent and put her hand to his head. The skin was warm but not hot.

Confused, she turned to Noelle. "He has no fever." Nicholas stirred.

"I never said he did." Noelle backed out the door, slammed it shut, and a click followed. Eva hurried to the panel and twisted the handle, but the lock held fast.

"Noelle, open this door at once!" she called. The response was a soft giggle, followed by the sound of retreating footsteps. "Noelle!"

Chuckles came from the bed. She discovered Nicholas staring at her, amused. "I see you are pleased," she snapped.

Eva was deathly weary of the manipulations of those around her, as well intentioned as they might be. She looked around the room to see if there was an object with which to break the lock. There was nothing but a tray of food on a table beside the bed, along with a bottle of wine and two glasses.

Obviously her captivity had been carefully orchestrated and was intended to be long in duration. "Were you involved in planning my imprisonment, Your Grace?"

He grunted as he changed position. "I am as innocent as a suckling babe," he said with a wink. "Though I cannot say I am disappointed to share a cell with you, love."

"Hmm." She shot him a skeptical look. "You, Your Grace, may not have been involved in Noelle's scheme, but you are no innocent. Many times I have been a victim of your less than innocent actions."

His half smile dissolved into a lecherous grin. "Indeed?" He held up the sheet to expose himself down to his navel and the dark hair trail leading farther south. "Join me, and I will put my vast experience to good use."

The man had been shot less than a day before, and yet

he managed to think with the part of his anatomy thankfully still hidden under the sheet. He was so very male, and cut from the same cloth as all men. They could find a stiff wind blowing up their trouser legs arousing.

"I think it best if you concern yourself with getting well, Your Grace." She narrowed her lids. "I plan to return to London by the end of the week, with or without you."

He dropped the sheet. "My heart is wounded. What a cold wench you are, Miss Winfield. You've thrown my proposal back at me, then refused a dying man a last few moments to escape the inevitable call of death."

"Death?" She scrutinized him from top to bottom.

For a man close to death, he was looking remarkably well. "Harold assures me the wound was in the muscle and missed all important organs. If you rest, you should be fit in a few days and ready to travel to Collingwood House. Then you can seduce half the women of London without fear of dropping dead."

"Had you proposed such rampant seduction a few weeks ago, I might well have considered the idea as having merit." He caressed his gaze down her body. "Unfortunately, a dowdy spinster has captured my attention. I desire no other. Now, if I can convince her to become my duchess, I will be content."

The warmth in his eyes and the affection in his words melted her insides. Why did life have to become so muddled? Why couldn't she slip beneath the sheet and let him do with her what he wished? It wasn't as if she'd not been naked and writhing beneath him several times. But this was different. Emotions added to the mix made for difficulties she couldn't ignore. The business between a duke and his courtesan was the sharing of bodies without love. His desire to wed her had knocked her off her feet.

And there was no convincing him of his mistake.

"I cannot, and I will speak no more of it," she said stubbornly, her emotions frayed. She was on the brink of launching herself headlong out the window onto the over-grown grass below. "You know, and must accept, the reasons for my refusal. It is best for all of us."

He watched her with his incredible eyes, and she struggled to remain stoic. How she loved him!

"My noble and self-sacrificing spinster will give up a chance at happiness to save everyone around her from the ills of the world."

"And what is wrong with taking care of my family? Is it wrong to protect my frail mother? She became a courtesan because she had no family, no one to help her after her aunt died. But she has me now, and I'll not fail her."

Nicholas pondered her statement before answering. "Nothing is wrong with protecting her, love. I admire you because of your devotion."

Unsure of what to do next and rendered speechless, Eva waited. Finally, he patted the bed. "If these are to be our last moments alone, I ask you to grant me one last wish: that I may spend these moments of our captivity holding you in my arms."

This was one wish she could grant. She gave him a shaky smile, strode to the bed, and kicked off her boots. He eased her down beside him and pulled her gently into his arms.

Careful not to jostle the bandage, she snuggled against his chest. Immediately, his warmth and essence infused her. She pressed her cheek to the light dusting of hair on the broad expanse and inhaled his spicy scent. He nuzzled his face tenderly into her hair. No further words were needed.

Sunset cast a myriad of lights over the white plaster wall above the bed as Eva stirred and opened her eyes at the sounds of excited voices drifting up from below. She hadn't realized she'd fallen asleep in Nicholas's arms until he stirred beside her and slid an arm around her waist.

The noise had pulled him from slumber, and his eyes opened, too.

"What is happening?" he asked, yawning, and rubbed a palm over one eye. His hair was tousled and scattered around his face. Her heart flipped.

"I don't know." She eased from the bed and crossed to the window. A huge coach pulled by six matching bays thundered to a stop before the house. She could see her courtesans, her sisters, and Harold, as well as several others she didn't recognize, lingering on the stoop. It looked like the entire household had come out to welcome the guest.

A thin footman in blue and silver livery climbed down from his perch and opened the door. A woman descended beneath a flurry of feathers dancing on her wide lavender hat, and went directly to Harold. She gave him her hand and he bowed over it as a proper gentleman should. Eva smiled.

"Do you plan to leave me curious, or will you tell me what you're staring at?"

Eva screwed up her face. "It is a woman. She must be of the nobility. She has the trappings of wealth." It wasn't the woman who drew her curiosity, but the tall man tucking her hand beneath his arm. "Harold is a servant no more," she said more to herself than to Nicholas. He carried himself with a bearing she'd never noticed before. Though an impoverished baron, he'd been raised befitting his birth. She tried but failed to imagine him laughing and dancing at the Pennington ball.

"Enough about Harold," Nicholas scolded, impatience raising his voice. "Tell me about the woman."

Eva turned back to the visitor. "I cannot tell the color of her hair, but she is petite. She is wearing a lavender hat, and it appears that her gown matches the deeper purple of the plumes."

He released a harsh breath. She turned to face him and frowned. "What do you expect, Your Grace? I can't see her face," she said tightly. "My view is limited by the distance and the angle of this window. Perhaps you would like to hobble over and see for yourself." When he appeared to take her comment as an invitation, she pointed her finger at him. "Don't you dare get out of that bed."

His Grace slumped back and crossed his arms. Satisfied, she returned her attention below. The household members had gone inside. All that was left was the coach and servants. "The footmen are clad in blue and silver, and a full half dozen bays are pawing up Harold's drive. There is some sort of crest on the side that I cannot make out. It looks like a stag, and a dog?"

Eva pursed her lips. She'd never seen a crest with a dog. It was an odd pairing of a deer and a canine.

"It's a wolf and a stag," Nicholas said, his voice tense. She peered over her shoulder and saw his face tighten. The woman was not unknown to him. She was certain of it.

"Do you know that woman?" she asked, and a thrill of jealousy prickled her spine. Though she hadn't had a good look at her, Eva was fairly certain the stranger wasn't Miss Banes-Dodd, and there was no reason for anyone else to know Nicholas was here.

Did he have a lover she didn't know about? Had he sent a message to her in hopes she would carry him back to London and her bed? Or was this visit unrelated to him?

"Nicholas? Tell me."

He met her gaze, and his eyes were troubled. "I know her very well. She's my mother."

Chapter Twenty

Your mother?" Bile burned Eva's throat. She was locked in a room with her lover while his mother, the dowager duchess, lingered below, in the company of a houseful of former courtesans. And not a one of them was discreet.

By the time Her Grace made it through the house and up the stairs, everything they knew about Eva and Nicholas would be laid out in vivid color for her perusal.

A *whoosh* echoed in her ears, and she felt light-headed. Had the window not been only two floors up, she'd consider climbing over the sash and jumping to her death. But at that height, she couldn't count on a fatal injury.

"Do something," she beseeched Nicholas, frantic.

"What can I do?" He didn't hide his amusement. His mouth twitched, and crinkles appeared at the corners of his eyes. "I'm injured and also imprisoned. I fear we will just have to wait for the duchess to mount a rescue."

The level of strain in her head threatened to turn Eva's mind to mush. She'd never met a duchess, much less the mother of a suitor. Though she hesitated to call Nicholas a suitor, she was his lover, and should be kept carefully hidden from his noble mother. Her Grace wouldn't be pleased to have their scandalous relationship flaunted in front of her. She'd likely snatch Nicholas from the bed and drag him back to London by his ducal ear.

"A duchess. I am about to be shamed by a duchess." Eva paced, as she'd done many times of late, and it had yet to offer her any solutions to her problems. "Who sent for her? Harold? Noelle? This would be just like Noelle. But what could she gain by bringing the duchess here? This will end badly, I know it will."

"My mother will not gobble you up, Eva," Nicholas said drolly. "She gave up such pursuits a fortnight ago."

Eva stopped. "I'm pleased you find this situation amusing, Your Grace." She wanted to dissolve into tears. "She is your mother, I am your lover. We are locked up together in this chamber of sin. Certainly you can see why I find this state of affairs troubling." She swung out her hands. "No mother wants to find her son injured, naked, with his whore."

A low grumble burst from him, and he pushed up on his elbow. His eyes darkened. "Call yourself that again, Eva, and I will pull you over my lap and beat the word out of your vocabulary."

She sucked in a sharp breath. "You wouldn't dare."

"I would. You are not a whore." The words weren't a casual threat. He was furious. "You are to be my wife and the mother of my children. You wouldn't be the first woman to share a bed with her future husband before vows were said."

"We are not engaged."

Nicholas sighed. "Do you wish to argue with me about this again, or would you rather help me into my breeches before my mother finds me like this?" He shoved aside the blanket to expose a halfhearted erection.

"You—you—oh!" She gasp-laughed, and her mood instantly lightened. "I am about to throw myself from the window to avoid your mother, and you find our argument arousing?" She stomped over to the chair and retrieved his soiled breeches. She threw them at him, and he caught them against his chest. "I will never understand men."

Pulling up a leg, he tried to slide his foot into the breeches. With the bandages around his waist, he couldn't bend far enough to manage the feat. Pain etched his features.

"My dear Eva, it isn't the argument that rousts my cock. Have you seen your delightful bum lately? Of course I'm aroused with your confounded hip swishing." He bunched the breeches in his hand and indicated his erection. "Since our first painful kiss, this is a condition I suffer with regularity. I fear you are the only remedy to my illness."

With a short, exasperated laugh, Eva moved to the bed and took the breeches. It was difficult to stay angry with him. With the thick bandage and his hair sticking up in patches around his head, he had a seldom-seen boyish quality she adored. His Grace was intensely aggravating but also entirely fascinating; the kind of man a woman could spend years and years with and never tire of the experience.

"If you think I'll relieve your suffering now, with your mother below, you are mistaken. But I can help you dress." She got onto her knees on the bed near his feet, and began the slow process of sliding the tight-fitting garment up his muscled legs. His cock twitched. Her mouth watered, and he grinned wickedly. She very much wanted to impale her body on it and ride him to a stunning release.

"If I guarantee a quick end, will you reconsider, love?" he said, and she wondered if he could sense the raw hunger seeping from her. One well-placed touch beneath her borrowed skirts and she would be lost.

"Lift your rump." She ignored his plea. The desire to strip off the dress and join him grew to a painful ache. If she didn't get him clothed soon, his mother's discovery of them, Eva's ankles about her ears and Nicholas pumping away in her like a randy stallion, was a distinct possibility.

He scowled, and did as asked. She tugged and pulled, and had managed to get all but his raging erection covered when the sound of a key rattled in the lock. With his hurried help, she got his breeches over his cock a second before the door swung open and Her Grace walked in, Harold and Noelle at her heels.

Panicked, Eva jumped to her feet to hide him behind her skirts as he jerked the blanket over his lap.

Clearly, the duchess thought they were up to mischief. Her brows went up, and something akin to dark humor tugged at her mouth. "Perhaps we should return later, Nicholas?"

Eva's face burned. The only thing worse than actually being caught in a compromising situation with Nicholas was for his mother to think she'd interrupted said situation. She wanted to explain the innocence of her actions, but her throat had closed off and she was struck mute.

Thankfully, Nicholas came to her rescue. "Miss Winfield was kind enough to help me with my breeches, Mother. I didn't want to injure your sensibilities with my nudity."

Pained, Eva squelched a groan. This was helpful?

"Hmm." The duchess ran a quick glance over her son, as if to check his condition, then crossed to Eva. Her Grace perused her face and dipped her gaze briefly downward to the shabby gown. Her lids narrowed slightly. "You are the Miss Winfield who so ensnared my son at the ball?" Eva nodded soberly. "I was disappointed we missed an introduction. I went home early with a headache."

Doubtless the headache had been caused by watching her son flirt with a woman far beneath them in every way. Her Grace had expected that her son would be engaged that evening, and Eva's presence had ruined her plans. How she must hate her!

Twisting her hands together, Eva softly said, "I do apologize for the pain my actions may have caused at the ball, Your Grace," and averted her eyes from the duchess's lovely face. She turned a pleading glance at Noelle, who shrugged helplessly. "And I also apologize for last evening. It was never my intention for your son to be hurt."

The stream of babbling ended when the duchess lifted her hand. "Please, Miss Winfield, no more apologies." She smiled softly. "If you haven't yet noticed, my son is a man who makes his own decisions, quite forcefully in fact." She shot Nicholas a stern look. "He chose to chase after you, and there was nothing I could do to stop him." The duchess returned her attention to Eva and reached for her. She tucked her arm around Eva's. "I am happy your Yvette is safe and my son is alive. Now let us leave him to rest. You and I have much to discuss."

Eva sent Nicholas a helpless glance as the duchess led her from the room by the elbow, as if she were a child. Harold and Noelle stepped out of the way and let them pass. There wouldn't be any rescue from that quarter. She'd been tossed to the wolves.

With her mind awhirl, Eva worked over every possible explanation and excuse in her mind as the duchess took her into the parlor and released her arm. Without a word, Her Grace positioned herself on the settee, smoothed out her skirts, and lifted her face. She cocked a brow.

"Do you plan to stand all day, Miss Winfield, or will you sit with me?"

Eva hurried to claim a chair opposite the duchess. She felt like a dusty church mouse in the presence of a queen.

The duchess was dressed in her lavender and purple finery, and the drab borrowed dress Eva wore was patched at the knees. Clearly Harold's sister had enjoyed outdoor pursuits. Climbing trees and crawling under hedges would be her guess.

"Miss Winfield," the duchess began. Eva braced herself.

"I could pretend ignorance and lead you to believe I am unaware of your relationship with my son. I know how forceful he can be, and that you were an innocent in his seduction."

Shamed, Eva felt all the blood in her body race to her face and pulse at her temples. The secret was out, and her humiliation was intense. She wanted to run from the room, from the house, all the way to the farthest reaches of the world. Nicholas, with his need for vengeance, had done this to her. Not only had he seduced her, he'd told his mother about it. She never, never wanted to face him again!

"I will remove myself from this house immediately, Your Grace." Eva stood with what little pride she had left and lifted her chin. "I'll be gone within the hour."

The duchess shook her head and indicated the chair. "Please sit down, Miss Winfield. There is no need to flee."

A desperate pull to escape weighed on Eva for a long moment before she reluctantly sat.

"It was not my intention to embarrass you, Miss Winfield. However, I do like to speak frankly."

Frankly? The duchess was brutally honest. "Lady Seymour suffers from the same condition," Eva said, defeated.

A smile broke across the duchess's face. "I have discovered that Lady Seymour, Noelle, has very strong opinions. I admire her for that." She leaned forward on the settee and encompassed Eva with her full stare. "I wish for us to talk freely and honestly, Miss Winfield. I realize you are very important to my son, and I understand your reasons for refusing him. What I want to know are your feelings for him."

Dejected and embarrassed, Eva knew she had little left to lose, so she would give Her Grace what she wanted, and take her punishment. She sighed. "I love him."

"I see." There was a long pause. When Eva lifted her eyes, the duchess was peering intently into her face, her expression unreadable.

Eva swallowed. "I realize my feelings are foolish. I assure you I have no aspirations regarding His Grace. I have told him I will not marry him. The problems between us are insurmountable."

The duchess stood without comment. She walked to the window. Mottled patches of sunlight danced around the walls and floor as it filtered through a tall elm. For all she'd just learned, her face was surprisingly serene.

"Fortunately, my son and I are of the same mind in regard to you." She tapped her fingertips on her crossed arms. "I think you and he are a fine match. If only we can convince you to accept his suit, you will give my son the love he deserves."

Eva uttered a surprised sound, and the duchess turned back to her. Had she heard correctly? "I don't understand, Your Grace."

"Then let me explain, Miss Winfield." The duchess fingered the drape. "When I was young, I fell in love with a bounder, a rake, though my parents warned me his intentions were dishonorable. He was a duke, I had no dowry, and my family teetered on the edge of poverty. They eventually relented and allowed me to wed him, in exchange for a large settlement from His Grace." Her eyes shadowed. "I quickly discovered he was everything I'd heard, and more. He was a despicable scoundrel."

She returned to the settee. "I lived twenty-two miserable years with that man. When he died, it was as if darkness had been lifted from my heart." Her Grace smiled tightly and apologetically. "I suppose it is awful to say so."

"We agreed to be honest," Eva said with a wicked glint in her eyes. It was impossible not to like the duchess and feel sympathy for her years of living in an unhappy and loveless marriage. Many women did so for financial security.

Her Grace laughed brightly. "I do like you, Miss Winfield. You are just the sort of woman to keep my son on his toes." She leaned an elbow on the armrest. "All I have ever

wanted for Nicholas was that he not make the mistakes
of his parents. I want him to have love and laughter in his
life." She paused. "Still, as I'm sure you have discovered,
he has much of his father in him. Both could be hard men
when crossed. Yet, he is not, and could never be, Charles.
He just doesn't know how to let his father's ghost rest and
accept that he is capable of love. I think that between the
two of us, we can teach him the error of his ways."

Eva sobered. "He is a good man," she admitted. It had
taken her some time to see that beneath his gruffness was
a caring heart. And then there was the fact that he'd risked
his life for her. "I'm certain your son and my sister have
informed you of my circumstances and about my mother,"
Eva said. "No, please don't deny it, Your Grace. Noelle is
set to match us, and of course she'd include you in her plot.
How could you know the details of my life otherwise?"

A slight nod confirmed her suspicions. Somehow, somewhere, the two women had conspired against her.

"I appreciate your kind words, Your Grace, and your
acceptance of me as a potential daughter-in-law. I know
having your son involved with a courtesan's daughter is
not an ideal situation, and I have my mother to think of.
Between the two, the wall is too high to climb over. I beg
you to accept my refusal and convince His Grace it is for
the best that we part now, before the truth of our relationship is discovered by the Ton."

Eva quickly excused herself and left the manor with a
heavy heart. Her Grace was a fine lady and cared very
much for Nicholas. She felt like she'd wronged them both.
Still, if she had to be stubborn, so be it. In time, Nicholas
would find a satisfactory wife, and soon enough his mother
would have grandchildren to love.

She walked along the weedy path in the expansive garden for some time, with no particular destination in mind.

She eventually stumbled upon a narrow bench near a row of trellises, and sat with her thoughts.

Not a quarter of an hour later she heard the rush of feet behind the trellises, and the sound of soft feminine sobs. The trellises kept Eva from discovering the identity of the distraught woman. She had readied herself to sneak away when the sound of heavy boots crashed through the underbrush as a second person strode up to join the first.

"Margaret, please," Harold's voice called out, low and pleading. "You must allow me to explain."

Eva froze on the bench.

"You lied to me, to all of us," Margaret said between hiccups and sniffles. "I thought you cared, Harold. How could I have been so foolish?"

Harold moved closer. Eva closed her hand over her mouth to muffle her breathing. If she ran off now, she'd draw attention to herself. She had to remain still and hope they would walk away. This was a private conversation. She had no business spying.

Still, she had to admit she was curious. Margaret and Harold? All sorts of questions filled her mind. When had their bond begun? How far had it taken them? Were they lovers?

"You were not foolish. I didn't intend to fall in love with you, Meg." He expelled a harsh breath. "I was a groom. You are a lady from a well-connected family. I never expected we would be friends, and certainly not anything more."

"But you were not a groom," Margaret protested, her voice rising. "You are a baron. You kept the truth from me."

"Would it have mattered? Do you think your mother would allow an impoverished baron to wed you?" Harold sounded anguished and his words were dejected.

Eva couldn't believe her stoic servant had fallen in love with her shy sister, and she hadn't seen a hint of the truth in either of them. Would the secrets ever end?

She pursed her lips to keep silent.

"You think I would wed you now, even if you had the fortune of a king?" Margaret sniffed. "You are not the man I thought you were, Your Lordship. You were part of Mother's plot to ruin Eva and her mother. I no longer know you."

"You know my reasons, and they were not so unlike yours. You also wished the worst for Eva before you knew her," he said gruffly, and moved closer to the trellises. Eva could see his blue coat through the latticework. She prayed he wouldn't look behind him and discover her eavesdropping. "I have refused to take money from Lady Seymour. I cannot betray Eva and Charlotte. Or you."

"Yet, you did betray me," Margaret said bitterly. "I loved you."

Harold stepped forward. Eva caught a glimpse of a faded frock. He stood close enough to reach for Margaret. This conversation certainly explained why Abigail-Margaret had fled the room when he confessed his identity and ownership of the manor. For once, it hadn't anything to do with Eva. He wasn't the groom Margaret loved. What an unwelcome discovery!

"Don't touch me," Margaret begged, stepping backward. "Don't ever touch me again." A sob cut off their conversation, and she fled toward the manor house.

Eva resisted the urge to go after her and commiserate over their shared betrayal by Harold. He'd lied to Margaret and had given Eva such trouble over the duke; he should be taken to task by both sisters. He deserved to suffer for his love as she had suffered for hers.

She smiled brightly and wanted to laugh. Her diminutive sister had taken down her bear of a servant with her love.

Eva must have made a sound that betrayed her presence. In the next moment, Harold was standing before her. She looked up with laughing eyes. Harold appeared ruffled and beaten.

"How much did you hear?" he said, his eyes accusing. Deep lines cut across his hard face. He *was* miserable.

"All of it." She beamed, and didn't bother hiding her satisfaction. "In all fairness, I was here first."

He snapped off a twig from the dormant rose bush and broke it into several small pieces before tossing it away. His wide shoulders slumped forward. "I have made a mess of my life. I never wanted to love her, Eva, you have to believe that."

Eva put a finger to her lips and looked him over. "I never imagined you falling in love or that you were capable of such a strong emotion. You were positively awful to me over my feelings for His Grace. I thought you were completely heartless."

Harold took a seat beside her. "Our situations are very different. I didn't take Meg's innocence."

"Perhaps you should have. She'd have been forced to marry you then," she teased. Eva tried to imagine her strong-willed servant wed to sweet, shy Margaret. Still, the young woman had rattled him to his core. Perhaps the match wasn't so impossible to imagine.

"I think you should take Lady Seymour's money," Eva continued. "That witch deserves to have her accounts lightened. I'll help you with an outlandish tale to tell her about Mother and me. She'll eagerly pay you then." She looked around the garden. "Then you can hire someone to find the grass beneath these weeds and paint the trim on the manor house. The mildewed carpets and drapes require a good airing out and cleaning, and the settees need new upholstery. If you want to marry my sister and give her a good life, you must have a house befitting her station."

Looking at her sidelong, Harold lifted a brow. "Margaret will not have me. She would rather wed a toad."

"Nonsense." Eva waved off his argument. From the emotion she'd heard in her sister's voice, she knew that Margaret just needed a little push to forgive Harold. "Do something outrageously romantic. She will be unable to refuse you."

*   *   *

Yvette proved more resilient than anyone expected. After a day and a half of rest, she joined them in the parlor for tea. Her face was weary, and dark smudges tinged the skin beneath her eyes. Otherwise, she was fit. Eva and the other women did their best to lift her spirits, and she rewarded them with an occasional weak smile.

She refused to speak about the earl or her time in captivity, and they respected her privacy. Yvette insisted that she be included in the upcoming party for the potential husbands and thanked everyone for saving her life.

An investigation had been launched to find the killer of the earl, and there were rumors about a mysterious woman, a fight, and a robbery, but no one at the abbey had actually seen anything useful. The Bow Street Runners were rumored to be leaning toward a robbery turned deadly.

"Do you think Yvette will ever be truly happy again?" Eva quietly asked Harold. Several times she'd seen Yvette look out the window when she thought no one was watching, and there was intense sadness in her face.

"It will take time, but she is strong," Harold said. He stared at Margaret, who refused to look at or speak to him. "She has suffered through much in her life. I think she is looking forward to a new start. I overheard her telling Rose so."

Eva nodded slowly and smiled warily. "And what of Margaret? Have you come up with a way to turn her heart around?" She'd spoken to Noelle, and Noelle was just as surprised as she had been to discover Margaret had had a secret romance with Harold. Noelle knew they were friends, but no more. "I have seen the glances she sends your way. I know she loves you."

Harold gave her a sharp, hopeful stare. Eva shrugged. "We women often see things with our hearts that men do not."

He expelled a breath. "Then perhaps you can advise me how to woo and win her hand. I cannot come up with a single idea of a grand romantic gesture."

She patted his arm. "You will. I have faith."

With Harold's help, Nicholas dressed. Three days abed without Eva had left him ill-tempered and short with everyone. Even his mother's happy chatter set his teeth on edge. The duchess had decided that Eva had descended from Heaven, complete with angel wings, and no amount of arguing could convince her that her son's stubborn mistress wasn't about to become his wife.

"These damnable bandages," Nicholas grumbled, shoving a finger beneath them for a scratch. Harold tugged Nicholas's shirt over his shoulders. "Next time I'm shot, let me bleed to death."

"There were times I wanted to shoot you myself, Your Grace," Harold said as Nicholas tucked his shirt into his breeches. The baron helped him into his black coat. "I shall have to live with the satisfaction of watching a footman take a chunk out of your hide instead."

After seeing the patched garments Eva and the courtesans wore, Nicholas was grateful his mother had brought his own clothes when Harold had sent for her. He scowled and flexed his shoulders. His forced inactivity had left him stiff all over.

"I am well enough to land a few decent blows if you'd like to take this matter outside," Nicholas said.

Harold's malevolent smile was the first he'd seen from the stoic man. The former servant turned baron, and now servant again, reached up and roughly knotted Nicholas's cravat. "Though the offer is pleasing, Your Grace, I think Eva has done more damage to you than I could do with my fists."

Eva. Nicholas hadn't seen her in days, though Mother

assured him she'd visited while he slept. She was avoiding further confrontations and any talk of marriage. She never once denied caring for him when she refused his proposal. It was all about her fears. Those he had to assuage.

When Harold finished, Nicholas critically examined himself in the mirror. "You make a good manservant, My Lord."

"It is interesting how you can learn to dress yourself when you lack a manservant." Harold leaned back on his heels. "I had many jobs during my travels and saw many things. Dressing you, I can do blindfolded."

"Is physician included in those professions?" The wound was healing nicely, and Nicholas had suffered through only a brief fever. There would be a scar, but Noelle assured him it would only add to his rakish reputation.

"I was in the army and spent time working in the infirmary." Harold smirked. "And when you are built like a pugilist, you are often challenged to prove your worth. I became an expert at patching myself up after fights. Carving the bullet out of your side wasn't difficult. It was not much more than a flesh wound."

"Still, I do owe you my thanks. I could have bled to death." Nicholas reached out his hand. The baron looked down, then closed his large hand over Nicholas's. They locked gazes. "Now if you can convince your stubborn mistress to marry me, you'll have my lifelong gratitude."

"I fear you'll have to put your courtship off a bit longer, Your Grace," Harold said, releasing his hand. "Eva packed up her sisters and her courtesans this morning and left for London."

Nicholas grumbled under his breath. "For a woman of steely strength, she is a coward when it comes to fighting for her happiness." He shook his head. "If you have any ideas on how to bring her around, please tell me. I have nothing."

Harold nodded slowly, and his expression softened. It

took years off his features. Nicholas realized then that they were probably close to the same age. He squelched a grin. Watching over Eva had been trying indeed, and the poor man was aging at an alarming rate.

"I have it on good authority that outrageous romantic gestures are the way into the heart of a woman," Harold said, puffing out his cheeks. "I think I have just the thing to save you both from a lifetime of misery, Your Grace."

Chapter Twenty-One

The day of the party at which the former courtesans would meet the men they'd selected began on a grim note when the weather conspired to ruin Eva's plans to hold the gathering outside. However, by noon the sun had forced its way from behind the clouds and made a valiant effort to comply with her wishes. The fragrance of spring blooms sweetened the air.

The servants dried the chairs and benches and set up tables. Cook pressed the two maids into service as her helpers while the courtesans readied themselves with the help of Eva, Noelle, and Margaret.

"My stomach is fluttering," Rose said as Noelle drew the ice blue day dress carefully over her head. Her red hair was pulled back and up with a few curls left to frame her face.

"I think I might be ill," said Pauline, who did look pale.

Rose giggled. "Don't get sick on your dress, dearest. You look too lovely to spoil the effect."

Pauline stuck out her tongue. She was clad in pink satin

and her blonde locks were braided and coiled atop her head. Sophie chose to wear lavender. The color and her happiness helped to take the hard edge off her face. Of all the women, she was the most desperate to find security.

Eva resisted the urge to remove her wig and spectacles. Though the courtesans knew the truth about her disguise and her desire to keep her two worlds separate, the suitors did not. She preferred to keep it that way.

She turned to Yvette, clad in red, and watched her hold earbobs up to her earlobes. Though Eva worried about her, she appeared to be outwardly well. As their eyes met in the mirror's reflection, Yvette smiled softly. Eva went to the jewelry case and removed a pair of beaded black earbobs.

"Try these," she said. Yvette put them on and nodded, satisfied with her reflection. She turned and took Eva by the hands, squeezing her fingers.

"Please don't worry about me, Miss Eva." She pulled Eva into a tight hug, and Eva felt her tremble. "This is a day of happiness," Yvette whispered. "I will have it no other way."

Eva held her for a moment longer and blinked back tears. If she had to drag every unattached man from Northumberland to Dover into this town house, and parade them before Yvette until she found her perfect match, she would do so gladly. She desperately wanted to see Yvette happy.

"Then I think we should ready ourselves," Eva said, and pulled back with a smile. She encompassed the entire clutch of former courtesans with her sweeping gaze. "We have just over a dozen men arriving shortly. We should not make them wait." She stretched out her hands, and they all came together. "I have confidence you will each charm someone today. And if you do not find a match, I will keep trying until you do." Tears welled. "I am so proud of all of you. You are courtesans no more."

They hugged, sniffled, laughed, and then headed downstairs just as two packed coaches finished unloading their passengers at the garden gate. When the men were assembled, Eva led the ladies outside and introductions began. When she finished, she stepped back and positioned herself discreetly off to the side with Noelle and Margaret, watching the women. It wasn't long before the young women were mingling with their potential suitors.

Middle-aged and young, charming and shy, the men were a collection from all aspects of life. Since Margaret had taken herself out of the group, the men greatly outnumbered the women. But Eva had promised them wives, and there was always the next batch of courtesans to choose from.

"They all look pleased," Noelle whispered as several men circled bubbly Rose and she laughed heartily at some jest. Pauline and Sophie each had two suitors, and Yvette was speaking with a rather stuffy-looking man with a sizable mustache. A few suitors held back, waiting for an opening. Mr. Reed, a handsome solicitor of thirty, peered over his spectacles at Yvette from a distance.

"I think Yvette has caught someone's eye," Eva said to Noelle, indicating the man with a slight tip of her head. "I might need to push them together." The three sisters shared a smile.

The day went smoothly except for a small skirmish between Mister Rhoades, a shopkeeper, and Mister Tipton, a painter, over who would bring cake to Rose. Eva got between them and explained that if they didn't behave, they would have to leave and would be taken out of her book. They quickly settled. Everyone knew that once Miss Eva took you out of her book, you were never invited back. Harold had vanished right after bringing the men, and Eva hadn't seen him all afternoon. She knew how difficult it was for him to spend time in Margaret's company, and her in his. It was nearing the end of the party when he finally made an appearance. And what an appearance it was.

Eva, Noelle, and Margaret gawked as he walked into the

garden, carrying a huge vase filled with a colorful explosion of mixed flowers. The immense arrangement all but blocked much of his upper torso and head. But when he lowered the vase to the ground beside the stunned Margaret, and dropped to one knee, Eva was able to fully appreciate the lengths to which he'd gone to impress her sister.

The cut and quality of his clothing rivaled that of His Grace, from his buff breeches to his snow-white shirt and cream cravat to the deep scarlet of his coat. His hair was neatly trimmed and his face clean-shaven. Eva almost didn't recognize him.

"Harold?" she said, but the sharp intake of breath from Margaret stilled further comment. Eva and Noelle watched a glint of amusement dance in Margaret's eyes.

He reached for Margaret's hand. She slowly released her fingers, and he encompassed them in his large hands.

"Lady Margaret Abigail Louise Seymour, I know I have made mistakes in my life and have hurt some of the people for whom I have cared the most. None more than you." He swallowed. "When I first saw you in the kitchen, while you were going over the menu with Mrs. Dunn, I was smitten. And my affection has grown every day since." A single tear broke loose and flowed down Margaret's face. "You would do me a great honor if you would consent to be my wife."

Eva stood open-mouthed as she watched the proposal unfolding. Never once in the time she had known Harold had he ever strung so many words together, and certainly not with such eloquence. It had to be desperation that had changed his normally gruff exterior to that of a man unafraid to show his love. It was easy to see that love in his eyes when he gazed upon Margaret.

Noelle was similarly affected by his proposal. She and Eva gaped like a pair of fish, then simultaneously clapped their jaws shut with matching smiles. The former courtesans and suitors all stood silent as Margaret stared at Harold as if he had grown a second nose. Clearly she hadn't expected such loving sentiment or such a grand and public proposal. Her face flushed pink.

"I—I . . ." She looked helplessly at her sisters. Eva and Noelle nodded. Margaret grinned and bent to put her free hand on his shoulder. "I will marry you, Harold."

He quickly stood and pulled her into his arms. He spun her around, then dropped her back to her feet before giving her a brief and very loving kiss. Margaret turned a deep red as the party guests clapped and the three sisters hugged and shared whispered words of congratulations. When Harold finally tucked Margaret protectively against his side, Eva walked over to put a hand on his arm, her eyes swimming. He bent to her, and she lifted to her toes.

"I am so happy to welcome you into my family, Harold. I've always considered you my friend, and now you will be my brother."

Harold pressed a kiss on her cheek and grimaced. "Someone has to watch over you three. Without supervision, you'll get into all kinds of mischief."

Eva laughed heartily. The day was lovely indeed.

While Harold and Margaret moved among the guests, Eva and Noelle watched their laughing sister and her beaming groom-to-be. Though Eva wouldn't have ever put the pair together, love was sometimes unexplainable. She knew this well. And sometimes it could not be returned. This was the affliction she suffered through every hour of every day. She knew rejecting His Grace was best for all, but it didn't keep her heart from aching.

"Well, one courtesan has been matched," Noelle said, smiling, and pulled Eva from her musing. She pointed to the solicitor, who was in deep conversation with Yvette. She was blossoming under the attention, and the wariness in her face had eased. "I think another is in the making."

Eva wrinkled her nose. "Margaret was never a courtesan. You made up her history as a ruse. So I'm not sure that counts as a match."

"Oh, but it does," Noelle insisted. "If not for you, Harold would have spied for Mother and then returned to his home. Your friendship and this school brought Margaret and him back together, to this happy end."

Perhaps she *had* matched them in an indirect way. Margaret and Harold would, of course, face the displeasure of Lady Seymour. However, Eva knew that between the two of them, and with Noelle encouraging the match, the woman stood no chance of breaking them apart.

Their discussion was interrupted by Mister Middleton. He was in his late twenties, owned a textile mill, and had a quick and charming smile. "May I speak to you, Miss Black?"

The seriousness of his tone lifted her brows. She nodded.

"I would like to ask for Miss Pauline's hand." He turned to face Pauline, and she inclined her head as if to offer encouragement. "I have a sizable house outside London with a full staff, and my business is doing well." He paused and darted another warm glance at Pauline. "I believe I can offer Miss Pauline a pleasing future."

This part was Eva's favorite. For whatever reason, the men always asked her permission to marry, though the women were old enough to do as they wished. She looked at Pauline, who pleaded with her hazel eyes.

"You have my permission, Mister Middleton." He let out an ear-piercing whoop and ran back to Pauline. He pressed a kiss on her cheek, and they spoke in low, excited tones. Within the hour and at the close of the party, not only were Pauline and Margaret matched, but Rose had whittled down her choices to two men, who would come separately to tea the following day so she could speak with them in a more private setting. Chaperoned, of course.

Mister Reed had proposed to Yvette, and she had told him she needed time to consider his offer. Eva thought it smart. After all Yvette had gone through of late, it was good to take some time to decide if he was what she really

wanted. Eva suspected that in the end, her answer would
be yes. He was a good and kind man; an ideal match for
Yvette.

Sophie walked over after good-byes were completed,
and Harold gathered the men to lead them to the coaches.
She'd received two offers, but her heart wasn't in them.
"I don't know what to do, Miss Eva. This is the first time
in my life I feel free. I'm not certain I want to wed." Her
expression was apologetic. "Are you disappointed in me?"

Eva took her hand. "Not in the least. My goal at this
school is not to force anyone to wed, but to offer husbands as a choice. What you do from here forward is your
decision."

Sophie's expression fell. Clearly, she was torn over
what to do. She'd always lived under the rules of her lovers. Freedom came with responsibilities. "I have no skills
except what you taught me." The lines around her eyes and
mouth deepened as she fretted. "What other choices do I
have?"

Eva pondered her plight for a moment as the coaches
pulled away from the town house. A solution came to mind.

"I need someone to oversee this household, to orga-
nize the books, and to help with planning the weddings.
The courtesans tend to arrive unannounced, and I am not
always here to take their information. I cannot pay you
much, but you will receive your room and board as well."

A slow smile lit Sophie's face. "I accept, Miss Eva.
Thank you." She hurried off to join the other women, and
Eva took time to collect her thoughts. The party had been
a success.

Tomorrow the final agreements would be made between
the women and their suitors. For now, only rest.

Noelle must have seen her squelch a yawn. Her sister
took charge of the maids and began the task of directing
the cleanup. Eva sent her a grateful smile and returned to
the house.

On her way to the privacy of the parlor, a knock sounded on the front door. Eva opened the oak panel and found a footman, dressed in His Grace's livery, standing on the stoop with a note in his hand. The large ducal coach was waiting in the street.

"I have a missive for Miss Black."

Eva wanted to refuse delivery of the note and slam the door closed. However, she was both curious and a bit alarmed over what the envelope might contain. It had been almost a week since she'd left the duke under Harold's care. She worried that Nicholas might have taken a turn and died, despite Harold's assurances that he was mending well.

"I am she." She took the note and tore it open.

Get in the coach, Eva. Please.

The note was simple and direct, just like Nicholas. He expected her to obey his wishes without question. This time, though, he did say please. It was a change from his usual barking out orders and expecting everyone around him to jump.

Eva tapped the note against her chin and pondered the plea. The footman stood politely and waited. Nicholas, His Grace; a flood of emotion washed over her as his handsome face filled her mind. She missed him dreadfully. The cowardly course would be to lock the door and be done with all this. But Eva was no coward. She wanted to see him one last time.

She wanted one last good-bye kiss.

Chapter Twenty-Two

❦

Eva was alarmed when, instead of traveling to his town house, the coach sped out of London. She tried to get the attention of the driver, but the man appeared deaf to her pleas. Not desiring to jump from the coach and risk injury, she jerked off her itchy wig and spectacles and settled back against the leather squabs to stew.

If he thought kidnapping her would keep her from cutting him from her life, he was sorely mistaken. She'd made her decision, and wouldn't change it because he bullied her to do so. Once he was in her sights, she planned to give him a set down that would set his ears ringing.

What seemed like hours had passed when the coach slowed to make a sharp right turn off the road. She looked out the window and saw a winding drive lined with trees and a perfectly cut lawn that spread as far as she could see.

There was a familiarity about the place, yet she was certain she'd never been here before. Then the recognizable spire atop Highland Abbey came into view over the treetops.

She gasped. Why would His Grace bring her to the place where he'd almost died? He couldn't be so desperate to control her that he'd lock her in the same dark room where the mad lord had imprisoned Yvette. Or could he? He'd been vengeful before. Was it such a stretch to believe he could be so again?

Worry twisted through her as the coach drew to a halt before the abbey and the footman opened the door. She knew refusing to alight wouldn't keep His Grace from having her dragged out. She accepted the young man's assistance and warily climbed down.

In daylight, the abbey was magnificent; a stone and glass monolith that took her breath away. There wasn't a hint of the evil hanging over the abbey that she'd felt the night of the rescue. Without the earl casting his malevolent shadow, she could appreciate the ancient building for the treasure it was.

"Don't look so frightened, Eva." The familiar voice spun her about. His Grace walked up the drive from the direction of an outbuilding. Aside from his white shirt, he wore all black, a savage figure befitting the backdrop of the carved stonework of the abbey.

His face, his frame, his confident arrogance sent shivers of need down her body and took her breath. She had to fight to hold on to her anger, when what she wanted was to drag him inside the coach and beg him to take liberties with her feverish body.

"Why have you brought me here, Your Grace?" she asked with forced disdain. Even with the narrow distance between them, she caught the light whiff of his scent on the breeze. It frolicked dangerously through her emotions. "I'm certain the earl's heirs won't appreciate our trespassing while they are in mourning. They have recently suffered a loss."

He ignored her comment and hooked her arm under his. "Don't worry, Eva love." He grinned and led her toward the entrance and its large rounded doors. "All traces of the earl and his nest of rats have been removed, and the linen's burned. There is no one here to protest our arrival."

They were alone? "You understand there are witnesses to my kidnapping?" she asked tightly. "Eventually Harold and my sisters will worry and search for me. They are a determined lot. You won't get away with keeping me captive for long."

Nicholas stopped and stared. "You think this is about kidnapping you and forcing my will?" He chuckled, and his lids crinkled at the corners. "You are a delight, Miss Winfield."

His humor rankled, and Eva's anger rose. "I shouldn't have gotten into the coach. I did so against my better judgment."

He lifted her hand to his lips and pressed a kiss on her knuckles. His green eyes drew her in, and for a moment she lost herself in their depths. She was so aware of him, of his sensuous appeal. Images of his lips on her, his hands caressing her flesh, made her ache to pull him into a shadowed corner of the abbey and lift her skirts.

"I hope that by the close of this evening, you will not regret your decision to join me." He led her inside.

She was struck by how different the abbey appeared in daylight and how the rays of sunlight spiraled through the stained glass windows in a wash of vibrant color that spilled over the walls and floor. It was like being inside a rainbow.

"It is so beautiful," she breathed, awed. "I have never seen anything like this place."

Nicholas followed the path of her eyes. "Noelle told me of your interest in the abbey."

Eva tensed. It didn't come as a surprise that Noelle was involved in this situation. She suspected the pair had shared secrets about her in an effort to get her before a priest. Her sister seemed to enjoy meddling where she shouldn't.

"My sister needs to stay out of my affairs."

"Was she mistaken?"

Looking up to the high ceilings and around the expansive space, Eva reluctantly shook her head. "I do love this abbey. I'm so relieved the mad earl can no longer stain its beauty with his vile presence."

"Excellent," Nicholas said, clearly satisfied by her admittance. He grinned. "I purchased it for you."

The shock on her face brought his laughter. "You what?"

He stepped in front of her and took her hands. "It is my wedding gift to you, love. I offered the earl's heir an outrageous sum he couldn't refuse."

The room warmed, and her legs wobbled. He'd purchased the abbey for her as a gift? Overwhelmed with both love and exasperation, she had nothing to say.

The man was incorrigible. No matter how many times she'd refused him, he wouldn't give up. He wanted to marry her, to father their children, and to cherish her all the rest of her days. How could she not love him?

Her heart soared, and she touched the side of his beloved face. If only she had the freedom to accept his suit!

"I—" Her refusal was cut off by the sounds of footsteps above. She looked up and saw her mother and Nicholas's mother on one of the balconies. The smiling pair looked down.

"There you are, Evangeline darling, we've been waiting for you," Mother said, her eyes dancing. "You should see my room, it is very pink. His Grace gave me a very large bedroom with its own sitting room overlooking the garden. And there is plenty of space for grandchildren."

The duchess nodded and winked at Eva. "Enough space for a full dozen babies and a huge nursery to hold them all." She and Mother shared a knowing glance while Eva's world took on a surreal quality. Mother and the duchess were here, together, planning for grandchildren?

She turned her eyes to Nicholas. "I don't understand. I left Mother this morning in London." She was painfully confused. Pressure pulsed at her temples.

Holding her hands firmly, Nicholas lowered himself to one knee and his face grew serious. "You have given up many things in your life to protect your mother from the ills of the outside world," he said softly. "I knew the only way you would ever agree to marry me was if I found a way to assuage those fears."

Eva's throat tightened, and she blinked several times.

"I purchased this abbey for you as a refuge for Charlotte, so she can be cared for and secure, where the outside world cannot touch her. This will be our home, and when we visit London, we will stay at Collingwood House." He paused. "What you decide to do with the Mayfair house is up to you. And don't forget, Margaret and Harold are only a quarter of an hour away by coach."

Tears pricked her lashes as she gazed lovingly into his face. He was everything she had dreamed, and more; her handsome and arrogant duke. She looked up at the smiling faces of two mothers who wanted desperately to see their children happy. But there was business to finish first. She couldn't accept him until they took care of a few final details.

"Do you love me, Nicholas?"

"I do."

"Will you forsake all courtesans and remain loyal and faithful to me for the rest of your life?"

He grinned. "My town house has been sold. No more courtesans, mistresses, or lovers."

She narrowed her eyes and frowned. "I will not give up matching my courtesans. Though Sophie will take some of the burden and help me with the daily activities, I will still run the school as I see fit."

A grimace passed over his face. "I didn't expect you would close the school." He sighed quite dramatically. "If I have to write out a contract with all your stipulations to get you to say yes, so I can get up off my knee, I'll do so gladly." He locked onto her gaze. "Marry me, Evangeline Winfield."

She laugh-sobbed and nodded briskly. "I will marry you, Your Grace." He rose to his feet and gathered her for a deep and searing kiss as her mother and the duchess cheered and clapped. Eva melted against him and knew she would cherish this moment forever. This man had overcome many obstacles for her, and she loved him with everything in her heart.

When he finally lifted his head, he ran a finger over the curve of her lips. "I do love you, Eva, very much."

"And I love you."

They looked up at their mothers, who were crying through their smiles. Eva saw a light of hope in her mother's face that she hadn't seen in a long time. Perhaps thoughts of grandchildren would help ease some of the sadness in her broken heart.

The duchess's eyes widened, and she looked at Mother. "We have a wedding to plan, Charlotte."

"We do, Your Grace." The two women hurried off, their excited chatter carrying throughout the three-story hall.

Nicholas chuckled and returned his attention to Eva. He drew a finger down her cheek. Intense heat burned from him, and she knew where his thoughts were. They weren't on a wedding, but a bedding; many, many future beddings.

"I fear we'll be still standing at the altar when our mothers will begin demanding grandchildren." He leaned down to nuzzle the side of her neck, and she giggled. "It is the practicing I look forward to."

Eva sighed. "If we were alone, I would suggest we not wait to get started." She slid her hands into his coat to clasp him around the waist, and pressed her hips enticingly against him. She felt him stir in his breeches.

"I know a storage room off the kitchen with a dusty old table large enough for two," he said mischievously and lifted his head. A slow smiled tugged her mouth, and her tongue made an appearance on her bottom lip. She ran her hands slowly over his buttocks and hips until he groaned and reached up to cup one breast. She felt her nipple tighten beneath the cloth. The room heated to an uncomfortable level.

"I'll race you," she said, and bolted toward the kitchen with a bright laugh, the dark duke right on her heels.

Epilogue

❦

One month later, Eva happily married Nicholas in a small and lovely ceremony in the tiny chapel on the grounds of Highland Abbey. She'd chosen the stone chapel for its simple beauty and because on these grounds her life had truly begun.

Her former courtesans were in attendance; Rose with her husband, the Honorable Thomas Stanhope, a baron's younger son; Yvette with her husband, Mister Reed; and Pauline with her husband, Mister Middleton, and possibly a baby on the way.

Noelle and Margaret had helped Eva dress in her mother's blue gown, with crystals in the sheer overlay to catch the light, and diamond pins in her hair. She looked like a princess. In the gown, she felt the love of her parents, and knew that somewhere her father was pleased.

Harold sat with his new wife, and Noelle, and Yvette, as Eva and Nicholas pledged their love. Never in her life had Eva been happier as Nicholas made his vows. He was hers, forever.

Never, she suspected, had two mothers ever been happier, either. The duchess and her mother had become fast friends, and Mother's spells lessened with the excitement of planning Eva's marriage.

After their honeymoon, Eva and Nicholas stayed at Collingwood House to finish out the last few weeks of the Season and to introduce her to society. She'd been terrified.

Speculation and gossip rocked the Ton over the surprise wedding, but with Nicholas at her side, and a few outlandish tales of love-at-first-sight spread by Noelle, Eva was soon the toast of society. They all kept Charlotte's secret, and most of society accepted the long-lost-cousin tale while her mother lived quietly at Highland Abbey. Even Lady Penn couldn't shake scandals out of the tales, and reluctantly accepted Eva into her fold.

"What about that one over there?"

Eva shook off her thoughts as Margaret's voice brought her into the present. She squinted and stared up.

"I think I see a sheep," Margaret said, pointing to a cloud with one hand as the other hand cupped the tiny bump growing beneath her day dress. The elder Lady Seymour had paid Harold generously for his scandalous information about highwaymen and ship wreckers he'd claimed were tied to Eva and Charlotte. She realized soon after that she'd been duped, and hied off to France to sequester herself from the betrayals of her ungrateful daughters.

"It looks more like a rabbit to me," Noelle said from her place on the other side of Eva. She closed one eye and frowned. "Look at those ears. It is a rabbit."

"I disagree, Noelle, it's a sheep," Eva said. "A sheep being chased by a cat with a mouse clamped in its jaws."

"A cat?" Noelle lifted her head and stared at Eva as if she'd been struck daft. "That is certainly not a cat or a mouse. I think that one is a naked baby with a rattle in his hand."

Eva pushed onto her elbows and grimaced. "Where did

you say Lady Pennington was today?" She looked around for signs of the dragon lady. They were, thankfully, alone.

When Noelle suggested a surprise visit to Lady Pennington, Eva wanted to refuse. But Noelle insisted it would firm up Eva's relationship with the popular, and feared, society matron. Eva was relieved to find her not at home.

"She apparently has gone off to dine with Lord and Lady Sherbrook," Margaret said. Noelle peered at Eva's concerned face and added, "Don't worry; by the time she returns, we will be gone."

Gone, leaving behind the lingering gossip from her servants about three women lying on their backs in her foyer looking up at her cloud-covered ceiling.

"Perhaps we should make a wish," Margaret said, flopping gently back on the polished marble. She had a happy flush on her cheeks. Impending parenthood had brought immense joy to her and Harold. "You only make wishes on stars, sister dear," Noelle countered. "I see no stars."

"I think a wish is a grand idea, and I'll start," Eva interrupted before her sisters began another of their frequent squabbles. She adored the impossible pair more every day. The elder Lady Seymour had done two things right in her life, and the two women were it. "Since Margaret and I found husbands and happiness, I wish for the same for Noelle."

"Hear, hear!" Margaret interjected with a nod. "I, too, wish for a husband for Noelle. He has to be strong man who will keep her out of mischief and has to have a big bulge in his breeches to keep her blissfully content."

Eva and Margaret laughed as Noelle gasped at the shocking comment.

"I don't need a husband, or anything else he might possess," Noelle huffed. "I plan to grow old and dusty and firmly settled on the shelf."

"I think I know a perfect suitor for her," Eva said, ignoring Noelle's protest. "He is wealthy and titled. Nicholas introduced us at Lady Dunleavy's party. He is a bit short and stout and spittles lightly when he talks. But he is a gentleman and has a wonderful braying laugh."

"I think I know him," Margaret added, her face turning serious. "He is called the Toothless Lord; homely but quite charming in his hunchbacked way."

"You two are not amusing in the least," Noelle grumbled, refusing to meet their eyes. Her scowl deepened as laughter echoed through Pennington Manor.

Read on for a special preview of
the next historical romance
from Cheryl Ann Smith

The Accidental Courtesan

Coming soon from Berkley Sensation!

Chapter One

Lady Noelle Seymour wobbled slightly on the trellis and bit her bottom lip to keep from crying out. Two stories up, the redbrick town house appeared much taller now than when she'd decided to go through with this ill-conceived plan and had slipped across the lawn and into the shadows of the building like a sneak thief. Still, the intrigue of having a grand adventure had caused her to lose any final hesitation as she donned a pair of rolled-up borrowed black trousers and a matching shirt and set off for the Mayfair town house of the Earl of Seabrook.

She weaved her hands between the scratchy climbing vines and gripped the trellis in a vise grip. If her sister, Her Grace, knew what she was doing this evening, she'd have her head handed back to her on a platter.

Yet she forced herself onward. She couldn't help herself. Prickles of excitement twisted through her. She was no longer a proper lady from a good family, but an adventuress without the encumbrance of society's rules and restrictions.

For this night, anyway, and she'd not let fear and common sense ruin her outrageous adventure.

Tomorrow she'd be tucked back in her corsets and stockings with no one the wiser. Prim, if not quite proper, Lady Noelle.

Tentatively, Noelle reached a toe toward the window ledge, her heart pounding loudly in her ears. Once her foot found a firm place, she let loose with one hand and clutched the windowsill in a death grip. If she fell, it would be more than bones or possible death that faced her. If she were discovered breaking into the married Seabrook's house in the middle of the night and dressed like a boy, the scandal would ruin her forever in the eyes of the Ton.

Mother would bury her so deep in the country, she'd shrivel up, dry and crackled, like a neglected daisy desperately deprived of water and sunlight.

Noelle grimaced and brushed a leafy twig away from her chin with her gloved hand.

Death was preferable to the shame of being sent off in exile. If she plummeted to the ground, she'd pray it was headfirst and instantly fatal.

"Almost there," she muttered for courage, and she slid her foot across the narrow stone ledge. Stubborn determination to see the plan through kept her going on. Ever so slowly, she eased her body to the right, skimming her belly against the brick, thankful the town house was blessedly quiet.

The earl was in Bath with his wife, according to gossip. This gave Noelle enough time to return the stolen necklace and save Bliss from prison or, worse yet, hanging.

Beautiful Bliss. The girl had the sense of a donkey.

Noelle smiled wryly. Clearly, at this moment, both were superior to her in intelligence. Neither courtesan nor donkey was about to commit a crime that might well land her into Bliss's adjoining cell at the horrible Newgate Prison.

Still, it was too late for regrets. She was almost there;

the darkened window loomed in her sights. In a few minutes the item would be safely returned and she'd be on her way home.

Gingerly, she leaned on her right foot to test the worthiness of the ledge and reached for the window. She said a brief whispered prayer, flattened her palms on the painted wood frame, and pushed the window up. Relief flooded through her as the pane opened easily with only a slight scraping sound.

She'd not have to fumble along the ledge for a second or third unlocked window. Clearly, His Lordship didn't expect anyone to make such a perilous climb to steal his valuables.

With diligence and extreme quiet, she first poked her head in to make sure the room was empty, then stepped gingerly inside. In the blackness, she heard nothing to cause her alarm. No snoring, no shifting of a body on a bed. The space was blessedly quiet, and she pulled in a deep, soothing breath to loosen the tightness in her chest.

According to Bliss, either this room or the one next to it belonged to the earl. The girl wasn't certain which, as her attention had been otherwise occupied during her brief visit with the amorous attentions of the earl. Though he kept a separate and smaller town house for his courtesans, some months ago, on a lark, he'd smugly snuck Bliss in when his wife was away enjoying the soothing waters of Bath.

Carefully and with outstretched arms, Noelle walked around the room, searching for the bed and the blue coverlet that would assure her she was in the right room. If she was to return the necklace, and lead the earl to believe it was only misplaced and not stolen by his former courtesan, she had to put it in a place where he could easily "discover" it as soon as he returned.

A task that turned out easier said than accomplished.

The blasted room was too dark! Not even the moon offered its cooperation by remaining well hidden behind the blanketing storm clouds. Lightning would certainly help, yet it had also failed to make an expected appearance.

Luckily, it took very little time to find the massive bed and less time to discover the coverlet was indeed dark blue, or black, or even a deep green. She squelched an explosive sigh and lifted the fabric to her nose to squint at it close up. She was fairly certain that it was green.

Blast! With no time to linger, Noelle dropped the coverlet and fumbled her way blindly across the room. With outstretched hands, she felt around for a door, then eased it open. Once in the dark hallway she turned right and followed the wall to the next room. She closed her hand around the handle and twisted. The panel creaked softly when she pushed it open, and she froze.

When no alarm sounded, she rushed inside and softly clicked the door closed behind her. The space was even blacker than the first room. Perhaps she should have waited until a cloudless night of a full moon before venturing out.

"You can do this, Noelle," she whispered. "Find the bed, make sure this is the right room, and get out."

She stumbled around the room, arms swinging in wide sweeps. Eventually, she knocked into a small table and beside it found the bed. Sheer luck kept her from upending a lamp. She leaned to squint at the coverlet.

Was it blue? Frustration mounted. She'd have to drag it over to the window and pray for a slip of moonlight to know for certain. Remaking the bed afterward would also be difficult in the dark. The maids would be suspicious if they found the bed in disarray and would report the incident to the earl. If the Bow Street Runners got involved, she could be in serious trouble.

In a case like this, desperate measures were required. She'd worry about the bed once the necklace was returned.

Noelle rounded the bed to the area closest to the window. She gripped both fists around the corner of the coverlet when an arm snaked out of the darkness in a flash of movement, and jerked her down on the bed!

"Oh!" she cried sharply as she bounced against a hard

body, before catching herself and cutting off a girlish scream. "Release me!" she said in her deepest tone. A hand clamped over her bum and she was dragged across a warm and naked chest—a naked and very male chest, by the feel of downy hair covering the firm, sinewy expanse.

The effort to sound mannish was rewarded with a low chuckle and a mumbled reply. "No man smells so sweet or has such delightful curves, love. Now give me a kiss."

A kiss? She couldn't see anything to give her a hint of his identity but did feel her captor's breath brush the side of her face. It had to be the earl. This was his house. But what was he doing here? He was supposed to be in Bath!

Think! Think!

Through her terror she managed to somewhat calmly squeak out, "Your Lordship, this is highly improper."

If she panicked, she could lose everything: her reputation, her freedom, and perhaps even her life!

"I shall show you improper," the stranger whispered with humor edging his voice. He removed the hand from her bum and slid it up her body in a quick exploratory caress. Then he shoved his fingers into her tightly braided hair, pulled her face down to his, and slammed his mouth awkwardly over hers!

Noelle stilled, shocked, her arms pinned against her sides. His firm mouth moved about in the dark for the correct kissing position until he found the proper place for his lips and claimed her fully with a searing kiss.

He teased and tormented her with his exotic scent and warmth, and she felt her limbs turn to hot pudding. Shocked to find a rising tide of tingles well in her body, she opened her mouth to demand a stop to the kiss. Instead of release, the bold stranger pushed his tongue between her teeth and she tasted some unnamed spirit invade her mouth. However, it was the strength of his hands caressing places they should not, and not his savage kisses, that tumbled her world off its axis.

The earl felt strong and untamed beneath her, unlike any of the tepid noblemen of her acquaintance. Beneath her open palms, his bare skin was warm and supple and his thigh rested hard and was honed with thick muscle.

A flood of desire poured through her body on liquid threads, and she went slack. She'd never been kissed like this before! This was no casual peck on the mouth, but the kind of kiss one partook in with a lover.

Her virginal mind went blank and her lids lowered as he rolled her onto her back and partially covered her with his upper body and a leg over her knees.

Why wasn't she fighting him? She should definitely be fighting him. But her body seemed unwilling to push him off. Suddenly, a horrified Noelle realized her arms were around his neck and she was hungrily kissing him back!

"So sweet," he mumbled when he broke the kiss, and then he trailed his mouth down her chin to nuzzle the base of her throat. There was something about him, his voice, that didn't fare well in her ears. Thankfully, it forced some reality into the situation. She felt a prickle of danger from this man and knew if she didn't get out of the bed immediately, she'd lose much more than her freedom in the blackened room.

He slackened his hold briefly to shift positions and Noelle took the opportunity to give him a great shove. The earl fell back in the bed, enough to allow her to roll out from under him and scramble to her feet. She bumped into a piece of furniture, a vanity, she suspected, and had sense enough to pull the necklace out of her pocket. The color of the coverlet no longer mattered. This was clearly the earl's room.

She heard the earl climb to his feet and she dropped the necklace on the smooth surface with a muted clink. Her breath came in short gasps, made worse by his unexpected assault on her mouth. She was disoriented by the kiss and the darkness. She wasn't sure which way was the door. All she knew was she had to get out before he reclaimed her.

His bare footsteps moved away from her and she heard him clatter around for a moment. Bright red coals sputtered to life as fire licked the sticks, or peat, he'd dropped atop them. Quickly, the room became infused with muted light.

Noelle knew her chance of escape was upon her if she made haste. She darted a glance about for the door and launched herself toward the oak panel. A few steps and she'd be free!

"Halt," he commanded behind her, and she jolted to a stop. Slowly she spun about, fists upraised, and braced herself to fight for both her freedom and her innocence.

"You are not a maid," he said and narrowed his lids. He gathered her up with his gaze and suspicion edged his eyes. There was no obvious explanation for her odd dress and boyish appearance. "I've stumbled upon a thief."

Fear chilled her limbs and she went numb. She was about to be arrested. She was a criminal, a thief in the eyes of the law. No magistrate would accept she'd come not to steal but to return the earl's stolen property.

There had to be a way out of this predicament. Think!

The fire flamed higher and she got her first good look at the earl, the half-naked earl. Her breath caught.

Though he was wearing black trousers, they were unbuttoned and sagged low on his narrow hips to a shockingly indecent degree. It was painfully clear he had nothing on beneath. Any sort of shift and the trousers could fall to his knees, leaving him without coverage altogether.

She flushed and pulled her eyes up from the thin trail of hair pointing downward beneath his waistband, to scan her gaze over the most incredible chest she'd ever had the fortune to gaze upon. Well, truthfully, she'd never before had the opportunity to take a close-up look at a male chest. Her experience was limited to one brief glimpse of a tenant's son in a distant field. Still, she was certain the earl's was magnificent in comparison to other men.

There was very little about Bliss's hasty description to recommend him as His Lordship. But Bliss had been in near hysteria when she'd described what she'd done, so Noelle took everything she said with a bit of skepticism.

Indeed, this man was tall, as the young woman had described, but he didn't favor the pale skin of his fellow members of the gentry. His sculpted torso was a golden bronze as if he'd spent all his time shirtless in the sun. His hair was light brown and streaked through by the same sunlight that darkened his flesh.

A pair of shadowed eyes peered at her from beneath a few strands of loose hair as he stalked toward her slowly and with a savage grace that wobbled her knees. In her mind he was an oddity, seemingly out of place in her world, yet she knew the earl was a well-respected member of the Ton and a noble; a picture that didn't fit the untamed beauty of the man before her.

Her heart flipped as she drifted her eyes to his firm mouth, the same mouth that moments ago had kissed her breathless. She backed up as he approached her, his confidence evident in the carriage of his perfect male form.

Just then she understood what it meant when her sister Eva explained the sensual feelings her husband, His Grace, invoked in her when he held her in his arms. Noelle had felt something for this man while sprawled beneath him on the bed and hadn't quite understood the feeling. It was a sensual pull toward a faceless stranger.

Sensual pull?

In that moment, a plan took root in her mind. If she could find a way to distract the earl, she could escape. And there was only one way for a woman to distract a man fully and completely. That much she'd gleaned from spending time around courtesans. So she stopped backing up and waited until he was close enough to reach out and touch.

Noelle settled what she hoped was a seductive smile on her lips, then lifted her hand and placed it on his chest. He twitched beneath her fingers. She had to remind herself to keep breathing as she stared at his mouth.

"I am not a thief, My Lord Seabrook." Noelle flicked her lashes and widened her eyes. "You mistake my intentions."

"Indeed?" He looked down at her clothing and reached to tug at the black fabric at her waist. The effort brought her a half step closer. "You are certainly dressed as such, Milady."

The dark clothes *were* difficult to explain. She had to redirect his attention. Quickly.

Slowly, Noelle drew her hand down his chest and the supple skin trembled beneath her touch. Curiosity and anonymity and fear of hanging led her to boldness. He was magnificent. She wondered if his skin tasted as exotic as it smelled. A virginal flush burned her cheeks and drifted all the way down to her boot-covered toes.

"I've heard you are casting about for a new courtesan, and I've taken these desperate measures to be the first to offer my services." She touched the tip of her tongue to her bottom lip. "I find you very, very desirable."

The last was not a lie and slid easily off her tongue.

A pair of brows shot up. A slow grin passed over his face, and yet, he didn't speak. Instead, he turned his attention to her hair, where golden strands had escaped the braid during her treacherous climb. He examined his find with a grin.

"I shall enjoy seeing it unbound."

The cool air of the room tingled across her skin. Noelle looked down to see he'd loosened her shirt while she was fondling his chest and pushed it up with his hands in an effort to expose her torso. Her lacy chemise kept her covered and safe from his perusal of her breasts. Barely.

Noelle forced herself to remain calm when he shoved up the shirt further to cup her full and thinly veiled breasts. Her nipples budded beneath his palms. A wicked smile tugged his lips and her mouth felt filled with sand. She ached to kiss him again with reckless abandon; to again taste his tongue mating with hers.

In this moment, with this man, she wasn't the proper and soon-to-be spinster Lady Seymour, but the reckless adventuress who climbed a trellis and into a window in the middle of the night, to return a necklace and kiss a handsome stranger with rigorous abandon.

"How desirable do you find me?" he said softly and tugged at a nipple through the thin cloth with his fingertips. She squelched a moan. Her legs threatened collapse and a warning chime sounded in her head.

There *was* something strange about this man that had nothing to do with his sensual appeal or the scandalous liberties she'd allowed him to take to save her hide. Yet, she couldn't put her finger on exactly what roused her suspicions, no matter how hard she tried to focus.

She leaned against him to stop the fondling and peered into his red-rimmed blue eyes. It was then she realized he'd had more than a few drinks this evening; enough to explain why he sounded and appeared slightly off to her. Not drunk enough to wobble or topple over, but enough for her to use to her advantage and extricate herself from the situation.

Noelle grinned. She'd found her opening. "The first time I saw your face in Hyde Park, I knew I had to have you, My Lord," she lied. She pressed lightly on his chest with both hands, and he shuffled slowly backward toward the bed. He cupped her hips and they walked in a bumbling synchronization, locked together.

"When I discovered through gossip that your courtesan had flown your nest, I knew I had to get to you before the other women discovered her flight." Noelle spoke in a hopeful, breathless tone. He stared down at her breasts and groaned. "Tonight, I plan to give you a taste of my many talents. Then tomorrow we shall come to an arrangement."

Her seductive smile drew his eyes. He stared hungrily at her mouth and grinned. "I shall need to see everything."

"Of course, My Lord," she purred. This adventuress relied solely on instinct and snippets of conversations she'd overheard from Bliss and the other courtesans on how to please men. Now was not the time to show her inexperience. He had to believe she was who she said she was. Her life depended on her acting skills.

Thankfully, the man was not a warty toad.

The back of his knees hit the end of the bed and he stopped. He slid his hands from her hips to cup her buttocks. "Where would you like to start, Milady? We have all night." He leaned to press his lips against her neck, and whiskers tickled her skin.

Noelle sighed seductively. "Here?" She lowered her hand to cup the large erection beneath his trousers and her face flamed at her boldness. She suspected he would be considered well endowed and required no padding to make it so.

Her innocent virgin sensibilities were replaced by more open curiosity as she caressed the bulge. What did an erect male member look like up close? Did it hurt the first time a man put it inside a woman? Would she eventually become used to having such a large thing inside her?

The earl's second groan was deeper than his first. He nibbled along the curve of her jaw and his warm breath sent tingles across her skin. "Thus far, you have moved to the top of my list of potential mistresses."

The flush on her face was a clear indication of her innocence, but she hoped he was too deep in his cups to notice.

"I have learned my craft well, My Lord." A courtesan would not flush while enticing a man with her hand. Her shocking curiosity led her onward. With anonymity a perfect mask to hide behind, Noelle felt positively wicked, truly scandalous.

She would do anything to save herself from Newgate— even fondle the earl if it kept him from summoning the Runners. His lids drooped and for the first time he wavered on his bare feet. He pressed a kiss at the corner of her mouth and it was all she could do to not turn her face to accept his kiss. It was proving hard enough to keep him upright.

Noelle bit back a smirk and splayed both hands on his chest. She pushed gently and he fell limply back on the bed. She'd waste no time waiting for his drunken snores to make her escape. The necklace was on the vanity and he couldn't place the missing piece in her hand. Even if he saw her at a social function, he wouldn't match the proper Lady with the courtesan. The dim light and shadows, mixed with his inebriation, would keep him from putting Lady Seymour and the thief-courtesan together as one person.

"Good night, My Lord," she said softly with one last look at his handsome face and hard chest as his lids began to droop over unfocused eyes. She shivered with regret.

And then she was gone.